UNCONSCIOUS
HEARTS

A HEARTS OF VEGAS NOVEL

Sir Kevin
McGingerpants

HARPER SLOAN

Unconscious Hearts
A Hearts of Vegas Novel, Book One
Copyright © 2018 by E.S. Harper

ISBN 10: 1718733771
ISBN 13: 978-1718733770

Cover Design by Sommer Stein with Perfect Pear Creative Covers
Cover Photography by Reggie Deanching of RplusMphoto.com
Model: Michael Joseph
Editing by Jenny Sims with Editing4Indies
Proof edits: Georgette Geras and Michelle Trelford
Formatting by Champagne Book Design

DEDICATION

This one is for my Alpha Babes.
To each and every amazing member of that group.
Your support and love has been one of the greatest gifts and
blessings.

A massive shout-out to two specific Alpha Babes: Melissa Massabni and Meggie McIntosh. You two are a big reason that this new world has a heartbeat that is so strong. What started as a simple contest in the group to name the two businesses in this world, quickly became a huge part of pulse to this series.

Thank you for your help in giving two incredible men the future they needed to find in life with The Alibi and Barcode.

I hope I did you proud with what your names brought to not just this novel, but any that follow.

ps … Happy Birthday, Virginia Carey! Thank you, for every year of your friendship. It means the world to me.

TO CONTACT HARPER:

Email: Authorharpersloan@gmail.com

Website: www.authorharpersloan.com

Facebook: www.facebook.com/harpersloanbooks

Other Books by Harper Sloan:

Corps Security Series:

Axel

Cage

Beck

Uncaged

Cooper

Locke

Hope Town Series:

Unexpected Fate

Bleeding Love

When I'm with You

Drunk on You

Loaded Replay Series:

Jaded Hearts

Standalone Novel:

Perfectly Imperfect

Coming Home Series:

Lost Rider

Kiss My Boots

Cowboy Up

UNCONSCIOUS
HEARTS

PLAYLIST

You Don't Do It for Me Anymore by Demi Lovato

I Think I'm in Love by Kat Dahlia

Perfect Symphony by Ed Sheeran & Andrea Bocelli

Make Me by Britney Spears

All of Me by John Legend

Code Blue by The Dream

Supermarket Flowers by Ed Sheeran

Bridge Over Troubled Water by Artists for Grenfell

Torn by Natalie Imbruglia

Kiss Me by Sixpence None The Richer

Beautiful Trauma by P!nk

Gravity Happens by Kate Voegele

Soldier by Gavin DeGraw

You Gotta Be by Des'ree

If You Ever Want to Be in Love by James Bay

I Have Nothing by Whitney Houston

Find the playlist on Spotify

PROLOGUE

Ari

Alone.

a·lone
ə'lōn/
adjective & adverb
having no one else present; on one's own.

No one.

no one
'nō ˌwən/
pronoun
no person; not a single person.

}T'S FUNNY, THE WORDS THAT SEEM TO COME SO EASY, MEANING nothing at the time they're whispered or spoken, hold all the weight of the world when you realize they're *meant* for you.

I spent years saying those words. Years hearing those words.

Over and over. They became almost meaningless to me. Not in the sense that I didn't feel compassion for those that they did mean something to, but it never felt relatable to me.

My story didn't start sad. It wasn't always a woe-is-me dance. I once felt that overwhelming happiness that comes with pure and wondrous love. I didn't know what it felt like to force a smile because they all came naturally. There wasn't a jaded speck in my vision. My parents were the best. My sister was my best friend. I was about to graduate med school with my boyfriend smiling by my side as we started a new chapter of our lives together.

Only, that chapter hit a major plot twist that not many of us saw coming, and there was nothing left but the backspace key—erasing each and every carefully constructed dream I had woven in the stars.

And the day it all was swept away—the day I found out what those words truly meant—I realized that, while I might still have people in my life, I was well and truly alone … with no one to blame but myself.

After all, who bases their entire future on the dreams they created while they had their head in the clouds?

Not me.

Not ever again.

I'll stick to being alone … with no one.

ONE

Ari

Aye aye, boss

MY HANDS, SHAKING UNCONTROLLABLY, REACH FORWARD and press the disconnect button on my office phone. The words left on my voicemail are just another reminder that I seem to always have eyes on me—the devil riding in the wind behind me, constantly on alert, ready, and waiting to tear me down the second I show a sliver of happiness.

I'm not allowed to move on with my life.

I'm in a purgatory of my own weakness.

Crippled by the fear my memories refuse to let me forget.

Keeping it bottled in and hiding it all from the one person the devil didn't rip from my life—my best friend.

Hiding my loneliness from even my own heart, I'm left to warm myself with empty daydreams of faceless men I'll never be allowed to have.

I can't even remember the last time I was able to go longer than a few months without a reminder slapping me back down.

Never leaving.

Always returning, invading my thoughts at the most inappropriate times, slashing me so deep it's pure luck I've been able to hide my pain.

"Knock, knock."

I jump, my knees slamming into the underside of my desk, when Piper's voice breaks through. It's as if my thoughts alone conjured up the one person I still have in my life, and that's because she's been by my side since we were soggy diapered toddlers. It's a miracle I've been able to keep her from seeing the magnitude of my deep-rooted loneliness. If anyone would understand, she would, seeing that the state of her own love life is cracking with its own pain.

"Hey. I thought you weren't coming in until later?" I greet, proud of myself for the practiced ease with which I push my issues back and swat the devil from where he's hanging over my shoulder.

Don't get me wrong, I'm not walking around in a constant state of depression. I still have fun. I love my job. I love my best friend. I love my cat—even if he is a jerk. I may be broken, but I'm not shattered. My life is what it is, and I've accepted that, but it doesn't mean I don't feel it cut to the quick from time to time.

I shift aside some of the inventory spreadsheets that have been giving me a headache for the past half-hour, then lean back and plaster a smile on my face. I can see, just by her expression, that she wants to call me out on what she walked in on—but, just like every other time before, she doesn't ask. Instead, she does what she always does, proving to me that I'm not completely alone by just being there for me and with me. It's easy to forget that loneliness when your best friend is determined to love you enough that you know you'll never be without her at your side.

She walks into my office and takes a seat on the couch opposite my desk, pushed against the wall. "Matt and I had another fight last night. I couldn't get out of the house quick enough this morning. Worst part, I'm starting to think all I have to do is wake up to set him off."

"Oh, Pipe." I sigh. Everything else forgotten, I place my pen down and push my chair away from the desk. "What was it this time?" I ask, while making my way over to the couch. Taking a seat next to her, I grab her hand, holding it tight and offering my support.

She lifts her free hand and waves it in the air. "Oh, you know, the normal. I'm not willing to quit my job. I don't wear the right 'sophisticated' clothing to all his fancy functions—even if the ones I wear cost more than what most people make in a month. My hair should be straight, not left in a 'disorganized bunch of curls that a toddler would favor.' How he can't see me ever being mature enough for children—not to mention the fact that I don't *want* to have children anytime soon. Just a normal day, so take your pick."

Anger swirls in my gut. I hate Piper's fiancé. If there was a stronger emotional response to someone other than hate, that is how I would feel about Matthew Scott. However, hate or not, he's the man she's chosen to spend her life with, and I learned my lesson when the one and only time I tried to talk her out of it went terribly.

"Pipe," I start, but just sigh when she shakes her head.

"I know. *I know.* It's just not that easy, Ari. I've been with him for almost fifteen years. I don't think I know how to start over."

"You guys started dating when you were too young to understand what a relationship should be about, babe. It might be fifteen years, but a big part of those were when you guys were just teens. You know I'll support you either way, but do you really think that staying with him just because it's what you've always known is the right answer?"

"No. I know it isn't. I just, I've got no one else."

"You have me."

Her worry lines relax slightly, and she gives me a small twist of her lips. It's not a full smile, but I'll take it.

"You're always there for me when I need you, Pipe. You always have been. What on earth would make you think I wouldn't do the same for you? Just think about it. Even if you just stay with me for a little while to get your head clear and straight. Maybe a break is all you two need to get back on the right path."

Okay, so I'm stretching it thin here—but I'll do just about anything to get her away from him.

"I'll think about it, okay?"

"That's all you can do, babe."

"Enough about my problems. Let me get out there and get to work." She doesn't wait for me to say anything else on the subject before she plasters a smile on her face and walks out of my office.

That is just like Piper to effectively get what was bothering her out, and then return to business as usual. Only, I know my best friend, and behind the perfectly put together blond bombshell dressed head to toe in designer wear—even if it isn't ever perfect enough for her man—she can still be just as broken and lost as I am.

Enough of this, Ari. It's time. You've let yourself be dragged down enough.

With a shake of my head, I stand from the couch and walk over to my office doorway. Located in the very back of my store, it gives me a perfect view of the large space before me. My eyes go directly to the massive glass jewelry case situated in the farthest corner from my office by the front door, where Piper is standing to get the computer turned on and the accounting program we use up and running before we open for the day. You would never know by looking at her right now that her personal life is a mess. Not my Pipe. She's smiling to herself, clearly aware that anyone inclined to do a little window shopping before store hours will be able to see her through the glass storefront, and everyone knows first impressions are everything in life.

I guess we've really both perfected that mask over the years—for different reasons—but we wear it well. I consider myself thankful for the fact we were able to hone that skill from an early age. It was our norm growing up as the daughters of very well-off families to often find ourselves in social settings that required a certain air of perfection. It's ingrained inside us to always put our best foot forward when in public. Of course, we also broke that rule and marched to our own beat—but it's true what they say, old habits die hard.

"Hey, Pipe?" I call out, and I wait for her to look over at me before I continue. "What do you say we head over to Barcode tonight for some drinks? It's been one of those days, and I think it's the best way to close out the week."

She doesn't answer for so long, I would have thought she didn't hear me if she hadn't been looking right at me. I was fully prepared for her to shoot me down, but with a nod that I'm sure is more to convince herself, she agrees.

"We can leave our cars here and Uber over if that's okay. That way we can enjoy ourselves without worrying about how we're going to get home."

"Yeah, sounds good, Ari," she answers. The hesitant sadness is not as dominant in her eyes as it was when she sat on my couch.

"I'm going to finish up payroll, then I'll be in the back cataloging and tagging some new items. I think Lily is coming in a little early today, but Hannah will be in at her normal time. Just yell if you need me, okay?"

"Aye aye, boss," she jests, looking back at the screen with her hand clicking away at the mouse.

It doesn't take me long to get through payroll. My store isn't huge, but six girls work with us in the store and another eight handle the online store and orders, so it takes me long enough to remember why I hate this part of owning my own business. It's hardly a career that makes a difference in someone else's life—but it's the hand I was dealt, and I wouldn't dream of not giving it my all. Even if it wasn't so profitable that I could essentially hire someone to do all this for me and just sit at home, I would still find a way to keep it growing.

When Trend first opened back in the early 90s, it was just a hobby of my mother's that she built with my father's help as a staunch businessman. She came from a very well-off family, and when her parents passed away, being an only child, she ended up with so much designer brand items, she could never have kept them all—not to mention more money than she knew what to do with. So she created Trend around just that, reselling designer items.

Over the years, her pet project turned into a thriving business that no one could stop. Before she died, Trend was turning a profit that guaranteed the rest of our family's lives would be spent breathing easy and breathing well.

She didn't have to work. My father had his fingers in so many pies there wasn't much he touched that didn't turn to gold, which is why I always thought Trend became so successful. But it was all her and her love for the store she created. People could tell when you were doing something you loved rather than doing it because you needed the money. She loved this place, and I loved my mother, so it wasn't a shock when she passed away that she gave Trend to me and not my sister—who never showed any interest in the business anyway. Knowing I didn't just share her love for luxury, but I loved and trusted her enough to take the gift she had given me, she wouldn't have done it without knowing down to her bones it was what I needed. Even if she hadn't left it to me, I would have fought tooth and nail to get Trend after the loss of my parents. This might not have been the future I originally saw for myself, but it's the only place I feel like I can still be near her. Plus, the only reason my sister wanted it was for the only thing she knew how to love—the money.

I stop walking when I get to the closed door in the back corner of Trend. Clearing my mind, I swipe my key pass and enter my code on the electronic keypad, then wait for it to signal the next step in our security process before placing my palm on the screen. The door clicks, and I reach down to the handle to open the large steel door that takes me into the cage—what we lovingly call the back storage room, which is really just a hallway made out of thick steel and concrete walls that take me to the warehouse behind Trend—where the magic is stored.

We had three huge consignment drop-offs yesterday, so I know I have a long day ahead of me in the back of the store, tagging and organizing what will go to the store or be loaded onto our online boutique. It's a long process, running both the physical store and the website, but ever since I made the move to the internet, our profits have been through the roof.

Trend only carries high-end designer items, so our security is so over the top, it would take a tanker to get into the cage area. What isn't out in the showroom is kept back here on shelving units organized by item and designer. Smaller vault style units for jewelry. Larger ones for clothes, and a mixture of the two for purses and shoes. It's a good thing that Trend is so profitable; otherwise, the cost of the security system and the night guard alone would put me out of business in mere days. Heck, maybe minutes.

It doesn't take me long to get lost in my work, only allowing my thoughts to drift where they always do when I find myself stressed—to the daydreams of a faceless lover, one who always comes back to me when I need the warm promise of something more than the nothing I allow myself.

In no time, though, my thoughts drift back to Piper. The trouble between her and her fiancé being too worrisome for me to think about much else. At least I got her to agree to accompany me to Barcode, one of our favorite local bars, tonight. We haven't been there in so long, and I know a huge part of that is because of Matt. He dislikes the place just because of its proximity to the most popular strip club north of the Vegas Strip. We meant to go back a few months ago when both establishments had a few theme nights that interested us, but Matt's distaste for the place stopped Piper, and without Piper I wasn't going. However, it's not lost on me that Matt's car has been seen parked in front of the same strip club that he says is full of nothing but trash and disease.

Well, tonight I plan to show my best friend that she is better than the emotionally abusive and manipulative man who she thinks she can't leave.

Tonight, I'm going to take the old Ari out of the box she's been stored in and help my friend see she deserves to have nothing but perfection.

Tomorrow.

Tomorrow I'll work on believing I can have that for myself again.

Maybe.

With a smile, I tuck my crossed leg out of the way when a customer enters the dressing room area. She takes the only open room out of the four we have without noticing me, or if she did, she didn't feel the need to share pleasantries with someone she assumed was just shopping. Most of my clients are repeat business, but every now and then, I get a socialite brat who, even though she's shopping second-hand, acts like everyone around her is beneath her.

I hear one of the doors open and meet Piper's blue eyes when she steps out of the dressing room, and a genuine smile curves my lips as I stand and walk over to where she's studying herself in the mirror.

Oh yes, red was a great call if I do say so myself.

I've always envied her body, tall with legs for days, a great butt, and an even more generous chest. With curly blond hair that literally bounces with every step, and eyes bluer than any Caribbean waters I've seen, Piper is the very image of perfection—even if she's lost the ability to see it over the years. But when you encase that body in a skintight red dress that hits her about five inches below indecent levels, well, you have a showstopper. Even if the neckline doesn't show off her cleavage, the tightness of the dress will turn heads.

"You're going to turn heads tonight," I tell her honestly, smiling and tapping my chin before leaving the dressing room area. Stepping out into the store, I look over at our massive collection of heels, and it doesn't take me long to find what I'm hunting for. Grabbing a pair of black heels that sport sleek red bottoms, I head back to her with my arms outstretched and the heels hanging from my fingertips. "And probably stop a few hearts while you're at it," I finish with a wink.

She turns in the mirror and smiles. "I've had my eye on this dress for weeks, Ari."

"I know. That's why I grabbed it a week ago when I saw someone circling it."

She runs her hands down her flat stomach and spins, taking the heels and lifting her feet one at a time to slip them on. "Well, what about you?"

I look down at my outfit: black pencil skirt that tests my ability to sit with its tightness, white camisole tucked into the skirt, a black blazer on top, and the sexiest pair of red peep toe heels to add some color. I shrug off my blazer, tossing it on the chair I just stood from, then start removing the pins holding my long black hair up in a bun. After placing them on the little table between the waiting chairs, I push my fingers into my thick hair and give it some good fluffing. Then I look at my best friend and raise a brow.

"Right. I forgot, you're perfect," she smarts.

"Ha." I snort. "Hardly, Pipe. Just got lucky I wasn't wearing jeans today."

"When do you ever wear jeans?"

I roll my eyes but don't respond because she's right. I always dress nice because it gives me an air of confidence I don't always feel. Plus, Piper knows I avoid them because *she* definitely wears jeans, and I'll do just about anything to be as different as I can from *her*. Again, not something I need to remind Piper about because she gave up jeans the second I did in some silent move of solidarity. She'll joke about my classy outfits, but she understands why I am the way I am.

"Let me go grab my purse and we can get out of here. Will you take care of the Uber while I'm shutting things down in my office and checking with the girls?"

When she nods, I head to get everything I need done so we can head over to Barcode, to give my best friend a girls' night guaranteed to take both of our minds off everything swirling around us.

TWO

Just like old times

"WHEN DID YOUR SISTERS START WORKING HERE?" I question in shock, looking at Piper's little sisters behind the bar at Barcode, wearing next to nothing.

"Uh, your guess is as good as mine, girlfriend." Piper's brows pull in, confusion only lasting a second before her anger flashes red hot.

Piper grabs my hand and starts dragging me toward the bar. With each of her stomped steps, I scurry and stumble behind her. *Well, aren't I just the picture of grace?* I hear her telling people to move, pushing us through the crowd around the bar until she has enough space to brace herself on the wood bar top, lean over, and turn toward the sister closest to her.

"Meggie Ross! Get your ass over here right now!" Piper yells, gaining her sister's attention immediately, even with the music as loud as it is.

"Piper!" Meggie exclaims. "One sec, big sis!" She holds up her finger, smiles, and then turns to the men she was filling shots for with a wink.

"Don't you one second me, Meggie." When she still doesn't get the reaction she was aiming for with her barked orders, she turns in the other direction where her other sister is still working, completely oblivious to the arrival of her insane big sister. "Melissa Ross! Get over here!"

"There a problem?"

At the question, I see Piper's head turn at the same time mine does. Her grip becomes painful on my wrist as she takes in the man who had spoken. I try to yank my wrist away, but before I can get loose, she tightens even more.

"Pipe, let go!" I yell with a jerk, stumbling back a little before regaining my balance.

"I said, is there a problem?" the man repeats, looking at Piper with an interest that I'm not sure has everything to do with her acting like a raging maniac. He's handsome, that's for sure. Dark blond hair, cut short, blue eyes, and a face that belongs on billboards.

When she just stands there, I lean in and look around her body to see her face frozen, staring at the stranger with an expression I haven't seen in her eyes since middle school and Bobby Turner grabbed her barely there boobs for the first time. I give her a beat before turning to the man, seeing both sisters moving in from either side of his body.

"Uh, sir, if you'll excuse my friend here, she's just being … well, she's their big sister and … okay, I'm not really sure why she's acting insane, but she's apparently forgotten how to speak. So, sorry? From both of us."

"Do Mom and Dad know you two are working at a bar IN YOUR UNDERWEAR!?" Piper finishes her rant with a scream, finally coming unglued and glaring at her sisters.

"You two deal with your family issues. I'll cover the bar, but fuck, for Christ's sake, do it in the back."

I look at Meggie, then over at Melissa and offer them a small smile. They just roll their eyes, not even looking the least bit mad at Piper for being an embarrassing nutcase.

"Follow us," Meggie says, walking down the long area behind the bar.

Piper grabs my hand again, pulling me with her as she follows her sisters in to what looks like a nice size break room. The second the door closes the loud sounds of the bar are dull enough that I can sit through the Ross sisters loving each other the only way they know how. Loud and louder. I laugh silently to myself, used to the craziness with them after a lifetime growing up beside the three of them.

"You two look like strippers," Piper snaps first, hands on her hips and glare aimed at the girls.

"And you look like a call girl." Meggie laughs, waving her hand in the air at her big sister's outfit.

"I think they like to be called escorts now," Melissa adds, giggling right along with her.

"Would you two stop it!?" Piper yells over their laughter. "And an escort wishes she could be as classy as me!"

One of them snorts when her giggle turns into a full belly laugh.

"Meggie, I think Pipe might be mad at us."

"I swear to God, I'm calling Dad!" Piper continues, reaching into her clutch to grab her phone.

"Ah, well, tell him we said hi! Even though we just saw him about two hours ago. You should try the Blue Moon Dad is always raving about. I haven't yet, but that's all he drinks when he visits us at work."

And that stops Piper. I roll my lips between my teeth to keep from laughing out loud. I'm not shocked in the least that Papa Ross spends time at the bar, supporting his girls ... even if they are dressed like strippers. When Piper joined me at Trend, he would pop in all the time for almost a year. No doubt that he loves his daughters.

"He did *not.*"

"Uh, Pipe," I interject, knowing these three could go on for hours. "I feel like I should point out that it isn't really any different than that summer you worked at Hooters."

Her head jerks around, curls going wild, and she narrows her eyes at me. "This isn't even close to that."

"Actually, it was worse because at least they have jeans on. You had shorts wedged up your butt."

"Whose side are you on?" Piper hisses.

I shrug. "I've only known you longer because they were born when you were eight. So I'm not picking sides. But I will add that you're being slightly irrational."

"My baby sisters are working at a bar that everyone knows is just an extension of The Alibi. Dressed like that, you know what men will think," she hisses, referring to the strip club in the large converted warehouse next to Barcode.

Melissa steps forward and takes Piper's hands in her own. "You know I love you, but seriously, what is the big deal?"

"Someone's projecting," Meggie adds, picking at her nails and looking bored.

"Don't, Megs," Melissa tells her, looking at her with annoyance before returning her attention to Piper. "What's wrong?"

"Why are you working here?" Piper asks, much calmer. "What happened with the hospital?"

"Nothing happened. We're just picking up a few shifts here on the weekends we're off. With the budget cuts, we both lost a few shifts. You know we're trying to save money."

"So come work at Trend!" Piper responds in exasperation, her voice picking up again, and I know she's winding up to keep this argument going.

"Piper, we're not going to work at Trend."

"You could if you wanted to," I add so Piper won't feel like she's on her own, fighting a battle that, in my opinion, doesn't need to be fought. "And, by the way, sorry about the budget cuts. That happened when I was at the hospital too."

"No thanks to Trend, Ari. No offense. We had a feeling they were coming. I completely forgot about when it happened to you. I bet you're happy you left that place," Meggie replies, changing her focus before her words even stop and finally walking over to her sisters. "Wild's a great guy, Pipe. He keeps us safe, and the tips here are unreal. And when I say he keeps us safe, I mean he keeps security at both ends of the bar and throughout the place. There has never, in the two months we've worked here, been someone who even had a chance to get close. We have fun. Bottom line, we've been here for what feels like a second and have already saved more than we could ever hope to put aside with just our nurse's salary."

"But what if someone gets the wrong impression and ..." She trails off, and the room instantly gets heavy as understanding dawns on the three of us. And just as swiftly as awareness dawns on us, the mood shifts. I can't believe none of us connected the dots to what had happened to Piper over a decade ago.

Easy to forget things, I suppose, when you're too busy burying your own pain.

"Pipe, we're safe. I promise," Meggie stresses with assurance—and understanding—in her tone. "I swear to you. Wild wouldn't let anything happen to anyone, employee or patron."

"Wild?"

"Our friend, well, boss. Wilder Fox."

"His name is Wilder Fox?"

"I know. Sounds like he was born to be a porn star, doesn't it?" Melissa jokes.

"Dad's really okay with you guys working here?" Piper continues, not laughing at her sister and ignoring the joke about their boss. Even if I wanted to laugh, I keep my mouth shut and have my best friend's back.

"Swear, Pipe."

"And you're safe?"

"Safer than we are at the hospital."

The silence ticks on until Piper lets out an audible sigh. "I'm sorry," she mumbles under her breath.

"That hurt to say, huh?" Meggie jokes, nudging Piper with her elbow before wrapping her arms around her shoulders and hugging her sister. "I love that you're protective of us, Pipe, I really do, but you have to let us live our lives. We're big girls, you know? Nothing will happen to us here, swear it."

"Even if we're going to be living our lives with our best bras showing," Melissa adds with a giggle.

"You do look hot," I add, joining the huddle and turning it into a group hug right before the door opens.

"You two done with the family reunion back here? I could use some help on the bar," their boss, who I now know is named Wilder, says before leaving just as quickly as he came.

"You obviously came here for a reason, so why don't you go find a spot at the bar and let your sisters take care of you guys for once?" Meggie suggests, smiling brightly before turning and walking out the door without waiting for us to respond.

Melissa gives Piper another hug, their blond curls dancing together. "I love you, you overprotective lunatic."

"I love you back, brat," Piper says.

We follow Melissa out, walking around the bar and into the sea of people around us when she goes behind the counter. I hear Meggie telling people to move because her VIPs were coming through, opening a hole dead smack in the middle for us. We sidle up, and before we've even had a chance to get our elbows on the sleek wood, two very full shot glasses are plopped down in front of us.

"Enjoy," Wilder says, giving me a warm smile, his blue eyes dancing before looking at Piper—his interest in my best friend clearly obvious in their bright depths.

Well, this is interesting.

Ignoring him, she takes the glass in her hand, turns to me, and lifts it in the air. I watch his eyes land on her engagement ring, and he looks almost pissed, but before I have a chance to study his odd reaction, Piper starts talking. "To girls' night and sister strippers!"

With a hoot of laughter, I'm thankful we quickly got past her reaction to finding her sisters took a side job as bra-wearing bartenders. Even if it brought up painful memories for Piper. I grab my own shot glass to clink against hers, then place the cool glass to my lips and down the shot. The burn of the tequila making me cringe.

Three shots later, we're both nursing a healthy buzz if the carefree giggles we are emitting are any indication. I'm not sure which one of us made it to the dance floor first, but the next thing I know, we're losing ourselves in the music, dancing like we were born to wear four-inch heels and make it look effortless. Both of us laughing with our arms in the air and not a single worry in the world. At that moment, we're just two friends having a blast after the healing powers of tequila and a best friend's love.

Just like old times.

Just like always when we lock our troubles away and forget it all.

By the time we head back to the bar for more shots, I can feel the cool bar air hitting my heated cheeks and damp skin, making goose bumps dance across my skin. When we reach the bar, I place my purse on the wood and grab my compact and red lipstick out of it to touch up what had worn off during the past hour of drinking and dancing.

I'm not sure what made me turn my head, but with my mouth still slightly open from applying my favorite red shade, I look over my compact and straight into the gaze of someone who defines the word carnal at the curve of the bar about ten feet away. I feel a punch to my heart as it awakens with arousal. My hands lower, my mouth closes, and I just stare. Even when I realize the rest of the man's face is hiding behind the woman he's kissing deeply, I still don't look away … and neither does he. Oh, he's giving his all to the woman his lips are savoring, but he's doing it with those eyes boring into mine. The only other part of him that I can see with her blocking the rest of his face and the dim lighting—aside from the thick, styled dark hair on top of his head—is one of his hands as he holds her head still. My whole body buzzes with awareness.

What is wrong with me? What kind of woman watches another's man with desire when he's clearly taken? I'm a disgrace to the sisterhood.

The woman's arms move up, and then I lose his eyes when, I assume, she adjusted their stance.

Holy crap.

If I felt that kiss from thirty feet away, I can't even imagine what she is feeling. Not that I'll ever know, that's for sure. As much as I would love to. I look down, putting my compact and lipstick back in my purse right as another shot is placed in front of me by Meggie on her way down the bar. Not waiting for Piper, I down it and don't even notice the burn. How could I when my body is on fire from something that has nothing to do with the alcohol I've consumed tonight and everything to do with the gaze of a stranger. I jerk my head back suddenly to where he was, only to find both him and his woman gone.

Stupidly, I feel the disappointment over his absence, knowing damn well I was about to attempt to memorize everything I could about that stranger's eyes so I could use the memory of the feelings they evoked to keep me warm when I get home to my empty house.

Clearly, it's been WAY too long since I've played this game of attraction if the past few minutes are anything to go by.

I push down my disappointment and do my best to forget him … even when I feel the overwhelming need to go in search of him.

Maybe I will *get another cat.*

And that's the last thing I remember before the tequila and good music take over my rational thought.

THREE

Ari

It's just Thorn

SMILE AT THE CUSTOMER, WAITING FOR THE NEXT QUESTION to come. It always does. Always. It doesn't matter that I've built a reputation of selling only authentic luxury items in my store. It doesn't matter that, in twenty years, there has never been a counterfeit sold in this store. People always ask. Some just with a little more class than others.

"You sure this is real, honey?"

The corners of my lips threaten to fall from my fake smile, but I hold them up and relax the impatience from my body.

"Yes, ma'am. As with all our items, they come with a letter of authenticity. However, I can assure you that this purse is one hundred percent authentic as it was purchased right in front of me in London about three years ago."

"Paris, you say?" the older woman asks with a tilt of her head.

I give her a shake of my head, spying her hearing aid, and repeat myself.

"Well, I've always wanted to go to Paris. I hear it's lovely. But London *is* one of my favorite places to visit."

"It is lovely," I respond, a familiar lump making its way up my throat.

"You won't go down on the price at all?"

Piper pokes my side from where she's kneeling next to me, placing some new jewelry pieces in the display case next to the register. She knows how I feel about London, and it has nothing to do with the city. I ignore her, knowing if I look down, she's probably just going to make a ridiculous face.

"Prices are firm, I'm sorry."

The older lady gives a wave of her hand, her sweet little face still alight with happiness. "Nonsense, sweet child. I probably would have paid more, but it doesn't hurt to ask anyway. I can't believe someone would part with a Louis Vuitton bag that looks brand new. My dear old Henry, he's put up with my spending for sixty years. Trust me, one little purse isn't going to make him blink now."

For the first time today, my smile comes freely. "I imagine he won't."

"I'll take it. And those earrings your friend is fiddling with. Are those Chanel?"

"Yes, ma'am."

"And they're real too?"

Piper stands, wearing a huge grin, the curls around her face bouncing with her exuberance. "Oh, yes. Ari here wouldn't dare have something fake in Trend. Just like your beautiful new purse, these beauts come with the same guarantee of authenticity as well as their original purchase documents and packaging. We just got them in the other day, too. Such a good find."

She reaches out, and one weathered finger grazes the studs. "That's good, honey. My great-granddaughter is graduating from college this weekend. Do you think she'll like these?"

I let Piper continue the conversation while I busy myself with pulling the paperwork for each item. Carefully folding them and stuffing them inside an envelope with the logo for Trend, I make a mental note to reorder before I go home tonight.

The two continue to chat while I ring her up, scanning both the purse and earrings before turning and wrapping them up—one of my favorite things to do while at work. I could spend all day stuffing tissue paper into boxes and arranging each item perfectly so it looks as if the items are lying on a tissue throne, before placing each light gray box into a lavender glossy shopping bag with Trend embossed on the outside.

Chic.

Sophisticated.

The perfect packaging.

Always.

Just like my mother taught me.

Make sure they get an experience, my sweet girl. The same as if you were to buy something lux brand new. The packaging is just as exhilarating as the purchase itself. Don't ever deny someone that experience.

My mother's voice wisps through my thoughts, sounding as if she spoke them right next to me. I smile at the bag, the familiar twinge of her memory pulling on my heartstrings as something I can finally remember without the searing pain accompanying it.

"Looks like Ari's got you all settled, Mrs. Larkin. If you need anything, just give us a call. I placed our business card in with your purchase receipts—both original to the items and the one for to-day. We also provide you with a care card for your purse. Just some basic information on how to keep the leather and canvas healthy," Piper says with a smile, picking up both the shopping bag with the purse and the gift-wrapped earrings before walking around the glass display case to stand next to our customer, Mrs. Larkin. "Now you lead the way, and I'll walk you out."

"Nonsense, honey. I might be old, but I've been shopping lon-ger than you've been alive, I imagine. The day I need help carrying my bags is the day someone should take my credit cards away from me."

Piper giggles. "That may be so, Mrs. Larkin, but walking you out gives me a chance to talk to you about that stunning Rolex you're wearing."

The older woman's eyes crinkle with humor. "I think I see now how you two manage to have such a lovely stock here."

"Now, Mrs. Larkin, are you suggesting I would try to talk you out of your watch?" Piper continues, guiding her right out the front door.

I laugh to myself softly. Piper's not shy when it comes to talking customers out of something she wants. I have no doubt Mrs. Larkin will be back with that watch and a handful of other items that Piper will convince her to sell with the promise of cash or store credits.

"Didn't you have an appointment at six?" Piper asks, coming back in and flipping the lock on the front door.

Glancing at the clock, I frown. "Yeah. I completely forgot. I guess he changed his mind about selling the collection we spoke about."

"Do you want me to stick around? Just in case he shows?"

"No, Pipe. I've got it. I have some accounting to do anyway."

"You sure? Matt and I don't have anything planned tonight."

Ugh, Matt. In the three weeks since our girls' night, he's been on his best behavior, so of course, it's all sunshine and roses for Piper, once again thinking he's not an evil jerk.

I open my mouth to respond, but shut it with a frown when the loud rumble of a motorcycle vibrates through the shop. Piper's head snaps in the direction of our front windows.

"Holy cow," she gasps a second later.

"Ditto," I breathe, not looking away from the tall man staring into the store from atop his big, black, shiny motorcycle.

Though he's still wearing his sunglasses when the sun has already dipped below the trees, I can feel his eyes on me. Whatever he sees, it must have been what he's looking for because a second later, he's removing his helmet. One long, jean-covered thigh flexes as he pops out the kickstand, then the other comes up and over the bike before he straightens, placing the black helmet down where he had been sitting moments before.

He's huge. Something I can tell without standing anywhere near him. Heck, even his shoulders top over the roof of my SUV he's parked next to. The black shirt stretched over those shoulders looks like a second skin on him, taking him from huge to massive.

"Pinch me," Piper gasps.

"Me first," I blurt, feeling my face heat instantly when Piper looks away from the stranger and studies me with a keen eye.

"No way!" she exclaims. "You'll definitely need to pinch me

first, girlfriend. Sweet little Ari Daniels, interested in a man! It's been so long since that's happened, I forgot you weren't a lesbian."

"Don't be a twit, Pipe."

"Oh, no you don't. Mr. Tall, Dark, and Handsome has awakened my best friend from her long nap of celibacy and disinterest in men. Where's my phone? I need to record this moment."

"You make it sound like I'm some spinster, living alone with my cats." One perfectly arched brow rises, and I narrow my eyes at my best friend. "I have one cat, Pipe. That doesn't mean I'm close to giving up on life and collecting more."

"Yet. You aren't collecting cats *yet*. But after six years, I'm just glad you've found a way to let those butterflies stir up attraction in your body."

She forgets all about me and my butterflies when a hearty thump comes from the front door. My heart feels like it's about to gallop right out of my chest when I turn and see the biker at *my* door, one big fist resting against the glass he just knocked on. Before I can do anything short of blink, Piper springs forward and unlocks the door, flinging it open.

"Hiya!"

He looks down at her, his expression giving nothing away. His sunglasses are gone, and from a few feet away, I watch as he takes in my best friend. It isn't a shock to me that he's showing interest in Piper—she's stunning—however, the disappointment I feel over it *is*.

I take a quick second to look him over now that he's closer than the parking area. His black hair is longish on top, shaved on the sides, and a complete mess from the helmet he pulled off moments before. I bet, when he takes the time, it could be styled perfectly in that rugged yet sophisticated way that men do. My gaze sweeps over his face, memorizing each attractive feature as quickly as I can—the strong nose, full lips, and powerful jaw that no amount of stubble could hide. He's the definition of perfect. I quickly glance down his body, seeing the tattoos on his arms and hands before going back to his handsome face.

It's during my perusal of his face that I realize my mistake. A tiny tightening of his jaw, making the area right near his ear flex, draws my eyes up, meeting his with a gasp I'm helpless to contain when I find him looking straight at me.

"We're closed, but if you want to come back tomorrow, we open at nine," Piper continues, not even fazed by the stifling electricity zapping around her, lighting an invisible path between this man and me.

When was the last time a man affected me so carnally that the attraction wrapped around me like a thick fog? I shift on my heels, not knowing what to do other than just stand here and gape at this man. His eyes narrow, but aside from that, he doesn't move to come into the store. I know exactly when I last felt a connection like this. Good heavens, what is wrong with me? Twice in a handful of weeks and I've turned into a lust machine I don't even recognize.

"Of course, I'm sure Ari wouldn't mind if you wanted to glance around a little while I finish cleaning the store up," Piper carries on, her voice sounding muffled through the pounding of my heart.

His gaze leaves mine, and he frowns down at Piper. Huge. I wasn't wrong. Piper's a few inches under six feet in flats, and this guy makes even her look small. Then again, being only five-foot-two, mostly everyone is a giant to me.

After a beat, his full lips open and his tongue comes out to wet them, rolling over his bottom lip in a slow and lazy glide that effectively kills any chance I had at regaining any rational thoughts.

Damn, that's hot.

"You both here alone?" he asks, his voice sounding rough and gritty—unused—rumbling out deeply. Something else I feel zap right through me.

"It's seven o'clock," I say as if that's explanation enough.

"Right," he grunts. "If I'm too late for my appointment, I can make a new one. Though I'll be late for that one too."

Well, if that wasn't enough to knock some of the lust drunkenness right out of my sails.

"You're Mr. Thorn?" Piper questions on a shocked gasp.

"Evans," he strangely responds.

"I'm sorry?"

"Last name. It's Evans. *I'm* just Thorn."

"Oh, uh, okay. Well, Mr. ... I mean, Thorn, we can keep your appointment tonight since you're here. No sense in making a new one if you'll be late for that one too," I confirm, walking back around the glass display and placing my hands on the cool surface before continuing. I hope I sound more put together than I feel because at this point, it sounds like he's just speaking Muppet mom. "Did you have someone else bringing the collection we discussed?"

His gaze moves to my hands and the case under them. I have no doubt my defensive move of placing something between us didn't go unnoticed. Piper clears her throat, waiting while volleying her attention back and forth between the two of us. When he steps deeper into the store, she moves to relock the front door, then turns and moves to the shelves of purses. Unlocking the glass door, she straightens a few of them—even though they were already perfect.

Nosy Piper. Her eyes remain on us and not the bags she's making a new mess of.

"I got pictures. Didn't want to drag all that shit over here if you weren't interested in taking it off my hands."

With great effort, I manage to keep my smile and not frown at him. "With all due respect, Mr. Evans—"

"It's just Thorn."

"Right, well, *just* Thorn … I'm sure you'll understand that, with the nature of what we do here, I need to inspect each item listed for consignment thoroughly to verify authenticity before I can make you an offer. Not just that, but the offer may vary due to condition and such."

"Yeah, I figured as much, but no way am I dragging that much shit over here unless it's something you're interested in. And I don't want consignment. You offer straight buyouts?"

I nod. "We do. Of course, you would make more if you went with consignment, though."

"Yeah, I get it. I don't care about making more. I just need it gone. Here are the pictures."

When he pulls out a thick stack of photos from his back pocket, my eyes grow wide. I knew he had numerous pieces from the message Piper took when he made his appointment, but I didn't know he had *this* many. The top image alone has my mouth watering.

"That's a Birkin!" Piper gasps, looking around his body at the same image that has my purse addicted soul crying tears of joy. We get Birkins every few years, but they always go quickly and, unfortunately, never to my own personal collection. I know Piper's been salivating for years to get one, but even with her employee discount, she's never bought one when it came in. Neither have I, though.

"I take it that means something?" he asks.

"Something? It means so much more than just something," Piper gasps with a giggle.

"Yeah, got that. Also, not interested in hearing why."

I don't look up, but I can only guess my sweet friend is shooting daggers. Lifting my hands off the glass, I reach for the stack of photos. My hands shake the whole time, something I'm sure doesn't go unnoticed. In my line of work, it helps to know what you're looking at. I can spot a counterfeit bag from a mile away at this point. Because of the guarantee we offer, I have to know what I'm looking at. Otherwise, I would spend thousands on something only to find out it's fake when I get down to appraising its authenticity? Nope. Not this chick. I didn't study myself into the ground to turn around and buy fakes. It doesn't hurt that, in each picture, you can tell these purses are coming from a very well-off household. Just the way they seem to be displayed alone is telling, but each and every one looks like it has never been used. You don't spend that kind of money to have this size of a collection, and apparently never use them, if you don't have an overabundance of money to throw away.

"I'm sure you understand now why I didn't want to drag all of this out of the house and across town. If you're interested, I can arrange to bring them here tomorrow."

"Interested is a mild way to express how I feel about all of these," I mumble, flipping through each photo with glee. "And the original owner?" I ask, hating that I have to.

"Dead."

I jerk my eyes from the photo I had been studying of a stunning Louis Vuitton trunk and meet his. My mouth opens a few times to try to speak, but finally, I take a deep pull of air before releasing it and nod at the odd indifference I see in his eyes.

Not just green, I muse, not giving myself time to analyze the look in his gaze. Stupid or not, that's all I can focus on. His eyes. They're the most hypnotizing mix of blue and what looks like a million different shades of green. Stunning.

"I can prove that I have ownership of them, if that's what you're needing."

I flip through a few more pictures, trying to get over the nervous butterflies this man has kicked up in my belly. "I mean no disrespect, but given the enormity of this collection and all ..."

When I get to the last picture, I still can't believe how many extraordinary pieces this man is parting with. Then again, what would he do with them other than sell if the original owner is no longer around to enjoy them? Not like he's going to carry them.

A little laugh escapes my lips at that thought, and my cheeks burn. I clear my throat, trying to play my laugh off, embarrassed by my inability to act like a grown woman around this man.

"When would you like to arrange a time for me to come and look at them in person? It'll save you the trouble of having to bring all this in."

His eyes spark, and those stupid butterflies start to flutter in pure chaos.

"How about now?"

"Now?" I squeak out.

"No time like the present. I have a busy night ahead of me and an even busier week, so now's probably the best I've got for at least a few weeks or so."

I glance down at the glorious photos, knowing stock like this would fill my bank account for a long time to come, but the thought of going off to the unknown with this stranger is not exactly how I planned to spend my Friday night. Plus, he could be some serial killer trying to lure the unsuspecting store owner off to her death.

"The house is over in The Orchard. If it makes you feel better, your friend over there can take a picture of my driver's license, and you can stay on the phone with her the whole time. I just need this shit off my hands, so I can finally sell the damn place."

And for what feels like the millionth time since he walked into my store ten minutes ago, my face goes from pale to red.

"Lead the way," I find myself telling him, not sure if I just made the biggest mistake of my life or the best decision for my business.

FOUR

Ari

The Orchard

"**T**HE ORCHARD. OF ALL THE STUPID PLACES I HAD to go in order to get to the promise land of luxury brand items, it had to be *The* freaking Orchard." I turn my signal on and follow the man in front of me, careful not to get too close to his black beast of a bike. "Piper, seriously, THE Orchard."

"I know, Ari. I don't blame you for not being excited about that, but just think about it this way. You get all of that in Trend, and you are *made,* girlfriend! We're talking house paid off, car paid off, and you can finally take me on that European vacation I've always wanted to go on. Plus, The Orchard is a huge development. The chances of you running into anyone you know are slim."

"It's not that huge," I grumble, my heart racing as we stop at the gate. The security guard struts out of his little house at the development's entrance to talk to "just Thorn." When both of their heads turn toward me, I wave like an idiot, all the while trying to keep my salad from lunch hours ago from coming back up. "And my car is already paid off, and Matt can take you to Europe."

The Orchard.

I hate it here.

In fact, I hate it so much, I haven't been back once since I moved out of this hellhole almost seven years ago.

The bike revs a few times as the gate opens, then "just Thorn" starts moving forward. The security guard just flicks his wrist at me to indicate I should follow. I keep my eyes on the back of "just Thorn's" bike—his butt really, that is. Well, what I can see of it. I refuse to look around as I drive, just in case someone who knows me sees me driving by. And let's face it, you can tell it's a really nice butt even while he's sitting on his bike. My only hope is that, if I'm noticed, they would be more shocked that I'm here than the fact I'm clearly following a man through my old streets. At least if I'm noticed, I won't have to face anyone.

"You know, for what it's worth, I don't think he's going to kill you after he gets you to his house." I jump when Piper's voice echoes through my speakers. I had been so far in my head, I forgot she was on the phone.

"Very funny, Pipe."

"I can drive out there if you're still worried. I have the picture of his license on my phone. I wrote down all the information on your desk and texted it to us both. That way, if you go missing, I know where to tell the police to start looking."

I sigh. "I'm not worried. You know how I get around attractive men."

"He's just a man, Ari. It's not like you don't have male friends."

"I have a few gay male friends, Pipe, but they're more like acquaintances, and you know it. Big difference. Seeing as I don't have the right equipment to attract them, there's no pressure. You know, even knowing that, I still don't have the easiest time talking to them."

"So? Just think of Thorn Evans as a gay acquaintance who doesn't want your equipment."

"Even his name is sexy, Pipe. Let's just say, by some small feat, I was able to convince myself he was gay and not into me, it would still be impossible not to want him. My mind would scream 'make him switch teams.' You saw him. He practically has 'I can make you forget everything you ever knew and love it' seeping from his skin. A man that lethal can do a lot of damage. God, what am I doing? I haven't felt like this in … well, probably about the same amount of time since I've been to *The* freaking Orchard."

"Don't let *him* ruin what could potentially be a great one-night stand, Ari." Piper's scolding voice is harsh, but the memory of the "him" she's referring to is what makes my stomach roil.

"You just had to bring him up, didn't you?" I turn, following the bike in front of me slowly, thankful we're not turning on the street where I had lived years before.

"Technically, you brought him up first. It's been too long for you to keep letting them take from you, and you know it. Hike that skirt up and, for once, take the bull by his horns and enjoy the ride." She's quiet, but before I can speak, she continues. "Honey, it's been almost seven years. They might still try to mess with you, but even that's slowing down. I think it would be a good thing for you to start trying to find a way to move on, so you can get on with your life and start working toward a future that doesn't include a house full of cats."

"Easier said than done," I mumble, turning to loop up a circular drive, more thankful than ever that I stopped telling Piper about the calls years ago. "I gotta go, Pipe. We're here."

"Hike it up, girlfriend!" she screams through the line. Disconnecting quickly, she leaves silence to fill the space around me.

I open my door, pushing down the nerves, and climb out. My heels clip against the driveway as I walk over to where Thorn is standing at the entrance of the large—very large—modern gray home. The glow of Vegas behind it and the shadow of the mountains to the side leave the golden light shining warmly through the many windows on the house behind him.

He doesn't speak when I stop next to him, just turns and unlocks the door with a quick succession of numbers keyed into the lock. Not expecting instructions since it's clear I'm here to follow him, I do just that. Stopping a few feet into the foyer, I wait for him to disarm his alarm, taking the time to look around what I can see of his house. Whoever decorated this place clearly had one thing on their mind—white and glass with the occasional accent of crystals and gold statues. One thing's for sure, there isn't a thing about what I can see that looks like Thorn Evans belongs here.

"Not what you expected?" he guesses, and I tip my head up— way up—to study him. I knew he was tall, but jeez, he's at least six-foot-four, if not taller. And every inch of that looks like rock-hard muscles.

"You could say that."

"If I gave a shit about the place, I would say take your shoes off, but I don't, so fuck it up all you want."

I gasp, looking down and lifting each foot to make sure I wasn't tracking anything on the white stone. Of course, the second I realize he was actually being literal, my face is already turning a million shades of red. *Get yourself together!*

"That's an odd thing to say about a home that obviously was put together with a hand that cared."

"Takes a lot more than what used to fill this house to make it a home."

"Well, still …" I lamely add, feeling even more foolish for resorting to the actions of a little girl and not the woman I am.

"Also, wasn't my hand."

"So not the point I was trying to make."

He turns his head slightly away from me, but I don't miss the small smirk playing on his full lips. I'm glad I was watching him closely too; otherwise, I would have missed it. There one second, gone the next.

"Shit's this way," he rumbles, walking down the hallway to our left.

What a confusing man.

I follow behind, watching more of his backend and the way it moves when he walks than the home around me. I'm forced to take my eyes away when we reach a staircase. Not wanting to fall to my demise, I climb with a hand on the iron rail, my shoes the only noise around us as the heels hit each step. Keeping my eyes down, I take each step slowly as my heart picks a different direction, it seems, and speeds up as we go. My feet afraid of the leftover pain from the cruel twists of fate in my past … my heart forgetting every second of that, ready for a new adventure.

"I've got calls to make, but take as much time as you need, and trust me, you're goin' to need it." He presses his thumb on a scanner against the wall next to the door, and the door—with no knob, I might add—slides open instantly.

Lights start popping on around the vast room, each placed over the display shelves lining the walls and even some placed over the island in the middle. My mouth drops, and I walk forward without hesitation, my palms itching to touch what is so perfectly displayed around me. My purse starts to fall from my shoulders and almost crashes to the floor. I catch it, just, but before I can hike it back up my arm, it's lifted from my hold. I look down at the large hand curled around the handles before following the arm attached to it up to Thorn's face. He tilts his head, and I follow his direction to a small table just inside the doorway, clearly meant to be the resting place of whatever purse was lucky enough to be the chosen one of use for the owner. He moves silently over to it, placing my bag down with a soft thud. Really, though, him taking care of my purse shouldn't be something that makes my body tingle. But it does because big, huge, manly Thorn Evans looks ridiculously good holding a woman's bag with care when you would assume he is incapable of showing that for something like a purse.

"Four doors down. You finish before I come back, that's where I'll be."

Then he's gone, moving quicker than any man his size should be able to.

And without the distraction of him, I can let myself enjoy heaven.

Almost two hours later with fifty-two purses, fifteen backpacks, thirty clutches, two huge trunks, and ninety-six small leather goods, I literally am in heaven. Well, my version of it at least.

I place my phone down next to the notepad I had been making notes in while taking inventory of the room's contents and doing a quick check of each item's authenticity. By the time I finish, it only felt like a second, but when I glanced at the total on the calculator app, I couldn't believe I had been here long enough to have a total of *that* kind of number. The sheer magnitude of what this kind of haul could do for Trend making me dizzy.

Over four million dollars of value in this room alone. If not more.

Four. Million. Dollars.

If I offer him just the base that we tend to use for buyouts, I'll stand to profit over a million dollars alone. We do damn good at Trend on a normal day, but I would make what typically takes us months and months to earn in just a matter of weeks with this inventory. I wouldn't struggle to resell a single thing in here.

Piper wasn't wrong. I could probably take us on a million European vacations for what we would pull in. A. Million.

"Holy freaking cow," I breathe, taking in the room around me again.

I have to brace myself against the center island I was working on, my arms holding my weight as I let my head drop on a roll to work the kinks out of my shoulders. My mind too busy spinning to do much else.

It seems silly to get this worked up over stuff that is just, well, stuff. I know a large number of people see me, see Trend, and assume I'm some stuck-up snob, but that couldn't be further from the truth. For as long as I can remember, I loved everything that came with fashion. Learning the history of all the fashion houses was akin to a trip to the candy shop for most kids when I was growing up. It was a love and appreciation I shared with my mom, learning to respect the brands and hard work that goes behind their growth. I studied the history of each almost as much as I studied my schoolwork—which was something I enjoyed. Not one person was shocked when I became a licensed appraiser before I graduated med school. Most people see purses, flashy outfits, and unnecessary gems ... I just see art. When I lost my mom—and everything else that followed—the joy these "things" brought to my life pulled me out of a really dark place.

Thorn has no idea, but by just bringing me here—on this weekend, of all weekends—he gave me the closest thing I could ever get to a phone call from my mother.

"Done?"

I jump when Thorn's deep voice breaks the silence around me as if my thoughts conjured him up.

Pushing all my heavy thoughts aside, I look back around the room before addressing him. "This is quite the collection you have here, you know. I'm shocked you're willing to part with it all. It certainly was a collection built with pride for luxury." I lift my head and look over my shoulder at the imposing man standing at the mouth of the room.

"It belonged to my grandmother. Cared more about this shit than anything else. Trust me, ain't a thing in this room I give a shit about, much less feel pride over when I have to look at it."

His words shock me. Not because of how much conviction I hear in them, but because that's the most he's actually said to me in one go since walking into Trend earlier. Knowing when to leave well enough alone, I turn and grab my notepad in one hand and my phone in the other. Using that time to take a few deep breaths, I pray they will give me a level of professionalism toward this man.

"I hate to ask this, and I mean no offense, but because of, well, all of this," I say, stumbling over my words and waving my arm in an arch to indicate the room as a whole. "Well, I need to see purchase receipts, as well as proof that you're the authorized owner to sell it."

Without responding, he turns and walks away. What the heck am I supposed to do now? Do I follow or stay? Glancing around the room as if it holds all the answers, I sigh and start walking toward the door. When Thorn reappears, carrying a thick folio folder, I stop abruptly, causing my notepad and phone to slip from my hold and crash against the floor.

Idiot.

A thirty-two-year-old woman should not be a fumbling fool around a man just because he's attractive. As a businesswoman, I should be able to stand confidently around him and not act like I've never been around someone attractive. I should. Yet … here I am.

I scold myself as I bend down, but because my mind was too busy, I completely missed that Thorn was already on the move before it was too late. I cry out when our heads collide, sending me to the floor with a teeth rattling bump of my butt against the cool flooring.

"Of course, I *would* fall at his feet," I mumble under my breath.

"Babe, usually doesn't take me this long to get a woman to fall at my feet, so don't beat yourself up for taking your time."

"Oh, my God," I all but wheeze when I realize he heard my mumbling. It takes me a second in the dress I have on, but I manage to climb back to my feet without humiliating myself further—or giving him a show. I make a mental note to buy some skirts and dresses that don't hug my curves so much.

Not wanting to draw any more attention to my behavior, I press on. "Is that for me?" I ask, pointing toward the folio he's still holding. Of course, I realize after the fact that my brain is still working at a snail's pace because where his arm is slack at his side—placing the folio about hip level—it looks like I'm pointing at his crotch. "Kill me. Please kill me now."

A rumble akin to thunder sounds from his chest and my cheeks heat while he enjoys himself at my expense.

"Okay," I breathe, closing my eyes and counting to three before looking up at his handsome face. "Let's just start over." I switch my phone to my other hand, notepad pressed in my arm against my chest and stick out my hand. "I'm Ari Daniels. I'm not normally so … clumsy. We can just blame it on this room and before that, the pictures that were just a promise of all this. I'll do my best to stop acting like a silly girl and get out of your hair as soon as I can."

With mirth dancing in his magical eyes, one hand comes up, and the second he takes hold of mine, fingers wrapping tight, I know I've just broken my promise. I'm such a silly girl.

"Thorn Evans, as you know, and babe, I'm thinking I like you here in my hair."

With a jerk, I rip my hand from his hold and try my best to keep things on whatever is left of my professional standing.

"Can you go back to short answers that don't really reveal much?" His lips twitch. "Right, never mind. Okay, Mr. Evans," I start, only to be interrupted.

"I told you, Ari. It's just Thorn."

"Sorry … it's hard to break the habit," I blubber, liking the sound of my name way too much when it's coming from him and that deep rumble he calls a voice.

He walks around me to the island and drops the folio down with a loud smack before opening it and starting to pull out paper after paper.

"All the receipts are kept in the bottom drawer under each of the cases. You just press in on it, and it'll pop open. Took me forever to find that shit, so I didn't spend too much time fucking with what was inside. But from what little time I gave it, I figured out that all the receipts and proof of spending way too much on that shit was filed in order it's displayed. I haven't checked them all, but if you find something missing, it shouldn't be far. The bigger shit, in here." He spins around a receipt that looks fragile and old. My eyes go wide when I see it's an original receipt for one of the trunks I know is from the early 1900s. "Also, here's a copy of my grandmother's will, as well as her death certificate. You'll see on the fifteenth page that it lists these items specifically as part of her estate left to me." He stops talking, and I just stare at him, incapable of doing anything else. "What?" he asks me when I just keep blinking up at him after he's finished speaking and pushing papers in front of me.

"I just didn't think you could say that much in one go."

Again, those lips twitch, and I give myself a little shake before focusing on the documents in front of me. Thankfully, I finally seem to be able to shake off the way he makes me feel, and it doesn't take long for me to get ahold of myself. I start scanning each of the documents he's laid out. When I finish, I look up and try to give him a sympathetic smile after reading the last—the death certificate. Even though his earlier comments made it clear he wasn't close with the woman who previously owned this collection, my manners wouldn't allow me not to express my sympathy for his loss.

"Thank you for getting all of this. I'm sorry for your loss, Thorn. I understand some people wish to part with things after a loved one has passed, but I must ask if you're sure you want to include everything in the sale. It would hardly affect your buyout if you chose to keep a few things back. Perhaps to pass down eventually?"

His eyes get hard for a beat before his features smooth back out. "Yeah, beyond sure. No one to pass this shit down to, and even if there was, I wouldn't be givin' someone ideas of materialistic bullshit if I did. More to life than all this shit."

"Okay, well, in that case …" I cough, not wanting to fight with him about our views when it comes to expensive wants versus needs. Last time I tried to argue the benefits of learning to care for and value something you work hard to buy, I had a black eye for almost two weeks. "In that case, I'm prepared to offer you a lump sum as a buyout for the whole collection, but I also want to mention, again, that consignment would be a more lucrative approach. Our buyout is just a standard percent of resale value, but consignment would allow us to mark up each to give you a larger profit."

"Told you, babe, want it gone. I don't give a shit about making it more lucrative. Look around you, hardly hurting."

"Still, it's my obligation to make sure you're informed."

"Consider me informed."

"Okay … so I can offer a tentative amount of three million. I would need more time to inspect each item in depth for any defects that could affect the value and also to research a few pieces I feel may be limited editions so that could also affect the value. Meaning that amount could go up or down, but I wouldn't expect it to be less than two point five or more than four point seven-ish. I wouldn't need but maybe five days tops, and I can come during the day if that works better for your schedule."

"You get this gone in two days, and I'll take one mil."

My whole body jerks back as if I had been slapped, staring at him like he was absolutely insane.

"That's absolutely insane," I tell him, voicing my thoughts.

"No, that's me not giving a shit and wanting it gone so I can get out of this place and sell it and all this shit some hand with care placed around each room. Woulda left this shit in and sold it with the house, but for some reason I'll never understand, you're here, and I still just want it gone. You don't need five days when I'm taking a two mil hit, babe. That would waste your time and mine, and I'm not a huge fan of wasting my time. Way I see it, you win, and I get a cold mil for some shit I didn't buy nor care about. So you get this shit outta here, and all I need is that."

"Thorn, I can't in good conscience accept that."

"Then dirty that conscience up and laugh your tight little ass all the way to the bank. Don't give a shit as long as it's gone, and I don't have to do anything to make it that way."

"This is insanity."

"Insanity would be tossing it all at the Goodwill drop-off. I'm making money. You're making money. Only thing sweeter than making money is doing it while I'm getting my cock wet, and babe, that only happens when my stock rises at the same time my cock does." He steps closer, and I back into the island, my chest burning as I hold my breath. "Course, never had four mil worth of shit to sell to a woman who makes my cock rise without even trying."

"Thorn," I whisper, placing my hand against his hard chest with the intention of pushing him back. Only, the second his warmth

46

burns through his shirt and hits my skin, I can't move an inch.

"Ari," he mocks, his eyes bright.

"I, uh, the paperwork …" I close my eyes and focus on my breaths and the words my mouth can't seem to form. When my heart slows enough that I won't die of a heart attack right here in heaven, I look back up at him. "You're breaking my brain, Thorn. Please step back so I can think clearly without my body trying to die on me."

The corners of his eyes crinkle as he continues to gaze down at me, but he does step back. My arm falling down to my side.

"As much as I wish I could have this room cleared out for you tomorrow, it will take at least until late Monday. I'll need to meet with you beforehand to have some legal paperwork signed for the sale due to its size. But my lawyer is an old family friend, so I can have that by tomorrow around dinnertime, if you wouldn't mind meeting me to take care of that. I won't be able to get the cashier's check until after those are signed, so late Monday is the best I can offer you."

"Want this shit gone, but it's hardly a hardship to wait a few more days if that means I've got a few more opportunities to try to make you want me as much as you want this shit around you," he says, his deep voice thick with desire.

"Good heavens, you don't stop, do you?"

"Not unless you beg, babe."

"I think it's best we went back to keeping things professional, Mr. Evans."

This time, it isn't a ghost of a smile on his lips. Oh, no. Not this time. If I thought he was handsome before this moment, I was a fool. Because Thorn Evans giving you his full, unhindered smile and a gaze so thick with unspoken promise as it washes over you and creates a fire of the desire you already felt … well, that expression on him turns him from sinfully hot to heart-stopping and irresistible instantly.

"It would take me five minutes to get you to beg me for it, *Ms. Daniels*. Admit it."

Offended at the thought that I'm easy, I narrow my eyes. *Finally*. At least anger is an emotion I've had plenty of practice dealing with. "I'm not sure what kind of women you're used to, but I promise you, I am *not* that type of woman."

"Maybe three," he oddly says, ignoring me.

"Three, what?" I snap.

"Minutes, sweetness. Three minutes and you'd be begging me for all this shit *and* my cock."

My mouth flounders, and I gasp.

"Though, pretty sure I could get that in less than a minute and get you doin' all the work while I watch from my back."

My arm is up, palm cracking against his cheek before I have the ability to do anything to stop it. "I think we're done here."

I walk around him, ready to find my way out and let him find someone else to take all of this off his hands even if it kills a little part of my lux loving soul. When his hand curls around my bicep—not painfully, but firm enough to make me stop—I look over my shoulder with a frown. For a man who was just slapped, he looks almost gleeful.

"One minute, Ari. Give me a minute and if you aren't ready to beg me for it, when those sixty seconds are up, you can take this shit and not give me a penny for it."

Walk away, Ari. Walk. Away. No amount of money is worth

being some man's whore.

Spinning away from his hold, I jerk my arm free and step toward him with a roll up to my toes, getting my face as close to his as I can. His scent overwhelms me. The subtle notes of his cologne fog my rational thought, making me drunk with need, and I sway slightly before correcting myself.

"Thirty seconds," I retort, my jaw tight with stubbornness.

I'm not sure who I shocked more—him or *me*. I have my answer, though, when I see victory flash in his eyes. Oh, my God … what have I done?

"You're on," he agrees, his eyes alight with the promise backed up by his devilish grin.

I nod, incapable of anything more. I stand there in shocked silence as he takes my phone, his thick fingers moving quickly over the screen. I vaguely hear a chime from his pocket and before I can so much as blink, he's handing me my things.

"Tomorrow, I'll text you. Paperwork first, then you beg."

I gulp, jerk my head in what I hope resembles a nod of agreement, and then … I flee.

FIVE

THORN
The King

"**Y**OU'RE GOING TO FUCKING WHAT?" WILDER questions again, frowning at me from the doorway of my office.

"Not a big fan of repeating myself, Wil."

"Yeah, well, it isn't every day my friend tells me he's just made the stupidest bet in his life. A friend, I might add, that I used to think was the only man savvier in business than I am. For fuck's sake, Thorn, you're about to throw away a million for a chance at pussy?"

"Not a chance, Wil. Guaranteed pussy and a million. Not really sure how you see that as the losing end."

"No pussy is worth what happens when you can't pull this shit off. How the fuck are you supposed to make her spread her legs in thirty seconds?"

I lean back from the paperwork I had been working on all morning and fold my arms over my chest. Wilder holds my gaze, searching for answers I'm not fucking giving him.

"Look, I'm sure you can meet this chick for dinner and just tell her you were kidding, get your cash, and be done with it."

"Not happening," I tell him firmly. Just the thought of not tasting Ari Daniels's sweet body is enough to piss me off. And just the thought of her sweet body is all it takes for my cock to swell uncomfortably in my pants.

"Pussy isn't worth that much work, Thorn."

"Hers is."

"I bet it isn't."

Leaning forward, I brace my arms on my desk and look over at my friend. "You ever known me to waste my time on shit I know I can't get?"

"Not the point, man, and this is not even close to the same thing."

"I don't see why not."

"Maybe because she's a fucking person and not something that can be bought or bribed? Or, I don't know, maybe because you're being a stupid fuck. No matter how much you want to sell the old bitch's shit and get that house on the market, risking any profit is just stupid."

"It's not like I need the cash, Wilder, and you know it. Once I sell the damn house, I'm looking at thirty more of those millions you're so worried about me betting."

"You might not need the money, but just because you're not hurting for cash doesn't mean you should be careless about it. Again, I stress, she's a fucking person. A person who, I'm sure, has real feelings and emotions. Not that you've ever been with a woman who was capable of that, and I know it's been a while since you've felt those things yourself, but they do exist for the majority of the world's population."

"You make it sound like I'm a fucking monster."

He shrugs.

He *fucking* shrugs.

"I want her. Simple as that. Not sure I see what, in that, makes me a fucking monster. I'm not going to abuse the woman. I'm not into the kind of pain that can hurt her. I'll make sure it's worth begging me for my cock, and not only will I still get my fucking money, but she still gets what she's after. Win, win."

"Not even close to the point. Has it been that long since you've had to work for something other than the easy bitches that fall all over you?"

"I'm forty-one, Wilder, not exactly new at this. I've had to work plenty hard over the years to get laid. Not sure why you feel the need to beat this out of me, but something's different about this one. If it takes a bet to secure my ability to find out what that is, then so be it."

"You could try asking her on a fucking date and seeing what that different is all about in a conventional way."

"I don't date."

"Yeah, I know you don't, but I think that bullshit about never wanting anything serious went flying out the window the second you were willing to toss away a million fucking dollars for some chick you don't know shit about. Makes me wonder, though, Thorn. Did you even stop to think that maybe, just maybe, she might be the one person who's capable of making you rethink the things you've always believed impossible? If you're already, in this short time, breaking all those damn rules of yours just to get in her pants, she might be something you've never considered possible for you?"

"Why are you busting my fucking balls so hard over this?"

He throws his arms in the air before dropping them to the desk and leaning over it. "This chick's friends with Megs and Mel. Those two don't even work every night, and the one night their sister finds them working at Barcode, she was ready to throw down World War III. Do you really think if you fucking treat that girl's friend like a woman who essentially needs to pay to get fucked that wrath isn't going to come tearing shit up again? I guarantee you, she does, you'll feel that shit in here at The Alibi even if a parking lot separates the two fucking buildings. So, Thorn, forgive me for not wanting to deal with the fallout when you eventually fuck up if you don't take a second and figure out what the hell this is."

"Is it too much to ask for you to just shut the fuck up and trust me?"

"Yeah, it really is, man."

"Then I guess we agree to disagree."

"You're a fucking idiot."

"So you've said, Wil."

"Jesus Christ." He rubs his hands over his face, then drops down into the chair. "Well, tell me the plan at least. Might as well help you so you don't fuck it up as badly as you could without the help."

I lean back, adjust my cock, and tell him my plan. When I finish, he isn't pissed anymore. Now, he's just shocked.

"It's been what, twenty years since you've gotten up there,

Thorn? I don't think I need to point out the obvious here and tell you that you might be a little rusty."

"Not exactly something you forget how to do."

"Says the man who fired that redhead chick just last week because she returned from maternity leave, and I quote, 'was stumbling up that fucking pole like she'd been snorting crack all day and fried every goddamn brain cell in her head, preventing her from knowing which end was up.'"

I shrug my shoulders.

"She was fucking rusty, not high!" he bellows.

"She wasn't rusty. Saw the bitch snorting that shit right after her disaster on the stage myself. You don't get rusty from pushing a kid out. You get rusty because your brain is replaced with powder."

He shifts forward, looking at me with disbelief. "Twenty years. That is rusty, my friend."

I stand, then walk over to the wet bar situated on the solid back wall of my top-floor office. The walls to my right and left have windows that allow me to look down at the floor below. Below the left window, the hottest women in Vegas get naked for anyone willing to throw cash their way. The right, men who make those Magic Mike chumps look like children … and exactly where I'll be tonight after I sign the paperwork Ari Daniels brings me.

After swallowing two fingers of brandy in one gulp, I turn to my friend. "Let me ask you this, Wil. You think, all that easy pussy you yourself said I have falling on my cock, I get that shit because I forgot how to move my body? You don't forget that shit when it's just as easy as breathing, and that, brother, is something you know damn well."

"Fucking some chick isn't the same as getting back up there

and stripping for a room full of them, T."

"And that is where you're wrong. Fucking is *just* like stripping, only instead of your cock floppin' around in the air with your skin soaked with fucking oil, your skin gets soaked by the sweat of a woman just as desperate as you are to have your cock drenched with her come."

"Sometimes, I wonder how you've made it this long without one of your women killing you in your sleep."

"For one, I don't have 'women.' Second, rule number seven is never let them spend the night."

"Fucking idiot," Wilder mumbles under his breath, standing and walking out of my office with nothing more.

I turn my attention to the window on my right and look down at the stage, the room empty except for the staff setting up before the doors open in a few hours. Rusty, my ass. I went from a boy to a fucking man on stages like that. When all the other kids my age were hating their time in high school, I was lying about my age so I could take my clothes off on stage for dollars and fuck cougars in the private rooms for a lot more than that. I worked my way up until I was the fucking best, having no choice when it meant keeping the roof of a shithole apartment over your head and having more than bread for dinner in the cabinets. It was sheer luck that I went from being no one to being the king. It was worth every one of those twenty-plus years that I fought through hell to get to where I am now. Worth every fucking second.

And there isn't anything that a king can't get.

Including a woman who stirred up shit that makes not one ounce of sense aside from the need driving me to take her.

A woman I've been thinking about since she made me fucking

burn when I saw her across Wilder's bar, only to become an obsession when, almost a month later, I unknowingly walked right into her store.

I'll quench the thirst for her first, and then I'll figure out the rest of that shit I don't understand after.

SIX

Ari

Red. Now.

ITH A FLICK OF MY WRIST, I TOSS ANOTHER DRESS, sending it sailing over my head to join the collection of rejects on the floor around me. When I catch the reflection of my haphazard and anxious expression in the mirror across the room, I give a huff and study myself with a critical eye, looking for something else to panic over but come up empty. My cheeks are flush with a natural blush, eyes wild, and hair all over the place while I stand here in my best lace freaking out about a thirty second bet.

My day started easier than one would think if they would have witnessed the insanity of my actions since walking into my massive closet.

It started off perfectly. I was relaxed, completely forgetting about the "I'll text" from Thorn until the infamous text came through, telling me where to meet him for dinner. That's it. A simple text with just the location and time.

And after that, I was a hopeless case of nerves, not letting myself text him back for fear I would back out of going.

I met with Joseph, my lawyer, for lunch, and together, we drafted the paperwork Thorn would need to sign, making sure to add a clause about the stupid bet. One that protected me, should he win, and for a reason I don't even understand myself, one that protected Thorn, should I win. Thankfully, Joseph was ever the professional and didn't utter a word about the changes. Heck, even if he had, I know there wasn't a chance I could explain it to him in a way that he would understand. How could anyone? *Oh, yeah, it's just to make sure I still get four million worth of product to resell no matter if I find him inside my body later tonight or not. No big deal.* Thankfully, I was safe from having to stumble over that scenario.

Piper started calling just after noon, but I managed to put her off without much effort by promising to fill her in on all the details tomorrow—even if my stomach pitches at just the thought of sharing Thorn. I might not understand what I was feeling toward him—or him toward me—but for the first time in my friendship with Piper, I wanted to keep it to myself for a little while. It made absolutely no sense. Thorn wasn't mine to keep, yet keep is what my heart beat for me to do. I think Piper was easy to put off because she had her own stuff going on with Matt again. No surprise there. Matt was being his normal pain-in-the-ass self again, keeping her distracted. I have no doubt that, had she been thinking clearly, I wouldn't have gotten off the hook that easily.

After my meeting with Joseph, I had to run into Trend to place the supply order I had completely forgotten about the day before.

I didn't stick around, trusting my staff to handle things, as they always do.

Then, with nothing left to occupy my time, I had the genius idea to clean my house from top to bottom. I usually enjoy my time spent cleaning the home I take great pride in, but that *genius idea* was just plain stupid. It was nothing but more trouble than it was worth because it just ended up pissing off Dwight, my orange tabby cat, to the point of no return. That meant tonight when I went to bed, he would get his revenge by torturing me all night. In the past, that could mean anything from biting at my feet every time I drifted off to attempting to smother me with his body while I slept. With Lord Dwight, you never knew what you were in for when he had his cat eyes set on revenge. Or murder.

If all that wasn't stressful enough, it ended with me standing here in my underwear, freaking out about looking good for a man who may end up getting me in a position I haven't been in, in years … and because of that, I spent the hour before my time tossing all my best outfits on the floor and grooming myself to the max— shaving, buffing, and moisturizing every inch of my skin. I've never been more thankful that I kept up my waxing appointments even after I had no reason to put my lady parts through that pain. If I would have had to add that to my shaving ritual, I would probably still be in the bath.

I walk over to the large black island in my spare-room-turned-master-closet-of-the-century and open one of the many drawers under the sleek granite I keep full of the best undergarments money can buy. Screw it, if this bet is going to end up the way I think it will, I might as well go all out and give myself something that makes the seven-year dry spell worth it with a night to remember and a sore body to walk away with from it. It's time. And who says I have to let him into my heart just because I'm letting him into my body?

With a plan in place and, thankfully, some of my anxiety dissipating, I grab the lingerie set I had in mind, toss the sheer lace on the island, and reach up between my boobs to unhook the bra I had on. The second the clasp is free, it opens without help, and my heavy breasts fall from the cups with a bounce. I step out of my panties next and kick them over toward the laundry hamper in the far corner before turning back to the mirror, eyes traveling down my naked form. Now that I've come to terms with what very well might happen, the flustered woman I saw in the mirror only minutes before looks almost sultry. I'm out of my depths due to what I like to call my "missing years" of experience due to my abstinence, but at least I don't *look* that part.

I know my nerves are almost completely to blame for those damn missing years, too. It wasn't that I couldn't find a reason to show my body off and gain the experience a woman my age would usually have under her belt; I just hadn't met a man I wanted to give myself to before now. Kind of ironic, considering my first reaction to this whole thing started with a slap across his face. Like it or not, what he was offering was just what I needed. No expectations other than sex. No risk.

The silver lining in it all—I may lack experience, but I didn't lose my body during those years. My stomach is just as flat and toned as it was when I was in my twenties. Of course, I spend hours working out daily to keep it that way. My breasts are still as high, full, and firm as they were when I was in college. I turn, look over my shoulder, and smirk because even with all of those things working for me, the one thing that did change only did so for the better. I went from lacking a backend worth someone doing a dou-ble-take over to one that you could bounce a quarter off of.

When the butterflies in my belly start kicking up dust, the rest of my nerves dissipate with each fluttered wing. Experienced or not, here I come.

I spin from the mirror with a slight bounce in my step and grab the bright red thong from where I tossed it. After settling the thin and very sheer lace straps against my hips, I grab the match-ing bra. Black would have been safe. Black would have been a good choice, but one that says you didn't give much thought to how the night might end. Red, however … well, red says you *wanted* the night to end with your body looking like it was wrapped with a big, bright, and see-through bow.

When I look back at the mirror this time, I do so with appreci-ation. Every inch of my tan skin glows. My eyes so bright, they look greener than the normal plain old hazel they are any other day. My cheeks, which I left free of blush because the heat my body generat-ed did all the work my expensive makeup would have, give me the perfect flush of color. Even with my hair being so wild from all my outfit indecisions, it worked for me.

Heck, I can admit it—I look hot.

Hot and seriously turned on.

I have no doubt that, if I were to reach between my legs right now, I would find more evidence that I am, in fact, excited for what tonight will hold.

Enough, Ari.

Stepping over all the outfits littered on the hardwoods, I walk directly to the back corner where I pull out the one dress I have been avoiding. But now that my mind is clear, it has no trouble guiding me straight to it. I bought it knowing I didn't actually have a reason for it—meaning a man to wear it for—but I couldn't resist the allure it held after seeing it on the runway of a Dolce and Gabbana show.

When the long zipper that starts just under my ass is pulled up and secured, I walk over to my shoe wall and grab the five-inch stilettos that will match my underwear perfectly and glide my feet into them with a practiced ease. After years of wearing only heels, the familiar pinch of the shoe hugging my feet no longer even fazes me.

Only then do I turn and look back at myself in the mirror.

"Bingo," I whisper and feel a pure rush of anticipation cascade over my hyper-aware skin.

The black lace that covers me from neck to wrists, stopping directly above my knees, hugs my body like a second skin. The solid black lining under the sheer lace is what sold me on this dress in the first place, though. Something I can see was definitely an instinct born of someone who knows how to spot perfection on a hanger … or in this case, a runway model.

When I turn back to my reflection, I know this is *the* dress.

The solid lining completely hides the red of my undergarments, but that's about all it covers. Everything else is just pure lace. The lace over my arms imitates intricate tattoos; the opaque lining against my legs is what makes this a showstopper. While the actual length of the lace is to my knees, the lining meant to keep me decent does that … just barely. That lining ends mere inches under my red lace covered parts.

Black lace and all legs. That's what this dress does. And with these heels, even someone as short as I am can look as if she has legs for days.

It was a dress that screamed for someone to crave me.

To take me.

To … use me.

It was a dress that was made to be on my body tonight. A delicate dress that was made for a man like Thorn. A dress that, I hope, gives me a slight advantage over Thorn when I essentially hand myself over to him in just under an hour's time.

"Ready or not, no matter what happens tonight, or after, you're going to enjoy yourself, Ari," I tell my reflection. Then I head back out of my closet, almost falling over Dwight when he refuses to move. His paw swats at my ankle in an attempt to start his torture early as I make my way back to the bathroom for some last-second touch-ups on my makeup and hair.

By the time I'm grabbing my keys to leave, I'm pretty sure I really don't want to be the victor of our bet anymore.

When I pull up to The Hunting Ground, one of the best steakhouses in town, I'm back to being nervous. So much for that confident Ari who left her house ready to start begging for Thorn the second she saw him. She fled the second I saw Thorn standing outside the doorway to the restaurant. He doesn't look like the biker I met last night anymore. No, tonight he's wearing black slacks and a black button-down—and even from a distance, I know they're high quality. His sleeves are rolled up to his elbows, and I see more bright colors and designs on his forearms. For a moment, I wonder just how much skin he has covered but then push the thought down before my hormones work up to dangerous levels. Tattooed men are a weakness I never knew I had. I can't have my wits going haywire this early, or there's no way I'll be able to hold my own next to him.

I feel his eyes on me when I step out of my SUV and start walking toward him, folder and clutch in one arm and the other rising to press the keyless lock button on my door handle to arm my SUV. I don't just see that I did, in fact, have his attention when our eyes clash, though. The warm buzz that accompanied it starts to heat my skin with each step I take toward him. There is no doubt about it— Thorn Evans likes what he sees. I can practically feel his eyes sear me physically as his appreciative perusal travels over every single inch of my skin.

Branding me.

Burning me.

I step right up to him, the tips of my red heels only an inch from his shiny, black dress shoes. I have no idea where this brazen woman has been hiding, but I watch my hand move of its own accord out of the corner of my eye, keeping my focus locked on his, and shock myself by resting my palm against one solid pectoral. The heat of him burns my skin through his shirt like a fire raging wild. His heart beating madly letting me know he's not as unaffected as he may look on the outside.

"You clean up nice, Mr. Evans," I tell him in a husky whisper.

"Fuck me," he groans, his eyes dropping to my red lips and staying there for a beat before he reaches up and covers the hand against his chest with his large palm, taking me from his warmth when my palm loses purchase of his delicious heat.

Shame and embarrassment for what feels like his rejection swirls inside my belly, but just as quickly as those emotions came— they left when, instead of dropping my hand, he shifts us until our palms connect and our fingers lace together. Then, and only when he looks up from our clasped hands with an expression on his handsome face that I don't have a chance to attempt figuring out, he leads us inside. Still, he doesn't say anything more than the two words I got when I arrived at his side. I use that time to smooth the shock from my features and attempt to figure out if this is part of the game … or something else.

His powerful steps and long legs have me rushing just to keep up with him as he stomps up to the hostess desk. The two college-age girls look close to passing out when he reaches them, and seeing the hunger in their eyes is all it takes for me to be right back in the thick of things. Oh, I can sympathize with their reaction, but what I see in their eyes gives me the rush only jealousy can cause to course through a woman. I pull my hand free from Thorn's, gaining a scowl from him as I adjust the items in my hand. It doesn't last, though. Not when I shift to push myself against his body, nudging his arm with my shoulder until he's forced to lift and drape the muscular—and heavy—arm over my shoulders. The folder with the paperwork now being held in the hand behind his back, allowing me to settle myself even tighter against his hardness. My clutch dangles from my wrist against his stomach as I flatten my hand high on his chest and look up at him.

"I'm just starved, honey," I breathe, biting the lip I had just been pouting up at him with between my teeth. His eyes drop to watch the show I am undoubtedly putting on for the two girls looking at him, still, with thirst, and I feel his groan against my body.

"Reservation. Two. Thorn," he barks in a harsh tone toward the girls but doesn't look away from my mouth.

I turn and give them a smile that is not even close to being genuine, raising my brow when they don't move. "Hey, girls. I'm sorry about his manners. We don't get out much, and we have really important plans tonight. If you don't mind, the reservation is for two under Thorn?" I feel a vibration against my body again when Thorn's enjoyment over the situation at hand makes itself known. The rush of power I feel for getting that kind of reaction from him makes it clear this is way too real to be a game anymore. All that I can do now is hold on and hope he feels the same way.

The two stutter and fumble over each other, but after a few hilarious seconds of silently watching them, we're following the one who managed to pull herself together to the back corner of the restaurant—the only section of the huge establishment that offers some privacy. Set far enough away to be secluded from the crowd, two people could forget they aren't alone. It's almost a private slice of dimly lit heaven made just for us.

Thorn takes the menus from the hostess before she has a chance to finish her job, and with a dismissive tip of his chin in the direction we just came from, he drops them on the table. I lose his heat when he walks behind one of the chairs and pulls it out for me, waiting until I'm seated before I feel him move.

Only, he doesn't move around the table to sit down.

My heart is beating rapidly as my thick hair is moved off my shoulder, and the cool air in the room bathes my fevered skin. I close my eyes and gasp when his warm breath leads the way for the tip of his wet tongue as it trails up the column of my neck, stopping just below my ear. He shocks me breathless when his lips press the softest of kisses to the sensitive skin there before lifting and bringing his lips next to my ear. His steady breathing, deep and clearly not unaffected, chills the skin where his tongue had wet as he holds me on the edge—not moving, not touching … just driving me wild in anticipation.

"You keep this up, and I'll fuck you on this table, babe."

Closing my eyes, I lean my head back and rest its suddenly overwhelming weight against his shoulder. Yeah, this is so very real and not just for me. This is one of life's delicious doses of reality.

Tonight, we both win.

Another barely there kiss is pressed against my skin, on my temple this time, before he straightens. His fingertips glide up my arms as he does, and then he walks around the table to his seat across from me. I use the brief reprieve to settle myself by placing the folder I was grasping down and moving my clutch off my wrist and onto the table, out of the way.

I open my mouth, but I can't think of anything worthy of following his last spoken words. Instead, I shrug, and his lips twitch. My hand shakes so badly when I reach out to take one of the menus that I'm surprised I didn't send the dang thing flying. His hand, though, doesn't so much as twitch when he takes his. Neither of us speak as we look over the menu, and I might as well be looking at Chinese because I'm not comprehending anything beyond the wild thoughts slamming around my head.

"Red. Now."

I glance up with a start at the authority of Thorn's rumbled demand. A terrified young server has joined us and stands next to our table with fear in his eyes. He nods, not wasting a second before he scurries off.

"That wasn't very polite," I scold, frowning when I see his expression.

"What it was, Ari, was effective. I'm not wasting time being nice when I know what I want and can get it quickly."

"You haven't even opened your menu," I accuse. "How can you possibly already know what you want?"

"Not the food I'm talking about."

"Oh," I breathe, understanding dawning.

"Paperwork over wine. Talk while we have our dinner. Then you're in *my* car."

"Have your thirty seconds started, and I didn't hear the warning bell?"

His lips twitch at my sass, sass I had no idea I was capable of in a moment like this. "Said you were in my car, not that you were on my dick. Yet."

My cheeks heat at his crass words when I realize our terrified server chose that moment to return. I can tell now what has him so worked up. Thorn looks capable of breaking him in two just because he's back and interrupting us.

"Have you both decided what you'd like?" he asks in a rush.

Neither of us break eye contact, manners no longer having a place here when his gaze is just as hungry as I feel. I vaguely hear his gravelly voice rattling off two dishes that I don't recall seeing on my menu full of Chinese words. I shift in my seat when another member of the waitstaff joins us to serve the wine. Thorn waves him off when he pauses to give him a chance to sample the wine and gives both our glasses a healthy pour—no doubt to ensure he wouldn't need to refill them anytime soon.

Then we're finally alone in our dim little heaven tucked in the corner.

Alone with so much sexual attraction zapping between the two of us I have a feeling I have greatly underestimated what just a handful of seconds can accomplish when it comes to Thorn Evans.

And I'm so freaking glad I decided to wear the red lace tonight—because I have a bet to lose.

SEVEN

Where evil belonged

ROM THE OTHER SIDE OF THE HUNTING GROUND, wrapped in the shadows and obscured by the tables between them, Anger was coiling tight in the belly of a beast.

No, not just Anger. Regret was also having a field day in those shadows.

The two opposing emotions sat in silent contemplation, ignoring each other while a different war battled inside them over what they were witnessing. Emotions only they could understand the reasons behind.

You see, there hadn't always been Regret for one—but the other had felt only Anger for so long, there wasn't a time in their deepest buried memories when it couldn't be found.

One had spent years vowing to make sure the woman in black, dining on the other side of the room, had nothing worth living for. A renewed strength of fury took hold, rushing through the veins of the devil. The devil had done a lot of learning over the years. From the words that could cause the most pain to the actions that would slice someone the deepest.

No, this wouldn't do, Anger thought, burning rage putting a haze of red over the room. *This wouldn't do at all.*

The angry eyes then moved swiftly and with purpose to the other side of the woman in black's table. It was then, with Anger swirling with a malevolent soul as recognition to what was happening between those two hatched a new plan.

While the Angry one's plan took on a life of its own and coated the air around the shadows with a tint of foul intentions—Regret remembered.

Remembered when years ago, there was happiness to be found.

Remembered what it felt like to be on the receiving end of the woman in black when that expression was on her face.

Remembered how it felt when evil didn't pollute the air and the devil wasn't in control.

Regret remembered, and Anger planned.

It was Regret that left first, making room for Grief to come play. Grief, however, could only mourn for when things had been different.

When the Angry one was in hell where evil belonged.

EIGHT

Ari

A Challenge

LEAN BACK IN MY SEAT, FEELING THE WARMTH OF THE WINE settle in my belly. I had swallowed the first glass down like a shot … and the second. Now I was just, well, oddly settled. No more nerves wreaking havoc. There's just something about Thorn that, while he undoubtedly is a force to be reckoned with, makes me feel at ease. Such a stark comparison to how I felt when I arrived at The Hunting Ground.

It's a good thing those nerves left because while I spent the past ten minutes attempting to go over the paperwork, Thorn showed me a side of himself I would never have thought he was capable of. Not him, a man who screams power and supremacy with just a glance.

"Would you just stop? You can't sign it through my hand, anyway," I tell the smirking man for what feels like the tenth time. He presses the tip of the pen between my fingers again, his tongue coming out to roll over his bottom lip and his eyes dancing with mirth.

"Thorn," I warn when the pen makes a wild slash, creating a bold T between two of my fingers.

"Ari," he jokes, somehow maneuvering another letter next to the first.

"Would you just stop and listen to me explain something? I mean it; you can't sign it through my hand."

"Move your hand, and I'll listen while I sign it."

"You aren't even listening to me now, so we both know you won't then either. Is it so hard for you to let someone else lead?"

The pen moves, this time lifting off the page. Calm as can be, he places it down next to where I had laid everything out earlier. He takes a deep pull of air, his whole body seeming to grow larger. When he tips his head and waves his hand out, silently telling me to continue, I'm not sure how to take his sudden change. Or if I can trust it. I watch, hesitantly, as he leans back in his seat and crosses his arms over his chest. The thickness of his biceps stretches the shirtsleeves deliciously; something I do my best to ignore.

"Are you actually listening now, or will you just finish signing the second I move my hand?" I roll my eyes when he shrugs, feigning annoyance. "You're hopeless. You know that, right?" I jest, enjoying our banter.

"So I've been told."

The heaviness in his tone makes me pause. There's a story there, but it's what I see clear as day on his face that has me wanting to pretend we aren't what we are. As if I have a right to know what that story is.

But that isn't us.

We're just having fun.

Scratching an itch.

Right?

Moving my hand quickly, I take the papers with me to gather my thoughts. I keep my expression neutral, not wanting him to feel like I noticed his change. He'd wiped his expression off his face, and he was back to looking at me like he was—again—enjoying himself.

If we were something different, I would ask him.

If we were something different, I would make it my mission to make sure that tone and *that* expression never crossed his handsome face again.

"Okay," I whisper, clearing my throat. "Let me start by saying, I don't intend to back out of our little … deal. Before I explain these," I add, pointing to the papers I'm holding against my chest, "I want you to know something that may change *your* mind."

Three little lines appear between his brows when he frowns at me. Other than that, he doesn't say anything; he doesn't even move an inch as he maintains his rapt attention on me.

Heat hits my cheeks, but I ignore it, determined to keep course. "I understand the allure of wanting what you feel is a challenge. I do. I get that what might be happening between us may be just that, some sort of challenge for you. I also want to be completely transparent by telling you I can understand why that might be the case, even if that comes with the added confession that I don't understand whatever it is I feel when you're in my presence or even in my thoughts." I suck in a much-needed breath, and when I pause, I'm hit with the realization that his indifference has shifted. He looks *very* invested in every word I've been trying to tell him since the food was ordered and wine consumed. "What?" I breathe, his intensity causing my every sense and nerve ending to zap with awareness to its power.

"Finish," he demands, pushing that one word out in a burst. Quietly, but with authority.

"Um, okay … where was I?" I mumble to myself, trying to get my thoughts back on track.

"Confessions and understanding," he offers, still exuding something that further confirms these confessions and emotions I don't understand.

"Right. Condensed, something happens to me when we're together. I feel it. I know you see it. Pretty sure you feel it. And I'm okay with it, if all that it is for you, is a challenge."

The frown lines are back. Great.

"And before we get to business, I need you to know that I'm okay with it if that's all this is. More than okay."

He leans forward, arms unfolding to put his elbows on the table, leaning over and getting closer—well, as close as one can get with a two-seater round table between us. The candlelight from the little glass holder makes his facial features look harsher. "Let there be no confusion, Ari. This was and never will be a challenge. I know what I want, and I know what I'll get. Calling this a challenge would imply I lack that confidence. What you do challenge, however, is my sanity. Finish the rest about 'understanding,'" he commands, nostrils flaring as he continues to give me his complete attention.

"I have no idea what to do with you," I admit breathily.

A gritty hum comes from his lips. "That's fine because I know exactly what to do with you."

"I'm being serious, Thorn."

"As am I."

He leans back when our waiter, looking less terrified than before, arrives with our food. He places two identical plates down in front of each of us. Steak, veggies, and potatoes artfully displayed and looking delicious. And as hungry as I am, I ignore the food and look back at Thorn.

"I haven't been with anyone in a long time, Thorn. I'm naïve about a lot of things shared between two people attracted to each other, but I'm not stupid. I know there's a very real possibility that tonight will end with me giving myself to you. I need you to know, regardless of how the lead-up to that happens, I'm not here because of these." His eyes drop when I lift my hand and extend one finger to the paperwork I'm holding against my chest.

Hunger flashing.

Need sparking deeply.

"Which is why," I rush out, "I had my standard contract for large consignments like yours—well, not like yours because I've never had *that* large of a consignment—altered." I shift, feeling the need I've sparked in him between my legs when I do. "What I've been trying to explain is that I'll keep our little bet, but you'll need to think of something else for the respective winner because I don't want what I don't understand to be tangled up as a business transaction. I'll finish with I'm sorry for slapping you last night when you made your intentions clear, but I will not be bought, and you don't deserve to be either."

His back slams against his chair, making the legs squeak against the floor. Intense pain slashing against his features briefly.

"What did you do?" he questions, words firm but with a hint

of … *fear?*

"*I* didn't do anything. I did, however, have Joseph—my law-yer—add that, no matter what the seller, you, and buyer, me, have on a personal level, our business deal will remain just that, a solid agreement that means you get what you deserve in financial com-pensation and what you need, being the removal of what I'm pur-chasing. Neither of us, though, will be exchanging monies of any kind for anything other than a business transaction."

"Ari."

My name, softly spoken from lips I already know hold a prom-ise of intoxication to my soul, just reinforces my resolve to separate business from the thick desire surrounding us.

"No, Thorn. It's important to me that you not think I'm using you to get what you're selling. It's important to me that you know I would want you even if all of that was off the table. It's *really* important."

"Give me the papers." When I don't move, he does. One long arm reaches over the table, papers gone from my grasp, and his dish shoved to the side carelessly. My breath speeds up as he lifts his pen back from the table and continues where his scrawled TH is wait-ing. His hold on the ink pen so strong I wouldn't be surprised if he somehow snapped it in half.

When he's done, he recaps the pen, then holds it out for me. My hand shakes as I take it, putting it next to my clutch to deal with later.

Neither of us looks away.

He repeats the move, picking up the papers and holding them out. And again, I silently take them and place them back into the folder.

Still, we just stare, and if the heat our connection is producing was capable, we wouldn't have to worry about our dinner spoiling.

"Eat. And eat fast, Ari. I'm suddenly finding I'm impatient to get to the part where your ass is in my car."

I nod.

He nods.

We eat.

Then my ass is indeed in his car.

NINE

THORN
When I win, I get you

A CHALLENGE.

She wasn't wrong. She most fucking definitely started as just that. The second I pulled up in front of her girly store, looked through the windows, and locked eyes with her, I knew I would stop at nothing to get my cock inside her.

That challenge she convinced herself was all I felt, though, only lasted seconds.

When she walked away from me, putting a goddamn counter between us, my fingers itched to explore, and I felt the shift. Something I had never experienced ripped from deep inside my body, creating an intense wave pulsing between us that was so severe, I felt the invisible strings tugging me with great strength in her direction.

She thinks she doesn't understand this?

Funny, because she's not the only one.

Only I'm not even close to naïve when it comes to what I want to do to her.

I haven't been with anyone in a long time, Thorn.

Her confession was spoken so damn softly, I almost didn't think I heard her correctly. But I did, and each of those ten words slammed into me with such force, what had cracked in my normal shield of indifference the second I saw her, started to rip apart even greater than before. The cravings I hungered to quench made my mouth water, and the hollowness inside me began to fill with warmth. I've never experienced a fucking thing like it. What I had experienced in my life told me to wrap my hands around what inspired such things and never fucking let it go.

Ari was giving herself to a monster.

She had no idea what she was offering the beast. Her naïvety even more apparent because if she had the experience, she would know to run. Run as far as she could and never look back.

It's unfortunate that I wasn't a better man. A man who would just sign the papers and let her go.

But I can't.

And more importantly, I won't.

Seeing her shift in her seat causes my hand to tighten on the steering wheel. My foot presses down on the accelerator, and with a loud vibration of my engine, my car speeds through the streets of Vegas. She changed the stakes, but I'm going to make sure the reward is just as sweet.

She will be mine in every way I can make it possible.

She will feel this oppressing weight that I've been carrying around when I make her want me as fiercely as I want her.

"What are we doing here?" she whispers into the silence of the car when I pull into the parking lot of The Alibi.

I ignore her, steering my car behind the building and into my parking spot directly between the two back entrances. One leads into the female's lounge area. The other, to the men's.

"Thorn?" she questions, this time with a twinge of trepidation.

Shutting the engine off, I climb from the car and walk around to her door, opening it and reaching down to help her out. When our hands connect, I feel the same buzz of warmth tingling from our connection as I did at The Hunting Ground. My eyes immediately slide to her legs when they shift to stand from her seat. I've been itching to bury my face between those fucking legs since she walked up to me in that dress earlier tonight. Instead of stepping back to give her room, I crowd into her, getting so close that she's forced to tip her head back to look up at me.

"Why are we here?"

"I've got thirty seconds, don't I?"

Her eyes roam over my face before shifting to the back doors. "But what does that have to do with this place?"

"Babe, really?"

She looks back at me; only this time, the sass she's shown me a few times is ready to come back out.

Fuck, she's beautiful.

"Yes, *really*. I thought …" she trails off, looks back at the door, and then, fuck me, her shoulders drop like she's disappointed.

"You thought?"

"It's nothing," she whispers, still looking fucking defeated.

Christ, she was right when she said she was a challenge. Not the way she meant it, though. She's a fucking challenge to understand.

"Don't keep yourself from me, Ari."

"I just didn't think this was where we would end up, okay? Happy? I thought you were taking me back to your place."

Didn't see that coming. At all. A challenge, indeed. "Who said this is where we will end our night? Got thirty seconds, Ari. Thirty seconds to make you beg. Then, and only then I can take you where I want you."

"And you want to do that … here?"

"What's wrong with The Alibi?"

"Well, nothing, I guess. I just hear things about how wild it gets in there, and I already told you I don't have a lot of experience, but Thorn … I really mean that. If you're thinking about doing stuff with other women or using those thirty seconds with another woman to win the bet we don't even have anymore, then maybe you should just take me back to my car."

God*damn* she's refreshing.

We were already close, but when I inch closer, it erases any space that remained between us. Her tits press into my chest, my cock into the softness of her belly, and the satisfaction I feel when she sways is intoxicating. She sighs when my hands frame her face, her eyes hooded, and lips parted slightly. I hold her where I want her and bend my neck to get closer, our breaths mingling and the sound that comes from her lips makes my cock twitch.

"I don't fucking share, Ari. Understand?"

She nods or, rather, tries to.

"Anything you heard about The Alibi, babe, wild would be putting it mildly. I didn't bring you for whatever you have running through that beautiful head of yours. You said I had to change the bet, so here it is. You win, you pick whatever the fuck you want, and I'll make it yours. I win ..." I close the distance between our mouths, closing my lips around her pouty as fuck bottom lip, and bite. Her whole body shakes, and her tiny hands grab my sides tight enough for her nails to bite into the skin through my shirt, and then, fucking fuck, she moans so deeply I know I'll never forget that sound. When I release her lip with a pop, I lick the spot I just bit before I pull back slightly. "When I win, I get you."

With the taste of her skin still on my tongue, teasing me, I promise myself that she will be mine. Even if I lose, I'm winning Ari Daniels.

No matter the cost.

TEN

Ari
Your time starts now

WAIT HERE.

Thorns last words echo through my mind; the two words on repeat as they continue to play over and over just as clearly as they did when he pressed his lips right on my ear and said them. Even with the music pounding through the room he left me in, it sounds like he's still right next to me.

But he isn't. He left me here alone. In a room full of screaming women, flying dollar bills, and half naked … and *fully naked* … men.

No one is paying any attention to me. Even the men—no, strippers—ignore me when they walk through the room, teasing the women and making sure they're the ones who get their dollars. No, that's not right. They don't ignore me, but they don't get close. The last one who walked by studied me so long, I almost ran out of here.

I take a chance that I won't almost get slapped in the face with a penis like the last time I tried to look around and one of them was walking behind my chair, and start to search through the screaming women and oiled men.

That's when my gaze collides with Meggie and Melissa's boss. He's standing off to the side where there's a door that says do not enter on it. I jerk back around, not wanting to be caught gawking at him. My lord, I really thought he had been looking at Piper with interest the night I met him. I never would have thought he was gay.

Oh, my God. Had I been that long out of the game that I couldn't tell when someone was interested or just being polite? No, I know I didn't get it wrong. There is no way. He wanted her.

I turn back, and he's still there. Still there and still watching me. I give him a small wave; not really sure what proper etiquette is for running into someone you kind of know at a male strip club. He shakes his head, smiles, and starts walking over to me.

Oh, my God. Oh, my God. What the heck am I supposed to talk to him about in this place? The weather?

"You look terrified," Wilder says, talking over the music and dropping down in the chair next to me, the only chair next to the small round table where Thorn had me sit ... right smack in front of the empty stage that looks all kinds of foreboding.

"I would say that's accurate."

"Relax. You're safe here."

I snort a nervous giggle. "I saw a penis, Wilder. A naked penis just bobbing all over the place like it was completely normal to walk through a crowded room with an erection. That same penis almost took my eye out when the man attached to it walked behind me. That isn't safe."

This time, it's Wilder who laughs. "I see it now."

"See what?"

He shakes his head. "Nothin', darlin'. Not a damn thing."

"There was nothing safe about that boy's penis either," I grumble on a huff, crossing my arms. "He could hurt someone with that thing."

"Do you say everything that you think?"

I shrug. "No, I was simply continuing my observation so you would understand how *not* safe it is here."

"It's safe, darlin'. Saw Matteo walk by. He wasn't that close. No one's going to get close enough to even chance touchin' you."

My brow pulls in, and I frown at him. "I hate to point out the obvious, but aren't you sitting right next to me?"

"I'm hardly a threat to you."

"I don't know you well enough to know if that's true or not."

"I'm not a stupid man. They're not going to get close because they're terrified of just the thought of what he would do to them if they did. Me? I know exactly what he'd do to me if I did, and darlin', those guys are smart to be terrified."

"I'm not following?"

He leans over, checking his watch as he does, and then smirks at me. "Sweetheart, you walked in here on the arm of the boss. That was not something missed by anyone. A woman who looks like you, innocent and gorgeous, would be surrounded by all o' them in seconds, had you not been on his arm. These men aren't weak. They aren't afraid of shit, but they do fear his wrath, and getting anywhere near you would ensure they felt it. You couldn't see his face, but everyone else in the room could. Trust me on that."

I gasp, fingers curling into my chair while I stare at Wilder with wide eyes.

"Now, as for me? You don't have to worry about me. I'm here because I wouldn't miss this for anything. I'm not afraid of him, and I know damn well he'll kick my ass for getting near you—even if it's for just a friendly chat—but there was no way I would miss watching him work so hard when he normally has easy being thrown in his face. Now, close your jaw and eyes to the stage. His ten minutes are up."

What the heck?

Then I remember the watch glance, and suddenly, I know exactly what's about to happen on that stage. When the music changes, the most sexual beat I've ever heard starts to play through the vast space around us. My skin prickles, each heavy thump seemingly vibrating throughout my whole body. Oh, wow.

Wilder bursts out laughing next to me. "Cliché," he grunts.

I don't pay him any attention. How can I when standing there in the middle of that stage is a shirtless Thorn Evans, looking like the answer to every woman's prayers. Something that every single screaming woman in the room confirms a second later when he starts moving with a grace I never would have expected from a man his size. I've never, not once, seen a man move like he was part of the music. His whole body creating a lust-filled energy of pure sexual demand making the room thick with erotic cravings by every pair of eyes witnessing this man move.

His tattoos come to life under the bright lights, but it's the carnal heat he's looking down at me with that does it—makes *me* feel as if I'll die without knowing what the man who can drive a room full of people insane with illicit hunger feels like when he's moving like *that* inside me.

"Your time starts now," Wilder continues.

Thorn jumps down from the stage and quickly straddles my legs—legs I have clenched together so tight, they hurt. Then he leans over my body, puts one hand on the back of my chair, and starts flexing his hips, grinding his crotch over me as if he was actually inside me. The sudden burst of jealousy I feel with others seeing him like this, when I have no claim over him, only makes me want to end this quickly. Then he grinds his erection against me, and I never want him to stop. My lord, he's making me be at war with myself.

"Five seconds." Wilder breaks through my thoughts. Thorn's gaze seems to heat, silently demanding me to give it to him, and he'll make it worth it.

And that's all it takes for the war in my mind to end. Rational thoughts break through, reminding me what we're doing here, and how I can get him to end this and take me somewhere where no one else sees him this way, *and* sate my hunger.

"Take me," I breathe, hypnotized by his scent, his expression, his ... everything. I could have sat here for the rest of the song and every single one that followed, this man lighting fire to every single inch of my body until I combusted, and I would die a happy woman. However, it's the thought of *this man* owning *me* that had me breathing those two words out of my dry mouth. My body so aroused, I feel like I might actually die *without* knowing what else the man grinding against me feels like when nothing separates us.

"Please," I continue at the same time Wilder calls time ... giving Thorn the one thing that he promised me I would do—beg him for it in thirty seconds.

The song continues, something I can feel with the deep bass, but every one of my senses is intoxicated by this man. He leans even closer, making me slide down until my bottom is halfway off the edge of the seat and he's touching me from crotch to chest, still rolling and thrusting his hips. His thrusts get slower, deeper, and harder against me as his head dips, and he bites the skin under my ear.

"I win you," he grunts, panting like he's out of breath.

When he lifts his head again, the male pride of his victory only makes him look more desirable. "Beg me again," he demands.

"Take me somewhere private and I will," I throw back, needing to get us alone right this very moment so I can do just that. Private means he'll stop teasing me, driving me insane with it, and make all the parts of me that feel empty, full.

He doesn't answer, but he does move with the beat to stand. My eyes travel down his chest, past the light dusting of hair that doesn't hide the ink that paints his skin, and over each hard ridge of his abdomen until they stop where his thumbs are hooked into the waistband of the sweatpants I didn't even notice he had changed into. Then he starts moving his hips in a new way; he moves each arm in tandem with the other, dragging each side of his sweats down with calculated measurements. *All* that is him, straining against the fabric as his pants drop lower. The short-groomed hair where the deep V of his hips ends makes way for what's begging to be let out to play—what I'm begging to come out and play with.

I'm going to die.

There's no way I'll survive it if he ... "Oh my God," I gasp at the same time he gives a jerk with both hands, and the sweats go down at the same time his erection springs free and slaps against his stomach.

I'm out of my seat, pushing against the table with such force it shifts under my weight, though I don't notice it for long because, with a leap, I'm in his arms, and the erection I want for myself is pressing against the very wet lace between my legs. I'm almost positive I felt part of my dress rip in my haste, but I couldn't care less if the whole back was wide open and showing the entire room my goods. Nope, not when I have Thorn's huge hands splayed over my ass, pushing me even harder against him.

There's nothing but desperation when I run my hands up his flexing arms until the slick skin ends and his silky hair tickles my fingers. There aren't words needed when my wetness is begging him for me. I lick my lips, causing his gaze to drop to them. I feel his groan against my chest, the music drowning the sound out and keeping it from me.

"I need you," I confess, tightening my legs around his back, feeling the heat of him against me. "I need you to fill me."

"Fuck," he hisses. "Don't want you out of my arms. Not at fucking all, but got to get my pants up if I'm going to get you where I can get my cock inside that pussy."

"Oh, my God, yes," I whine on a low moan, sliding my hips in a roll against him before I reluctantly untangle my legs and, with his strong hands on my hips for support I very much need, stand on my feet.

He doesn't miss a beat, reaching down and jerking his sweats up. The room gives a sound of disappointment when the show ends, and I belatedly notice another song playing. When that happened, I couldn't tell you. Heck, I couldn't even tell you if that was the only song played after the first one. Everything's a blur after hearing Wilder call time.

I jump when a shirt comes flying from my side. A shirt that Thorn must have expected because he catches it without looking away from me and shrugs it on. He grabs my hand, pulling my body against his side. I look up at him; the pulse at the base of his neck beating so violently, I can see it clearly in the dim room.

"Keys," he demands, and the haze of lust clears, reminding me I had been sitting with a man. I look over my shoulder at Wilder just in time to see him toss a set of keys to Thorn, wearing a roguish grin on his face. Thorn starts to turn us in the direction that we entered but turns back. "Never call me fucking rusty again, asshole."

Wilder's laughter follows us out into the warm night, the promise of what's to come still letting us ride high on its wave.

ELEVEN

Ari
Please

THORN'S SLEEK SPORTS CAR TAKES THE STREETS OF VEGAS dangerously fast as he speeds expertly through traffic. The haze of desire I've been dizzy with since witnessing his performance on stage at The Alibi has caused me to hang precariously on the cusp of awareness ever since I did, in fact, beg him in thirty seconds to take me. I've never witnessed anything like it, but even in a strip club full of strangers, it was just him and me … and what he did to my body. Now, here we are, rushing to parts unknown. The only sound heard over the purr of his car is our equally choppy breathing.

His deep and rushed, only broken up by the occasional grunt and deep vibrations from his chest. Without his confirmation, I can only assume his heaving is caused by wanting me as badly as I want him.

Mine, short and pained, my need ever-present in each inhale and exhale.

Mine, well, mine are also completely because of him *and* the hand he has between my legs.

Just thinking about how we got to this point makes my insides clench around his fingers and the coil deep inside my body tighten further. The strength of my arousal monstrous, climbing higher and higher with each ministration of his ridiculously talented fingers.

Thorn hadn't made it but a few steps from where I had been sitting in the club when it became clear I wasn't going to be able to keep up with his rushed steps. Only it had nothing to do with his giant-size legs and everything to do with the war raging inside my body rendering me slow and klutzy. I was up in his arms before I could blink, and it seemed a second later, we were both in his car, speeding out of the parking lot. Before we reached the first traffic light, his hand was on my thigh. When a whimper left my lips, he started moving that hand slowly toward the apex of my thighs. However, I'm pretty sure it was my needy gasp echoing around us that had him hooking his fingers into my panties to move them out of the way and entering me without pause a moment later.

The rest, every second that passed that led us to where we are now, is just a blur of arousal and unimaginable talent from him. He was stringing me tight, and I was seconds away from snapping.

It would be huge.

It would be overwhelming.

It would be … *everything*.

"Don't come," Thorn strains through tight lips. His hand, the one between my spread legs, shifts, and the two fingers inside me go impossibly deeper. I hiss in a breath, close my eyes tightly, and roll my head against the leather holding it up. "Don't you fucking come until I get my mouth on this pussy."

"I can't … it's too much … oh, my God, what are you doing to me?" I shudder, feeling it build higher inside me.

It takes everything I have in me to hold back. The instant attraction I've felt toward this man since the first time I saw him walk into Trend just proving I was right in trusting my gut about this— the powerful rush of sensations roaring through me is like nothing I've ever felt.

Nothing.

Mind and body.

All-consuming.

Overwhelming.

Full-bodied.

There isn't an inch of my skin that doesn't feel the burn of my need. Not a single sense that isn't drowning in him. The desire for more making me feel drunk with need. For *him*.

"Thorn. Please."

"You won't come. Don't you fucking dare," he grunts, his fingers twisting and plunging into my body.

The car takes a turn that has me shifting against the door, him not slowing down, and I hear the wheels screaming in complaint against the asphalt. Not once does his hand stop, the rhythm holding steady. The tail end of his car jerks side to side for just a second before I feel the jolt of us accelerating again. My thighs press together against his hand. Unfortunately for me, instead of that stopping his movements, it pushes his fingers deeper and allows him to continue while hitting something delicious.

"Ohhh," I gasp. "I'm going to…" My belly tightens and jerks in tandem with my core, and I feel the flutters of my orgasm starting.

Then he jerks his hand from between my legs. The loss of him instant.

"Fuck!" he bellows, slamming his palm against the steering wheel. The same hand that had been only a second away from giving me what promised to be the most intense orgasm I have ever felt in my life.

I roll my head against the seat and look at him through hooded eyes. There's no indifference in his handsome face now. He's clearly just as impatient as I feel. He glances over and lifts his fingers to his nose, inhaling deep with a groan before looking back at the road. One that I echo when he places those fingers between his lips and sucks.

"God*damn*," he hums. "Never tasted anything better."

I don't look away, watching him clean my arousal off his fingers. When he finishes, placing his hand back on my thigh and leaving it there, I still can't look away. I was so lost in him, I didn't even realize until we stopped that we weren't at the house I had visited in The Orchard.

"Where are we?" I ask, my voice wobbly.

"Does it matter?"

I think about his question. Do I care where I am? I should. I should, but I don't. It makes no sense at all, but I trust him not to do anything to me that I don't want. Reckless? Maybe. But I'm not going to ignore how he makes me feel or overanalyze what this is between us.

He's given me back something I lost for a long time … desire for another, and confidence in myself, without the fear I normally have holding me back from connecting with someone.

He's given me no promises aside from what I know will be a ride worth taking.

I don't need hearts, flowers, and promises of forever.

That didn't work the last time.

So, this time, I'm going to finish living in the moment with no regrets.

"No, I don't think it does."

I know I answered correctly when he gives me something I hadn't seen often from him—his full-blown and heart-stopping smile.

Holy. Cow.

Yeah, this will be worth it. In the morning, I'll figure out what to do next. Tonight, I'm going to enjoy the heck out of this man.

"Wait there," he says deeply, shutting the car off and swinging out.

I keep my eyes on him as he walks around the hood, coming to stand at my door. I have to clench my legs together again when I catch sight of his erection pushing against his pants.

Good heavens above, that alone is worth whatever happens when this night is over.

The door opens, and with his help, I'm standing next to him. The intensity in his gaze makes me sway on my heels. His hands are on my hips before I can do so much as move an inch, preventing me from falling at his feet. We stand there, staring at each other until I can't take it any longer. My intention must have been clear as day because all I do is bend my legs slightly, intending to climb this man like a damn tree, and he's helping lift me off the ground until my legs are around his hips and that beautiful bulge between his legs presses against my oversensitive parts.

"Please hurry," I beg, licking my lips before nipping the skin on his jaw. His answering growl vibrates my chest, making my nipples even harder. I rub against him, chest and crotch, needing so much more than I could even imagine. "Kiss me," I continue, needing to know what his kiss tastes like.

"No." His rejection stings, but I push it down, taking what I can get.

His first step jolts my body, making me gasp. His hands tighten on my hips painfully. I continue to hold on, kissing and licking his exposed skin. I couldn't even tell you how much time passed. The second he started walking, I became incapable of doing anything more than running my lips and tongue over the thick column of his neck. His bruising hold on my hips thrusting my body against his rock-hard heat with each step, purposely driving me insane.

It isn't until I'm flying in the air, the clutch I just noticed was between our bodies going flying with me and I land against silken sheets, that I get a sliver of awareness back. He stands above me, next to the bed I landed in, panting rapidly and stripping his clothes away.

He doesn't look away, and neither do I. Even when he's pushed the last layer off his body and down his hips. Even when he reaches down to place his hands on my ankles, yanking me to the edge of the mattress with a tug, I hold his gaze.

I gasp.

He grunts.

Then one of his brows is up, and I'm being spun to my belly.

I jump when his fingers graze the top of my dress's zipper, a low mewl leaving my lips when he drags it down. His lips trail his touch, kissing my skin as he exposes it. I relish in the tenderness of his actions. That is, until he gets to where he exposes my bra, then I lose the soft care, and the beast comes out. A hiss of appreciation bursts from his mouth, and then the rest of the zipper is jerked open, ripped from my body quickly, and I'm once again on my back. His hungry eyes roam over my body, stopping to enjoy the red lace that's left covering me.

"Planned on taking my time. Didn't expect this, though." His words, whispered but strangely harsh, make me shiver. His fingertip glides over the top of my lace bra, right on the swell of my breasts. His eyes looking down between my legs. "Tell me to fuck you. Tell me I don't need to play with this pretty pussy for you to be ready for me. Tell me to fuck you so hard, you'll never forget how I feel filling you up."

"Please."

He shakes his head, his finger moving down my stomach and stopping at the top of my lace panties.

"Tell me to own your pussy, Ari."

"*Please*," I gasp again, feeling like I'll pass out if I don't have everything he's offering at that moment.

He leans down, mouth hovering over mine. "Say it."

I shake my head, my hands reaching out until the heat of his back is against my palms, and I try desperately to pull him on top of me.

"*Fuck* me, Thorn. *Own* me, Thorn. Make my pussy *yours*, Thorn," he continues. "Say. It. Now."

"Please." I gasp as his mouth closes around one lace covered nipple, biting and sucking. "Fuck me, Thorn. Own me and make my pussy yours," I rush out, needing it.

I hadn't even finished before he was lifting his body, hands to my hips, and ripping my panties from me with little effort. He only pauses to reach over to the side of the bed, coming back with a condom in hand. My hands roam over his exposed chest while he makes quick work of rolling it on. His abs clench under my fingertips, skin dancing with goose bumps, showing me what his words aren't.

Then, my God, then he pushes my body up the mattress at the same time as he surges inside of me. He goes so deep, I cry out in pain while begging him to never stop in the same breath. Stretching me unlike I've ever felt. Our bodies coming together wildly. He flicks my bra open with practiced ease before bending and pulling my nipple into his mouth, sucking deep. He moves between the two, his hands curling around my shoulders to pull me down against each powerful thrust.

I do the only thing I'm capable of doing. Hold on. His muscles ripple against the hold I have on his back, and I curl my fingers until I know my nails will leave a mark. My legs, hooked around his hips, make it easy for me to rock my hips to meet each jarring thrust. Mouth open, I scream out my pleasure as I clamp down around his length. My whole body coming alive as my orgasm rushes through me.

Giving him me.

Being owned.

And I feel the scary knowledge enter my brain the second he seats himself impossibly deep, twitching inside me and shoving his face into my neck with a groan ... that I will never be the same.

Then he moves again, grunting as he finishes enjoying his own orgasm, a rush of wetness leaving my body as I come again, just from one deep glide of him finishing inside me.

Unfortunately, it didn't even occur to me that, while I was experiencing something so magnificent, the man who gave me that hadn't once kissed me. It didn't even enter my thoughts that, as he climbed from the bed and walked toward a doorway across the room, I might be in over my head.

Nope. I was too sated to do anything more than shift when he came back, pulling the sheets around us and dropping down with a groan, my body moving to curl around his without thought. If only he hadn't been so good at owning me, then maybe I would care that the only parts of him touching me were the parts I was curled against.

But as sleep claimed me, all I could feel was beautifully used.

THORN

My skin tingled. The soft weight of Ari's body against my skin burning deep to the bone. My cock, still fucking hard, begging me to push her on to her back and get into that hot fucking pussy again.

I've never, not once, felt anything tighter than her pussy.

Never.

She was so tight, I checked for blood before flushing the condom down the toilet, half convinced she was a virgin. She admitted it had been a while, but it felt like it had been more like never. The thought alone thrilled me more than it should.

Staring up at my ceiling, I continue to ignore the urge to take her again. I don't let myself reach down and pull her tighter against me. I refuse to press the delicate hand against my chest tighter. I deny the whispered voice inside my head that screams at me for being too fucked up to know how to offer her something that would keep her in my bed longer.

I should be happy. I got what I wanted. I've had her. I can let her go and be satisfied that I didn't even have to work *that* hard to get another available pussy in my bed.

Only, I'm not because, fuck me, that wouldn't all be a lie.

Wilder was right when he said no pussy was worth working as hard as I did to get Ari's—even if it wasn't really that hard at all. Only, he was also wrong because now that I've had it, I know I would have worked a hell of a lot harder to get not just her pussy … but her.

"Shit," I hiss, rubbing my face with my hand and finally allowing my other arm to curl around her body, pulling her deeper against me.

I knew something was between us. I fucking knew it. But I didn't prepare myself for that shit to be so fucking strong. I was willing to forget all the lessons I've learned in over forty years, and be a man a woman would want to work past all my goddamn issues for.

And because I'm so fucked up, I have no clue what to do now.

Ari moves, interrupting my thoughts, and lifts one leg up until I feel her wet pussy against my thigh, relaxing even further against me. Her hand leaves my chest in a glide that has it resting at my side with her arm across my body. Only then does she stop moving and a content sigh leaves her lips.

Fuck it.

I allow myself to move, pulling her slack body closer, tangling our legs together, and dropping my free hand to hold her arm against my chest.

Tomorrow, I can figure it out.

Tomorrow, I'll do my best to convince her to keep giving herself to me.

Tomorrow, I'll do the one thing I've never fucking done in my life.

Make a woman more than just a body to fuck.

I take a deep breath, careful not to stir the sleeping woman in my arms, and look down at the beautiful face tipped just slightly to be looking toward mine in her dreams. Only then do I bend my head, bringing my lips down to press against her slack ones. I feel that one-sided kiss with so much brute force, it's like the iron box my heart's encased in might—for the first time in my life—have found a weakness against its armor.

TWELVE

Ari

London

WARMTH.

So much warmth, I'm burning alive from the heat.

That, and the sheen of sweat I'm covered in because of it, are the first things I notice when my sluggish mind starts to come awake in small degrees.

I start to stretch, my whole body feeling like I have run a marathon, and come awake instantly when I feel the hardness behind me that could only be one thing.

A man.

Or, more specifically, a Thorn.

Oh, my God.

Everything we shared comes rushing over me, so overwhelming that I can't handle the enormity of what I'm feeling. I just know I need to get the heck out of here. Panic wins over every emotion I feel pulling me in different directions.

It takes what feels like forever to pull his heavy arm from where it's resting over my body. He doesn't so much as twitch when I start to slide out from under it, quickly grabbing a pillow from his mammoth bed and replacing my body with it, careful to lower his arm back down around it. The chill from losing his warmth bathes my naked skin in chills.

He looks so peaceful. The hardness that I had become used to in his features, nowhere to be found. The imposing power that I have no doubt he holds, not as intimidating when he's relaxed in slumber. I force myself to move, not taking the time to enjoy the exposed skin not covered by his dark navy sheets.

I ignore my bladder, rushing around the room to grab my clothes—or what I can find of them. My dress and shoes on the ground next to the bed are the first things I grab. My clutch a little farther away, reminding me how it went flying at the same time I did last night. When I find my underwear, I drop them back to the ground when I realize they're useless with the sides ripped.

Where is my bra?

I whip my head around frantically, but when my phone starts to ring in my clutch, I rush from his room, naked, not even caring that I'll be doing the walk of shame without anything under my dress, if that means keeping my phone from waking him before I can make my escape.

It takes me a second, but I manage to get my phone out without dropping my dress and shoes, quickly accepting the call before the second ring can start. I pull my dress up my legs without dropping my phone as I jam my cell between my shoulder and ear.

"Yeah," I gasp, not paying much attention as I push my arms in and halfway zip it up. Silence greets me as I step into my heels and start searching for a way out of this house, finishing the zip on my dress while I do. I almost drop my clutch a few times, but by the time I find the stairs, I'm able to take my phone in my hand and hold on to the banister with the other. "Hello?" I repeat, rushing down the steps.

"You keep popping up where you shouldn't be."

I stop dead at the base of the stairs. The large foyer registers slightly as nothing short of stunning, but my sister's voice paralyzes me.

"For years, you don't pick up! You keep yourself gone like you're so good at doing, and without the constant reminder of *you,* I finally was able to make *him* happy. Then you're everywhere in just a handful of days! And all I've heard in those fucking handfuls of days is *Paris* this and *PARIS* that!"

"London," I whisper.

"No, Paris. You've ignored my calls and my messages for too long. It's time to listen to what I have to say. I did my best to erase you from our lives, but you just won't fucking go away so I can! On the weekend of the anniversary of Mom and Dad's death, of all times, you're fucking everywhere! Do I need to remind you ONE MORE FUCKING TIME what you took when you tried to keep a man?! What was lost because of *you!*"

I don't reply, unable to speak past the lump in my throat, and disconnect the call. This time, I rush toward the door with a different feeling filling me. One that is full of pain. The memories of the past slam into me; it's a miracle I'm able to even get outside, and at some point, in my sprint down the driveway, I get an Uber ordered.

It isn't until my Uber arrives ten minutes later that I stop hyperventilating. The shaking doesn't stop until he's dropped me off in the empty parking lot of The Hunting Ground. But, the tears still don't come. Not on the drive home. Not in the run from my garage to the house. Not until I'm in the closet of my guest room with pictures thrown all over the ground around me.

My sister and me, around sixteen, well before we left for college, and she started to hate me.

My parents, alive, one Christmas morning a few years before they died.

My mom and I at Trend.

My sister and dad in the garden.

My sister.

My parents.

My heartbreak.

Dwight joins me, curling into my side where I had collapsed, and I feel the pain of just hearing her voice over and over.

This is why I have no one.

This is why I keep to myself, not letting my heart open for something that could hurt me like they all did. I thought I knew pain when we lost our parents. Even if London had started hating me for reasons I never understood before that, losing them meant I lost the one connection that guaranteed I wouldn't lose her completely. Only, she made sure that connection was severed in a way it would never be whole again. And, in doing so, ensured I would be alone forever because of it.

The only person I had left is the one who refused to leave—Piper.

I gasp, a sob getting caught in my throat, and clutch Dwight to my chest when I stand. I trip over my own feet, still feeling the soreness from Thorn in my tired muscles, and grab the landline phone next to the bed in my guest room. Dialing Piper's number, I curl my body into a ball on the bed.

"Hey, girlfriend! I didn't think I would hear from you *this* early! Tell me—"

"I need you," I cry into the phone, interrupting her.

I don't hang up until she's told me she's on her way. Then I disconnect and let the phone roll from my fingers and onto the ground. Dwight, for once, lets me hold him tight without complaining.

It doesn't take Piper long. It feels like only seconds, but not long after I had hung up with her, I hear her loudly entering the house. Front door slams, her keys, and whatever else, falling to the floor, then her rushed steps echo throughout the house. All the while, she's screaming my name at the top of her lungs.

"Oh, my God, Ari! What happened?!" She drops down on the mattress, causing Dwight to hiss before scurrying off. She places one hand against my arm and dips down until she's looking in my eyes. "Did he hurt you? If he hurt you …" She trails off, and I hate the pain I hear in her voice.

"He didn't hurt me," I whisper, closing my eyes tight against the memories of Thorn.

"Then *who* did? He was the last person you were with!"

"I don't think he would hurt me," I confess.

"Don't or *didn't*?"

"He didn't hurt me! He doesn't even know I'm gone!"

I look up to see her confusion and sigh.

"London called. London called, and I was too busy trying to sneak out that I didn't even think to check the caller ID on my cell before answering. London called, and I was too busy running scared from the way Thorn made me feel to check. I always check!"

"Oh, Ari."

"I forgot, you know. It's been so long since I let someone get close enough to make me feel *more*. I hadn't remembered what it felt like when they inevitably left. I forgot what it feels like. I can't believe I did, but I still forgot."

"Ari, stop," Piper begs, her voice thick with emotion.

"No! Don't you see? I forgot. Seven years of always remembering, and I just forgot. London just reminded me what happens when I stop being alone. When I let someone close, just like I did with Thorn, I just hurt others."

"Your sister is wrong. Nothing that happened was your fault. Your parents wouldn't want you to be alone, honey. How is getting close to Thorn hurting anyone? He's single. You're single. It's not messy. You deserve a chance to have something not messy."

"She must have seen me," I continue, not hearing Piper. "She must have seen *us*. I don't know when, but I know I didn't look unhappy in his presence once last night. I should be. I should be, especially so close to the day I found out what real pain is! I FORGOT! I forgot!"

"Would you stop it!" Piper yells, jarring me with a shake of my shoulders. "You didn't forget, dammit! You've started to heal! I've waited so long to see that happen, and I refuse to let that bitch sister of yours try to ruin things when you are finally on the way to letting it all go and healing. All the twisted things she's said and done to you, *that* is what you are forgetting. And thank God you are. You're busy putting the pieces back together, and honey, that's not forgetting, that's learning how to live again!"

I shake my head, not believing her.

"But it was my fault," I gasp, my tears falling faster. "I don't deserve to live again!"

"Yes! Yes, you do! You deserve a beautiful life again. They died, and it was tragic, and the timing sucked, but it wasn't because of you."

"They wouldn't have been out that night if it wouldn't have been for me."

"Wrong. So wrong! How many times do I have to tell you that?"

"It doesn't matter."

"It damn sure does if, because of London stirring this up again, you're going to push away someone who I've seen make you come alive for the first time in seven damn years!"

"It's done."

"What's done?"

"Thorn. He got what he wanted. Papers are signed. It's just … done." Admitting that, feeling the taste of those words on my lips, makes me want to take them back.

"Don't do this, Ari."

My mind all over the place, I push my pain down and sit up. My movement forces Piper from her lean over me.

"I'm going to need you to cover things at the store if you don't mind. I think I need to take some time to get my head straight."

"Of course, but Ari, we need to talk about this."

"Do you want to stay for brunch? I can cook us something." I look at the clock on the dresser across the room and frown.

"Ari," she continues.

"Actually"—I sigh, not listening and needing to concentrate on something that will take my focus somewhere else—"I'm not sure what I have as far as brunch food, and it's close enough to lunch that we could probably just have that. We could order in, or I can still cook us lunch?"

"I'm not fucking hungry!"

I blink at her, then stand and start to walk out of my guest room.

"Ari, seriously."

I keep walking, reaching behind me to pull my zipper down on the way to my bedroom. Stepping out of it with a kick toward the hamper, I enter my master bathroom. I turn on my shower, my sister's words echoing through my mind. Only, they all vanish when I hear Piper gasp from the doorway.

"Are those handprints?" she screeches, her eyes on my body.

I glance at the mirror across from me, seeing Thorn's mark on my skin, and push down my initial thoughts—the ones that tell me to run back to him—before meeting Piper's shocked face and shrug, feigning indifference. "Yeah."

"Yeah? That's it? Just yeah?"

"What else do you want me to say?" I yell, twisting to narrow my eyes at my best friend. "Yes, they're handprints? Handprints from the most amazing experience I've ever shared with a man? That they're a reminder of just how explosive that experience was? That the tender bruising will be the only thing I feel from him again because IT'S DONE!?"

"Honey," she says softly; sadly, her tone full of pity. "We need—"

"No. We aren't talking about that. I need you to be here with me and take my mind off what my sister said. I need you to be the best friend who refused to leave when I lost everything and didn't try to talk me into anything I wasn't ready for. That's what I need. I'm going to shower so I can't smell the memory of last night anymore. Then I'm going to cover my body up so I can't see what I shared with the man I can't let myself have. Okay?"

She studies me, then nods sadly. "Okay, Ari. Okay."

"Okay," I repeat, stepping into the shower and rinsing off my beautiful night. The pain of losing the scent of him off my body— losing him—almost as strong as what my sister's call did to me— making me remember what I had allowed myself to forget.

Almost.

THIRTEEN

Ari

Come back to life, Ari

MY PHONE RINGS … AGAIN.

I feel Piper's accusatory stare. The same one she's been giving me all afternoon since I refused to speak about what happened this morning. I don't move. I ignore her burning gaze and keep my eyes on the show we've been watching. Television is safe.

"You should get that," she tells me for the millionth time that day, breaking the silence.

Millionth.

Millions.

Thorn.

I close my eyes.

Everything I've watched on television today, small scents hitting my senses over the hours, or even pictures in the magazine

I flipped through earlier … have been constant reminders of the man I ran from. The hold he has on me makes no sense. Even the dog food commercial that played during the last break got me. I instantly wondered if he liked dogs or cats. Seriously, I was on the cusp of losing it over a man who I, for all intents and purposes, don't even know anything about. Well, aside from our ridiculous chemistry, that is.

My ringer continues, and I know without a doubt that it's him calling. With Piper still here, I can't think of anyone else who would be calling me over and over. Plus, there's the little fact that I ran out on him this morning. Something tells me a man like Thorn Evans isn't used to women fleeing the scene. Ever.

The ringing stops.

I let out the breath I had been holding.

He'll give up.

He never said he wanted more than what we shared. He wanted me to beg him to take me, and I did. He wanted *me,* and there's no doubt what we shared last night was what he meant by that. He had *me.* That's hardly cause for him to put forth this much effort to break through my silence. In a different world, I would have woken up with him and asked him straight up for more. But that's not my reality.

He'll move on to someone easier.

The ringing starts again.

Or maybe he'll move on after this call.

"Seriously. This is so ridiculous. I've let you sit there and be miserable all day, but enough, Ari Daniels. Enough! I don't care what you *think* you need; I'm going to give you what I *know* you need."

I don't open my eyes. I keep my head back, resting against the couch. I also don't correct her. She's right; I've been stewing in my own pain and misery all day. I'm not that person—the one who sinks to the bottom and doesn't try to get back up. But I also am. I very much am. I sink to the bottom, then I climb back up, but I remember what made that fall possible in the first place and avoid the pain of hitting my knees again by holding those memories up like a shield.

That's me, Paris Avoidance Daniels.

"I'm going to say some things that I should have told you years ago. I'm going to say them, and I don't give a shit if you like what I have to say. I don't care if you think you aren't ready to hear it or hearing what you think you need. I refuse to let you be sucked back into that depression your bitch sister always succeeds in putting you in, closing yourself off from finding that beautiful life you deserve. So, ready or not, it's time for some harsh truths, my friend. First, letting someone get close does not mean you're going to lose them. You don't need to keep your heart locked away from feeling. Look at me, honey. I've been here, and our friendship doesn't mean you will feel pain. I'm as close as it gets, and you won't lose me. Your loss, their lives, that shouldn't be something that keeps you from finding more in life! They died, Ari! They died on their way to you because they loved you so much; the thought of you being upset was too much for them to sit at home and ignore. Tragic— God, it was—but knowing that, can you honestly say they would want you to use their loss to keep from moving on and finding that 'something more'?"

I keep my eyes closed, my tears starting to fall through my closed lids. Her words slam deep into my soul, ripping me apart.

Oddly, with each rip, it feels like something else is following to mend it back.

Word by word.

Stitch by stitch.

"I was there," she continues. "I was there through it all, so I *know*. I was at your side while you were living your dreams, and I was so unbelievably happy for you. But I was also by your side when those dreams turned into nightmares. So, I *know*, Ari. You didn't ask for everything that happened and the changes they put into motion for your life. You experienced something that truly was heartbreaking—that isn't up for debate—but because I've been at your side, I can say you've been using that heartbreak as a crutch. Preventing you from moving forward and finding new dreams. You deserve to find those new dreams. Never did you deserve all that happened. Never. You also never deserved to stop living because of it."

I hiccup a sob, feeling as if that had all happened the day before and not seven years earlier.

"If anyone's at fault in this room, it's me, Ari. I'm to blame for letting you go this long without helping you find a way back to those dreams when I could see so clearly that you were keeping yourself from finding your way back there. I'm to blame for not saying something when you stopped going to your therapist. And because I love you, I'm willing to do whatever I can to make sure I don't add to what faults I hold."

At that, my eyes open. "Pipe."

She holds her hand up. "No. Enough. You want to take a few days and grieve the loss of your parents, do it. I can't imagine what it feels like to lose parents, but I think it's completely normal to continue to feel the freshness of losing them every year after. The anniversary of losing them will never be a day without pain for you, and I know that. There is never going to be a moment when taking more time to miss them isn't acceptable. But you do *not* get to carry on doing that for days and months and years anymore, using it as a reason to keep yourself from *living*. Ari, you got through the actual anniversary of losing them, and it didn't break you—not like it used to. That was days ago. Why don't you take a second and ask yourself if you really forgot, as you claim, or if you took that day on and remembered them without sinking to where you are right this moment. Do I really need to point out what—or should I say who—walked through the door that same day? You used to believe in signs, and girl, that's got to count for something. Your parents loved you so fiercely; they would be heartbroken to see you like this."

In the distance, my phone rings again, and Piper stops talking to frown in the direction of its ringing.

I keep my silence. Her words penetrating. But she doesn't.

"I'm not saying Thorn is the man you'll spend the rest of your life with, Ari, but I *am* pointing out that he's the first one who's come into your life and made you remember—even if that wasn't conscious on your part—how to start living past what's held you back, and that, my friend, counts for a whole hell of a lot. You want to take some time and ignore life, get your head with the program, and stop believing what London's spewed at you to be true, that's cool. Just because she can't handle her own guilt over what happened and continues to live in the past, that's on her, not you. Maybe, just maybe, in that time, you'll remember all the little signs you felt over the years that made you believe your parents were watching over you. Then think about, again, what day Thorn popped up in your life."

I sniff, my chin wobbling, and wipe the tears from my face.

"Now, I'm going to silence your phone and head home. I love you, and I hate seeing you upset. If you don't want to talk to me, that's okay, but you need to talk to *someone*. It's time to come back to life, Ari."

She gives me a hug after she stands, and I'm left staring off into the space where she had been when she walks out of the room.

The ringing stops.

My thoughts do not.

I let everything drain out of my tired mind, making room to replay what Piper just said one thing at a time.

She's right. I did spend the anniversary of their deaths remembering them fondly. I was sad, but instead of spending the day unable to stop the tears, I had cried in the shower. By the time I stepped out, the tears had stopped, and only the happy memories remained. I had only a small fraction of sadness left. I cut a few roses out of my garden before I left for work, the same kind of roses my father had painstakingly grown in his own backyard, and put them in a beautiful vase that had belonged to my mother. They were still sitting on my desk at Trend. I wore my mother's pearls that day, feeling their weight like a hug straight from her. I spent the day wrapped in their memories—happy memories—and even though I did it with a sad fondness, the pain *had* eased.

She's also correct that my parents would want me to be happy. They wouldn't want me to live my life in limbo because of my fear to let someone close, only to lose them. And it's time. Time for me to find a way to let go of the guilt I feel over their deaths.

My thoughts shift, and I picture, clear as day, my parents meeting Thorn and what they would have thought of him. Just as quickly as the vision comes, I push it aside. My thoughts drifting to London.

My twin sister.

I gave her everything. My heart, my loyalty, and my trust. Even when she started hating me, I still held onto hope that one day we would find our way back to the relationship we had before college.

I also gave her the power. The power to put all the blame on me when … "God," I gasp, Piper's words echoing in my mind. *Just because she can't handle her own guilt over what happened and continues to live in the past, that's on her, not you.*

All these years, I let her convince me that I was solely to blame. Not once did I see things differently because she worked so hard to never let me forget. To never let me have a break from the subtle reminders long enough to see the loss of our parents any other way.

My past was tragic.

It was gut-wrenching.

But Piper's right … it also wasn't completely my fault.

Dwight meows deeply, jumping on the couch and eyeing me. Giving me a hiss, he swats me with his paw, his claw connecting with a small prick of pain. He doesn't stick around to clue me in on what pissed him off, jumping away as quickly as he came, in favor of the sun spot on the floor. Then he looks over, lifts his leg, and starts cleaning himself.

My thoughts shift back to Thorn, my grumpy cat reminding me of him with those eyes that seem to say everything without saying anything at all.

Maybe Piper's right, and his timing in my life isn't a

coincidence. But she could just be grasping at straws. One thing's for sure, I know that when you let someone get close, they have the power to bring you to your knees. Could I really, with that knowledge, take a chance on someone who has given me no indication that he wants more than what I already gave him?

Remember what his touch did to you.

Remember what he made you feel.

Remember, he isn't your past.

And isn't that just the scariest part of all? In a few short days, he was able to make me feel in a way that was so powerful and huge. I know that anything I had experienced before he rode into my life was just a cheap imitation.

He made me dream again.

He gave me that faraway look that my mom had when my dad was around and she was dreaming wide-awake. He looked at me with the same heat my dad looked at my mom with.

Piper's words slam into me again. *Maybe, just maybe, in that time, you'll remember all the little signs you felt over the years that made you believe your parents were watching over you. Then think about what day Thorn popped up in your life.*

Days, I've known him for days and felt the earth move … days that started on the same weekend as their anniversary.

I look up. "If you sent him to me, prove it," I whisper to the ceiling.

They don't answer—of course, they don't—but that doesn't mean Piper's words don't continue to play back in my mind.

I hate seeing you upset. It's time to come back to life, Ari.

Come back to life, Ari.

Come back to life.

FOURTEEN

THORN

She's different

YOU HAVE TO BE FUCKING KIDDING ME.

I toss my phone on my desk, knowing if I don't get it out of my hand now, it'll be sailing across the room.

"What's your problem, T?" Wilder questions, walking into my office like he owns the place.

I scowl, ignore him, and pull my email up on my laptop.

"You've been in such a shit mood; I've had your employees complaining to me. What the fuck is going on with you?"

Again, I ignore him, continuing to busy myself with my computer. Looking up the email address I need, I plug it in, skipping the subject line, and move my cursor to the body of the email.

"I see they're not wrong or exaggerating about your bullshit mood. Let me guess, she wasn't worth the work after all?"

That gets my attention. My head snaps up, and I glare at him.

"Shut the fuck up."

"Or maybe she was, and there's something else wrong with her."

My fingers move over the keys, making short work of telling my private investigator the information I need. Namely, the address of one Ari Daniels. When I start detailing what I actually do know, I just start getting more pissed. This time, at myself.

I have no doubt that, after our short time together, I know her better than a lot of people do—something she admitted herself when she not only told me how little experience she had, but also showed me when I sank my cock in her tight body. Unfortunately, knowing how someone feels coming apart, naked in your arms and around your cock, won't help you find them when they've been ignoring you for a goddamn week.

A whole fucking week. Nothing but silence and, recently, a full voicemail. But did I stop trying? Not even close. I've called her so many times I feel like a chump for it.

"What's the problem?" Wilder repeats, this time not sounding like the cocky bastard he was moments before.

I send the email, lean back in my chair, and exhale loudly.

"She did a runner on me." His eyes go wide, and I doubt he expected to hear that. "Woke up feeling lighter than I had in god-damn years—if fucking ever—and the only sign she had even been there was two tiny as fuck scraps of red lace."

"You usually can't get them out quick enough, man. What's the problem with her leaving before you had a chance to push her out? Wouldn't that save you even more work?"

"Because, unlike the women I normally wake up to, her presence was wanted."

121

He drops back in his chair, a long whistle leaving his mouth.

"I've called. I've texted her. Nothing. If she was done with me, the least she could do is tell me."

"Yeah, well … I guess the tides have finally turned, brother."

"Shut the fuck up."

His head tilts, and he studies me. "Shit. You're serious, you're that into her?"

The tension in my neck has me bringing one hand up to try to rub some of it out. "Don't understand it myself, but that would be putting it mild as fuck."

"You know where she works. If you want her that badly, make her tell you to your face that she's done. Then at least you can do your best to convince her otherwise."

"Tried that. She hasn't been in all week. A few of the little girls who work there were too busy trying to remember how to talk, so I didn't get shit from them. The friend she was with the night I met her, now, she had plenty to say, namely that I was scaring the employees with my 'intense alpha male grumpiness,' and that Ari was 'taking some time to figure things out.' Whatever the fuck that means. I pressed her. Could tell she had more to say, was written all over that chick's face, but she just shook her head and told me not to give up. Pretty sure I left there more confused than when I walked in."

"Told you more than you knew before then, riddles or not."

"All of it just as confusing as the nothing I had before, though."

"So go to her house. Didn't you pick her up the other night?"

I shake my head, the tension just getting worse and the beginnings of a migraine creeping through my skull. "She met me at the restaurant. Didn't even think about picking her up. Fuck! Of course, she ran off on me. I take her to dinner, play her up until she's dying for my cock, and then I fuck her like it meant nothing but the challenge she accused me of making her. I might as well have slapped her on the ass when we finished and said thank you."

"So," he draws the word out. "What you're saying is … you're rusty?"

I narrow my eyes. Not this shit again. "I am *not* fucking rusty."

"Right. My bad, T." He laughs loud and long. The arrogant fuck. "You're right. You aren't rusty; you're just clueless."

I bite back my knee-jerk reaction to tell him to fuck off. He's right. I'm clueless. I'm a grown man who's never had to even try. Hell, never wanted to try. Now I'm faced with a woman I want more of, and she won't give me the time of day.

"I even left a message with her about picking up the shit she's buying, but I got some bullshit email from the store, not her, telling me that someone would be in touch about arranging pickup. The next day, a fucking courier dropped off a cashier's check for one point five million and a note that the rest would be deposited into the account of my convenience after the pickup and appraisal of that bullshit."

"She just sent that kind of money? That's it? Jesus."

"No, that's not fucking it. It was part of the contract I signed at dinner last weekend. Some kind of holding fee, I don't know. I know *that* only because I found it in my car the day after she left and read it front and back, trying to find some clue about locating her from it. I was too busy trying to get through dinner to actually read it. Read that shit again when, after I had dropped the original off with the protective little bulldog at her shop, it was attached to that goddamn check the courier dropped off."

"Damn. I guess I was wrong when I thought you stripping for some chick was working hard for pussy. You'd do less work training and completing a cross country marathon."

"Shut the fuck up!" I bellow. Wilder doesn't so much as flinch.

"Look, I hate to point out the obvious, but did you consider that maybe it just wasn't that good for her, and she's letting you off the hook easy?"

A humorless bark of laughter bubbles up and out.

"What? It might be possible that you couldn't impress this one. No matter how skilled you think you are."

"She was … impressed," I fume through a tight jaw, not liking telling Wilder about my night with Ari—another thing different, since I've never kept details about who I sleep with from him before. Impressed, though? What a joke. It was so much more than that. The fucking earth shook for her just like it did for me; I know that to be true down to my bones. Only, knowing she felt that didn't mean shit when I woke up ready to convince her for more, and she had run scared because of it.

"Yeah, running out on you while you're still sleeping screams impressed, Thorn. Happened to me plenty of times."

I ignore the twinge in my chest over continuing to discuss what we shared with someone else. Sharing her. Sharing us.

"She's different."

"Yeah, got that."

"No, Wil. She's *different*."

The humor leaves his features, and he leans forward, elbows to knees, and I watch as the realization clicks. "Shit, Thorn."

"Never, not fucking once in my life, have I felt this shit. Learned a long time ago, something you know, that women aren't worth the trouble of getting more than a decent fuck from. All the women I've known in the past only care about three things: money, using a man's money to buy shit, and using their cunts to get both. I met Ari, a woman who owns a store that caters to those types of women, and still, I was thirsty for her. Never been fucking thirsty for someone like that in my goddamn life. I knew damn well from experience what I was walking into. Didn't stop me, though. I knew all o' that, and I still carried on like I could fuck her, move on, and she would be out of my system." I run my fingers through my hair and relax against my chair.

"You stop to think that maybe you just want her more because she's the only one who has ever left without you pushing her out the door?"

I grunt, shaking my head.

"Seriously, T. You say she thought she was just a challenge before, and now, she's basically made herself one. Only, she's an even greater one now."

"She might have started out as a challenge, but she stopped being that the second she pulled that contract out and told me how important it was that I understand she wasn't there to gain something from me unfairly. How important it was that I know she wanted to be there to explore how I made her feel and not because she could potentially gain a fucking lot for nothing. All she had to do was make it thirty-one seconds, and she'd have all that shit and not have to give me a cent. I'm good, damn good, but if she was playing games, she could have easily resisted and gained a fuck ton. So, tell me, Wil. Why even bother if she was planning to run out on me anyway? Why did it matter enough to her that she took the time to explain that shit and tell me how I made her *fucking feel*?" I pick up the glass paperweight and hurl it across the room. It lands against the wall, leaving a dent in the drywall before falling to the ground. "She could've even just fucked me, run, and made a fucking mint off me without all that trouble. I've seen what it looks like when a woman has my cock in her body and wants me to believe it's more than sex. I've watched them fake that shit, wanting to use it to get more, but I've never seen one actually mean it until her." I take a deep breath, pissed all over again that she got away from me … and kept herself away for a week. "And I've never seen that same shit looking back at me in the mirror every day since."

Wilder doesn't so much as blink.

"And fuck me; I can't just let it go. I can't just let *her* go."

"So don't."

"Tell me then. I get her to finally pick up the phone, and by some miracle, we figure out how to explore this shit, I'm supposed to offer her what?"

He scratches his head. "I'm no expert, but maybe start with seeing where it goes, and if it keeps going good, a future you both enjoy?"

"You know my past. She won't want much of a future with me. Not with that shit riding my back."

"Right, well, you've already made it this far past your usual hang-ups. First, I think what you do know about her proves that she isn't like the women who gave you those fucking hang-ups to begin with. Second, just because you believe you're like your piece of shit parents doesn't mean you are. Can't use that shit to convince yourself she won't want something more. Not with all that shit you just told me. Got this far, so maybe see what else she can make you want."

Everything. The thought pops into my head immediately.

"Whatever you do, drain some of that anger you're wearing like a second skin before you find a way to get her to stop ignoring you. You might not be the only one with shit fucking with your head. You go in as pissed as you are, might as well not even try."

Wilder gets up and walks out of my office, not saying anything else, but he doesn't need to. He's given me enough to think about. Given me enough that I know he's right. And if I'm able to get past some of my shit, who says I can't help her get past whatever made her run?

I just have to find her first.

My email chimes, and I check to see a message from my private investigator telling me that he'll have what I need before the end of the day.

Soon, Ari. Fucking soon.

Until then, I might as well use all this pent-up energy and formulate a plan that will ensure when 'soon' comes, she'll be begging me all over again.

Only this time, she'll be begging for a whole lot more than before.

FIFTEEN

Ari

Day by day

"**P**ASS ME A TISSUE," I CRY, CLUTCHING MY NEW KIT-ten to my chest. The new kitten I picked up last week when I decided that I was, in fact, going to start my life as a cat hoarding spinster, doesn't wake from his nap. He doesn't even flinch when I choke on a choppy breath, only to have it come rushing right back through my lips a second later; the mother of all sobs assaulting my body as I continue to bawl.

"I can't," Piper wails next to me.

I wipe my eyes on my new baby's fur and sniffle, my heart continuing to break in more tiny pieces.

"Oh, my God, this is so hard. Why does it always have to be so hard?" I gasp out.

"I can't take it anymore. I can't, Ari. This is the last time we do this."

Dwight jumps up on the couch, takes one look at us, and jumps back down, clearly deciding we're too unstable to tolerate being near us. Jim, my new baby, doesn't miss a beat and jumps from my arms. I hear Dwight hiss before the sounds of them taking off in chase begin a moment later.

"No," I cry when I focus back on the television. "Oh, no!"

Piper grabs my hand and clutches it tightly, and together, we silently—well, with the exception of our loud crying—watch in heartbreaking horror as Mark Greene's wife finds him dead. Our distress over what will always and forever be the most depressing death in all of television makes us belligerent as we continue to weep.

"Why did we have to watch *this* season of *ER*!?" I yell at Piper after the end of the episode, having just finished another crying fit through the credits after the final scenes showed some of our favorite characters, who had left the show, making an appearance at Dr. Greene's funeral. "We need to go back and watch the episode when Carol has the twins." I reach forward, grab a tissue, and blow my nose. "That will take this pain away. Plus, Mark's in that episode, so we can pretend none of what we just watched actually happened."

"No way. Last time you watched that one, I had to listen to you carry on for a week, yelling about how Doug should have shown up during her labor with their twins, giving Carol a grand gesture of love because that's how their fairy tale should have played out."

"Well, he should have!" I argue, tossing the tissue into the huge pile on the floor at our feet. Or what's left of the pile since the cats have taken great pride in ripping every piece they can to shreds. "The writers really screwed that up. They had the opportunity to give viewers the most epic romantic act ever. I know it in my bones!

Doug was supposed to rush into the room—just in time, I might add—thank Mark for being there until he could, then kiss Carol. They could have made plans for her to turn in her notice and finish her last couple of weeks at County before packing up and heading off for their happily ever after in Seattle."

"And then how would we have gotten deeper into the tortured love life that is Luka Kovac?"

"Don't even get me started on Kovac," I deadpan. "I'm still bitter he took so long to realize who he was meant to be with." I could go on for hours about the *ER* characters I love.

"I can't believe I let you talk me into watching this season."

I ignore her, knowing she doesn't mean it. It was her idea to start season eight anyway. She persisted even when I reminded her that season eight was *that* season.

We clean up our mess of tissues and the snacks and drinks we've accumulated over the past day and a half. When she showed up yesterday with more junk food than we could possibly consume and the promise of letting me watch anything, I didn't even have to think about it. I picked *ER*, she picked this season, and we lost our Saturday (and most of our Sunday) to the roller coaster of emotions induced by this show.

And that brings us to now.

"I'll be back at work full time on Monday," I tell her, coming back in from the kitchen. I head to the couch with my portable vacuum to clean the many crumbs left from our binge watch session.

"So you said," she replies. "Are you sure you're ready?"

"Yes. Thank you for covering things for me. And," I add, stopping what I'm doing and looking at her so she sees the sincerity in my words, "giving me this time."

"Did it help?"

I shrug and go back to the vacuum, letting the soft hum of it fill the silence of my non-answer. We haven't talked much about how I've spent my past two weeks since she essentially woke me up. Not because I'm keeping it from her, but because I didn't even really understand where I was mentally until the other day.

"Well?"

Standing from my crouch, I turn to face her. "I'm not in the middle of an emotional breakdown anymore. So, I would say it did."

"That's good. And?"

"And what?" I hedge.

"And … what about the rest?"

I walk away, returning the vacuum to my laundry room just off the kitchen.

"Ari, I haven't said one word since you asked me to give you time. I kept my mouth shut when you called after his message about the pickup and insisted on sending him a check through some messenger service. I didn't say a word when you told me what to include on the note with that check either. I kept my lips zipped and held back from doing more than check in on you during that first week. I even went against my better judgment and didn't even say anything to him when he showed up at the store trying to find you. But I've given you your time until you told me you were ready— which you have repeatedly done since I showed up this weekend— and now you're going to tell me what you've been going through for two really long weeks."

"I'm working on all of that. The Thorn stuff. I really am." I know that's not exactly what she was hoping I would start with, but

I know it's a big part of what she wants to know.

"Have the calls picked back up?" she asks, unnecessarily, seeing as she saw his name on my phone last night when he called.

"You know they have."

"Right, then don't you think 'all of that' should have taken a front seat long enough for you to have something better than 'all of that' when referring to your situation with him? A day of blowing him off, I understood. Two days, even. Then days passed and you pulled that check crap, and I was starting to *not*. Now, it's been two weeks, he's still calling and you're still blowing him off. All of this and you're going to have to eventually see him when you go supervise the packing of that small fortune you bought from him. So, tell me, is that when you're planning to ... deal with figuring out 'all of that'?"

I flinch. Hearing her lay it all out just makes me feel worse. I might have screwed it all up by taking this much time and giving him a whole bunch of nothing, but it had to be done. It had to. If I lose him before I even had a chance to get him, well that's on me. The least I can do is find him to thank him for being part of the catalyst that pushed me into healing myself.

"He calls every night at the same time," I admit, looking out the window and continuing to whisper. "Like clockwork. That started two days after he received the check. He never leaves a message anymore, but he follows each of those calls with one text. 'We're not finished.' That's what I got after the first week passed. Now, I could read into that one text in so many different ways. We're not finished ... sleeping together? We're not finished ... with our bet. We're not finished ... with our business deal." I shrug. "But, as I said, he never left a message or sent another text to follow that one up, so I'm not sure what 'we're not finished' means for him. Three days ago, he started adding a countdown to those three words. First up was just the number three. Yesterday was the number one. I imagine, unless he wants to change it up, that either zero will come tonight … or something else. To be honest, I haven't let myself think about what happens when he gets to zero OR what that something else could be."

The doorbell rings, and she rolls her eyes, clearly exasperated.

"Food's here," I say with a weak smile and an apologetic shrug, moving around the couch to go answer the door. I stop when Piper holds her hand up.

"No, you stay here and think about what you're going to tell me about *all of that* when I get back. I mean it, Ari."

She stomps off, leaving my living room. I lose sight of her when she turns the corner to go down the hallway toward the front door. What does she want me to say? I know I screwed up when I let my silence go on for this long. I owe him an apology for my silence as well as for leaving, and then maybe, if he forgives me for that, well … then I see where we stand after that. I knew I would try, though. Try for his forgiveness. Try to move on. Try to let him close.

The weekend I ran from him, the one where I silently begged my parents for a sign and got one, set me on the path I've spent the past two weeks traveling. Maybe it's silly that I believe it was a sign, but no sooner had I asked the ceiling for one, my silenced phone had crashed to the floor, and when I picked it back up, it was vibrating in my hands with Thorn's name on the display.

Bright and clear.

My sign.

I'd left him running scared, but that sign had jump-started my past two weeks. I went from that day on with more clarity than I had ever felt in my life—wanting to make myself better than what I had become. Knowing, even if I didn't get him, what I needed to do to make sure I was able to truly move on.

After almost a year of silence from me, my therapist happily welcomed me back with open arms and understanding. After the first visit—the day after I ran from Thorn's bed—we set the course of daily visits and the plan of intense therapy that has brought me to where I am now. I figure, if he's meant to be more than the person who pushed me to start healing, something else will happen to tell me so. If he was just supposed to come into my life to show me what I was missing, it would suck, but I would find a way. I knew I was strong enough to now.

"Ari."

I drop the remote, spin with a gasp, and almost pass out when I see him—Thorn—standing in my house.

How's that for a sign?

"Shut up," I mumble, not needing my inner thoughts to start the 'I told you so's'.

He narrows his eyes.

"Not you," I rush when I realize he was narrowing them because he heard me. How humiliating.

His eyes look around the room, I'm sure trying to find someone else in here. Well, if he's not going to call me on it, then I'm not admitting that I was talking to the voice in my head.

"Where's Piper?"

"Leaving," my best friend answers, squeezing past the imposing man standing at the mouth of my hallway. "I'll see you Monday. If that changes and you need more time off, for a six-foot-huge kind of reason, let me know, and I'll open the store. If it's for any other reason, forget you know my number and you can open the store your damn self. Also, dinner's coming with me. I'm hungry and emotional. And I deserve it more." She grabs her purse off the sofa table, the pizza box still clutched in her hand, and turns back around to look at Thorn. "Good luck, big man."

Then she's gone.

"You've been crying," he says, his face impassive but those stunning blue-green, magical eyes of his looking almost … concerned.

"It's nothing." I wave him off.

"If it was nothing, you wouldn't have cried over it."

"How did you know where I lived?"

"What made you cry?"

I throw my hands up and roll my eyes. "If you must know, I was watching a show."

"A show? A show made you look like that?"

My eye twitches, and I purse my lips. "It was a sad show."

"I see," he replies. Yet judging by his incredulous expression, he's clearly not actually "seeing."

"How did you find out where I lived?"

"Why did you leave me?"

"Thorn." I draw his name out.

"Why. Did you. Leave?" he repeats.

I don't answer, and instead, my gaze takes him in. He looks good; though, I'm not really surprised. Dark jeans, distressed enough in all the right places that you know he didn't pay for them to look that way. Gray shirt tight across his chest and around his arms. Short sleeves showing off his brightly colored, muscular arms. When I reach his face, I take my time, not even caring about the stretching silence.

He hasn't shaved, making him look even more imposing with the hair on his jaw. His lips stand out more against the black hair. His eyes hold mine when I reach them in my study of him, and I quickly slide past, avoiding their intensity. The long hair on top of his head wasn't styled like it had been the weekend I begged him to take me, but instead, it's unruly and falling across his brow. Just like it did when he walked into Trend after wearing his helmet.

When I look back down at his eyes, giving him my attention again, I notice how tired he looks. My breathing speeds up, matching the rapid tempo of my heart.

"Why did you leave me?" he asks again, his deep voice rough but laced with something that I can't quite put my finger on.

He almost sounds … vulnerable.

It's because of that slight vulnerability that I finally feel the tension in my shoulders dissipate, and not even a second later, my mouth is moving, my whispered confession making me feel the vulnerability I heard in his voice slam right into my chest.

"Because I was scared."

"Of what?"

He doesn't move. I wonder briefly if he wants me in his arms as badly as I want his arms around me. I shake my head, letting everything I had come to terms with and worked through with my therapist keep me strong.

"You," I admit.

"Why?"

My shoulders lift, offering him a shrug because I didn't know how to put the rest into words. I don't want to freak him out when we're already on shaky ground thanks to my disappearing act.

"Why?" he says again, stressing the word with force.

This time, I shake my head.

"Why!" he bellows, still not moving, making me jump.

"Because!" I scream back. "Because! Because I have never felt that before, Thorn! Because I spent one night with you and woke up feeling like I needed to get out, away from those feelings immediately, before I got hurt!"

His head jerks back as if I had physically slapped him.

"You think I would have hurt you?"

"At that time, yes. The things I knew about that kind of hurt leading up to that moment had taught me that anytime someone makes you feel anything, especially that kind of intensity, it will only ever end in pain."

A flicker of understanding flashes.

"I've had enough pain to last a lifetime, Thorn. So I ran. I'm not proud of it, and I'm sorrier than you will ever know, but that's all I could do at the time."

"You aren't the only person to feel pain, Ari. Don't take your lessons from that shit and refuse to learn from them."

"I learned. I learned that it's not worth opening yourself up to the chance of more if you can help it."

"Then you didn't learn shit."

"Excuse me?"

He stalks toward me, his long legs making the short distance in half of what it would take me. "I know pain. I know the kind of pain the devil himself would hesitate to inflict on his worst enemy. You aren't the only one to feel that lick your soul and sear it deep. I know that, and I still woke up that morning ready to take that pain, those lessons, and open myself up to more. Only, where I expected to find the woman who woke that need inside me, she was gone. So, tell me, Ari, what pain makes you so scared?"

"I'm not sure I'm ready for this," I breathe, my nose burning. I go to walk around him only to stop when his hand closes around my arm, tugging me with care to his body. "I thought I was …"

"Tell me."

I close my eyes, drop my forehead to his chest, and try to calm myself with slow, deep breaths. His heart pounds against my head, the beat rapid and telling. He's not calm. He's far from unaffected. I soak up the feeling of being this close to him, though, letting everything I learned focus my thoughts. Using the tools from my therapy sessions, I sort my thoughts and organize my mind.

"You got in," I confess softly. His other hand comes up and around my back, pulling me tighter against his body. "For seven years, no one but Piper has even come close to touching that spot inside me. And you didn't just get in, Thorn. You were in deep and had started filling the emptiness inside me. After just one night, I could feel it getting smaller. One night."

"Ari," he rumbles.

"You wanted it, Thorn," I remind him. He asked for the truth of my disappearing act.

"Yeah. Still do. Why did it scare you that I got in?"

I exhale. "I felt that in a few days of meeting you. *Days*. As strong as it was in those days, I couldn't give it time to get stronger."

"Why?"

Just say it, Ari. Rip it off like a Band-Aid. They can't hurt you anymore. YOU are in charge of your future.

"Seven years ago, people I loved were lost to me forever. My parents were two of them. My sister another. And the last, well, after last weekend, I know the last person never even came close to making me feel the way you did that night, and I wore his ring."

He hisses in a breath, and I finally have the courage to look up.

"Days, Thorn. I felt that zapping between us in just days. Each time I looked into your eyes, what started as simple attraction had grown into something more. If losing them almost killed me, I couldn't even imagine what would happen if I let that kind of power closer to me, let it build into something even stronger, only to have it taken away later. So I ran."

"You'd just give that up without sticking around to see what could happen if, instead of it being taken away, it just kept growing?"

This time, it's me who frowns up at him. I hadn't expected him to understand this well.

"Yeah, I see you've only thought about what could happen if we went bad. You aren't the only one who felt it. You also aren't the only one with a past giving you a reason to believe it might turn bad. However, I laid awake with you in my arms that night, and instead of letting that bullshit win, I went to sleep willing to take a chance and see what would happen if we continued building more. I woke up knowing that if I lost it all in the end, at least it would be worth the ride."

"Thorn, it's not that simple."

"Oh, it is. Day by day. You take the time to explore something that you feel, in your gut, is going to keep burning bright. You don't just toss that away. In the end, if this doesn't keep going the way I feel it will, the way I hope it does, we won't lose each other. You won't lose me. This turns out to be something else, Ari, I promise I'll still be here. You're meant to be in my life; I have no doubts. All that said, though, my gut is never wrong, baby. I know why you're meant to be in mine. Now I get to show you why I'm meant to be in yours."

"I haven't let anyone close enough in all those years, Thorn. I wouldn't have known how to do day by day before I left."

He bends down, way down, and when his eyes are level with mine, he speaks. "And I haven't let anyone close enough to explore anything with in my *whole goddamn life*." His words fanning softly from his lips to mine are so close I can taste him.

The shock of his confession dances over my face. He doesn't move, continuing to hunch down and search my eyes.

"You scare me," I remind him. "What I felt in days made me scared of you."

"Well, baby, you terrify me. That night, my world shook, and it still made me want to grab on with both hands. Day by day, Ari. Give me that, and I promise, no matter how long we're meant to explore this, I'll do everything to make sure you don't feel pain."

I swallow, the loud gulp echoing around the room. As the silence ticks on, his touch brands me. I don't look away as my heart drowns my remaining fears. Even after all the healing I've experienced in the past two weeks.

And then, I nod.

SIXTEEN

Ari

My best friend is back

AFTER WORKING ON PAPERWORK ALL DAY, I DROP THE LAST bit into the tray on my desk marked "to file" and lean back with a sigh.

Today was busy. Now, that's not right. It was beyond busy. Today, I didn't even look up from going through the piles that had amassed in the past two weeks I was absent from Trend. Well, not absent, but popping in for a few hours here and there isn't exactly the best way to stay on top of my duties.

Piper walks by my office door, catching my eye, and I call out to her. We haven't talked since she left my house yesterday. Well, not about anything aside from things that had to do with Trend. I know she wanted to ask, to discuss everything *and* find out what happened with Thorn, but she also knew how much work was waiting for me. Even though I wanted to talk to her as much as she wanted to listen, before now, I needed to get my work done so I could focus.

"You've been busy," she says, leaning against the doorframe, looking over at the desk that had been a complete disaster when I sat down this morning.

"Yeah. Remind me never to put off everything for two weeks again."

She scoffs.

"Hannah here yet?"

"She clocked in about an hour ago."

"Good," I say, picking up my phone and pressing the button that connects me to the front desk.

"This is Hannah," she answers with a smile in her voice.

"If you're good, Piper and I are going to have a meeting in my office."

"We're all good, boss. Hayley and Jess are already here, so we're set for the afternoon."

"Let us know if you need anything; otherwise, Pipe's done for the day."

"Okie dokie."

I hang up and smile at Piper. "Remind me again how we functioned without Hannah?"

This time, she does laugh. "We didn't. You were stretched thin, even with me getting Matt to agree that I needed to be full-time, until we found her. Sometimes, I pray she never leaves, and we don't lose the best manager—aside from myself, of course—that Trend could have."

"Better knock on wood," I joke. "Come on. Shut the door and sit down."

She shoves off where she had been resting, knocking on the door as she closes it. She doesn't waste a second sitting down on the couch and exhaling loudly after ensuring our privacy.

"You know I love you. You're more than just my best friend. It doesn't matter that we don't share blood; you're my sister, and I'm so thankful I have you in my life. You deserved more from me than what I've been over the years, and I'm sorry for that."

"Ari, you make it sound like you haven't given me just as much over the years."

"It's not the same, and you know it."

"I don't keep tabs. That's what I know. It's what we are."

"I know. I know. But I want you to know how much I appreciate your support through the years. And for pushing me to see things differently that morning when I couldn't get there myself. I don't know that I would have taken the steps I did over the past two weeks if it hadn't been for that shove."

She shrugs. "Like I said, it's what we are."

"It was like I had been sleeping through my own life, Pipe. All I could see was everything that led up to losing my parents. You're right; I've been using that to keep me from living. Dr. Hart has really helped, too. I don't think I would have started the intense therapy he's been pushing me toward for years had you not forced me to listen. Forced me to see. I know I'll never be able to say thank you enough for what your hard truths brought me."

"Ari, don't give me all that credit. You were ready, and I believed it. I just needed you to believe it, too."

"And you nudged me along to start the process of believing it."

"Whatever. I'm not comfortable taking all the credit, but for the sake of you telling me about the past two weeks *and* what happened with Thorn after I left yesterday, I'll say you're welcome and I'm happy that you finally believe."

"You know, two weeks ago, I never would have thought I'd be thanking you."

She laughs but doesn't say anything. I know she's waiting for me to continue. She doesn't hide her worry for me well.

"Dr. Hart, he finished opening my eyes the rest of the way. The first week, I felt every single emotion imaginable. Every one. It was ugly. It was unbelievable, but it was what I needed. Every single day that first week, I spent four hours in his office, and by the time I was dropping into my bed at night, I felt another shift. Last Monday, I went into our session with the acceptance of what happened, and the guilt was completely detached from my mind. We spent this past week working through the grief I have over losing my family. It still feels like something is empty inside me, but I know that's okay … even if it never fills back up completely. It's okay, and more importantly, I'm okay."

She sniffles.

"Half of the past week we talked about Thorn and why it was okay for me to keep you close but believe I couldn't let anyone else in."

"And?" she breathes, hanging on my every word.

"And I didn't freak out completely when he showed up yesterday because of what I've gained from my sessions with Dr. Hart."

"God, Ari. That's great."

"I know I can't control what happens in my life, but I also can't continue to live half a life. Dr. Hart taught me a few exercises in case I freak out about it again, but he doesn't think I'll be back in that place again to need them. My therapy will continue bi-weekly for just an hour, though, instead of four. I won't stop seeing him again. Even if I get to the point where I don't need him, I'll still continue to go."

"Really?"

"Really. It's been a hard two weeks, but I don't want to lose this strength I've gained since returning to my sessions. One day, I'll get to the point where I only need him once a month, maybe once every few months, but that's a while down the road."

"My best friend is back," she whispers, tears falling freely.

"Yeah," I confirm, leaving my chair and walking to where she's sitting. She stands the second I'm around my desk, and we meet, wrapping our arms tightly around each other. "I'm sorry I couldn't find my way back before now."

"Shut up. All that matters is that you're back, here with me, and ready to move forward."

"He woke me up, Pipe. He did, but it was you who made me understand the fear my nightmares had festered while I slept. You did that and pushed me to realize I needed Dr. Hart's help to finally believe what you kept telling me."

We hug for a while, neither of us willing to let go. When she pulls away, her red-rimmed eyes study mine.

"I'm really happy you're back."

"Me, too."

She takes a deep breath. "What about Thorn?"

"How long have you wanted to ask me about his visit yesterday?"

"Since I woke up this morning. No, actually, I wanted to call you last night, but I managed to hold back. Barely."

I giggle, releasing her to sit on the couch. I wait until she's back on the cushion and fiddle with my bracelets.

"I told Dr. Hart how I met him, you know? I told him about the visit to The Orchard, the contract, the bet ... all of it. While he might not have agreed with the way it started, he felt like it was okay for me to continue exploring things with Thorn if I felt like something was unfinished between us. However, he did express his concerns that I take it slow until I knew where Thorn was after everything that happened, and ... well, until I knew how genuine his interest in me might be. It helped that I shared the calls and such I had received from Thorn since I had left with him. Dr. Hart felt that, had I just been the bet, Thorn wouldn't have continued to try to contact me after I left the way I did."

"That's good, right?"

"It's something." I laugh uneasily. "What it did, however, was open the door for us to discuss my fear of letting someone else into my life. Only more in depth this time since this is different from my relationship with you. I could never see past the pain of losing my family to see things differently. I let that pain and my fears cloud everything else. I might not completely believe that letting someone all the way into my life will be worth the pain if I were to lose them, but I'm willing to try. I'm willing to open myself up to finding my dreams again, and if it isn't with Thorn, I'm at least going to take it day by day while I find out."

"Does that mean that last night went well?"

"Yeah. I think it does." Last night comes rushing back, and I'm once again enveloped by the warmth of my decision ... well, Thorn's and my decision.

"Anddddd?" she prompts, drawing the word out and wagging her brows.

"He knows why I ran. Well, he knows I lost people in my life, making me afraid when what we shared was more intense than I had expected. He let me know he has some stuff in his past too, and the rest we decided to just take it as it comes and see where we go. He also made sure I knew exactly where he stands."

"That's all you can do, girlfriend. I have a feeling about that man, though. So, tell me, what happened after you guys decided that?"

The smile on my lips dips down a little, something Piper doesn't miss. "He ordered another pizza—you know, since you stole the one we ordered—and we talked while we waited. And after it was delivered, we talked while we ate. Well, I probably did more of the talking and he listened, but it was nice to share normal get-to-know-you things with him. I know his favorite color is black, which I shared wasn't really a color, his favorite movies, shows, and books. He knows the same about me, minus the black, but in addition, he knows about my weakness for Hershey's Kisses, chocolate-dipped cones from Dairy Queen, my Kindle being an obsession I should buy stock in Amazon over, and my propensity to read trashy magazines while watching even trashier television. I guess it was the kind of thing two people, who are whatever we are, share when they're new. He hung around for about an hour after we finished eating, then he kissed my forehead and left after I promised to answer his call next time. I'm not really sure what kind of timeframe that next time implies. It's been a while since I've been on this particular bike."

"You mean the tall, dark, and handsome bike?"

We both laugh, lightness in the air and in the pit inside me … it feels good.

I start to open my mouth, a joke about riding that tall, dark, and handsome bike on the tip of my tongue, but stop when a knock sounds on my office door.

"Uh, sorry, guys," Hannah says, poking her head in. "I would have waited, but I didn't want it to melt."

I look from Hannah to Piper to back at Hannah, then stand to walk toward her. "Didn't want what to melt?"

She opens the door wider and thrusts her arm into the office. "This."

Piper starts laughing like a crazy person.

Hannah waits with a smile. A confused smile but a happy one nonetheless.

And I have a good feeling I know what kind of timeframe Thorn is calling with now.

Only, this call is in the form of one melting chocolate-dipped cone and an armful of trashy gossip magazines.

SEVENTEEN

THORN

I don't care if I haven't seen you for an hour, you kiss me

"I DIDN'T THINK YOU WERE REALLY LISTENING TO ME," ARI whispers, her voice coming through the phone and hitting me right in the gut. The two weeks I spent with her silence made me feel like a fucking caged animal, but hearing that softness over the line made it worth it.

"Babe, looked at you the whole time you were talking."

"Yeah. I mean, I know … but I talked, uh, a lot. *I* probably would have tuned me out."

She isn't wrong. She did talk a lot, but she was also nervous. I could tell even without her rambling about everything just how nervous she was. I'm pretty sure I wouldn't have been able to get a word in edgewise, but fuck if I didn't enjoy the hell out of just listening to her talk. Not once did I want to tune her out, though. Not fucking once.

"And I listened a lot," I reply, wanting to keep hearing her whisper to me through the phone.

The low giggle I hear isn't felt in my gut this time. No, that one went right to my cock.

Slow, Thorn. Not going to do you any fucking favors if you make her think you just want to sink into that sweet as fuck pussy again. Well, it won't if she thinks that's all I want.

"Thank you, Thorn. Thank you for surprising me. Thank you for not letting me screw everything up and for accepting my apologies. Thank you for thinking I'm worth the trouble."

Damn, this girl has no clue. Not one fucking clue. Any other chick, I would have written her off the morning I woke up alone and found someone else to wet my dick and wash her off. But Ari? No. She wasn't the only one who felt something in one day. That's all it took for me to know she was different. All it took was her sweet fucking smile aimed right at me over a plate full of steak and potatoes to confirm it. Two weeks apart hadn't even dulled an ounce of that. I saw that she was fragile with my own eyes even when I kept my distance. A few days after she ran, I had everything I needed to ensure I could keep watch over her until I knew she was ready for me. Like a fucking stalker, I watched her come to her store three times. The first time, she looked like the weight of the world was on her shoulders. The second, it was still there but not as heavy as before. The last time, four days ago, was when I knew she was ready. Ready for me. She wasn't moving like every step was difficult anymore. She looked like she was lighter. So I set my shit in motion.

"You don't need to thank me for that, Ari," I tell her, honest as fuck.

"Maybe not, but I mean it." She clears her throat, the moment gone. "The ice cream was just what I didn't know I wanted today."

I step from the wet bar and walk over to the window that looks down on the female side of The Alibi, my eyes scanning over the servers and bartenders getting ready for the night.

"I wasn't sure it would make it," I tell her, pushing aside my annoyance that, once again, I see one of the girls coming from the back stumbling on her heels. Fucking coke head. I make a mental note to deal with that after my call, moving away from the window so I'm not distracted.

"It was a close call," Ari replies, bringing me down from the anger boiling inside me. Just like that.

"Wish I didn't have to, but both of my floor managers are out until Wednesday. Unless you feel like coming here, it's looking like I'm not getting you back in my car until Thursday night, at the earliest. That's not working for me, Ari."

She hums, and my cock twitches. Fucking Thursday.

"Do you want me there?"

"Not sure there's much of anywhere I don't want you."

"Chinese or Mexican?" she oddly asks, and I frown.

"Not following, babe."

"Dinner. You need to eat but have to work. I don't have to work and like to eat. So Chinese or Mexican?"

"Surprise me," I answer instantly, feeling my chest get tight, liking that she wants to spend more time with me just as I do her.

"Okay, Thorn," she says huskily.

"Text me when you're here, and I'll come get you. Pull around back and park next to my bike."

"Yes, sir." She laughs.

"Fuck."

She doesn't say anything else, disconnecting with another laugh, but it's that throaty laughter of hers that I hear long after pocketing my phone that has me feeling as if I've just been given some kind of gift. Lightness. Fuck me, pure goddamn lightness settling deep in my bones.

Yeah, two weeks in a cage wasn't shit if this is my reward for being patient.

Then I wipe the smile from my face and stomp down the stairs to fire another one of my dancers because she can't keep her nose out of the fucking powder.

I'm here.

I was out of my seat and heading down the second I saw her name appear on the screen. Those two words settle deep, cooling my sour mood instantly. I ignore the guys from security who start waving me over when I open the door that takes me onto the floor of the male side, eyes on the back door, and push through into the night less than a minute after her text came through. When my eyes land on her, leaning against her car with two bags in her hand and a shy smile on her face, I'm done for.

She could tell me to bow and kiss her feet, and I'd fucking drop to my knees in a heartbeat.

She doesn't move. I stay where I am, holding the back door open so it doesn't lock, thankfully remembering the second I pushed it open that I left my keys up on my desk. I use that time to get my control in order so I don't drop to my knees for a whole different reason.

"I went with Italian," she says with a shrug, and that shy smile is joined by two pink cheeks.

"Babe."

"I probably should have texted you first to make sure you liked Italian, but I figured, who doesn't like Italian?"

Fuck, this girl.

"Babe," I repeat.

"You do like Italian, right?" she asks, looking at me with a frown.

My fingers itch to touch her. To pull her into my arms and against my body. To feel her.

Fuck, enough of this.

"Ari, get the fuck over here and kiss me."

Her eyes widen, and those pink cheeks turn red. I'm about to let the door go, not even giving a shit if I have to fucking walk us around the building to get back in. Not if that means I get my hands on her. I take a step forward, one arm stretching out, almost coming off the door. Then she moves, and before I can so much as adjust my hard cock, her body is against mine and her head is tipped back so she can look up at me.

I bend, not needing to see that she's as close as she can get, standing on her toes.

She gives a little bounce, confirming that she's rolled up as far as she can and needs a little more help than simply bending can give.

I dip my head down another inch, and then those lips are on mine.

I kick my foot to the side to hold the door, and move my hands to push into her thick hair, taking control of our kiss. She moans when I tilt her head, taking her mouth deeper. When I lift away, she doesn't open her eyes, and I lick my lips, her taste on my tongue making me want more.

"Next time, Ari," I murmur low and deep, need in my tone that can't be disguised. When her hazel eyes are on me again, I continue. "Next time, I don't care if I haven't seen you for an hour, you kiss me."

"Okay," she breathes. Instant. Certain. No fucking walls in the way to make her hesitate.

"You like that?"

She nods. "I like that."

"Then, baby, give me those lips again."

We finally make it back up to my office after I get a longer taste of those sweet lips. I've managed to ignore the voice inside me telling me to push her down on my desk and take more. I managed, just, and helped by clearing off my desk to make room for our dinner. She was still smiling by the time she finished unpacking all the food she brought. My hunger for the deliciously scented food she set down replaced the hunger I felt for her. She had so much food, all I could do was watch as she pulled more and more out of the bags she had carried in. Complete with plates, cutlery, and napkins.

"What'd you do? Order one of everything they had?"

"Close." She laughs. "I know the owner, so I just called and asked for an assortment of their entrees. I wasn't sure what you would like or how hungry you would be, so I … uh, well, I wanted to be sure you would have something you liked."

I say nothing, but when her blush comes back, that hits me just as hard as her wanting to make sure I was taken care of. I laugh to myself and grab a plate, silently loading it full with a little bit of everything from each carton my girl brought me.

My girl. Yeah. I'm thinking I like the sound of that a whole hell of a lot.

"So, tell me, how does one become the owner of a strip club?" she asks after we had settled into our seats.

I look up, over my mountain of food, and glance only briefly at her plate, smiling at the differences between the two. "How anyone does, I guess. Worked my way up."

She takes a bite of the lasagna, and it's the furrow of her brow that makes me drop the fork full I was about to eat back down to the plate. She wouldn't ask. I know she wouldn't. But I know she isn't satisfied with vague answers.

"It found me." She swallows, that frown growing. "Sounds pretty stupid when I say that out loud, but it did. Grew up on the streets, even during the years I had a house I could've gone to. It was easier there, believe it or not. I was young, but I was fucking smart. It didn't hurt that, at sixteen, I looked much older. Before me, Harris was the owner here. When I showed up looking for a job, he had no reason to doubt my age when I could provide him with proof that I was old enough to be there."

"If you looked even a little close to how you do now, I bet he would have believed you without proof." She laughs.

"Not much has changed in over twenty years 'cept a few more gray hairs."

Her mouth drops, and her eyes roam over my face. "Over twenty years?"

"Babe." My lips twitch, and I take a bite of my food.

"Did I wake up this morning and enter some world where people are immortal? There is no way you're old enough to be able to say 'over twenty years.'"

Her blush comes back when I bark out a laugh. "A lesser man would fish for some more compliments to stroke his ego."

"Yeah, well, you definitely don't have cause to lack any confidences over all of that," she smarts, using her fork and waving it around. "I mean, I guess I can see why you wouldn't need that."

My shoulders shake, more laughter vibrating my chest. "Turned forty-one earlier this year. I might not look it, but there are mornings that I damn sure feel it."

"Wow," she breathes. "I would have pegged you closer to my age."

"Nine years isn't that far off."

She looks down and stabs her fork into the spaghetti before twirling it, worrying her bottom lip between her teeth before releasing it. "I shouldn't be surprised you know my age. You did find my house with whatever resources you have at your fingertips. Anything else you already know about me?"

She looks up, and I'm thankful I didn't press for more than the basic background check when I see her unease.

"Know where you went to high school and college. Aside from your age and that you own both Trend and your house outright? No, Ari. The rest I wanted to learn straight from you."

Her shoulders drop as the tenseness leaves, and she takes a deep breath. Yeah, I'm fucking glad I trusted my gut when I thought she would be less than happy to know I used my reach to find out more than the minimal.

"Harris," I say, finishing the bite I had been chewing. "He

owned The Alibi for a few decades before my sorry ass showed up. I could tell he didn't believe me, despite my flawless ID, but he put me to work. I was dancing for over a year before he called me on it. Might not have felt it then, but I was lucky to end up here. After the day he pulled me into his office to ask for the truth, he started grooming me to take over."

"Just like that?"

"Yeah, babe, just like that. He had a son, but he wasn't interested in The Alibi. Back then, it was just the one building," I say, pointing toward the male side. "I didn't add the female entertainment until about five years after he retired. Even then, his son wasn't interested. Didn't have a thing against strippers, seeing as he danced on the same stage I did, but it just wasn't the future he saw for himself. Me, though? It was the only future I had let myself plan, so I took what I learned and built this place into what it is now."

"Um ..." she mumbles softly, licking her lips, eyes on me.

"Don't get shy, Ari. You want to know something, ask me."

"Okay," she breathes. "Did you ... dance for a long time?"

"I won't lie to you, but fuck if I'm not worried that my honesty will make you run again."

She wipes her mouth and leans back in the chair she had pulled up to the edge of my desk. "I won't run."

"You sound sure of that."

"We all have pasts."

I scoff. "Ain't a single thing about mine that isn't tainted with filth."

"It still made you the man you are today. I won't hold your past against you."

Fuck, if she only knew.

"I promise, Thorn," she stresses softly, eyes beseeching.

"Twenty-five years ago, The Alibi wasn't a club known for just dancing. I started dancing, but when I realized the back rooms were where the money was, dancing wasn't the only thing I did when I took my clothes off. That was before I had the future Harris gave me when he retired and left The Alibi to me, so all I could do was work my ass off to make sure I didn't end up back on the streets. Showed up here at sixteen and I was down there on the floor using the only thing I had, my body, for almost five years. Spent more time helping Harris run shit and just dancing here and there, after. Until I danced for you, I hadn't been on the stage since I was twenty-two."

"Um, I hate to make a joke about what I can tell was a hard time for you, but Thorn, if you moved like that after twenty years, I'm pretty sure I wouldn't have lasted fifteen seconds back then."

This time, the laughter that boomed from deep in my belly didn't sound as rusty as it had each time before. True to her promise, she not only didn't judge me for that shit, but she also clearly wasn't repulsed by the fact the man she was getting to know allowed others to pay for the enjoyment of his body.

"You're just full of surprises," I tell her.

"Like I said, we all have a past. So you've owned The Alibi since you were twenty-two?"

"No, babe. I haven't danced since then. Harris pulled me off the stage and spent a few years teaching me everything he knew. Ran this place by his side until he retired. I was twenty-eight or so. Took a while to get the addition of the female side built. Had to completely close for a few weeks while they tore the roof off the old building and built my office up. After more headaches than I sometimes think were worth it, we had everything in place to reopen both sides. When he saw the profits after the first year of both clubs being open, I did more than prove he was right in pulling me off the stage and giving me the business he had started from dirt."

"I might not know a lot about what you do, but even I know you have one heck of a place here. I don't know what it was like then, but in the short time I was down on that floor, it clearly doesn't lack happy customers."

"You one of them?" I joke, dropping my fork and downing half the bottle of water she brought.

"Depending on who's on the stage, I think I could become a regular."

"You want more of that, and I guarantee you it won't be in a room full of other people."

"Other people?" She chuckles. "That's funny because I didn't notice anyone else."

"Fuck," I groan, leaning back to adjust my hard cock. "You flirt with me, Ari, you do it on my lap, so I can feel something other than my pants when you make me hard."

She looks down but jerks her eyes back up when she realizes what she did, shifting in her seat. "I really liked watching you," she whispers. "Does everyone enjoy watching people take their clothes off and move to music like that?"

"Ari," I warn.

"Do you think some of the girls who dance here could teach me some moves so I could dance like that?"

"Fuck it."

When I push back my chair, it crashes behind me as I stalk around the desk. Her eyes widen with each step. Even with the fire blazing inside me, the fire she lit the match to, I reach out and, tender as fuck, pull her to her feet. She keeps those wide eyes, but they're full of the same heat I feel. I bend, hands on her hips, and pull her against my body. Her hands land on my chest, my cock pressing its hardness against her soft curves. When a groan vibrates against her hands, she smiles with pride.

"It's hard enough to keep my cock from getting back into your pretty pussy, Ari. Keep talking like that and I'm pretty sure I'll prove to both of us that I suck at going slow."

"I don't want slow. Not with you."

I drop my forehead, keeping our gazes connected.

"Not going slow made you run from me. I'm not fucking this up before I give us both what we want."

She tips her head to the side. "And what's that?"

"More."

I don't give her a chance to say anything else. I close the distance, take her mouth, and drive her as wild as I feel. With each second that we spend locked against each other, her body grows heavier in my embrace until I'm forced to adjust my hold and lift her against me. Her fingertips roll against my scalp as she reaches up and grabs the longer part of my hair. When her legs part, wrapping around my hips, and the warmth of her pussy hits my cock, I growl against her mouth, and our kiss turns wild.

It's a fucking miracle that I'm able to pull away minutes later. Seeing the dazed as fuck expression on her beautiful face, I'm determined never to have a day without her in my presence that she doesn't look up at me with that exact fucking look.

That dazed look dims slightly, and she blinds me with her smile. "I think I'm going to like finding more with you, Thorn Evans."

Goddamn. If I didn't know better, I'd swear my knees just shook. "Yeah, baby, you damn sure will."

EIGHTEEN

Ari

Definitely second best.

I YAWN, ROLLING MY SHOULDERS IN THE POINTLESS EFFORT OF shaking some of the tiredness off me, and turn my car off. It's been like this all day. Even the quick hour-long power nap I took this afternoon on my couch at Trend didn't put a dent in the tiredness I was dragging around. It was worth it, though. So worth it.

The past two nights after leaving Trend, I've gone to Thorn's office at The Alibi. After our first dinner, we didn't make out on his couch more than we talked, but after the second time he was pulled down to one of the floors, we stopped acting like horny teenagers and spent a few hours getting to know each other a little more. Of course, it was more me running my mouth and him listening. Last night, I had dinner with Piper and, unfortunately, Matt. After that, it had been late, but I stopped by after asking if he wanted me to bring him something from the restaurant. He shared a little, but not much, and again it had ended with me talking more than him. Both nights, he made sure that, no matter what, we were connected in some way. Either with our hands holding each other or him holding me. Hours of just sitting in his office felt nothing short of magical.

And tonight, his managers are back, so we're going on a date. Though it's not technically our first date, it feels like it is. Which would account for the nerves.

I grab my mail and purse off the passenger seat and step out of my car, waving at Doreen, my elderly neighbor, before walking up the pathway to my front door. I enter the code on my lock and step into my dark house. After telling my Echo to turn on my front room lights, I go to drop my purse and the mail down on the table off to the side of the front door, only to come out of my skin when I see Dwight sitting where my purse belongs. He blinks, and I swear those cat eyes of his narrow.

"Go on, you big jerk!" I scold, waving the mail in front of him.

He doesn't move.

Of course, he doesn't because Dwight is a big freaking jerk that thrives on making my life more challenging.

"Dwight," I fume. Pushing him with my purse, I earn a hiss immediately. "Move, you mean beast!"

Hiss.

My phone rings, and I glare at him. When it becomes clear he is definitely there to stay, I shove the mail into my purse and grab my phone out of the side pocket.

"Hello," I greet, turning and walking to the wall on the other side of my foyer to drop my burdens onto one of the two chairs.

"You okay?" Thorn's deep, yummy voice asks.

I sigh, turn, and curse my stupid cat. The cat that is now gone from the spot he was determined to claim.

"Do you want a cat?"

Silence.

"I could tell you he's the biggest sweetheart in the world and talk him up so you would really want him, but that would all be lies since he's the devil."

"Babe."

"You don't look like a cat person, but even the devil needs someone who will let him do hellish things. You're bigger than me; maybe he wouldn't be too vicious."

"Hellish things?"

"You have no idea."

"Do hellish things mean you want to skip the movies tonight?"

"Uh, no, they definitely do not. In fact, you would be doing him a favor by taking me out of this house before I call the vet and leave a message that I need an appointment to have the devil's balls removed."

No sooner than the words leave my mouth does Dwight saunter back into view. He stops, looks right at me, and hisses. Jim comes prancing into the foyer happily, his body tries to stop, but with the hardwoods under him, he only ends up in a crash of hisses and fur when he collides with Dwight.

"What was that?" Thorn asks, laughter in his voice.

"That was hell cat being a jerk to his little brother."

"Fuck. Stop being cute, Ari."

"I'm not doing anything, Thorn."

"Exactly." He grunts low. Before I can explain it's impossible to be doing nothing at the same time as doing whatever makes him think I'm cute, he continues. "I'll be there in ten. Try not to let hell cat win."

"Right," I answer, stepping over said hell cat as he licks the balls he's so fond of. "You hear that, you evil jerk. Just ten minutes and if you make it that long, those balls of yours might live for you to keep licking them for another day."

"Fuck."

Then the line goes dead, and I hurry into the kitchen to feed the cats so they won't be waiting up late for their dinner. Jim gives me a lick when I place his bowl down, earning some ear scratches. Dwight just sits there and waits for his human slave to do what is expected. Jim takes a few seconds to stick his paw into Dwight's food, earning another cat glare from the beast before he goes back to his own bowl.

With the cats sorted, I head into my closet to switch my tight shelf dress out for something better suited for a movie date. The flowy black dress I grab hugs my chest, the swoop neck giving way for a generous cleavage display, and hits me just above the knee. Flirty, casual, and effortlessly sexy. I leave my strappy heels on, change my jewelry out for just some simple bangles, and pull my hair down from the twist I had it up in all day. When I step in front of the large mirror, I smile at myself. I might feel tired, but the excitement over seeing Thorn again tonight is enough to heat my skin with a healthy glow, making me look far from tired.

The soft waves of my long, thick hair frame my face. Highlighting just how excited I am with a freshness that betrays working for over twelve hours on a few hours of sleep. Even with the long hem on this dress, my legs still look longer than they are thanks to the four-inch heel. Just a little gloss and I'll be ready to go.

I grab one of my favorite shoulder bags and head back to the entry to get the purse I had carried today, then head into the kitchen to switch out my essentials. I have just finished when I hear my bell ring. Jim scurries from his dinner at the chime, and Dwight just looks up annoyed at the interruption. Clearly, the thought of continuing to eat is just too much when he feels the need to let me know I've angered him.

"Jerk."

My heels click against the floor, and my heart picks up speed as I walk to the door. I can see him through the decorative glass, and I lick my lips. Another dress shirt. I've come to realize I like him in all levels of dress, but this might be just as good as naked Thorn.

"Hey," I greet when I open the door. I glance down, seeing he's rolled up the sleeves to his elbows, showing off his tattoos. The top two buttons on his collar open to show his golden, tattooed skin. Definitely second best.

"Second best?"

"I need to work on keeping my whispered thoughts quieter so you don't hear them." He doesn't say anything. He just stands there, and I start shifting on my feet. Oh, fine. "You in a dress shirt, like that," I continue, using his silence as him wanting me to clarify what he heard. "That's second best to my favorite version of you."

"Your favorite version?"

"This really is kind of embarrassing."

"What's ahead of this?" he asks, pointing at himself.

"Uh, naked you?"

One of his brows goes up. His lips twitch.

"It's not kind of embarrassing. It's definitely embarrassing."

"Babe."

"What?" I snap, feeling the heat of my confession on my face.

"You can be embarrassed if you want. Shouldn't be, but you can. You forget something when you were too busy rating versions of me?"

Now it's my turn to be confused.

"Kiss, Ari. You see me, no matter how long, I get your mouth."

This time when I roll my eyes, it's with a smile as I walk to him. "When you're bossy, it almost makes dress shirt you even with naked you." I press my lips against his, but pull away before he can get more than a peck. "Though, that's only if naked you has a sheet over the bottom half. Otherwise, I'm not sure anything can beat fully naked you."

"Fucking kiss me, Ari."

"Bossy," I smart, smiling against his mouth.

"Stop making my cock hard."

"I'm not doing anything," I tell him, peppering small pecks against his lips, but not deepening the kiss to give him what he wants.

His hands rise, framing my face and stalling my movements. His eyes burn into mine, his labored breaths hot against my mouth.

Then *he* kisses *me*.

NINETEEN

Not even hell could keep this evil caged any longer

BACK IN THE SHADOWS WHERE ONLY THE EVILEST OF BE-ings felt at home, Anger was burning hot. The heat all-consuming, turning and churning like the very acid that flowed through its veins. Anger was no match for that heat as it quickly became apparent that the very flames destroying Anger were set ablaze in order for Rage to come forward and finally take Anger's place. For good.

Over the years, Rage had sated its needs by spending a few hours, every couple of days, drinking up the vision of the woman in black who sat a few rows ahead of the monster inside the crowded theater. The woman never saw Rage, but Rage was always there. Waiting.

The same shadows that were licking her skin this very moment were the ones that kept Rage fed and sated. After all, Rage was something born of pure evil, living on the fears and pain only something so dreadful could create.

It's a shame that Anger wasn't stronger because Rage had a thirst to play. The devil started to reach forward, the desperation to claw the woman in black to shreds with its claws erupting from deep within.

She would feel pain, Rage vowed.

She would regret the years Rage had been kept from what it needed to keep the devil happy.

Just when Rage was about to lash out, the veil clouding Rage's vision cleared for the briefest of moments. That's when Rage saw the man at the woman's side. The man's arm, what Rage was focusing on, as it held the woman was unknowingly the only thing protecting the woman from Rage's desperation.

For now.

The cloak of darkness kept Rage hidden as the devil retracted its claws. The wickedness only roiling faster through Rage, coating the air in sticky putridness.

Rage blinked, the red haze not dimming in the slightest.

How dare the woman leave the void of nothingness that Anger had make sure she never forgot, Rage thought, bitterness joining in the poisonous vat of hate deep within Rage's belly.

This wouldn't do.

Rage had allowed Anger to become complacent. Complacency, it would seem, had allowed the woman in black to betray the shell of herself Anger had crafted. Though, it was clear Anger had been weak because had Rage been allowed to surface before now, the woman would know better than to step out from where she belonged—in the dungeon of Despair, waiting for the beast to come claim her soul.

Rage knew one thing; the woman wouldn't forget her place next time.

Rage would make sure of it.

At least Anger had done one thing right over the years. Anger had ensured that Rage would never have to worry about the woman in black and the pesky annoyance that had been Grief becoming more than they were. The woman in black may have found a temporary break from her void of nothing, but Grief would never be that lucky. For Grief hadn't done the job right. Anger had made sure Grief paid.

Rage would then be able to put the woman in black back where she belonged. Then it would be her who felt nothing but Grief for as long as Rage allowed her lungs the air they needed.

After all, the man at her side wouldn't always be there.

As new plans started to ink themselves in Rage's mind, the sinister smile formed on the mouth of the beast.

Not even hell could keep this evil caged any longer.

TWENTY

Ari
You do it breathing easy

MY ALARM BLARES, AND I REACH OUT BLINDLY TO SHUT IT off, dropping my hand when I reach the distance I've all but committed to muscle memory. Only, instead of my alarm silencing, I get a grunt of pain.

I jerk up, hearing another grunt, only deeper sounding.

"Watch the elbow," Thorn's sleep-thickened voice gasps, and I lift my arm up from his belly. "Christ."

"Sorry," I mumble, carefully climbing over his body—his deliciously void of clothes body—to turn off my alarm.

"Why the hell is your alarm set for seven in the morning on a Sunday?"

I lift the strap of my nightie and shrug. "I don't like to waste the day."

"You don't like to waste the day?" he echoes, looking at me as if

I am all kinds of insane.

I blink back the sleep and roll my eyes.

"That's what I said."

His eyes crinkle at the corners, and he reaches up to pull me back into his arms, settling us back in bed. I sigh, the warmth of his skin soaking into mine. God, I could really get used to waking up like this.

"Not seeing how a day in bed with you is a waste."

I don't respond, but I silently agree. His breathing starts to even out, and I relax more into him, the arm around my body giving me a small squeeze. Still sleepy, I blink toward my window, but I know it will be impossible to go back to sleep. The early morning sun peeks through the crack in my dark curtains, supporting my internal alarm that seems to just know when I'm wasting time lying around. Now, I know I'm the one responsible for setting the cycle of getting up with the sun, but come on! How can I be punished for never sleeping in for years when I've got this man in my bed?

My mind, wide-awake, starts thinking about the many ways I could stay in this bed and still not waste the day away. Oh, no … it would definitely not be a waste. Now, if anyone is to blame for the turn of my thoughts, it's Thorn.

It's been two weeks of the day by day with this man, and aside from the most delicious kisses and learning each other's bodies without losing our clothes, he hasn't done anything to move things further.

I know why he hasn't made the move to go past that.

And I know I have no reason to hold back from giving him my more. Not when he's shown me on every one of these day by days what he wants from me—more … everything.

We might not have gotten deep, deep in getting to know each other's pain, but aside from both of our pasts, in the course of our two weeks together, we've opened up a lot. I know he hates anything but cheese on his pizza. He doesn't mind sitting through *ER* but can't stand *One Tree Hill*. He thinks the guys are pussies and the girls have more drama than are worth the trouble of having. That might have been our first fight; though, that's about the only thing we've disagreed on.

Last night, I introduced him to my favorite British trash show, *Geordie Shore*.

I lost the remote control privileges after one episode. I didn't mind too much because when he lifted the remote from my hand and turned off the television, his mouth was on mine, and the rest of the night was history.

Delicious history that ended with us getting further than we had since the night I begged for him.

"Your mind is louder than that fucking alarm was," Thorn grumbles, and I smile against his chest, squeezing the arm I have draped across his stomach.

"What happens next?" I question, not giving myself a chance to wuss out.

"Next? Figured I would take a piss and see if you had a toothbrush I could use."

"I didn't mean this morning. I mean with our day by day."

His chest shakes, moving me with his silent laughter as small rumbles vibrate from his chest. He's enjoying my awkwardness, but I don't mind. I know he isn't laughing at me, and to be fair, I like that I can make a man as hard as Thorn is let loose.

He pats my ass and starts to move out from under me, done

with his hilarity. However, I'm rendered thought-drunk when the sheet is flung off him, he climbs out of the bed, and all I can focus on is his naked backside.

Is there any inch of him that isn't perfectly made? I'm pretty sure there isn't.

With each step toward my bathroom, his cheeks flex and harden. I can see the heaviness of *him* between the gap of his legs as he walks, and I press my hand against the mattress to lift myself off for a better view. It was dark last night when he shed his clothes for bed, keeping me from getting a good view of his penis. I lose my show of him when he enters the bathroom and fall back on the bed with a sigh.

Day by day is pretty darn perfect when it starts with a wake-up like this.

I hear him moving in the bathroom, the toilet flushing, cabinets opening and shutting, and the water running. I keep my eyes on the ceiling and listen to him, knowing deep down that I don't think I can see ever getting sick of this feeling. I was so focused on my thoughts that I almost jump out of my skin when Dwight leaps on the bed.

"Good morning, Dwight," I coo, reaching out to pet him, drunk off Thorn thoughts and forgetting the little ginger is an evil jerk.

He swipes his paw at my hand and glares at me. He's going to murder me in my sleep one of these nights. I'm convinced that is what he's planning when I get those eyes from him.

A soft meow comes from the ground, and I ignore Dwight's evil hisses to lean past him and look down over the edge at Jim's green eyes blinking up at me from the floor. Now, where I swear

Dwight can glare, I swear Jim can smile.

"Hello, handsome," I sing to him, picking him up and curling him in my arm.

Jim purrs loudly, loving my scratches.

Dwight hisses. I narrow my eyes at him and stick out my tongue.

When Thorn steps out of the bathroom, unfortunately with his black briefs covering him up, Dwight looks away from me and studies his next victim of the morning. Thorn's spent a few nights at my place, but we've spent a lot of our time at his place. In the times that we've been here, both cats have been oddly absent.

Thorn eyes both cats, then walks over to sit on the edge of the bed. Dwight, the little jerk, struts his ginger butt over to Thorn and rubs against his side. The second Thorn places his giant hand against the grumpy beast, I hear a loud purr come from him.

"You have to be kidding me," I gasp. Jim twists in my arm, then jumps from my hold and goes to see what Dwight's so excited about that he's purring—something that never happens. Only the minute he gets close enough, Dwight euphoria slips, and he shows his true colors again by swatting the little guy to the floor.

"I swear, I'm going to take you to the vet and have your balls removed," I grumble again, bending over the edge to pick Jim back up. "Dwight's sorry, Jimmy baby. He's just a big evil jealous jerk."

"You named your cats after *The Office*?"

My cheeks heat, but I ignore it. "So what if I did?"

"Cute," he mumbles with a small smile on his delicious lips, still scratching Dwight.

"He doesn't like anyone," I tell Thorn, nodding at the cat sucking up his attention and trying not to be jealous of my evil beast.

"I'm not just anyone."

My cheeks burn again, this time not from embarrassment.

"Do you need to feed them?" Thorn asks.

"Yeah." I start to toss the covers off my lap, scooting to the other side and leaving the warmth our bodies had created. I get both feet on the floor and stop when I hear a low growl coming from Thorn. Looking over my shoulder at him, I find his gaze no longer on Dwight, who is very aware that he's lost his new slave, and instead directly on my legs. "What?"

"It was dark last night. Didn't see how short that thing was. But I also didn't have a window telling me how see-through it was either." He takes his time gliding his eyes up my body to my face, the burn of his perusal lighting a fire across my body. "Should probably go feed your cats before they miss their breakfast."

I jump, then hurry through the house to the kitchen. Getting two bowls down, I arrange their separate meals in each. Dwight comes trotting in when the sound of his food echoes through the house, wearing a smug look on his face now that his human slave has given him a new peasant *and* is preparing his feast.

Jim, still learning the sounds of his meals but more determined to follow the larger cat around, is hot on his trail. I wait for each cat to settle into their breakfast before turning and walking back down the hallway to my room.

Thorn is back in bed when I enter the room, the sheet covering his lap and his back against my large fabric headboard. His eyes track my body as I move around to the empty side and lift the sheet to climb back in bed. He lifts his arm, making room for me, and circles it around my shoulder the second I get close, pulling me into his warmth.

"Day by day?" he rumbles against my ear.

"I like our day by day, but I'm ready to give you my more, Thorn," I admit, needing him to understand without words what I'm stumbling to voice.

"You're finally catching up with me," he oddly says.

"What?" I shift, looking up at him from my position against his side, head on his shoulder.

He glances down and winks—freaking winks. Who is this man I've woken up to?

"I'm sorry I left," I tell him, for what is probably the thousandth time.

"I know, Ari. Worked out in the end so stop beating yourself up about it."

I start swirling my finger around his abs, tracing lazy outlines against the deeply defined muscles. My tracks only veering off to trace the occasional tattoo line that intersects a few of them.

"I'm *really* sorry."

He grunts, tightening his arm, but otherwise remains silent.

"I know I've said it before. I know you don't hold it against me, but I know you still have been waiting for me to tell you why I ran."

"I'm a patient man."

This time, it's me who laughs. "You're many things Thorn Evans, but patient is not one of them."

"You'd be surprised."

I know what he means. As much as I would love to discuss the sex I wish we were having, I need to get this out.

"I wasn't in a good place. Even if I had stayed until you woke up, it would have just ended the same." I get a reaction then. He moves us, lifting and adjusting me until I'm sitting in his lap. His hands drop from my hips to rest on each thigh, spread wide to accommodate the man between then.

"Give it to me, baby," he rumbles, eyes searching. It isn't lost on me that he instinctively moved me closer when it became clear where this conversation was leading us.

"I was already kind of freaking out when I woke up. As you know, you were the first man I had been intimate with in a long time. I didn't know what would happen after how intense our night was, and to be honest, I think I was afraid you would wake up and act like it meant nothing when it felt like everything to me."

His eyes dilate, and his chest moves quicker as his breathing speeds up slightly.

"I was in the middle of finding my clothes when my phone rang. Not wanting to wake you up, I answered without looking to see who was calling." I look at his lips and pause when I see them press thin. I take a deep breath, look back into his eyes, and continue. "My sister is one caller I haven't actually accepted a call from in five years or so, and well, she had a lot to say. Things that she normally leaves on my answer machines and I delete before I hear too much. I think it was the shock of accidentally answering that made me unable to hang up. She brought up a lot of stuff I had been feeling the pain of since our parents died … and things that happened during the days surrounding their death. The point is, I was already running scared of my feelings before she called. I don't know what would have happened had I stayed, but I know if you would have seen me after she called, it wouldn't have been pretty."

"I don't mean to say this without care, especially after you've given me all of that, but I thought you said you lost your sister? You got more than one?"

I shake my head. "I might not have lost her like I lost my parents, but she's gone to me, regardless, after what happened."

"Explain that," he orders, his thumbs rubbing soothing circles against my legs. Encouraging me. Supporting me silently. Giving me the courage to keep going.

"This is what we've been dancing around while we've been enjoying our day to day. You know that, right?"

Some of the harsh lines leave his face, his lips twitch, and he nods.

I dance my fingers across his warm skin, the light dusting of hair on his chest tickling my pads. My heart pounds, knowing I'm about to let him the rest of the way in to a place that I've only allowed Piper near since the day my world started falling around me.

"Three weeks before the day I was supposed to be married …" I pause when anger slashes across his face.

"Not easy to tell me this, Ari, I know that. Don't let the jealousy I can't hide from you just thinking about you almost never being right here with me keep you from letting me all the way in."

I nod. He has no idea what gift he just gave me with that, but I soak it up, knowing he's just as far gone to me as I am to him. Especially if he's angry just thinking that I almost married someone else.

"Ari," he urges.

"Right, sorry. So, there I was three weeks out of that day when I walked in on my sister sleeping with the groom. They saw me but didn't stop. Sometimes, I can picture it in my dreams as clear as the day it happened." I shake my head, ignoring the anger that is back on his face. "If it wasn't for those unwanted flashbacks from that moment, I don't think I would have seen clearly what happened after. I don't remember everything. To be honest, I think I blocked it out. One thing I do remember is they didn't stop. I never had trouble remembering that, but it was how wild they became when I caught them that sneaks back into my memories. I think they got off on it. Whether they meant to get caught, I don't know, but when they were … I'll never forget the sounds he made after that. I just stood there in shock while my heart was breaking. I just stood there, tears burning down my cheeks, and didn't even move when he pushed her off and climbed from the bed. Do you know what he said when he walked over to where I was standing in the doorway?"

A deep grunt comes, Thorn's stomach clenching with the sound. "What?" he asks, teeth clenched and jaw tight.

"He thanked me for saving him a trip, then held out his hand, and told me to give him back my ring so he could make sure the sister that didn't just lay there like a dead body got it this time. He said we might share a face, but she's the wild I couldn't give him to tame."

"You're fucking kidding?"

"I wish."

His frown deepens. "What did you do?"

I shrug, looking down and resuming my exploring of his muscles. "I took it off, my tears betraying what I didn't want him to know he was doing to me, and threw it at his crotch. I got a tiny bit of satisfaction when it bounced off his erection and landed on the floor. I ran after that. Ran from the house where I had been living for two years before that day."

"Jesus Christ."

"I didn't see them again until my parents' funeral. I didn't pay much attention, but Piper told me a few years later that my ring was, in fact, on London's hand."

"London? That's your sister."

I nod. "Yeah. Paris and London. Our parents were travelers, and those were their two favorite places. Though, my father always joked that they were lucky to have twins since they wouldn't be sure which of the two cities they conceived us in." I smile, remembering with fondness how many times my parents would joke about that.

"I've always been fond of Paris, myself," Thorn says, breaking into my thoughts and easing some of the pain I feel when I think of my parents. I smile at him.

"I miss them. Even my sister, in her own way."

"Not sure she deserves that."

"Maybe not but still, I miss them all the same."

He doesn't speak for a while, his thumbs continuing to glide against my legs and my fingers continuing to explore his chest. I had moved on to tracing his tattoos when he spoke again, but his next question causes my hands to still.

"How did you lose them?"

"Car accident." I pause, frowning at the ink on his chest, my hands shaking as they hover over the line I had been following—the one that ended after the word "pain" that was inked in thick black directly under his left pec. How appropriate.

I trace back over the word with my eyes before losing the ink and following the golden tan skin up his neck, not stopping until the intensity in his eyes wraps me in their comforting concentration—patiently waiting for me to finish giving him my more. "There was a heavy storm moving in that night, but I had called them upset, and they rushed to be at my side. They died instantly when another driver lost control and hit them on their way to me."

He doesn't need me to connect the dots; I can see him figuring it out, the timeline of my tragic past taking root in his mind. This time, I'm sure the anger I see has nothing to do with jealousy and everything to do with the pain that followed two people's selfish actions, forever changing the lives around them.

"Part of my sister's call," I continue, feeling brave and safe enough to tell him the truth of those nights—something I hadn't told anyone outside of Piper and Dr. Hart. And whether it's because of Thorn himself or the progress I gained from all my sessions with Dr. Hart since that morning I ran from Thorn's bed, I actually want to let him in. No, I need to. I need to not only to keep my momentum toward letting it go, but also because I want him to understand exactly why I was so scared. Giving him the final part of me. My more. "It's all part of a little game she likes to play with me. One that has her constantly telling me where the fault lies with their deaths, never letting me forget. I don't understand it, but she has spent the past seven years almost intentionally hurting me over and over."

The transition on his face as he loses the sympathy and rage takes its place is brilliant in its display, momentarily rendering me speechless.

"You're fucking kidding," he barks, making me jump. "You believe that shit?"

"I used to. That morning, yeah. I'm not proud of it, but it's still the truth. I'm working on seeing the truth, though."

"Working on it?"

"Like I said, I wouldn't have been in a good place after her call. I got home, Piper showed, I lost it, and she gave me a dose of tough love that she had been keeping from me since it all happened. It wasn't pretty, Thorn. It really wasn't. I hit rock bottom, and it had everything to do with that call, but it was because of our night that I wanted to see things from a different point of view—the one Piper painted for me. I think I'll always feel some guilt over it being my call that had them rushing out in that storm, but like I said, I'm working on it."

"Don't you fucking dare hold on to that."

I move my hands, gliding them up from his chest and wrapping them around his neck. "I'm getting there."

"You won't hold on to that shit." He keeps going as if I hadn't spoken. "Don't you, for one second, feel guilt that your parents loved you enough to need to be there when your sister caused you enough pain to need them in the first place. You put that blame where it belongs, which is on her and that motherfucker."

"Thorn, honey."

"Fuck, Ari. You'll always remember it, know that, but do that without guilt. My parents, not people who would feel the same, but I have no doubt that yours wouldn't want that."

"I know, Thorn," I agree, trying to speak but pausing again when he continues.

"I get it now," he says, nodding and moving his hands from my legs to wrap his arms around me and pull me to his body. "No clue how to promise you that you won't feel that pain again, but I can guarantee you, I would take a bullet for you if it would mean you didn't have to feel the burn of it. I don't need day by day to know where I want to be, but I'll give you whatever you need as long as you know I would never, not ever, make you feel pain I could keep from harming you, and you do it breathing easy, knowing that, no matter what the future brings us, I will never fucking burn you like that. Ever."

My chin wobbles, and his eyes drop to it for a beat before looking back up.

"No one knows what the future holds. No one, but I know you're worth figuring out what it does with. I might not have known it at the time, but for those two weeks after I ran, I spent working through the mess of shredded pieces they had left inside me. Every inch of that, I worked to piece as much of it back together as I could with my doctor. They're not all stitched back together, but they're getting there. You gave me that, Thorn. You, the promise of you … and the promise of us you keep giving me day by day. So while you'll never know how sorry I am that I ran, I'm thankful at the same time because it made it possible for me to find my way back to the life I thought I didn't deserve anymore."

One of his hands leaves my leg, and I feel it glide up and over my thin nightdress, our eyes saying so much in the silence. When he stops, his hand resting between my breasts and my heart beating against his palm, the most overwhelming calm settles around me.

Yes, this right here, this is so much greater than any life I could have ever imagined when I thought all I would ever have, was no one.

This right here is worth every second of pain I felt when I thought I was alone.

I lean forward, press my lips to his, and it settles a second time. Only this time, I feel more of those shredded pieces stitching together—mending—and that void in my gut getting a little fuller.

TWENTY-ONE

THORN

That woman is *not* you

I walk into Barcode and when I see Wilder behind the bar, I give him a tip of my chin.

"I thought you were busy with Ari all day," he says in place of greeting.

"I am. Stopped by on my way to pick up dinner for her and Piper to see why you were acting like a dick last night when you called about watching the game today and I told you I had plans."

"I wasn't being a dick," he defends.

"You were being an asshole. That better?"

"Fuck off. Seriously, why are you here?"

"Just told you."

"Aside from that?" He cuts a few more slices off the lime he had been working on, then looks up and frowns. "How are Ari and Piper? Haven't seen them in here for a few weeks."

"You want to know how my girl is, or how her best friend is?" I ask, knowing damn well he doesn't want to know about Ari. Wilder's done a shit job of hiding the fact he's interested in Piper. He's just not done shit about it because of the ring on her finger. Still, he can't hide that shit from me.

"Shut the fuck up, T," he grumbles.

"Right. Denial is a fun playground, isn't it? I'm here because I had some time to kill, saw your car when I was leaving The Alibi, and walked over. Figured I would stop in to see what you're doing here all by yourself."

He points at the limes, ignoring my jab. "Most of the bartenders are out with some fucking stomach bug. Perks of being the boss. They get sick, and I'm stuck covering for them. That shit land over at The Alibi yet?"

I cringe, just picturing what would happen if it did. "No. Thank Christ."

"Yeah, imagine that wouldn't be good. Not the same as the boss covering for sick fucks here as it would be for you over there now that you have yourself a woman."

"She didn't seem to mind it last time I got on the stage."

Wilder laughs. "The second you whipped your cock out, she was in your arms and hiding it from all the hungry bitches screaming around the room for it. You get this bug over there, and trust me, she'll mind."

I ignore him, reach behind the bar, and grab the canister of nuts he has to restock the bowls he keeps on the bar when the place is open. I palm a handful and toss them back.

"So what's going on? It's been a while since we've just had time to ourselves catching up. It's either work or whatever the fuck shit you two invite me to because Piper doesn't want to be a third wheel—which still makes me wonder why you always call me and not her fiancé. And no, you don't need to give me more shit about denial. Trouble in paradise?"

"Not even fucking close," I answer, feeling every word and ignoring his mention of Piper—again.

"Goddamn, Thorn. Never thought I would see the day the mighty fell."

The familiar burn I've become accustomed to, even welcomed, starts back up in my chest. Just thinking about Ari causes it to slam into me. I'm just able to stop myself from reaching up and rubbing the spot in the middle of my chest; the power that blows into me when I picture her in my mind would knock me to my fucking knees if I was a weaker man.

"Not going to deny it, huh?" Wilder asks, cocky as hell.

"Not for a second."

He stops slicing, glances up, and really looks at me. No clue what he's hoping to find since I still don't understand what I'm feeling myself half the time. He shakes his head, a smile forming.

"I'm happy for you, man. I really am."

I lift my chin, nod, and reach for the container of mixed nuts again, tossing a handful in my mouth.

"I take it that means you two got past all that shit that had her sneaking out on you then? Christ, what was that, like a month ago?"

"Seven weeks, give or take."

Wilder snorts. "Give or take, huh? Something tells me you know exactly how long it's been."

I lift my middle finger.

He laughs, grabs the limes he cut so far, and tosses them into the bin attached to the rest of the separated containers full of the various produce he'll need throughout the night.

"We're good, Wil. We talked about it a few weeks after I got her back. She let me in, I get what happened, and it's not a big deal. Not to our relationship, that is."

"Relationship, huh?" he asks, smirking like the cat who ate the fucking canary.

"The word fits. It's what it is."

He nods, but there's no way he knows what I mean. The word might fit, but fuck if what we have isn't a hell of a lot stronger than just a simple relationship.

"I told you she was different that day in my office, and that was after one night and knowing her for a weekend, Wil. She went from being the girl I saw across this very bar one night, shocking the shit out of me when I walked into her store and saw her again, to someone I don't just want to see every day but need to. You find a word that fits what we have better than relationship, and that'd be us."

He drops the knife, wipes his hands, and leans back against the wall of liquor bottles, crossing his arms over his chest with a low whistle.

"Damn," he finally says after studying me intently.

"'Bout sums it up."

"So what's the problem?"

I toss back another handful of nuts. We're different people now since that night I saw her around the face of another. She didn't recognize me as that man when I walked into Trend, but fuck when I told her, she didn't even care I had been kissing someone else. She could only focus on the fact that, since first glance, we've had something powerful between us. It probably fucking helped that I told her, after seeing her, I had walked away from that woman and spent my night with only Ari's face to keep me company. Something so simple as seeing a beautiful stranger across the room had hit me right in the chest and changed my life … starting the wheels in motion to heal hers and, fuck, probably mine too.

I don't like talking about the things Ari's shared with me—the things that make me sure she's healed. It feels like a betrayal of her trust, but fuck if I can wrap my head around the way I felt when she laid it all out for me. Wilder might not have tons of knowledge in this area, his own relationships few and far between, but he knows more than me—a man who's spent the majority of his adult life avoiding any kind of attachment past one night.

"She's been working through some shit. The same shit that made her do that fucking runner in the first place. I get it, Wil, I really do, but I'm worried for her if she really hasn't let it go."

"Vague, but okay. She told you she let it go?"

"Yeah." I nod. "Told me but shows me every day, too. She didn't just wake up the next day and forget it. She's been seeing someone since the Monday after she ran. Every Tuesday and Thursday night since we started our thing back up, she's been in his office. Just last week that dropped to only Tuesday nights."

"I'm not exactly an expert in this stuff, but I would think if she's down to one day, she probably really is letting it go."

I pick through my thoughts, eating a few more handfuls before handing the container of nuts over when Wil reaches out for it.

"I've held her in my arms when she talks about this shit, Wil. When she first told me about it—about the sister who has caused every fucking slash of pain in her past—it felt like I was the one getting those lashings when I heard the pain in her voice. What happens if that bitch pops back up, and Ari's tested on just how much progress she's made over the past two months?"

"What's really bringing this on? If she hasn't given you a reason to think she's not really moving past her issues with the sister, then why are you sitting here, eating my shit and worrying about some hypothetical situation?"

I shake my head, then give him the smallest bit of Ari's past with her sister. Mainly, that her sister slept with her ex close to the wedding and that her parents died the same night she caught them. I skim over the rest, not wanting to betray her trust any more than I might already have, but needing to get some advice from him at the same time to make sure she's covered if she's here and I'm not.

"Are you kidding?" Wilder bellows, scowling at me. His reaction isn't a shock in the least. He and Ari connected instantly, and the few times we've hung out together have brought out some big brother tendencies with him. She's been at Barcode a few times since we started our day by day and never did I worry about her—before and after knowing about her sister—but I know I'll feel better with him knowing what he does, keeping a closer eye on her when she's here because of it. I asked him once how they got so close in such a short time, but when he said they bonded over dangerous dicks, I shut the fuck up about that. My girl and the closest thing to a brother I have being close is a good fucking feeling.

I shake my head. "I wish I was. Some shit can't be made up even if you tried."

"I can see why you're worried about her, but man, she's not given you a reason to worry. From what I can tell, you two are solid … and so is she."

"The sister also hasn't been in contact since that morning, either."

He pushes off the counter, grabs two beers, and pops the caps off, handing me one and keeping the other.

"Ari asked me to leave it be. Told her I would … unless that bitch calls again. All bets are off next time."

"I'm shocked you agreed to leave it be in the first place."

"She wants to move on, and her doctor is helping her do that. We've talked about it a lot, too. I know she's stronger based on what she's told me about her past. I get why she wants to just move on, but that doesn't mean I like it. Goes against my instincts to not do something about it, but I care about Ari's feelings a lot more than I care about my own."

"Not like you not to take charge no matter what someone else asks you to do. Hell, I probably would have called the bitch myself just based on what you told me."

"Yeah, well, as I said, you didn't hold Ari in your arms when she ripped her heart out to explain why she almost let her past get in the way of us. Telling me about the pain she carried because of that bitch was enough that I'll be happy if I never have to see her relive that again."

Wilder hums and takes a drink. I look over his head at the game playing on the televisions around the room, not seeing a damn thing as my thoughts get away from me.

If you would have told me two months ago I would be sitting here with Wilder talking about my relationship, I would have laughed. If you would have told me I would be this far gone over someone, I wouldn't have believed it. We've spent every chance we had between both of our businesses demanding our attention together. The only exceptions being the time we spent with our friends alone—which was rare. Living us day to day, just like we agreed, there hasn't been a single one of those days we weren't together, or that we didn't speak on the phone. Our lives have effortlessly woven together in those two months to the point where I can't imagine a day without her in my life.

She stopped looking at me like she was terrified to let me in a few weeks ago. I didn't just think she was different than other women anymore because I knew she was. What she said she felt building between us in just days has only grown stronger in our weeks together. We hadn't even slept together again yet, and she was effectively taking place of The Alibi, Wilder, and Harris as the most important thing I've ever been given in my life.

I was done dragging my feet and playing it safe because I was letting my past scars stand in the way. I wouldn't push her away. She was mine, goddammit. She gave me her more, and as soon as we finished up with that shit at the house in The Orchard, I'd give her mine.

The door opens behind the bar, pulling me from my thoughts, and I watch a few of his servers walk in—all female—and ignore them to glance back at Wil with a raised brow before taking another pull of my beer.

Two of the girls walk away, off to set up their shit around the room, I'm sure. I nod at one of Piper's sisters, Meggie, looking around but not seeing Melissa. Meggie frowns, but before I can ask her about it, I feel a hand on my arm. I glance down, frown, and follow that hand up the arm and to the body it belongs to.

"You're touching me why?" The anger I feel when I see the lust in her eyes—having someone's touch that isn't Ari makes my skin crawl, and I don't need to see my reflection to know I probably look like a mean bastard.

Wilder barks out a laugh, joining Meggie's softer one. I, however, don't find anything funny about this at all. I deserve it, though, and I know that logically. Logic doesn't matter, though. Yeah, I used to be the type of man who would take that flirty smile and lust-filled gaze and give her what she wanted, but that man stopped existing when Ari blew into my world.

"Uh, hey, Thorn." The girl bats her eyelashes. All I see, though, is the thick clumps of her mascara and the heavy hand of her make-up, instantly comparing Ari's effortless beauty to the woman next to me.

"Remove your hand," I demand through tight lips. So out of depth with what I'm feeling. Unable *not* to be rude when I've never had to deal with something like this. I don't want to be what I used to be to the easy women I went through. Fuck. For the first time, I actually regret the life I lived before I found Ari.

Her hand drops, but she doesn't move away, standing way too close to me. Her perfume making my head hurt.

Wrong.

Too strong.

Not Ari.

"I haven't seen you around in a while. I, well, Marcie said she hasn't seen you hook up with anyone since her, and she was months ago. I just thought maybe, if you were free later and all," she trails off, and those eyes start going crazy again.

Yeah. That regret isn't just there, but it churns up something nasty in my gut. My own self-loathing just makes the scowl on my face grow. It's not this girl's fault. She knows the old me. She knows the man who just used women. She's never met the one who only breathes for one. The one who made me a better man. The best man. *Her man.*

"Excuse me?" I lean back when she crowds me again, putting space between us.

"She said she didn't mind if we hooked up. If that's what you're worried about."

I bark out a laugh. "She might not, but I sure as fuck do."

"Oh, well, I mean … if you want her to join, I guess that's cool. I didn't think you and Marcie were a thing."

I look at Wilder, glance at Meggie, then back at my friend. Wilder doesn't look like he has the answers for me. "Is this shit happening? How is this shit still happening?"

"You can hook the ball and chain on the man, but that doesn't mean anyone else can see that shit."

"Yeah, well, now you know why it's been so long since I've just stopped by."

He snorts.

"Does this happen when Ari is in here without me?"

He doesn't answer, but I can tell by his face that it fucking does. Now that shit I like even less.

"Need to make that ball and chain more visible," I mumble to myself. I can't do shit about my past. I can do whatever I can to show everyone around me that I'm not that person anymore. Ari, though? She's the most beautiful woman I've ever seen, so there's no shock that she would attract other men. I know in my gut she doesn't do anything more than just be herself. She can't help that her natural perfection is the most attractive thing ever—especially when she has no fucking clue that she is just that.

"You could put a fucking ring on both of your fingers, and it would still happen. Get used to it, you good-looking bastard. Unless one of you wakes up less attractive, it's your life now."

I flip him off.

Apparently, the chick at my side didn't appreciate being ignored because instead of her hand, she presses her hard tits against my arm this time. I might not understand why her hand on my arm had made me angry. Might have tried to mask that then. But I'm hopeless to keep it checked now. All I can think of is Ari seeing this and assuming I encouraged it. Fuck, the rage that flows through me at the thought is palpable, I'm sure.

"You've lost your fucking mind, woman," I thunder, jerking away from her. She wobbles on her heels and pouts. "I don't give a shit what you and your friends chat about. Forget it all. You hear my name leave any of their lips again, you tell them to forget that I fucking exist. You see me, they see me, look *through* me. I don't give a shit what any of them had or want from me. I'm off the market. Understand?"

She nods, but it doesn't appear to hit home because she goes to press her hand against me again, and I lose it.

"One woman has permission to put her hands on me. One woman. That woman is *not* you. Hear what I'm saying to you. You take that and go back to *Marcie* or anyone else who still thinks I'm fucking free, and you express with certainty that I'm most fucking definitely not *free!*"

She finally gets me and rushes off. I look around the room, seeing about six other girls eyeing me.

"Any of you have one of these chats with Marcie too?" I snap. They shake their heads, looking at me like I'm the possessed one.

They're not wrong. It's not their fault that girl stirred up shit I didn't like feeling. I don't want to be a fucking bastard about it, but when I imagined what Ari would see if this happened in front of her, I couldn't be nice about it if I tried.

"You brought that on yourself, you know. You've never had a problem with easy before, and you haven't been around here enough with Ari since you two started. All they knew was that you cut them off. You became some sort of golden prize to claim before with the no attachment, no relationship speeches you gave every chick you hooked up with. You created this game they didn't know had ended." Wilder stops talking and isn't even attempting to be a professional boss and keep his enjoyment to himself by keeping his voice down. He's holding his gut and laughing like a fucking idiot.

"Made plenty of mistakes in my life, Wil, and I'm not proud of them at all. Before Ari, that was the only man I thought I would ever be. Fuck, it was all I thought I deserved. Not once did I think I would find someone who blew not only what I learned out of the water, but made me want to be someone different than who I was for the first time ever. Don't make it sound like I let anyone before her think there was a chance at more. And don't fucking rub this shit in my face. You make it sound like I fucked every woman who works here."

"You want to stop by same time tomorrow? Different shift is on. I wouldn't mind watching that again and making you eat those words."

"Fuck off, you lying bastard," I hiss, standing up to leave. I glance at Meggie, just remembering that she was standing at the bar, and cringe when I think about how that looked—and what she might tell Ari. Only, with how she's smiling at me, I'm pretty sure the only thing she's going to be telling Ari is just how good her man is.

"Well, he didn't fuck Melissa or me, so at least he's safe with two tomorrow," she jabs, laughing. "Don't worry about it, Thorn. It's a good look on you, what you have with Ari being something you want to protect. It's even better knowing she's finally got someone who feels that strongly about another person other than her being near him. I don't know you well enough to say, but I'm pretty confident I'm right regardless. You might regret whatever you were to get Kirsten to act like that, but don't let that fester. Everyone has a past, just like everyone has a future. You got both now, and something tells me you've earned that just as much as Ari has."

She winks and turns to go farther down the bar, beginning her work instantly.

Fuck, now *that* felt good.

TWENTY-TWO

Ari

I wouldn't have stopped chasing you

PIPER AND I HAD JUST CAREFULLY STORED THE LAST ITEM from the huge collection of Thorn's—or the one he had been willed, I should say—into the van we rented for the day. Piper had been driving back and forth between the house in The Orchard and Trend all day. When the van would fill up, she would head off and monitor the offload by the cage staff, then head back to help inventory, store, and load another trip. Luckily, this was the last load because we were beyond exhausted at this point. I knew the collection was extensive before we started, but I didn't think it would take us this long.

We've been here, in this huge house in The Orchard, for hours now, and I feel like I could crash any second. Heck, we've been here for so long, it seems as if days have passed since this morning when Piper came to pick me up from my house in that huge van. In reality, that was really only eight hours ago. Eight really, really long hours.

Thorn greeted us with breakfast when we arrived this morning, but he took off shortly after to head over to The Alibi to get some work done. I frown when I recall the tense set of his shoulders when we walked into the house earlier. I wanted to ask him about his reaction to this place, but I didn't—just like I hadn't the other times we discussed when I would come and pick up everything or the sale of the house that just went under contract the week prior. Knowing he doesn't like being here is one thing, but pressing for him to tell me what makes him so uneasy about this place, especially when we aren't alone, wouldn't be right.

"Remind me the next time some tall, dark, and handsome man shows up at Trend with promises of grand riches to deny him before he can so much as blink, okay?" Piper complains with a laugh, pressing her hand to her head before making a dramatic show of dropping to the floor. She rolls onto her back in the middle of the now empty closet, her curls even more wild than normal after working so hard today running all over the place. Even tired, my friend looks beautiful. Aside from her unruly locks, she looks like she is ready to strut her stuff in an activewear runway show.

"I shouldn't agree with you for the sake of Trend thriving and all, but right now, I think I would shut the door on that hypothetical tall, dark, and handsome man myself. I can't believe how sore I am." I drop down next to her, the carpet soft against the exposed skin around my tight workout clothes.

I smile, remembering how Thorn had reacted when I got out of the van this morning in my racerback tank and short spandex shorts. My very short spandex shorts. We've been together for a while now, but he's yet to see my workout gear. I vowed right then and there, while I watched as he adjusted himself without shame, that I would make an effort to work out when he's around. Instead of fitting it in whenever I could find time between our time together and my schedule at Trend. Plus, if I go back to my morning workouts, chances are he'll be there to join me. Getting to see Thorn working out, getting all hot and sweaty while displaying his delectable body? Not even close to a hardship. But to see all of that while getting a reaction from him like I did this morning? UH, yes please! I make a mental note to add some equipment to my home gym, just in case and all that.

"I hurt in places that shouldn't hurt, Ari!"

"You and me both, Pipe. I thought I had discovered all the muscles I had that could ever get sore, but I found new ones today, that's for sure. I mean, I didn't get this sore after being thoroughly worked over by Thorn, and trust me, he knew how to work me hard in a way that I should have already found these stupid sore muscles. So either I've become a lazy bum over the course of the past two months, or I need to throw down a new bet with him."

A throat clears across the room, and I lift my head from the carpet to see the very man smiling from the doorway.

Of course. Of. Freaking. Course.

"You heard all that, didn't you?"

"Babe," he says with that tone that I know exactly what he wants. I know what *that* particular babe means, and if he's going to play like he didn't just hear me, that's A-okay with me.

I roll my eyes and drop my head back on the carpet, rolling it to look over at Piper. "He thinks I can actually move from this floor. Do you believe that?"

"Uh, I'm not really sure how to answer that." She leans closer to me. "He didn't ask you to get up, though. You do know that, right?"

"Yes, he did."

She just blinks at me, and I can tell she thinks I've lost it. For someone who doesn't know Thorn speak, I get it.

"Babe," Thorn calls again.

"Don't you babe me, Thorn Evans. I'm dying down here, can't you see! You want it, come and get it."

"What exactly is going on?" Piper asks, mumbling the question more to herself than actually wanting an explanation from Thorn or me.

"Not going to tell you again, Ari." Impatience mixed with desire-driven need laces his words.

"Oh, wow." Piper sighs. "Doesn't even matter if you two are talking in code. That's hot."

"Even if you give me that 'babe' again, you're still going to have to walk your hunky self over here and peel me off the floor to get it anyway."

"Ari. I come over there, you're going to find out there are still a few spots I can make sore that you haven't discovered or even dreamed of. Get over here before Piper gets a show."

"Holy shit, girlfriend. I'm pretty sure I've just learned I'm some closet slut for authority or something. It doesn't even matter that I have no clue what your sugar muffin wants, but for Christ's sake, whatever it is, give it to him."

I lift my tired arm and point a finger at her. "You say that now, Pipe. The second you have a demanding alpha throwing all of that authority around all the time, you might change your tune."

"Ari." This time his tone is all parts impatient. Even if he's smiling when I glance back at him, I know he wants me off the floor and in his arms. I'll be honest, knowing he's not willing to come over here because he wants me too much isn't a hard pill to swallow, either.

"Actually, Pipe, that's a complete lie. There's no way anyone would change their tune."

She giggles, and Thorn says my name again, only deeper, rougher. Severely stressing what he demands without words—or those deliciously spoken babes.

"Oh, fine. Keep your panties on, mister."

"No, please, don't."

I ignore Piper, get to my feet, and roll my sore shoulders before walking toward him. He doesn't move from his position leaning against the doorframe. He looks like the epitome of a relaxed man with not one care in the world, but I know it's a ruse. He's holding himself back from taking more than the kiss he wants. It isn't until I make it to him, stepping close and tipping my head back to look up at his handsome face, that he straightens to his full height. Sometimes, it's easy to forget that he's over a foot taller than I am. I'm either wearing tall heels, we're sitting or lying together, or I'm in his arms.

"In tennis shoes, you handsome giant. You want your kiss, you're going to have to lift this girl up so she can reach her man's mouth without breaking her neck or back trying to give it to you."

His hands are at my hips, and I'm in the air before I even finish speaking. My hands immediately land on his shoulders, and my legs wrap around his waist. I smile, not even annoyed that my man gets impatient when I take too much time to greet him with my mouth each and every time he sees me—no matter how long we've been apart. Just last week, I left him on my couch watching some sports thing so I could shower. I don't think I was gone more than twenty minutes, but sure enough, he gave me that *babe*, and I gave *him* his kiss.

I reach one hand up, running my fingers through the thick hair that had fallen from the stylish mold it had been gelled to this morning. A few pieces falling across his forehead. My fingers move to the sides of his head when I'm done, loving the soft buzz that tickles my fingertips, then settle my hands back on his shoulders.

He didn't shave this week—his beard more of a shadow against his tan skin than anything—but it looks so good on him. It feels even better against my skin when his kisses are driving me crazy. I tighten my legs, trying to ease the ache between them, and sigh when I can't find the friction I need. Something he doesn't miss at all. His lips curl up, his white teeth flash, and I get one of those rare full-to-blinding smiles from him.

"Hi," I mumble, smiling back before leaning into him and pressing my mouth to his. Complete and utterly hypnotized by that open proof of happiness so seldom given by him.

Our kiss is brief but unfathomably hot. He groans loud enough that I know Piper won't miss it, but the one I give him in return is soft and just for his ears. He pulls away first and adjusts his hold on me, his wide hand burning through the material covering my bottom as it slides from my butt cheek to the center of my bottom, freeing up his other hand. He lifts it up, one finger moving in, and presses it against the frown lines that must have appeared between my eyes when he cut our kiss short. I'm not surprised. I felt the loss of his mouth the second he stopped kissing me. I felt it deep.

"Now you know how it feels when I want my kiss, and you

make me wait for it."

"Very funny."

He grins, not the same as the smile before, but no less heart stopping. When he looks away and starts roaming those bright green eyes around the room, his grin vanishes in seconds. He covers it quickly, though. Just not quick enough for me not to notice. If I hadn't been this close, I may have missed the pain that slashed over his face for just a second before vanishing. His eyes do another brief sweep before he looks down at where I had just been lying on the thick carpet.

"Piper," he greets with a nod. "You need help getting yourself or your jaw off the ground?"

I toss my head back and laugh, feeling the lightness his joke was meant to induce.

"You know, it really isn't funny to make fun of the wounded, Thorn."

"Wounded?" he questions, brows furrowing. "You hurt?" he asks me; even though she said it, assuming, without even considering that it was a joke, that I had somehow become injured in the time I haven't moved from his hold. Or that she might be hurt. He automatically heard her and made sure I wasn't part of her implication. Now, that's nice.

I pat his shoulders. "I'm sore, but fine. Let me down, honey, so I can go pull the sarcastic gawker up from the floor."

He drops me carefully, and I turn to go help Piper but stop when he moves around me and offers her his hand instead. She reaches up, places her hand in his, and plants her feet on the ground. It probably wasn't wise on her part to push off at the same time he gives a barely there tug because instead of just letting him lift her up, she basically goes flying.

"You didn't tell me you were dating He-Man, Ari. Christ," Piper admonishes when she finishes getting her bearings. "Were you planning on tossing me through the roof or just out of the room so you could finish pillaging the innocent?"

He shakes his head, laughing softly.

"I mean, I bet you do sex like some kind of animal, don't you?" she continues, moving over to the island that we had turned into command central today. She packs up all the power cords, stuffing them into her tote bag with efficient speed. Next, she carefully closes her notepads full of detailed notes on the items she had handled today and places them neatly on top of her closed laptop before tossing her phone in her bag. She huffs a curl away that had fallen in her face before turning to look back at us. "It really makes sense now, why you've stopped spending every waking moment at Trend. If Matt hauled me around like that, I probably would stop living at Trend, too. Though I wouldn't lie around on the ground when the big brute wanted to haul me around like it's just no big deal, either. Really, Ari. When you jump back on the saddle, you really jump back on a beast, don't you?" She moves her attention to Thorn, then a wicked grin appears. "And getting her to finally stop spending fifteen plus hours a day at the store? Never been done before so well done, He-Man. I guess that makes Ari your Castle Grayskull, huh? Though, Ari, you should watch out when he starts hoisting his sword around."

"Pipe, seriously." I blush, looking at her with wide eyes. Eyes that scream use your filter. Giving her the look that tells her to shut the heck up. Even if her nerd talk is funny. She doesn't know that we haven't had sex again since that first and only time. Who am

I kidding, Piper any other way than my inappropriate best friend would just be weird. It's who she is, and I love her, no filter and all. Even if she did know we hadn't had sex again yet, she would still make her jokes.

"I'm going to take this last load over to Trend and transfer it all to the cage until tomorrow. I'll deal with inventory and cataloging over the weekend, so the online team can start with photographs for the site on Monday without having to wait for me to do that. It's the smallest load we've had today, so I don't need to pull DeMarcus out of the security room to help me handle this one. Poor guy is probably just as tired as we are after dealing with each drop-off to-day. You two stay here and have fun in this big old house. Enjoy being manhandled, Ari. I'll see you guys in a few hours. We did decide on that Mexican place over by He-Man's den of sin, right?"

"Yes. What time do you want us to meet you and Matt over there at?" I ask, not commenting on either her nickname for Thorn *or* the one she has for The Alibi. It would just encourage the no fil-ter little nerd if I did.

"Eight, I guess. It's half past three now. It won't take me long to get all of this offloaded and locked up. DeMarcus is proving his worth as head of security and already has the weekend set for two extra people until we get everything settled. I'll head right home and get ready after. I'll shoot you a text if I need more than four hours. I wouldn't count on it, though. Matt gets grumpy when we eat late." She shoulders her purse and holds her laptop and notepad to her chest. "Later, kids. Be good … or good at it." With a wink, she's gone.

"I would apologize for her lack of shame, but I think you know her well enough by now that it would be more shocking to you if she wasn't running off at the mouth like that. Even when she's getting tongue-tied around Wilder, she's still just ... well, that."

He smiles, but with Piper gone, I can tell he's letting his guard down. His eyes roam the empty shelves again, taking in the room. Normally, when one of us brings up our two friends' weird behavior around each other, we tend to test theories on why that happens. It's what I see that makes a chill wash over me, and I know any of the joking moods we just had aren't coming back.

He's silent. Pensive. Almost ... saddened.

"What's on your mind?" I ask, moving closer and wrapping my arms around him.

"I thought it would feel different when I finally saw all this shit gone."

I tip my head back and study him, his attention still on the room around us.

"What *do* you feel?" I hold my breath, waiting for him to share with me—to open up.

There's no denying we've gotten extremely close, but there's still so much about the man who's quickly owning my heart that I don't know. I knew that the stuff in this room was more than just some "shit" he was given when someone passed away. You don't hold that kind of odd resentment for materialistic items unless there's some deeper significance at play.

"Come on," he finally says, dropping his arms from around me.

Not answering me.

I actually have to work hard not to exude the disappointment I feel over him brushing my question off. I want him to open up, so much, but I won't push him—no matter how much I wish he would let me in. It will happen when he's ready. And if it doesn't, well, then what we're building together clearly isn't what I feel deep down inside it is.

I walk over to the island, quickly packing up and grabbing my stuff. Silently, I follow him out of the room. He leads me down the hallway, going in the opposite direction of the main stairs. I frown but follow just a step behind him. My position gives me a front row seat to study Thorn. His tense shoulders, eyes directed in front of him, completely ignoring the lush opulence around him. It only drives home what I already knew. This place, it has a hold on him, and not a good hold.

When I first came here, over two months ago, I'll admit I was curious about what the rest of this house held. The urge to open the doors and peek in each room had been strong. Especially after I had seen the room full of heaven we just left for the first time. Then Thorn happened, and my heart cared more about the negative effect this place had on him. No longer did I care to snoop. I didn't want to know what other brilliant trinkets and treasures may be hiding around the corner. He invaded my heart, and instantly, I hated this place. I hated this house almost as much as I hated the development it was built in. All because I could see it was a place that hurt him on some level I didn't understand.

I'm pulled from my thoughts when he stops at a staircase I hadn't seen before. I look over my shoulder, seeing the room we had just left farther down the hallway, and even knowing it's the same house, I can't help but notice the difference between what I've seen of the house and what I see down those stairs. Halfway down the steps, it seems to get darker, less lavish. There's no natural light for one thing, but it almost feels like the air around us is different. It's so strange.

After a quick glance at Thorn, I know my assumptions are right. His jaw flexes as he clenches his teeth tightly. Okay, maybe he isn't shutting me out after all. Unless this is some hidden passageway to exit the house, something big is happening right now, and I have a feeling I might have jumped to conclusions with the disappointment I felt when I thought he was keeping himself closed off.

He reaches over, taking the giant tote I had stuffed full with everything I had packed up before he appeared. He transfers the handles to the hand opposite of my body, the bag looking tiny compared to him. After I hear him roll his head, popping his neck, his free hand takes mine, lacing our fingers together tightly, and he clears his throat before beginning his descent. Slowly guiding us down the stairs and into the unknown.

Everything looks the same, only dank and dark without the many windows the rest of the house boasts. Oppressive. It feels despotic against my skin.

My grasp on his hand tightens, but I follow his lead silently even though my instinct is to pull him back and out of this house.

When we reach the bottom, there's another shorter hallway to our right where I can see an empty garage type space through an open door. The other side holds a few doorways, all closed and with no windows. Thorn goes left, leading us down the longer hallway. He passes each of the closed doors at our sides before stopping in front of the one at the very end. Every other part of this house screams money—but this looks like an afterthought built off dollar menu building supplies.

Thorn drops my hand, then reaches out and opens the door. I don't know what I expected, but it wasn't the sun-room before us. Though, calling it a sun-room would be too generous. The huge growth of trees surrounding each glass wall blocks any sun that could ever try to shine inside. Just like the rest of the hallway that leads into it, it's run down compared to the rest of the house. There's a few couches and chairs, end tables on the ends of each, and a metal card table tucked into one corner. It all screams second hand but still well cared for.

"What is this place?" I ask, looking around some more but not seeing anything personal aside from a few decks of cards carelessly stacked and a puzzle only halfway built on the metal table. Even though I just walked through the house, leaving the extravagant, I never would have believed we were still in the same house had I not witnessed the change myself.

"This would be the servants' quarters. I'm sure it isn't lost on you that the rest of the house looks like it's never been lived in, yet this room does. I'm sure that isn't because the staff actually had time to enjoy their lives in this room, but because this was the only space—aside from their bedrooms—where they were allowed when not working. When I met them, shortly after acquiring this house, they would tell me about this section of the house. About their lives. No expense was wasted on them. I doubt the furniture in this area of the house even comes close to the cost of just one of those fucking bags you worked so hard packing up today. Even so, this room probably held more happiness for those who worked here than any other room in this place ever did." His dull voice makes me ache to hold him. "Money can buy a lot of shit, but the abhorrent pride of an evil soul couldn't even afford the price of happiness others get for free, just by being decent human beings."

"Thorn?" He glances at me, coming out of the stillness he had fallen in while staring off at nothing. "What is this place to you?"

He lets out a rush of air. Looking back around the room, he then pulls us toward one of the threadbare loveseats—if you could call the small two-seater that. It looks more like a bigger version of the small chair near it. He carefully leans my bag on the ground against the side before dropping his large body down and looking up at me with a silent invitation. I don't hesitate to place my knees on each side of him, climbing into his lap. The second my bottom hits his thighs, I take his face in my hands, studying the pain I see there. My knees dig into the poorly supported cushion, but I don't adjust myself, knowing he needs me.

"Your more?" I test.

He nods. My heart races because I hate seeing my strong man like this. I hate knowing his more holds the pain he told me in the beginning that he understood.

"I left home when I was sixteen. You know this." I nod, and a huge exhale leaves him. "I escaped that hell I grew up in, Ari, and I don't regret leaving, not for a second. Even when I lived on the streets, I was better off. Growing up, fuck, it was terrible with the parents I was stuck with. My mom was a junky who left just a year before I did. I found out years later that she killed herself about six months after that. My old man, I couldn't do justice to the piece of shit he was if I tried. Not one thing about him could ever be redeemable. Fuck, for a long time, I had been sure he was the devil himself. Which would make sense, seeing as he's currently doing life in prison. We didn't have shit, baby. Lived like shit. Hardly had food, clothes were whatever I could steal for myself when they stopped caring about that, too. What little they earned by my old man whoring my mom out went to fund their habits."

He stops talking, looking away from the void of nothingness

he had been staring at, and frowns when he sees the tears falling from my eyes.

"Ari. Baby, don't you fucking cry for me."

I hiccup. "How can you ask me not to? I can't just turn off my feelings for you."

His eyes flash. "Just because that shit wasn't pretty doesn't mean I kept living that nightmare, baby. I survived. Not just that, but after I dusted myself off and met Harris, all o' that meant I wasn't stupid with the future he put in front of me. That shit, those memories, they became my drive. I don't want you to cry for that shit."

I nod, biting my tongue to try to keep myself from crying more. My heart breaks for what Thorn lived through. When a tear falls from my eye, I know I can't fool him.

"You want the rest?" he asks softly, shaking his head and swiping the hot tear away with his thumb.

"Yes," I whisper thickly through the lump in my throat.

"It's not as ugly but still isn't pretty. When I met Harris, I gained a real father figure in my life. He's one hell of a man and more than makes up for the one I had for the first sixteen years of my life, Ari. With him came the closest person I have in my life to this day, aside from you, that is. The son I told you about?" I nod, and some of the pain leaves Thorn's eyes when he smiles. "I wouldn't be the man I am today without the two of them. The day I met Harris's pain in the ass son, I knew it would be Wilder and me against the world from that day on."

My jaw drops, and Thorn laughs at the shock on my face.

"Told you Harris had a son who wasn't interested in The Alibi, but what Wilder did want was Barcode. His father opened that place two years after I showed up, gave it to Wil the day he handed me The Alibi. Wil would have hated all the shit that comes with running The Alibi. He enjoyed his time dancing there, but it was just part of him loving the thrills of fast and easy. But that bar, he fucking thrives there, and he's never alone with the crowd he has every single night. He can be who he wants to be, get what he wants, and he can do that with his clothes on."

"Why didn't you tell me who Wilder was?" I gasp.

"I just did."

I narrow my eyes. "Not the same thing. I mean, I knew you two were close, but he's your family, Thorn."

"Just didn't think about it, I guess. He stopped dancing a little after I did, and it's been a while since The Alibi was something I shared with Wil. Easy to forget the time before it became mine when I've spent so long with it being just that, but you're right. He's my family. I'm new to this whole sharing thing, remember?" He smiles—not a big one, but I'll take it.

"No wonder you were so successful as a stripper. You two together? That's dangerous." I grin when he starts to get that jealous glint in his eyes. "Stop. There's only one man I would want to stuff his weird man G-string with dollars for."

He shakes his head, then just as quickly as the lightness comes, it's gone again.

"I didn't know she existed until I had been stripping at the club for a couple of years. At the time, Harris wasn't happy that I wouldn't take his offer to help me move into a better apartment. My place, it was shit. A cardboard box would have offered more. Not only that, but it was also in a bad area. I could take care of myself, but that didn't stop Harris from worrying. He knew about my mom. Knew my old man was doing time. But he thought if I knew I had other family out there, it would help. No clue how, but he somehow managed to track down my old man's mom. Someone I didn't even know about until Harris brought me to her. Brought me … here."

I shift, my legs stretching more to accommodate the man between them. He wraps his arms around me and pulls me closer, leaving them there like steel bands around me. I do the same with my arms around his neck and hold on, somehow knowing I needed to be closer to him for the rest.

"The first time I met her was in this room. I was a nineteen-year-old kid, old enough to be on my own, but I still walked into this room actually feeling hopeful. It took two minutes for her to fuck up that tiny part inside me that my parents hadn't managed to damage. That hope? Fucking shredded. She wouldn't sit when she walked into this room. She stood the whole time and looked down her nose at me from the doorway. Before I could even open my mouth, she informed Harris that we were in that room because she couldn't trust that her precious belongings would be safe if I was anything like the 'filthy trash' my father was. Let us know, if it was money that I was there for, she could put me to work as part of her staff, and I could earn my meals like the rest of them."

"My God," I gasp.

"She let it all hang out. Told me that she may have birthed my father but she'd disowned him years before, and he had stopped being her son that day. She knew I was stripping. She knew I had escaped the life I had been born into. She didn't know the man I was forced to become at sixteen. Didn't know anything else about me. Unlucky for me, I look just like my old man, always have, and because of that, she hated me on the spot. Harris spoke first, throwing her bullshit back in her face. She laughed at me, her own flesh and blood, and told me to get a good look on my way out because it was the closest I would ever come to having a life like hers. I listened to about ten seconds more of her telling me what type of man she had convinced herself I was before I walked away without ever looking back. Never did see that fucking house, seeing as I came and went through the garage down here."

"I don't understand," I whisper. "How did all of this become yours?"

He scoffs. "Ironic, isn't it? The riches she was so sure I was after, she ended up giving me in the end. From what I was told, she had some kind of come to Jesus moment when she got sick. Cancer. Ravaged her body and twisted her soul. The way those who lived here, in this part of the house, tell it—the few who were still here in the end—this was her way of buying her ticket of forgiveness for the fucked-up way she lived her life. I had a lot of time to get to know her staff, getting to know those who lived here through their stories since she died a few months before I met you. I don't think I'll ever understand her motives, but now instead of just being angry, I'm thankful that, in the end, everything I resented about her brought something into my life I never imagined I'd find. I made sure every person who was here after she died found new employment with someone who wouldn't treat them badly."

"Thorn," I breathe, dropping my forehead to his.

"She wasn't the first but just another in the long line of women who made me the man I had become. Then you come along, and it turns out I didn't fucking know a thing. That night when you told me about those changes you made to the contract?"

215

I nod, my head moving against his.

"I'll never, not ever, be able to tell you how much it meant to me that you went through so much trouble to show me that you were there, with me, because you wanted to be and not because you wanted some materialistic bullshit or easy money. I'll be honest, Ari, I wanted you so fucking badly I was willing to overlook the possibility that you could have been there just to get that shit and make a fucking mint off it. Ever since I was old enough to understand women were made of something different than men, I thought I had them figured out. I built that wall up and kept myself detached, used easy women, and made sure they knew where I stood. That didn't stop each one from trying to gain something from me. They saw the money and my opinion of women, relationships, and it just deteriorated further over the years. Then there was you. You brought a new truth to the table, and everything I thought I knew went out the window."

"Honey," I say meekly, my heart beating wildly, all for this man.

"You ran, but Ari, I wouldn't have stopped chasing you. Not after that. Not ever."

"Please, stop," I beg.

"I never needed that day by day I promised, but for the first time in my life, I was going to fight for a woman and do what it took to get what I never thought was possible to find. You needed that day by day, but I never did. I was fighting to give myself to someone completely, and I knew I could trust that you would never hurt me like the women in my past had."

The tears return; only this time, it isn't for the pain this man endured, but for the strength he embodies. Unbelievably proud to call him mine. That he saw something in me that allowed him to give me the gift of him. Made me believe I could trust him with me in return, and that's something I will never stop trying to give back to him tenfold.

His thumbs move to my cheeks, swiping at the tears in vain. When it becomes obvious I'm not going to stop anytime soon, he leans in to close the distance and kisses me deeply. I hold on, giving just as good as I'm getting. When he pulls back, dropping his forehead back against mine, I smile—weakly—but at least my tears have stopped.

"Told you I knew pain, baby," he softly says. "It's because of that pain I can sit here with beauty in my arms and feel thankful for every fucking day I lived through it. Life brought you to me, and I know it's because of what I've lived through that I could recognize what I was being given. Everyone experiences pain. Some more than others. It's how you choose to learn from it that determines your future. To live through pain, the kind that cuts a deep mark on your soul, and survive? That means I can truly appreciate when the last thirty seconds of my past ended and I got my future of beauty."

"Thorn," I breathe, swallowing the thick knot of emotion lodged in my throat.

"What, baby?"

"Take me out of this horrible woman's house and get us home. Let me show you, somewhere that isn't haunted with the memory of someone so nasty, how I feel about what you just gave me."

TWENTY-THREE

THORN

Wild and raw

I LEAN INTO THE TURN, AND ARI'S ARMS AROUND MY WAIST tighten as my bike speeds through traffic. Her words before we left The Orchard replaying through my mind.

Let me show you, somewhere that isn't haunted with the memory of someone so nasty, how I feel about what you just gave me.

This time, when I feel that burn in my chest, I welcome it. Starting to understand it.

Get us home.

Home. Goddamn did that rock me.

She has no idea—not a fucking clue—what she's come to mean to me. Telling her that shit back there, watching her cry for me, fucking gutted me. I knew she needed my "more," though. I probably would have given it to her before then, but I didn't want to tell her that shit before she was ready to take it on. Not after the heaviness of hers had hung around for weeks after I got her "more." I imagine she needed mine just as much as I needed hers, though, and that's the only thing I regretted during the time I kept my past from her.

One thing's for sure, I don't regret waiting to give more of myself to someone until her. Didn't know I was waiting for her to come into my life at the time, but fuck did she make it worth the wait. She owns me. Completely. Just like I own her. I don't need my résumé of broken relationships to tell me what I already know. That what I have with Ari is as real as it gets. I know what stains mark her past. With her, what you see is what you get. No games. No bullshit. No lies and manipulations. It's because of that, I know down deep that she hasn't given herself to someone completely either. Even if she was engaged to that sorry fuck.

When I stop at the light, I reach my hand down and rest it against her bare thigh. Her whole body trembles against my back. She rocks her hips, the thin material of those fucking shorts not hiding her heat from me. Even through my jeans, she's burning hot.

The light changes, my pipes roar, and I take off. She presses closer, hands pressed flat against my stomach, and I feel her smile against my back.

My girl, she loves my bike.

Her hands begin to roam the closer we get to my place. I'm wound so tight, knowing I'm about to have her back in my bed, it's a fucking miracle I can even drive. I've been patient. She's been blossoming around me for weeks, but still, I waited. I meant it when I told her I wanted more before we got between the sheets again. I wanted to know her better, know what made her who she was, but I wanted to give *her* that of myself just as badly.

Before her, I would have thought it was a fucking joke to keep my dick in my pants and make sure a woman knew how much I cared about her before fucking her.

Now? Now, I might not regret waiting to find Ari, but I hate that she knew I wasn't even close to a saint in those years my pain kept me trapped

I'm going to savor every fucking inch of her, and I'll make sure she knows all I see now—all I'll ever see—is her.

I turn down the drive to my house, hooking to the left instead of following the drive where it loops to the front of the house, and head down to my underground garage. The sensor, having picked up the chip on my bike, already raising the door, and I pull right in. My bike sounds even louder against the walls.

I don't even think. I have us both off the bike and our helmets tossed carelessly away seconds after shutting my beast off. I hear one of them hit something solid, and glance briefly over at my McLaren to see both helmets resting on the ground near it. If it's dented, it'll be worth it. I roll my neck, then turn and grab Ari by the waist. She laughs, wrapping herself around me. Just like every time she's done it before, the second her body is clinging tight as fuck to mine, something settles deep inside me. A calm that betrays the irrepressible hunger to own every inch of her.

Fucking perfect.

Her mouth lands on my neck. My hands flex against her ass, the firm flesh feeling so goddamn good in my hands. When I get to the door, I push it open, and it slams against the wall in my haste. I don't even need to hold on to Ari when I let go to punch in the alarm code because she's doing all the work for me with her body clinging to mine.

"You going to need a shower before we go to dinner later?"

She hums, confirming that she will, but doesn't stop kissing the skin around my jaw. When her teeth nip at me, my cock jerks against her violently.

My hands move to her hips, gripping her tight and moving her hips against my length. Our breaths are loud in the silent house as I move to the stairs and climb them while I drag one hand from her hips, behind her ass, and trace the line of her crack until I can feel the wetness of her pussy against my fingers. Then I press, roll, and make sure every inch of her sweet as fuck pussy knows who owns it.

I lose her mouth when I start rubbing her clit. Her head falls back, arms stretch out, and she leans back with a firm hold around my neck. I hit the top of the stairs and move my hand, going between our bodies. Her new position giving me a better angle. I look down, pull the waistband back, and slip my hand between her tight fucking shorts, diving between her folds.

"Oh, God," she cries, tremors shaking her body when I push two fingers deep. "Yes, honey."

"Your pussy is hungry for me," I tell her, the scent of her arousal making my mouth water. "Fuck, I'm hungry for you."

She makes a low whine, her hips trying to take what I'm not ready to give her.

I drag my fingers out slowly and hold them at her entrance. I step into the bathroom, looking at her, and wait for her to focus on me.

"Thorn," she gasps, her chest moving rapidly, wiggling her hips when I don't move my fingers back in where she wants them.

"Need me to fill you up, baby?"

"God, yes," she answers immediately.

"Climb down," I tell her, not liking the fact that I have to let go in order to get inside her. It's irrational, the anger I feel over having to release her in order to get us both naked ... and my cock inside her. "What are you doing to me, Ari?"

Her feet touch the floor, and she pushes her hair out of the way, looking through her lashes at me while toeing off her shoes. She lifts her foot, one at a time, slow as fuck, and pulls her socks off.

I reach out, impatient to have her back in my arms—against my body—but she slaps my hands away. I narrow my eyes at the same time my cock jerks.

"Take your clothes off, Thorn," she orders, pulling her shirt up and off. She drops it to the ground at her feet, her thumbs sliding against her sides and into her shorts. Then she stops. "Now."

I clench my teeth.

"You gave me something back at that house, Thorn. Now listen to me. Get naked, and let me show you how I feel about you giving me your more."

"Fuck. Me."

She smiles, smug as can be, when I do what she wants. If she wants to run this show, I'll do my best to let her ... for now. I doubt I'll be able to hold off for long anyway. Just seeing her tits straining against her bra is enough to make me want to ravage her tight little body.

Her hands leave her shorts, gliding against the skin I want against mine, until she's pressing her delicate fingers against the center clasp of her bra. My mouth waters when they fall free, swaying heavily as she continues to undress.

I kick my pants to the side, my cock slapping against my abs and the wetness of my pre-come dripping from the tip.

My eyes roam her naked skin. The dusty pink nipples point, straining toward me, begging for me. I slide my eyes down her flat stomach, licking my lips when I see the wetness on her pussy. Every inch of her, perfect. When she's like this, naked and vulnerable, it reminds me how fragile she is. Petite, a body that has just enough meat on it to welcome mine as I take her. The only part of her that isn't tiny is her tits. If I hadn't already had her naked and those full tits in my mouth, under my touch, I would swear they were fake based on her size.

I reach out, wanting to get the wetness that's making the trimmed curls between her legs dewy, against my tongue.

She skirts my reach, though, walking around me to step into the shower. She turns on both of the showerheads. The water falling like rain from each. Then she points at the bench between the dual heads.

I raise a brow but do what she wants, walking into the steamy air.

My ass hits the cool marble when I sit.

She bends, my gaze leaving her face to watch her tits sway.

"Eyes up here, big guy."

She moves the hair from my eyes, the steam from the shower not helping, and it just drops back down. She, again, pushes it back. This time, she leaves her hand in my hair and smiles at me.

"Thank you for not letting me stay stuck in my own past, Thorn Evans. Thank you for being patient, gentle, and knowing what I needed even before I did. Thank *you* for changing the course of my life with the same thirty seconds that changed yours, even if it took me a little longer to see it. Thank you, honey, for giving me beauty too."

My chest burns, and my throat moves as I swallow. The need to pull her into my arms climbs higher. I'm just about to say fuck it and get her where I want when she slowly lowers herself to her knees. If I thought I was testing my control before, when she leans back—ass to heels—and the water falling from the showerhead starts rolling down her body, I realize I never knew temptation until I had Ari Daniels naked and wet, kneeling before me. She smiles, her eyes hooded, and rocks forward while pushing her wet hair back.

My cock jerks when her hands glide up my thighs from my knees. I grind my teeth, breath through my nose, and feel my whole body rock when one hand cups my balls and the other wraps around my shaft.

And when her mouth closes around my swollen cock, I swear I feel the earth shake. I lean my weight onto one hand, the other going to her head. My thumb sweeps against her cheek, resting near her mouth to feel my thickness stretch between her lips while she feasts on my cock. My fingers wrap around the back of her neck, flexing on every downward glide and flexing my ass at the same time she takes my length until she gags. I watch her go as deep as she can, her eyes never leaving my face, and lick my lips when her tongue presses against the tip of my cock. A small burst of come shoots into her mouth when she puts pressure against that hole with her tongue, lapping the small sample of me up and humming her enjoyment against my length.

The iron grip on my control snaps when I watch her shift her hips, rolling them, searching for what only my cock can give her. Needy for it, just from sucking my cock.

She cries out when I pounce. She's off the ground and in my

arms with her back against the shower wall in seconds. I press my hips against hers, the lips of her pussy opening to make room for the thickness of my cock. I glance down our bodies, seeing the angry red tip of my cock, her pussy hugging my shaft, and bite my tongue. I'm a big man, but us like this makes me wish I could slow down and give her gentle.

But I can't.

Not this time.

The hot water falls from the shower down my back. The heat against my back not even close to the heat from her.

My hips pull back, the length of my cock slowly losing the warmth of her pussy, until just the tip of me is gliding against her. I only look away when I feel the searing heat of her entrance kiss the tip.

"Ari," I call out, my voice rougher than normal. She stops watching my cock, her arms tighten around my neck, and she gives me those beautiful eyes. "Fuck, baby," I breathe; all the words I want to say just vanish when I see her looking up at me like that.

Her legs tightening around my body is the only hint she gives before her heels dig deep into the skin above my ass and she pulls herself up with her hold she has on my neck. One second, I was trying to find a way to get past the loss of my control, and the next, she had every inch of my cock buried deep, taking what she needed. My roar that follows her sliding that tight heat over every fucking inch of me should have shattered the glass walls surrounding us. She cries out, her walls clamping down around me, rippling and constricting against me. The wetness of her arousal coats my length, and I feel my balls pull tight, instantly ready to give her what she's milking from me.

I move my hand to the back of her head, holding her there while I start to feed my cock into her body and making sure her head doesn't crack against the wall when I start to slam into her roughly a few thrusts later. Her screams of pleasure continue to pick up, and I can feel my own grunts vibrating through the stall. Each time I bottom out, deep inside her, my balls slap against her body. The sensations of it all causes me to lock my knees in order to keep my balance.

Her pussy ripples against my cock.

Her nails claw at my back, shoulders, and neck. Everywhere.

Her tits bob as she struggles to catch her breath. They jiggle violently when I slam deep.

The whole time I fuck her, I know this is different from anything I have ever felt. Even wild and raw, it's so much more than just fucking. As I'm pounding into her, she's meeting me thrust for thrust, our bodies moving as one. The dance fucking magnificent as we reach for the peak.

"Thorn!" she screams, and I push deep, rolling my hips, then reach between us to pinch her clit between my fingers.

When she starts to come, the wetness dripping down my balls has nothing to do with the shower raining down my back. The blinding rush of my own orgasm has me dropping to my knees in the middle of her climax. She yelps, her legs tightening during my fall, and that only pushes me deeper when I land. I drop my head forward, open my mouth, and bite down on her shoulder when the sensation becomes too much. The sound that leaves her mouth, I'll never forget. Her pussy starts to constrict my movements, and I know she's coming again. The shower floor unforgiving against my knees and shins, but I wouldn't dream of moving when heaven is still wrapped in my arms, sitting on my cock.

I couldn't pull out of her tight pussy if I wanted to. And fuck me, I don't. I empty myself into her, feeling her ride out her pleasure.

Then I thank Christ that her beauty is all mine.

TWENTY-FOUR

Inside the devil's house

REGRET WAS OUT OF CONTROL.

The only thing left was a deep-seated fear unlike anything Regret had ever felt. Regret hadn't just been remembering all this time, no … Regret had been trying, for so long, to find a way back. To fix everything that had unraveled.

To escape the prison that Regret had made from the help of another.

Regret could no longer feel the happiness from the forgotten days.

Regret could no longer remember when the person Regret had loved deeply, loved Regret back.

Regret could no longer remember a life where the devil didn't feast on what parts it could successfully slash away or carve out.

All that was left for Regret now was fear, worry, and the almost nonexistent sliver of hope that Regret had been hiding from the evil beast.

The only break Grief had was when Regret came back out to plan when the misery became too great of a companion to bear.

Grief could remember one thing, though … how to mourn the life that Regret so foolishly threw away because weakness and fear bowed in the face of terror. No fight to be found.

Regret, Grief, Fear, and Pain.

They had one thing in common now.

The room they shared inside the devil's house.

And each day, new tears of blood dropped from flesh inside that room.

Yes, Regret was indeed out of control.

Out of control and grasping onto that tiny sliver of hope. Though, Regret knew it was probably far too late for it to do any good anyway.

TWENTY-FIVE

Will that be a deal breaker for you

E WERE LATE.

I'm *never* late.

Ever.

Late is Piper's gig. It is not mine.

"They're going to know why we're late." I sigh, shifting in my seat. The soreness I feel now has nothing to do with the hours I spent working earlier today.

"So."

I turn with a gasp. "So?"

He glances over and gives me a crooked grin, one that tells me he's proud of himself, and then looks back at the road.

"You know, if I couldn't actually feel how well you earned the right to have that cocky attitude, I wouldn't find it as attractive as I do."

"Even if you didn't know I could back it up, Ari, you would still fucking find it attractive."

I harrumph and cross my arms over my chest. He's right—he knows he's right—but I'm not going to feed the cocky beast by divulging it.

"Babe."

I open my eyes, turn my head, and study him. He changed into a dark gray thermal, which I admitted to him the second he stepped out of his closet might be slightly hotter than the button-down shirt, sleeves rolled to his elbows version of him. On top of that, he paired that hotness with a pair of dark wash jeans that fit him just right all over. Drool worthy. He just laughed and walked into the bathroom to do whatever it is he does to make his hair look perfect. When he stepped back into the bedroom, looking and smelling like heaven, I almost called Piper to cancel dinner. Almost.

I somehow found the strength to keep my hands to myself and started getting ready—after he left the room, of course. I only have so much willpower.

During the course of our relationship and the constant back and forth between our separate homes, we had accumulated a shocking number of personal things at each other's houses. It made it easier, to be honest. We often wouldn't decide which house to settle in for the night until the last minute. The first time I stayed at his house without a change of clothes and had to pull on my previous day's clothes, I had a little bit of a freak-out, remembering the first time I rushed from his house. We had been together for a month at that point. Thorn, being Thorn, walked into his closet and grabbed three suits and two pairs of dress shoes. He didn't need to have me waffle on about how sorry I was about running from him because he forgave me, and when he kissed me goodbye at my car, he loaded his stuff in the back seat. Just like that, he was letting me know where I stood. Well, that and the "better bring enough that you never have to feel like this isn't just as much your space as it is mine."

I brought some things the next time we stayed at his house. He brought more of his when he came to mine, but he also took more of my stuff from my closet when he would leave. I didn't realize it, not at the time, but standing in his closet earlier, I was knocked over with just how merged our lives had become.

I had a ridiculous number of heels here—even a few of my favorites I had been looking for at my house for weeks. Enough dresses that I could probably go two weeks without going back to my place at all; if it wasn't for the cats, that is. He'd even stocked his bathroom with my favorite brands of toiletries. Best part, thanks to the fact that he has an invisible fairy who comes to clean his house and do his laundry, my clothes ended up laundered and hanging in his closet before I realized what had happened. Which was probably why I hadn't realized how much of my stuff had ended up here.

I tried not to let myself love the way my brightly colored clothing looked hanging next to all of his dark ones. It was a sea of black and gray, making my clothes only stand out more. It was futile, though.

Seeing our lives mix only made me imagine what it would be like if we permanently shared space. I stood frozen, the dream of that just too incredible to break away from.

It was the shoes, in the end, that did me in.

It's no surprise that a man as tall as Thorn would also have a giant foot. No surprise at all. I'll admit, the first time I realized how big his feet were, I gawked but only for a second. I couldn't help it. I had never seen feet more than double the size of mine. When my shoes shared closet space with my ex, his didn't strike me like Thorn's. They were also about four sizes smaller too, but not the point.

Thorn had giant feet.

Thorn had giant shoes.

But it was seeing my dainty size six heels, arranged so perfect and neat, that made me wish for things I had no business wishing for this early in our relationship. They shouldn't look like they were made to sit together, but boy, did they. Just like Thorn and me, we fit … perfectly.

I felt another shift deep inside me, and there, standing in my underwear, the significance of what made me pause to begin with struck me hard.

The emptiness I had lived with, what little was left since Thorn started making me feel again, filled so fast with a giant rush, I couldn't feel that void any longer.

Someone who shared closet space with her man was not alone in life.

Someone who had her shoes mixed and displayed so effortlessly with someone else's didn't have "no one" to share her heart with.

No, she definitely had someone.

A giant someone.

A perfect someone who was made for her.

"What are you thinking about?" he questions.

"I like the way my stuff looks mixed with yours in your closet," I utter, not wanting to keep something that means a great deal to me from him. His fingers tighten on the wheel, the hand resting against my thigh jerks. "I like it. I really like it. It sounds silly, I know, but I've never looked at my things, sharing a space with a man's, and perceived them like I did when I was getting ready. Even when …" I pause, swallow, and wait for him to ease up on his grip of my thigh. "Even before … well, it's just never resonated like that before. It's odd, but there you have it."

"Ari, you want to talk about your life before me, don't hold back. I don't just want some parts of you. I want it all."

"It's not important. Or the point."

His hand lifts off my leg, downshifts while steering around a slower car, then I feel his warmth again when he resumes his speed and steadies the wheel after passing the other vehicle.

"His name?"

"Pardon?" His question throwing me for a loop for a second.

"Your ex. What is his name?"

I frown. "Thorn, we don't have to do this."

"Ari. His name."

"Tommy. His name is Thomas Vale."

"All right, Ari. Way I see it, Thomas Vale might be a son of a bitch, but he's still the son of a bitch you have a history with. As much as I would like to erase the pain from that history for you, I can't. And, baby, even if I could take the pain away, that history would remain. It's a big part of you. It made you the woman I need. Don't keep that from me because you think I can't handle it or I'll fly off the handle because of it."

I keep my eyes on the road. We're only about ten minutes away. "I don't think you can't handle it, Thorn. I just don't think you should have to. It's not like he's someone we have to deal with."

A deep chuckle escapes his lips. "As much as I hate to admit it, the chances of us running into someone from my past aren't slim. Just because you're the first who made me need more, it's bound to be something you're going to have to deal with. That motherfucker, though? The odds are high I'll never have to find out if I can be near him without strangling him for hurting you. You telling me what's on your mind isn't me having to deal with him. It's me letting you know just how much I want every piece of you. Good and bad, Ari. It made you the woman you are today. Don't overthink it. Now, tell me about little Tommy."

"I would rather have a root canal. You know what would be more enjoyable? If we talked about our shower earlier."

"You can tell me all about how much you love my cock later."

"You're so bossy."

"Ari."

"You want every piece of me? Even the bad?"

"Especially the bad."

"Okay, honey." I take a deep breath, letting the memories he wants come out of their box. "I met him my freshman year at University of Nevada. We were both studying medicine, which is what opened the door to us dating. We stayed together throughout school, and he eventually got his medical license. At that point, I was a registered trauma nurse, but back in school working toward certification as a physician's assistant. We both were focused on our careers. He asked me to marry him just after I turned twenty-three. I remember when it happened because I didn't saying yes right away. Still, it did eventually happen and only slightly altered the ten-year plan I had mapped out."

I glance at Thorn before continuing, worried he wouldn't

handle talking about Tommy well, but I find him calm and attentive.

"Anyway. The plan. We wanted to open a practice together, instead of him doing it alone and me going to the ER as I had originally planned before our engagement. We would have two kids after a few years, some cats, and a minivan in the driveway." I sigh because the rest was not pretty. However, it was something I had accepted and put behind me—thanks to Dr. Hart. "I should have seen the signs, you know? London stopped speaking to me about a year after I became engaged. Things were strained before that but not terrible. Eight months before the wedding, Tommy started complaining and snapping at me for the stupidest things. Things he felt I was lacking. Everything from the way I dressed to how I was … uh, in bed. That didn't bother me as much as him comparing me to London. What I lacked that she had. Four months before the wedding, he dropped a bomb on me and admitted he had a vasectomy. Who does that? Who fakes a business trip only to stay in town and get sterilized without telling the woman they're supposed to be starting a future with? A future where kids had been planned. Anyway, I realize now that what I had with him was unhealthy. Even if he and London hadn't had their affair, Tommy and I never would have lasted."

He's quiet. His hand, like a lead weight against my leg, gets heavier as the silence trickles on. I know he said he wanted to know about Tommy, but his actions aren't exactly backing that up.

"Thorn, I'm—"

"Kids important to you?"

I frown at him, confused. His question throwing me for a loop. Out of everything I said, that wasn't expected. I replay what I told him about Tommy, and the lightbulb clicks. "If I say yes, will that be a deal breaker for you?"

"Depends. If I tell you I never want to ruin a kid by passing on the shit I'm made from, is *that* a deal breaker for you?"

The air rushes from my lungs, my body jerking back into the seat, his words like a punch right between my breasts—straight to my heart.

The shit he's made from? My God. I get why he thinks that—I really do—especially after everything he's told me about his life before he found Harris. But just because I understand why he would think that doesn't make the sting any less knowing he doesn't see the man I do.

"I'm ... I'm not sure."

He sighs, the soft rush of air falling from him heavy and thick with importance. "We're new, Ari, but even so, we're solid in a way that the day-by-day stuff ended weeks ago, and the possibility of an end to us stopped being an option. We're new, but we're also very much not. The things we've shared? Only two other people know my shit, and I'm sure not many more know yours. That says a lot about just how big what we have is. You've changed the way I look at things, a lot of things I never thought I would change my mind on, but I'm not sure kids would be one of those things even the beauty of you could fix."

"I understand," I murmur. And I really do. He didn't have the family I did growing up. The one with two parents who loved each other so much, but loved their kids even more. The childhood that made me want nothing more than to show that to my own children. Could I give that up? Could I give up something I've always wanted if it meant I would never lose Thorn?

"Like I said," he continues, flipping the turn signal and steering into the parking lot, "we're new because of how little time we've had so far, but not when you take into account just how much we've overcome to get here and stay here. There's nothing but time for us now, Ari. Two months ago, I would have dropped a chick off at the bus stop if this conversation even started, but you're different. Table it. Don't let it worry your mind. I won't let my issues keep me from hearing you out later as long as you keep an open mind to me being enough if I can't give you that. You think about it, I'll think about it, and I promise I won't run off and get snipped in the meantime as long as you can promise not to run from me again because you're worried about it."

I unhook my seat belt and nod. "I promise."

He opens his door and climbs out, but dips his head back down. "Though, probably should remember a condom next time I fuck you."

He winks, meaning it as a joke to lighten the mood, and shuts his door.

Meanwhile, I try not to freak out over his words.

It doesn't escape my notice that, even though that was some heavy stuff, it doesn't actually feel like the end of the world. He fills me up. He really does. If I feel that with just him now, maybe he really is enough that I wouldn't feel the void of no children. That being said, I still feel in my gut that it would be a shame not to give the world more of this incredible man.

When he opens my door, I climb out with his help, mindful of the short hem on my dress. I smooth the skirt out when I stand, looking at how well we match when he pulls me to his side, and leave my thoughts behind. My dress—the same gray of his shirt, only covered in light pink flowers—looks perfect next to him.

"You want your phone?" he asks, tipping his chin in the direction of his car where I left my phone in the cupholder.

"I'm good, honey." I've never liked being one who cared more about their phone than their dinner companions. Plus, I know it's safe with his dark tinted windows.

He nods, then takes my hand in his. Solid. Warm. Everything. He doesn't ease up on his hold, guiding us to the restaurant with the ease of a man used to having a woman at his side. Which I know he isn't. We just really do fit effortlessly. Even when I stumble, my heel getting twisted on a hole in the sidewalk, he's instantly there to hold me steady.

"I'm on the pill, you know," I tell him softly right before he opens the door.

His hand stills, the door open just a crack, and he looks down at me. "Not a good time to tell me that I don't need to wear condoms, babe. Not when I can't do shit about it until later."

I shrug. "Something to look forward to, I suppose."

None of the heaviness from our conversation remains. It's not forgotten, but seeing him looking almost carefree, without that stoic sternness on his face, settles a contentment around me. He holds the door with a gesture for me to go first, kisses my temple before I can walk past him, then takes my hand once again and follows me through.

"Hey, guys," Piper greets, standing up from the seat where she had been sitting near the door in the restaurant's version of a waiting room.

I pull from Thorn and give her a hug, noticing her tense smile immediately. "You okay?"

She doesn't answer, pulling back and stepping away instead. I look over her shoulder and find Matt standing behind her with his disgusting, ever-present frown in place.

Lovely. Douchie Matt is here tonight.

"Matthew Scott, let me introduce you to Thorn Evans ..." I look at Thorn and smile. "Thorn, honey, this is Matt."

Thorn reaches out, offering his hand. "Nice to meet you," he says when Matt's hand hits his. Matt's arrogant expression tells me he didn't notice Thorn's tone, but I did, and I know he didn't mean a word of that.

"So what are you? Some dude she hired to be her date tonight?" Matt laughs, playing it off as a joke.

He did that when he first met Tommy, too. Though, Tommy laughed with him. Thorn doesn't find it funny at all, judging by the grunt that leaves Matt's mouth a moment later. His egotistical face now pinched with pain.

"You don't know me, but it would be wise never to say shit like that again."

Holy cow.

He drops Matt's hand and pulls me close ... even closer than before with his arm around my shoulders.

"Matt," Piper hedges, earning his scowl. "You know I told you Ari was bringing her boyfriend tonight."

Matt just barely catches himself before he rolls his eyes. Over the years, he's made no secret of his opinion of me. I heard him tell Piper once that Tommy lucked out when he got the better sister before it was too late. I shouldn't be surprised that he would assume I couldn't get a man like Thorn without paying for him.

The silence while we move to our table and order our drinks is beyond awkward. Matt wisely keeps his crap to himself, but when he glares at Thorn for the second time after we've sat down, clearly judging him, I've had enough.

"Pipe?" I call across the table.

She looks up from her menu, and I stop myself from wincing when I see the dull look in her eyes. I hate seeing my boisterous friend like this.

"You wouldn't believe the size of Thorn's closet. I've never seen anything like it."

I see Matt frown out of the corner of my eye but don't pay him any attention. One thing Matt hates is when someone else might actually be more successful than he is. Even when most of that success is in his own arrogant mind. And he's so far out of Thorn's league, he's still playing T-ball while Thorn is in the World Series.

"There's no way his closet is bigger than yours." She laughs, some color coming back to her cheeks. "I mean, hon, you convert-ed a whole bedroom to get yours. What'd he do? Buy a whole sepa-rate house for his?"

"Yeah, actually, when you put it that way, his makes my con-verted bedroom closet look like a postage stamp."

She jerks her gaze and stares at Thorn in disbelief. "Is she kidding?"

He laughs low. "Postage stamp would be an exaggeration, but no, she isn't kidding that it's a little bigger."

"A little bigger, he says." I snort.

"God, Ari, what did you do, order him on up mister perfect dot com?"

Everyone but Matt laughs.

"Seems like it sometimes," I tell her, looking at Thorn and meaning every word.

"I guess that means it'll be an easy choice for you when you guys have to decide which house you'll keep when you move in together," Piper jokes.

I feel like I've stopped breathing. That is, until Thorn's hand lands on my lap and gives me a gentle squeeze. Oh, my God. He's probably freaking out at just the thought of that step in our relationship. I mean, sharing closet space is one thing, but sharing one house is completely different. He gives me another squeeze. I bite the side of my cheek, suck in a breath, and look over at him. Only, he looks nothing like a man who has a problem with sharing a house with his new girlfriend. No, he's looking at me with a soft smile, and something that looks real close to reverence bright in his green eyes.

"Nothing against your place, baby, but I've got the garage for all my cars and one hell of a view from every window in my house. You got The Strip lights but not the mountains. Closet's good, but you're right; it isn't mine."

"Uh," I lamely offer.

"Should also point out you don't have the pool, theater, a bigger gym, or the kitchen you like to remind me is the best thing ever."

"Whoa, big guy, I was just kidding." Piper laughs, but even she doesn't seem sure if he's serious or just playing off something she made awkward.

"You mighta been. I wasn't." Oh, okay. Wow.

The waitress comes up to our table, and we order. We make small talk, but all I can hear is Thorn admitting he was serious. His "I wasn't" plays in my mind over and over. Thankfully, Matt's massive jerk attitude doesn't take long to resurface, distracting me from my thoughts.

"So, Thor, what is it that you do?"

"You want try that again? We both know you know my name."

Matt's façade doesn't crack even though he was just called out. I have a feeling he thinks his question is a way to put Thorn down. He used Thorn's casual dress to wrongly assume that Thorn isn't successful just because he isn't wearing something else. Of course, Matt's still wearing what I imagine he had on for work. He wouldn't change for a relaxing meal with friends when he can wear his outfit like a mask, showing off like he's way more important than he is.

"I own my own business," Thorn answers vaguely. That's my guy, recognizing Matt's play instantly and playing the game right along with him. Only he's one step ahead.

"Oh, yeah? Doing what?"

"I guess you could say I'm in entertainment," he answers, pausing and leaning back with a smug smile. "I own The Alibi."

I don't look away from Matt, and when I see panic flash over his face, I feel that like a victory. Not what he expected, I'm sure. Not even close to what he might have assumed. Piper might turn a blind eye to what her fiancé does when he has a few hours to spare, but I'm sure he'll be finding a new strip club to frequent now.

"Your boyfriend owns a strip club?" he asks, covering his initial shock. I should have anticipated that. Matt doesn't just give up. Not when he thinks he found a way to gain the upper hand. "You sure do know how to pick them, Paris. Next thing you'll tell me is you picked him right off the stage."

I tighten my jaw. I hate that he always calls me Paris.

Thorn moves, jerking up from that relaxed position, and slams his open hand against the table with a loud crack. I jump, and Piper lets out a little squeak. I look over at her and hate Matt a little more than I already do when I see her mouth say that she's sorry.

"You'd do best to show *Ari* respect, Matt." Thorn sounds venomous.

"It's okay, honey." I sigh, reaching over and taking Thorn's now clenched fist and bringing it back down to my lap, rubbing circles against his skin until he relaxes some. "Not that it's any of your business, Matt, but the day *he* picked *me* was one of the best days I've ever had. And even if he was on the stage and not in the office, I would still feel the same. So get off your high horse when you're far from being some bright, shiny star. You work for your dad. We both know that's the only reason you have that job."

"Piper, we will be discussing this later," Matt fumes toward Pipe.

I see her chin wobble, and I hate him for it, but I also hate that I let him get under my skin.

"Talk about what?" Thorn interjects immediately, wisely picking up on the shift.

"If you must know, not that it's any of your business, I expect Piper to uphold a certain image. She's going to have a few things to think about when it comes to her association with Ari."

A tear falls down her cheek.

She bats it away before Matt can see it.

"Matt, please." Piper reaches out and wraps her hands around his forearm, but he jerks it away.

"If you'll excuse us," Matt hisses at Thorn and me. Grabbing Piper by the bicep, he basically drags her toward the restrooms.

"Tell me he isn't going to hurt her, and I'll stay where I am."

"He wouldn't," I answer.

"Fuck," Thorn snarls.

Thorn doesn't stop staring at the hallway they disappeared down. I can tell he wants to follow them to make sure Piper's okay, but he manages to stay seated. Our food comes at the same time they rejoin us. I can tell Piper had been crying, but she just shakes her head and places her napkin in her lap. Her red-rimmed eyes don't look back up once.

"Well, let's eat," Matt says, chipper as can be.

Thorn leans over the table. "You'll do well to make sure your fiancée doesn't ever have that expression on her face. Not when I'm around and not when I'm not. Her association with Ari? That's got not one fucking thing to do with either of us. Remember that. You try to pull the two of them apart with your bullshit, knowing damn well they're close as family, and we're going to have problems. Understand?" His voice is scary low. Sitting at the table while they were gone cost him when he saw Piper's tears, I have no doubt, and he made sure to let Matt know just how much in a way that wouldn't embarrass the person he was defending.

Matt nods, but I have a feeling even Thorn knows he's full of it.

What a nightmare.

TWENTY-SIX

Ari

In every way possible

"**W**HAT'S THE STORY WITH PIPER AND MATT?"

I shift in bed, turning in his arms, and sigh. I knew this question would come sooner than later, and I'm honestly surprised he waited this long to ask it.

We got back home—my house this time—a few hours ago. Dinner ended just as strained as it began. I was mentally exhausted from dealing with Matt and feeling nothing but sadness that Piper was with someone like him when she deserved so much more. I know it cost Thorn to keep his cool. Had it not been for Piper and me being there, I know he wouldn't have.

The only thing I had enough energy for when we got home was kicking my shoes off, feeding the cats, and pulling one of Thorn's dress shirts from a few days before from the hamper and slipping it on. He switched his jeans for an old pair of sweats and lost the shirt. After we got comfortable, we settled on the couch. I watched some of the recorded shows from the past week, and he checked his emails, returned a few calls, and basically humored me through an hour of *The Real Housewives of Beverly Hills*.

That brought us to now.

"Aside from her fiancé being the biggest jerk in the world, you mean?"

"That I already sorted out. I'm just trying to figure out what the fuck she's doing with him when he's not only a fucking dick, but she's also clearly not happy."

"I don't even know where to start, to be honest. He grew up with us. They started dating young. Middle of high school, I think. At the beginning, it was really more like passing notes and the occasional date. Even back then, though, even when they were too young to have more than the label of a couple, it still wasn't a good relationship. Piper's been in love with the idea of love since we were kids, so even when he would ignore her or make fun of her with his football teammates and followers, it didn't matter. I think he's made her feel like she couldn't do better, that she would never do better, so she stuck around. I know deep down she doesn't love Matt, but instead of thinking she couldn't do better, she's now afraid of him. He's made her that way, but because that young girl who fell in love with the idea of love is still in there somewhere, she's basically convinced herself things will change. I tried getting her to move in with me once before they got engaged, but she said she would be a burden and wouldn't hear anything more on it. Her parents are divorced, both moved about an hour away when we graduated, but they don't have a lot of money to help her anyway. Her sisters couldn't help even though they would. Everything she earns from

Trend goes toward the lifestyle Matt tries to keep up with. To her, he's her only option, I think. I keep hoping one day she'll wake up and realize she's better than him, but until then, I just keep making sure she knows she actually does have other options."

"Has she ever tried to leave him?"

I nod, resting my chin against the hand I have on his chest. "Back in college, before things got worse. Some stuff happened to her when they weren't together, stuff that isn't my place to share, but it spooked her into being afraid of being without someone more than being with someone she feared. I think she took him back because she felt safer with someone who doesn't care about her as long as she wasn't alone."

"Does he hurt her?"

"Emotionally, yeah. Physically? I-I'm not sure. I've never seen any bruises, but you saw how he is. I try to talk to her about it, but she gets real mad when I do. Last time, she didn't speak to me for almost a month."

"Right. You give her that offer again to move in with you, Ari. Keep trying until she agrees. It's time for us to get her the fuck away from him. You can work on getting her to realize what she does deserve after you hand her the keys to your house."

I blink at him. "Did I miss something?"

"You sat in my car when I told you we were solid in a way that there was no end, weren't you?"

A rush of air leaves me. He did mean what I thought he did. "It's been two months!"

"You going to change how you feel about us after another two months pass?"

I snort. "Highly unlikely."

"Then, Ari, get your girl in your house. Tell her whatever the fuck you need to, but starting tomorrow, we work on getting her the fuck away from that guy. All that matters is getting her safe."

"Okay, Thorn."

I settle back into his side.

"One stone, two birds, baby. She's safe, and it'll be a lot easier for me when I can make sure you don't have to worry about selling this place when you move to mine."

I widen my eyes, stare at the television, and try to figure out if I've just somehow agreed to move in with my boyfriend.

Sleep didn't come easy that night, but I finally managed to drift off about an hour before my alarm went off. I groggily move from the bed, silence the alarm, and head to the bathroom. I grab my robe off the hook on the door and cover up my naked body on the way. It's a miracle I managed to leave the bed with Thorn looking as good as he did with the sheet just barely covering his naked body.

After taking care of business, I wash my face and brush my teeth. When I hear my alarm go off again, followed by Thorn cursing under his breath about better ways to wake up, I smile at my reflection. He enters the bathroom a minute later. I turn, place my butt against the counter, and watch his naked body as he moves to the little closet area where the toilet is separated from the rest of the bathroom. I don't look away. He glances over his shoulder and shakes his head.

"Babe, really?"

"What?" I smirk and try to look innocent.

"Watching me piss has you looking hungry as fuck."

"You look really good in the morning. It can't be helped. And, well, it's not you using the restroom that I'm thinking about. It's just hot to watch you touch your penis, no matter what you're doing. It's really hot."

Heat flashes in his eyes.

"Cock, baby. Penis is for chumps who don't know what they're doing with it."

I blush. I'm not used to such candor. I lost my virginity to a man who didn't deserve it, but he was the one who always made me call it a penis. Thorn's right; that is most definitely for those who don't know what they're doing.

"Fuck, you're cute. You like watching me touch myself, baby?" he asks, stepping up to the sink and washing his hands before grabbing the toothbrush he keeps in the little decorative holder with mine and brushing his teeth. Effectively easing my mind from where it had veered.

My eyes roam over him, every single hard inch, and I lick my lips. He laughs the best he can with a mouthful of foam, then bends to spit and rinse. He drops the toothbrush onto the counter, then pulls me against him. I don't even care that he's missed the holder for the brush because, with my robe wide open, his naked bits are against my naked bits.

"We've got a problem, babe. You feel me?" he asks, flexing his hips to make me feel just how big of a problem we have.

"I feel you, honey."

"Then get your ass back in bed so we can take care of it."

Heat licks across my skin from the rush of arousal caused by his words. I spin when he releases me, letting the robe fall from my shoulders and onto the ground. Before I can climb back into my bed, Thorn's hands are on my hips, spinning me back around. My belly flutters, and an eruption of heat pools between my legs. His mouth is on mine, our tongues sliding together. Kissing me deeply, he moves us so that my back is on the mattress with his body over me. He keeps inching our bodies across the mattress until my head is just inches away from hanging off the edge.

Then he lifts his mouth from mine and starts kissing a hot trail down my neck. His mouth closes around one nipple, sucking it deep and swirling his tongue around the sensitive peak. His hand causing heavenly torture to my other breast. I cry out when he bites down, soothing the pain away with a lazy lick before looking up at me. He doesn't glance away, keeping his eyes on me while he starts kissing his way down my body. My erratic breathing mingling with the hungry sounds he keeps making from deep in his throat, tickling my skin. Just when I think he couldn't possibly drive me any higher, he grabs the back of my thighs and lifts my hips off the mattress.

Then he winks and drops his mouth to my pussy and feasts. There's no other word for how his mouth and tongue are moving against my core. His sinfully talented mouth takes me to the top and over the crest in seconds. I cry out his name, blind with desire. Even though he shows no signs of relenting, I hold him to me until my body quakes with aftershocks. Still, he doesn't stop. He growls against me, his tongue sliding into my body before gliding back up my slit.

"More," he demands, his lips hovering over my pussy as he looks at me up the length of my body. He leans back down, inhales, and then I get his eyes again. "Fuck, you smell just as good as you taste."

"Thorn, please, baby."

"Give me what I want, then you can have what you need."

He opens his mouth, covering so much of me, and sucks hard. His tongue flicks against my clit, driving me right back up the peak I just crashed down. He shifts, his lips moving over me, and nips at the sensitive flesh. When two thick fingers enter me, curling deep, he drops his mouth to my clit and sucks so intensely I swear I see stars. My whole body jerks, my back arches off the mattress, and I grab the back of his head again. Only this time, it's not to keep him there as much as it is to use him to get there faster. I start rocking against his mouth as every inch of my body comes alive.

Seconds later, I scream his name and feel a burst of wetness leave my body. I almost feel embarrassed, not understanding what just happened, but if the sounds he's making are anything to go by, he's a very happy man and I shouldn't worry. I keep gasping for the breath I can't seem to find. His fingers continue to pump inside me, slower this time, even though I'm well and truly spent. The wet sounds from my body get louder with each twist and push of his wrist.

"Fuck me," he hisses, lifting his mouth and looking down at his busy hand. "You're just full of surprises, aren't you?"

I cover my face with my hands. I've watched enough porn while I kept myself entertained over the years that, now that my mind isn't in the throes of ecstasy, I know I just squirted … all over his face.

"Ari, look at me."

I shake my head.

"Now, Ari."

Slowly, I drop my hands. My eyes widen, and my mouth parts

slightly. I hadn't felt him move, but my God. I hadn't even felt his fingers leave my body. At some point, he did, and now he's kneeling between my legs, giving me the most sensual show.

"You see what you did to me? Don't you ever fucking cover yourself up like you're embarrassed that your body responds to me. Not fucking ever. You see how hard my cock is for you? Goddamn, baby. You have no clue how hot that was."

He continues to thrust his erection into his fist, twisting his wrist and grunting softly. His other hand comes up, closing around the rest of him, and I watch while he jerks himself off.

"That ever happen to you before?"

I shake my head, not looking away from the carnal sight. He picks up speed, both his hands moving in sync around his length.

"You see how wet my cock is? That's from you, Ari. Fuck, I'll never grow tired of watching you come alive under my touch, but when I can make you respond like that." He trails off, one of his hands swirling around his tip, inducing a deep vibration from his chest. "Magnificent, baby."

His harsh breathing picks up speed when his hands do. The muscles of his abs tensing every few thrusts. Good God, I could go again just watching this.

"Tell me again. Tell me what you like watching me do."

"I like watching you touch yourself," I breathe, goose bumps firing all over my skin.

"You like me touching my *what*?" he continues, pausing and bending slightly so he can drop one of his hands between my legs, not stopping from jerking himself with the other. I jolt off the bed when he glides his hand through my folds. "Drenched," he praises, gathering my wetness and bringing it to his red and angry erection to coat himself with more of me.

"Your … your cock."

"Yeah, baby. Tell me what you want me to do with my cock."

I gulp, feeling like I really am about to come again. My eyes soak up this sight before me, branding it to my memories.

"I want you to fill me up."

"Fuck, yeah, you do."

"But," I continue, feeling empowered by him, "I want *your* come on my skin, too."

Something purely animalistic erupts from his mouth, and he releases himself, falling over me. He's inside me a second later, his mouth dropping to mine before he's even given me all of him. I taste myself, but instead of being grossed out, it just makes me want it more. I pull his head closer and lift my hips, searching … needing.

He pushes into me slowly, so painfully slow. Deep and lazy glides of his huge cock keep me on the edge. He lifts his head, bites my bottom lip, and flips us so his back is to the mattress and I'm sitting on top with him impaled deeply.

"You have to decide where my cock empties now, baby. Where do you want it more? Inside this tight pussy?" He jerks his hips off the bed and hits the deepest part of me. "Or on your skin?" He reaches up, pressing his hand between my breasts, sliding it down my stomach slowly until his thumb presses against my clit.

Color is high on his cheeks. I've done this to him. I've driven him to this remarkable state. It's stimulating every one of my senses. I don't need any more encouragement. My hands go to his chest, and I take over. He feels so deliciously good inside me, I never want him to leave. His thumb speeds up, pressing against my clit harder. Rolling, gliding, and driving me mad. His other hand lifts to one of my swaying breasts and grabs the heaviness, pinching my nipple between his thumb and finger. I pick up speed, bouncing, rocking, and rolling my hips against him. His enjoyment vibrates from his chest, against my hands, as he stares at me with hunger in his gaze. It only fuels me.

"You have about ten seconds to figure out where you want it, Ari," he hisses through tight lips. "Fucking hell, your pussy is greedy."

"Can't. Want. Give it to me, baby." I rock my hips, so close to the edge. "I need ..."

"I know what you need." He grunts, his hips lifting off the mattress to push himself deep. I scream when a tiny bite of pain joins the pleasure, tipping me over the edge.

I collapse, falling over him, and he wraps his arms around me. He lifts his legs, the position pushing his softening length back in when he starts to fall from my body. I don't need words to know he wasn't ready to leave me, just like I wasn't ready to lose him. His heart pounds against my cheek, my own answering each frantic beat with one of its own. We don't speak, but words aren't needed. That was intense. It was so much bigger than just sex. We connected in every way possible.

Body ... and heart.

Our hearts are saying everything words aren't needed for.

Beat for beat.

He's filled my emptiness, awakened my heart, and brought magic back to my life.

I just hope he's falling for me just as deeply as I've fallen for him.

TWENTY-SEVEN

THORN

All the way to my fucking marrow

I LEAN BACK IN MY CHAIR, RUBBING MY HANDS DOWN MY FACE.

Fuck, I'm tired.

Tired of the long hours at The Alibi—something I never minded before. Tired of not seeing Ari. Both of us being so fucking busy, our time together had been cut out completely. Real tired of sleeping alone in my bed, too. Fucking sick of it.

I've been stuck at The Alibi for so damn long, I feel like I've moved in. I haven't even had time to take my girl to lunch, let alone see her. I'm here from lunch until around three in the morning. Four days ago, the stomach bug that hit Barcode hard for almost three weeks found its way here. That nasty shit started almost two months ago, proving how strong of a virus it was when it started moving through my girls.

As of today, I was still down five dancers and my best bartender on the girls' side. Yesterday, I had to send two of my boys, one manager, and three guys from security home on their side. I've had the cleaning crew in here so many times since that shit started there shouldn't be anything left. I had each dancer restricted to only stage and table routines. Customers didn't give a shit that the back rooms were closed down and they weren't getting lap dances on the floor. I'm about ready to just close the doors for a few days at this point and not because my staff keeps getting sick. They're spreading that shit around each other because they keep fucking in the break rooms, giving me a bigger headache by keeping that shit going. Closing the damn place down wouldn't just make it harder for them to fuck stomach viruses between each other, but it would guarantee me some much-needed solid, uninterrupted time with Ari. Even though I know that shit's spreading because half of my staff is sleeping together—something I'll be addressing at the next staff meeting—I know that's why I haven't gotten it. Hasn't stopped me from being afraid to get near Ari on the off chance I'm carrying the bug around from just being in this place and breathing the air. Irrational, I know, since none of our daily regulars have gotten it, and they've had their faces all in the tits and ass of some dancers' who were the first to get it.

It's been a week since I had her.

Five long fucking days since I've seen her.

And, looking down at my wrist, twelve goddamn hours since I've talked to her.

My phone rings, and I grab it off the desk, smiling when I see it's the very woman I can't get off my mind.

"Babe."

"Hey," she says, soft and sweet. "You sound exhausted."

"I feel exhausted."

"How were things tonight? Any better? I would have called earlier, but I worried it was another insane night like the last couple for you. I didn't want to pull you away."

I sigh, rolling the tension in my neck. "I've got enough dancers on both sides that it's not a fucking cluster fuck like it has been the past three nights. So I guess that's better. Next time, though, don't wait to call. Nothing is important enough for you to think a call from you would pull me away. Nothing, Ari."

"Okay, honey." She giggles. "I'm glad things were better today."

Just like every other time she calls me honey, that word hits me right in the center of my chest. Women have called me terms of endearment before, but it was just words until I heard Ari give me that soft honey for the first time.

"How's Piper?"

Ari's sigh comes through the line, and I know she's upset. Another reason I'm fucking tired of being here. I hate knowing she's stressed over Piper, and I can't do shit about it. Ever since that dinner two months ago, she's spent a lot of time crying on my shoulder, worried more each day for her friend. She's been trying, just like I asked, to get Piper to move into her house, but nothing has changed. Piper withdraws more and more each time Ari brings it up. It's breaking my girl's heart, and feeling like I can't fix what's hurting Ari, isn't a pill I've been able to successfully swallow.

"I tried again yesterday. I mentioned to her that I'm hardly there these days, and the cats are feeling neglected. I figured since I hadn't brought it up in a few weeks, she would really believe me. She didn't buy it, though. Just like she hasn't bought any other reason I've thought of to get her to move into my house. She still remains firm that she's fine where she is, and it doesn't make sense to move out of the place she shares with the man whose ring is on her finger. I did find out why she's been acting weird. Matt, apparently, has been giving her a hard time about quitting Trend. She admitted that it's put a strain on her but assured me that she has no intention of leaving. I've known that man for over twenty years, and he's never tried to pull us apart like this, Thorn. Never. I need to figure something out soon, though. I'm worried if I can't come up with a reason for her to move into my house and get her away from him soon, he's going to make that divide growing between us snap."

"Don't give up on her, baby. You'll figure it out." I'll fucking kill that motherfucker if it starts to look like he isn't going to go away quietly. I'm sick of hearing how Piper's suffering, and I really fucking hate how that rubs off on Ari.

"I hope you're right. Anyway, let's talk about this later. I've been upset about it enough today. Tell me something that will distract me."

"Okay, baby. How about we talk about how it's been five days since I've had you in my arms? At this point, I'm real fucking close to having the staff start to clear this fucking place out and close the doors for the night. You called just in time to stop me from pissing off a lot of customers. Now that I hear you in my ear, that's all I need to get me through long enough to finish some of this paperwork and pull Devon off the floor. He can keep an eye on things for the rest of the night so I can get the fuck out of here. I have my regular night managers back tomorrow, which means we've got a weekend to ourselves. Meet you at my place in two hours?"

"God, you have no idea how happy I am that you said that.

I was considering working for the first weekend in almost three years if you were going to be tied up over there again just to have something to keep me busy. As it is, I'm so far ahead with every-thing here, I could probably take all of next week off and still come back with nothing to do."

"Not a bad idea," I mumble, thinking about what I would need to do around here to get a week of uninterrupted silence.

"Well, unfortunately, even if I wanted to, I can't this week. Another reason I've been worried about Piper. She asked me this morning if she could have the week off starting Monday. I couldn't tell her no even if I wanted to, not when she hasn't taken a single vacation day in the six years she's been at Trend. She said she needs to be home and show Matt that she can be the attentive fiancée and keep her job here. So I might not have any work to do, but Piper does, and now she won't be here next week."

I frown, looking across my office. My gut tells me she was right to be worried about this time off. I make a mental note to contact my investigator next week about looking into Matt. I've had him on standby with Ari's ex after a week trailing him didn't tell us shit, might as well give him some work until I decide what to do with Thomas fucking Vale.

"I'm sure it's nothing, though," she adds, almost like an after-thought meant to convince herself.

"Keep your finger on her pulse, baby. All you can do until you have more than a gut feeling."

"I know. That's what I don't like. Anyway, I'll see you at your place in two hours."

"Babe?"

"Yes, honey?"

"Bring the cats. Once I finally get my hands back on you, there's no way I'm letting go. You'll have the weekend to convince me why you have to work on Monday."

This time, the breathy sound that she exhales is almost as sweet as hearing her call me honey.

"Bring the cats. Got it. Crap, hold on." She moves the phone away from her mouth, but I can still hear her talking to Piper about some customer being upset when Piper told her that her bag wasn't authentic, whatever the fuck that means. I don't speak purse. "Baby, I have to go. Apparently, someone is here trying to sell a counterfeit bag. They're mad Piper rejected the sale and asked to speak to me. I'll meet you at your place, but I might be a little later, depending on how long it takes me to deal with this."

"All right, babe. Don't keep me waiting too long. I need you."

"Okay, honey. Love you."

She ends the call, and I can't move. The phone is stuck to my ear. My heart pounding wildly. But, fuck me, it's not because I didn't like what she said. I'm not even sure she realizes she said those two words. Her frazzled tone and rush to get off the phone and deal with her problem at work meant she had her mind on other things, but that slip wouldn't have happened if she didn't feel those two words. No fucking way. I replay her words, each of them wrapping around me tightly, so tightly I feel them dig deep down to the center of me.

Love you.

"Jesus," I breathe, rubbing my chest.

Love you.

"Fuck." I know what that burn is now. Crystal clear, I understand what my body has been telling me.

Love you.

Her words envelop me whole, squeezing tight.

So unbelievably tight.

I feel them dig deeper, winding from that burn in my chest and throughout my body—constricting the air in my lungs as they seize. That sensation produces wave upon wave of warmth as those two words settle all the way to my fucking marrow, latching on to every inch they pass on the way—bonding, mending, and *Christ* … I feel my own tattered pieces of the past, the same kind that Ari spoke about having inside of her months ago, start reaching out for that warmth, begging to be healed.

Love you.

I toss the phone and start packing up my shit. I'm not fucking sitting around here after that. After I get her in my arms, I'll try to focus on what work I have left over the weekend. Way fucking after.

If I thought I knew what it was like to need her in my arms before those two words came through the phone, that need is absolutely immeasurable now.

TWENTY-EIGHT

Ari

Not a shadow left in the sky

MY HAND LOWERS. THE DEATH GRIP I HAVE ON MY PHONE is making my fingers smart. My heart feels like it's just completely stopped.

Okay, Ari. Maybe he didn't hear you. And if he did, just tell him you were talking to Piper or something. There's really no reason to panic over it. Oh, my God, but there is. I just told the man I've been dating for a little over four months that I loved him. The same man who has never been in a relationship and basically avoided ever being in one his whole forty-one years. I should have waited for him to say it first!

"He's totally going to freak out," I whisper to my empty office.

Or maybe—the tiny voice of hopeful reason chirps in my mind—I shouldn't underestimate someone who's given me no reason to assume he doesn't feel the same love for me that I do for him. Over the past four months—not counting the two weeks after that morning I ran from him—he's shown me on more than one occasion just how deeply he feels for me.

"There's nothing I can do about it now," I grumble.

Not only that, but there's no sense in being upset about a truthful slip of the tongue.

I *do* love him.

So much it overwhelms me at times.

If he can't handle it, then maybe what we have isn't what I feel.

I stand from my desk, rubbing my sweaty hands down the form-fitting sheath dress I wore today. Business. Let's focus on that. I'll worry about whatever comes from my "love you" later when I get to Thorn's house.

I step out of my office, feeling a whole hell of a lot calmer than I did a moment ago. I walk toward the front counter, grinning at the expression on Piper's face. She's annoyed and not even trying to conceal it from the woman standing in front of her. Now, I normally would care, but this woman must be the one trying to sell a counterfeit bag, and that isn't the kind of customer I care about losing their business over.

"Sorry about the delay," I tell them both, walking around the counter and stepping next to Piper, smiling sweetly at the woman. "Hi, my name is Ari Daniels. I understand you wanted to speak to the owner, and that's me. How can I help you?"

"You can start by telling me why this one told me you can't accept my bag! I've had it for less than a week, and there's nothing wrong with it. It's brand new!"

I nod, letting her assume I'm listening. I can already tell she is going to be a headache. At least Piper was at the counter when she came in. If it was one of the other girls, I wouldn't have been able to have the upper hand when I walked up. Piper, though, she knows her stuff, and if she says it's not real, then it isn't. Of course, I confirmed that for myself in the brief glance I got of the bag when I stepped up to the counter. I cross my fingers, hoping I can get her out of Trend before she makes a scene. I hate when they cause a scene. At least there aren't any other customers in here at the moment. A rare break that will cushion any fit this woman may pitch.

"How about I take a look? That way I can better assess why my associate felt we couldn't accept your item. Here," I say, pulling one of our policy notecards from the side of the register and sliding it across the glass to the woman. "If you wouldn't mind, this is our policy on how we base our decisions for buying. It outlines the things we look for that could potentially reject a sale. That way, when I'm done, maybe we can compare notes and see what we can come up with."

She grumbles under her breath but takes the card anyway.

I carefully slide the purse closer. At least the woman—whose name I still don't know because she skipped past good manners and jumped right to angry—was right about one thing; it does look brand new. However, that doesn't really make one bit of difference in the value of her purse because it's definitely fake. A good fake, really good, but fake all the same. Sometimes I'm shocked at just how good counterfeits can be.

It's the nature of my business to deal with counterfeit bags. It really sucks when you can tell the person trying to sell it had no idea, but that rarely happens. As in, maybe once a year. With the price tag on luxury items, people usually do their homework when they're buying from someone outside the actual store. No one is willing to part with thousands of dollars without a guarantee that what they're purchasing is authentic—which is why we offer a money back guarantee if there is ever anything sold that isn't authentic from Trend. A guarantee we have never, not once, had to honor.

It's the people who come in here and automatically have their defenses up and show us all their cards before we even have a chance to exchange names.

Just like this woman.

I keep inspecting the bag, making sure that she sees me as I check every inch of the purse. At this point, I could give her a full-page checklist of the things I found, but I'll give her the easy and indisputable ones so that I can speed this up.

"Well, you done? I'd like to get my money and get out of here."

Smile plastered on, I neatly lay each handle on the side of the canvas, but keep the bag near so I can show her where her purse maker screwed up the most. "Unfortunately, ma'am, my associate was correct in her first assessment." She starts to argue, but I just shake my head. "Please, if you don't mind waiting to ask any questions, I'll tell you why."

She grunts, crossing her arms and narrowing her eyes. "Go on then."

"Certainly." I pull each side and open the top of the purse and turn it so she can see the heat stamp on the inside pocket. "Right here, on the heat stamp, the font isn't correct. Louis Vuitton has a few little tweaks to their font that never changes. The leg on the L is too long. The O's are too oval. The space between the two T's in Vuitton is too big. And the leg on the R starts in the middle of the hook above it. There are, of course, a few exceptions to every rule of thumb, but not with this particular model." I reach inside and locate the date code tab, pointing it out to her. "These, however, never change. Always two letters, indicating the location of the factory, and four numbers arranged specifically to tell you the exact week and month it was made. With much older bags, there wasn't a date code, but we're talking before the 80s. With yours, the code is saying—with the first two letters—that it is a bag produced in the United States. However, if you look under the heat stamp I just showed you, it states there that it was produced in France. You will never have a bag where those two things don't match."

"Look here, lady. I know this bag is real. I bought it myself."

"That might be the case, but I can guarantee you it wasn't Louis Vuitton that manufactured this purse, regardless of when you bought it."

"Just because some bullshit letters are the wrong shape and some screw-up with a hot stamp?"

"Heat stamp. But, yes, those reasons as well as a number of others. If you would like, I can show you those too, but it won't change the fact that we won't be able to buy this purse from you."

"Bullshit, bitch. I want to speak to someone above you."

I steady myself so I don't lose my cool. "There is no one above me. As I stated earlier, I'm the owner of Trend. As much as I wish I could help you, everything I just explained to you is also listed on the buying policy I gave you. You might have also read on there that we reserve the right to deny an item for many reasons other than just lack of authenticity. I assure you."

"You can take that assurance and shove it up your ass."

She grabs her bag and stomps toward the door, slamming her hand against the glass and shoving it open. I keep my eye on her while she strides angrily to her car. When I hear the rustling of a bag, I look from the car as it peels out of the parking lot and frown at Piper. She's still watching the parking lot, small smirk on her face, chewing on a chip she must have just put in her mouth.

I snatch the bag from her and frown.

"Hey! What the hell, Ari! Give it back. That's my dinner!"

I pull it farther away when she tries to grab it back. "I don't think so. You know the rules about eating on the floor. You want your chips, take them to the break room and I'll cover the register until you or Hannah get back up front. You better not be eating out here when I'm not here. What kind of example does it set for the rest of the staff when my number one is breaking the rules?"

"Give it to me," she complains, holding her hand out. I place the bag back in her hand and arch a brow. She starts walking toward the break room. "You know what? If I want to eat my feelings, I should be able to without you making a hostile work environment. Just because you don't like snack time doesn't mean others can't enjoy it!"

"Oh, hush," I chide, giggling when she sticks her tongue out at me. Thank God there aren't any customers in here. Piper throwing a fit over food would just be the icing on the cake after the pleasant fake bag pusher. Even if she is joking.

"Just for that, I'm going to drink all your Cokes from the fridge while I'm back there!"

She walks into the break room, and I'm left laughing even harder now. Bethany, one of the newer girls, comes from the back, wheeling a cart full of new stock behind her. She looks around before stopping in front of the counter.

"Is Piper okay? I thought I heard her yelling."

"No! I'm not okay. The snack warden is being a food bully!"

Piper yells from the break room door, standing just inside the room with the tips of her shoes just kissing where the show room technically starts. She has a Coke in one hand and her chips in the other. "Good news though, Bethie. We've got free Cokes on Ari for the rest of our shift!"

I have to hold my sides from the cramp my laughter is giving me. It's been weeks since my funny best friend has cracked a joke. Even if she was breaking the rules, it was worth it to get a little part of her back.

"What the *fuck*?" Piper hisses, dropping the bag on the floor inside the break room and hustling toward me.

I swipe my eyes, my amusement dying instantly when I see the expression on her face. The bell chimes over the door, but I'm too focused on my friend to turn.

"Pipe?" I question. "Are you okay?"

She's still glaring over my shoulder, something murderous in her eyes.

"You are *not* to be believed!" she snaps, still looking behind me. When she gets close enough, she slams the unopened Coke down on the glass counter, continuing toward the door at my back.

"Ari?"

My eyes feel like they're about to bug out of my head when I hear *that* voice. Piper's brilliant display of madness makes sense now. Everything seems to move in slow motion as I start to turn around. Bethany's confused face is the last thing I see before I finish turning the rest of the way. Piper looks seconds away from unleashing the uncontrollable energy vibrating off her.

It doesn't even faze *him*, though.

No. He's just standing there, a step inside the store. If seeing him isn't enough of a shock, the desolation on his face damn sure is. Piper's right, he is not to be believed.

"Thomas," I say coolly, proud of myself for sounding a lot better than I feel. He flinches, and I know the use of his full name hit the mark I meant to strike. Just as I hate Paris, he despises Thomas.

"You have a second?"

I frown. Piper growls.

"A second for you to turn around and march right back to whatever snake den you slithered from? Yeah, she has a second for that, Thomas Vale!"

"Pipe, love you for this, but it's okay."

She whips her head to me. "It's okay?" Disbelief in her tone.

"Yeah, it really is." I don't blame her for the skepticism. She watched me suffer for years all because of what this man's actions set in motion. She picked me up so many times, I would be more concerned if she wasn't shocked. But ever since that morning four and a half months ago, she hasn't had to save me from myself once. It's because of that morning, the man I ran from, and the help the sequence of events that preceded that run led to, I know I really am okay.

"We'll be in my office," I tell Piper. "Thomas," I add, turning and walking away without checking to see if he follows.

I feel my calm strengthen as I keep walking. Each clip of my heel against the floor acting like a soundtrack of proof to how much I've healed and grown.

I'm not lost.

I'm not alone.

I have people in my life who care about me. Nothing Thomas can say will change that, and for once, there isn't a single bit of pain to be found smothering me.

He's no one now.

The door to my office shuts quietly at the same time I glance up from the chair I had settled in behind my desk, steepling my hands together on the wood surface. My eyes track his movements as he takes a seat in the chair across from me, his gaze doing a sweep of the room as he does.

"What do you want, Thomas? It's been an awfully long time to just show up for a chat."

His hands move, and I catch the glint of light that reflects off the shiny gold band on his hand. Funny, seeing that there actually does nothing.

"I, uh …" he starts, his Adam's apple bobbing when he stops speaking to swallow. "You look good, Ari."

I snort and lean back. "You're a ghost for seven years, and now you pop up to tell me I look good? Thanks, but that isn't something I need you to tell me."

He flinches. Aside from the odd shadow of unease, it doesn't look like he's changed a great deal. His blond hair duller but still sporting the same cut he had since the day we met. Short and boring. His suit is perfectly pressed, gray with a light blue shirt as he always wore. I couldn't help but notice he's even kept his lean runner's body over the years. No beer gut for him.

So different from Thorn, my gentle giant. Seeing Thomas after all this time, I'm struck by just how different they really are. Dark against blond. Blue-green magic against dull brown. Powerful body against wiry and almost thin. Tall against … average. The man who owns my heart against the one who never deserved it.

Just as quickly as the image of Thorn popped through my

mind, I feel the rush of courage loving him has given me flourish.

"This … it's not easy being here. Seeing you."

A laugh bubbles free. "You 'see' me every day, if I'm not mistaken." Reminding him of his wife—my twin.

His eyes flash, stark white agony and sadness tangling together. He's not even trying to hide it. Heck, it's almost like he's intentionally projecting it toward me.

"I see someone who looks like you, Ari, but will never come close to being anything more than an imitation."

"I hate to point out the obvious, but"—I point at his hand, the one with the wedding band—"aside from the evident proof that she had to have been something more to do what you both did to ensure that band was placed on your hand by her and not me, I believe you told me you got lucky and had the right sister the last time we spoke."

"I've seen you," he whispers uncomfortably, shifting in his seat and leaning forward, elbows to thighs.

"There sure does seem to be a lot of 'seeing' accounting to your confusing state, Thomas."

"I thought I was right, you know," he continues, ignoring my sarcasm. "I really thought I had the right one."

"Such a blessing for you that they had twins at the pick-a-bride store. Heaven forbid you pick incorrectly." I roll my eyes.

"It wasn't like that, Ari."

I toss my arms in the air. "It pretty much was, Thomas. Look, I don't know why you're here, but please just get it over with so I can get to the rest of my plans for today."

Something washes over his face, a wave of emotion that is gone too quickly for me to understand. "You never moved on. I always wondered if that was because I was wrong, and you were waiting for me to realize that. I would remember things that you would do, things London doesn't do, and just fucking wonder. Always popping up in my mind. Then, almost instantly, you would hit my memories, and then like I conjured you up myself, you would just appear."

"Thomas—"

"Are you happy?" he interjects.

"Unbelievably so."

He glances down, looking at his feet, and his head nods slowly. "I thought as much."

"You've seen why I'm happy, haven't you?" I question, knowing that could be the only explanation to why he would just show up after this long looking upset. He doesn't want me, but he doesn't want anyone else to either. He just didn't know that until I found Thorn, my time alone, with no one, ended for good.

He keeps nodding, then looks up. I have to fight the urge to flinch when I see his misty eyes.

"I needed to know. I had to hear it from you. Needed to see for myself that what I did wasn't still affecting your life."

"Then please, Thomas, hear me. I'm beyond happy. You and London, you don't even cross my mind anymore. The only thing I think about from that time is my parents. If anything, I should thank you. If it wasn't for what you two did, I wouldn't be able to really understand just how beautiful my life could be."

He doesn't speak. Heck, I'm not even sure he's breathing.

"I'm where I was always meant to be, with the person who I undoubtedly know was made for me. So, thank you for ensuring I was ready for him when fate brought him to me."

He blinks.

"Forget about whatever it is that you've held on to, Thomas. I have."

Silence ticks on when I finish laying it out. The open door to his emotions has closed, and he's become stoic and still.

"Thomas, really, you came here because you said you needed to see I had moved on. You got that assurance. I've said all I wish to say. If there's more, please get on with it. I have somewhere I really want to be."

He frowns but gives the tiniest nod. "You're right. I just needed to see for myself that you were what appeared to be true." He stands, and I stay in my chair. "I hope he can keep you that way. For what it's worth, I'll always remember the good times we had, and I'm sorry for my part in what happened back then."

"It's in the past, Thomas. Go back to your wife."

He lets out a heavy breath, then turns and grabs the doorknob. But I call his name before he can open it.

"Tell my sister to stop contacting me. No more calls. I mean it, Thomas. I've had to deal with her constant bullshit, misplaced guilt, and angry rants for far too long."

"I'll take care of London. Be happy, Ari." He waits, clearly hoping for something more from me, but when it becomes clear that I'm well and truly done, he opens the door and exits my office.

The chapters of my past—the ones I felt a heavy-handed backstroke had erased from existence—no longer feel like they were lost years to me anymore. The binding of my life's book shifts inside my mind, making room, and replacing those old chapters with something rewritten. Rewritten with the lessons I had to be taught from the pain I no longer felt.

Until that moment, I don't think I realized just how far I've come in the time since Thorn came into my life and gave me more than I could have ever dreamed of. Thorn gave me the drive and Dr. Hart gave me the tools, but *I* was the one who took those gifts and built a path of courage toward the beautiful life I deserved. The one Thorn was at my side step by step for.

I look toward the closed door that Thomas left through and feel a symbolic door inside me shutting as closure settles.

The past locked away behind it conquered with a finality.

The future before me bright with promise, not a shadow left in the sky.

TWENTY-NINE

Ari

All the beauty that is you

PULL INTO THE DRIVE AT THORN'S HOUSE LATER THAT NIGHT. It's a miracle that I was only thirty minutes past the two hours I told Thorn I would be here by. I had left Trend with more than enough time to be here, but in the end, it didn't matter. Not when I have a cat that seems to have only one job on this earth … to terrorize me. He's been wailing loudly since we left my house. I swear my ears are seconds away from bleeding. He started tossing himself against the sides of his carrier about five minutes ago when his complaints went unappreciated. Five very long minutes.

I knew from past experiences that Dwight did not travel well. As in, at all. So the carrier had become a must. It's also why we rarely brought the cats over from my place. It had never been this bad before. That was also because Dwight didn't show his ass much around Thorn, and each time before, Thorn had been with us.

At least I could count on Jim. He started purring in my arms while I held him and loaded everything in the car. I decided to test his car riding abilities before going in to chase down the cat beast, Dwight, by doing a quick spin around the block with Jim. He curled up in the passenger seat the second I turned on the car and hasn't stopped purring once.

Thorn is waiting for me when I pull into the empty space in his massive garage. A space I knew he made possible. Not only because I watched him free it up himself, but because he had told me the night before he did it that he was making sure I had a spot of my own.

Making room for me.

Making it known he wanted that before it had even been something I thought of.

"Hey, honey," I greet softly when he pulls my door open for me.

"Babe."

"You know, you wouldn't have to babe me if you would have just waited a second for me to get out of the car and give it to you. Now you've said it and you want it without giving me some space to stand." He continues to look down at me for a second before stepping back—which wasn't much of a step, if I'm being honest with myself. Jim gives an adorable kitten meow, so I scoop him up before climbing up from my seat into the sliver of space Thorn allotted me. "Bend down, honey."

He bends instantly.

"Hi," I breathe against his lips, then press mine to his and kiss him with everything I've got.

He makes a sound deep in his chest, his hands sliding into my hair as he holds me close. Jim wiggles and twists. I lose him when I feel his little body lift off my arm. I feel him move so I know he's safe but don't stop greeting my man the way he likes to be greeted. I pull away first, even though that's the last thing I want, because I have an evil cat to free before he harms himself.

I grin up at Thorn, lick my lips, and go back to press one more quick peck against his soft mouth. Then I see my sweet Jim perched on his shoulder.

"Uh, how did he get way up there?"

Thorn, not even fazed by the friend on his shoulder, shrugs. "Climbed."

"Climbed? As in, he climbed you, and you didn't take him from me and put him there?" I don't let him answer, pulling his shirt up and searching for claw marks on his skin. I run my hand over his stomach and chest, bending and twisting my head to check the spots camouflaged by his tattoos.

"Used my shirt, Ari, but even if his claws had got me, I wouldn't have felt that shit. Not when you're finally back in my arms."

"Honey." I sigh. "You make it sound like it's been years."

"To me, it sure felt like it."

And, that's what a full body swoon feels like.

"You know, for a man who's never had a girlfriend before, you sure do know how to give good woo."

He cocks a brow. "I don't have a fucking clue what a woo is, but if the truth gives it to you, guess that's no hardship."

"Yeah, Thorn, it's definitely no hardship."

He opens his mouth to say something but closes it with a shocked glance toward my back seat when Dwight gives a particularly powerful sign of his impatient anger.

"How about you hang on to the one that's content, and I'll get the beast?"

He reaches up, lifts Jim gingerly, and hands him to me. "Go on inside and let me deal with my Dwight. Jim at least knows how to share."

For Pete's sake. If he wants to deal with the demon, I'm surely not going to argue. It should bother me that Dwight tucks that evil in when Thorn's around, but it's seriously the most adorable thing I've ever seen. Well, tied now with the vision of Jim sitting like a proud little thing on his shoulder that is.

Dwight stops his nonsense the second Thorn opens the door and holds his hand to the carrier door. I don't stick around to watch Dwight's pitiful act of sanity return just from sniffing Thorn. I walk around to the other side, grab my bag and purse, and head inside. The heavenly scent of food lures me to the kitchen. I see a covered saucepan on the stove and the oven ticking down with twenty minutes remaining.

"They need to eat?" Thorn asks, coming into the kitchen behind me.

"Yeah," I answer, walking to the corner that Thorn had set up as the cat's, grabbing what I need from the cabinet closest to prepare their dinner. Neither cat wastes a second digging in when I place both dishes down next to the obviously fresh water. I love that he thought to do that.

"Dinner smells good," I observe, leaning against the island and taking the wine that Thorn had poured for me while I fed the cats.

"Stuffed peppers. You mentioned wanting them early last week, but things got busy. Figured it wasn't a long shot that you'd still enjoy them."

"You weren't wrong."

He takes a drink of his beer, places it on the counter, and then pulls the glass he just gave me from my hand after I take a sip. His hands land on the island, close enough for me to feel their warmth on my side. He bends close, and his eyes search mine silently. The intensity in his gaze making me shift on my heels.

"You woke something up inside me that had been unconscious for a long time, Ari. I'm not even sure there was a time it wasn't just beating through life, completely worthless aside from the job it did to keep me breathing. God, baby." He exhales, licks his lips, and gives a little shake of his head.

My heart pounds wild and fierce. Everything in my mind goes blank except this man before me. I lift my hands, palms to his cheeks, and … hold on.

"Knew you were different, baby. Even when I didn't realize why I could know that with the certainty I felt deep. Felt that from the jump. Then you, all the beauty that is you, just kept giving me more proof that I wasn't wrong."

"Thorn, honey," I whisper, his words affecting me profoundly.

"Love you, too, Ari. More than you could ever fucking know."

My chin wobbles, drawing his attention.

Which is precisely the moment I burst into tears.

His strong arms pull me in, and I cry against his chest, feeling that heart beating against my cheek. Each thump against my skin doing what it always does, calling out to mine until their rhythm is matched, beat for beat. There's no doubt in my mind that his wasn't the only heart beating away, unconscious and incapable of doing anything more than giving life to the body it resided in.

"The time I'm willing to wait for you to be settled here, where you belong, just got cut short," Thorn tells me, his voice deeper with my ear pressed against him. "A lot fucking shorter. As in, it's gone."

"Honey."

He leans away, and I'm forced to move before I fall on my face. His finger presses lightly under my chin, pulling my eyes to his. "You aren't there yet; a month is as generous as I feel like I can be. Spent over forty years living without feeling in my own life. Each year, I felt like I wouldn't ever find more than what I had fought to have. I don't feel like waiting anymore now."

"It's so soon."

"It's not soon enough. I wanted you here two months ago, Ari."

"You really want me here? Me and my cats?"

"I really want you here. You and the damn cats."

"I woke you up?"

"Wide-awake, baby."

"You gave me back my life," I confess, clearing my throat and trying really hard to push through the emotions burning up my throat. "You weren't the only one asleep, Thorn. You love me?"

"Woke my heart up, Ari. Beats for only you now."

"I love you." A sob makes my whole body jerk. His face gets soft, and he puts me right back where I want to be—pressed tightly against him. "I'm going to fill up your closet."

He moves us, maneuvering our bodies, and lifts me to sit on the island, stepping between my legs.

"Then I'll buy a bigger house. You finally moving in with me?"

I nod, tears still pouring down, and smile so big and wide it makes my cheeks burn.

Two hours later, dinner was also burnt.

THIRTY

THORN

There's nothing I wouldn't do

ARI'S PHONE CHIMES, AND SHE GROANS. THE PAINFUL sound reminding me of what happened last night. Well, what happened much later last night, that is. I wish I could take her pain away, but I know she needs to get it out.

Last night, after I showed her how I felt about her giving me all that she had, we tossed the burnt dinner in the trash and ordered Chinese. She hadn't even finished hers before she was running out of the kitchen with her hand over her mouth. She was on her knees heaving into the toilet when I got to her. I've never felt so helpless—not once in my life—and fuck knows there were plenty of times I should have. I held her hair, wiped her neck with a cool washcloth, and then carried her to bed after she'd emptied her stomach and didn't have anything left to come up.

She slept hard.

I didn't sleep at all.

And that goddamn phone was too far for me to reach and silence.

The big cat shifts against my back, the same place he's been since I pulled Ari into my arms last night. I can't see the clock on the other side of the bed, but judging by the light filling the room, it's still early.

The reminder of the text sounds, and Ari grumbles.

"Leave it, baby," I tell her, not wanting her to get sick again.

"Piper's week off starts today. I told her before I left yesterday that there was no sense in her waiting until Monday when the other girls can handle it over the weekend. I can't ignore it in case it's one of my openers, though."

I lift my arm and let her move out of the bed, kicking my ass for moving it in here and plugging it in last night after I had cleaned the kitchen. She goes to the bathroom and not the table across the room where our phones are charging.

I throw back the covers and follow her. Even though I can hear she isn't getting sick, I don't want to be a room away if she starts again.

She's brushing her teeth when I walk into the room, looking tired but fucking beautiful. She finishes while I'm walking back to the sink after using the restroom. I kiss her temple and wash my hands before brushing my own. She moves slowly but goes to the toilet, shutting the door behind her—something I find fucking cute as hell that she gets shy about. Almost as cute as her blushing when she comes back to wash her hands before leaving the room. I just keep brushing and shake my head.

It happened when I lifted a handful of water to my mouth to rinse.

A sharp gasp burst from her.

I heard it over the sound of water running.

Fear.

I'm at her side a second later, ripping the phone from her hand.

"The fuck?" I roar when I see the text on the screen.

London: You need to watch your back.

"What does that mean?" Ari cries, falling into my arms and clinging to me. "Oh, God!" She pulls back and looks at me with wide eyes. "With everything that happened last night, getting here and … well, everything, I didn't even think. I meant to, I did. Then you told me you loved me, and nothing else mattered. Even if it means feeling this way right now, it was worth the ugly not sticking to the memories of what we shared last night. I need you to know I didn't mean to forget, honey. I really did mean to tell you!"

She's frantic and not making any sense. I feel the truth of what I can understand in her tone, but it's the desperation and her tight grip on me that makes me feel like I'm not going to like whatever it is she forgot to mention last night.

"Just tell me, Ari."

"T-Tommy," she cries with a strangled breath.

Rage consumes me. That fucking fuck.

"I didn't mean to keep it from you! You have to believe me."

It takes a lot of effort to push down the beast roaring inside me, knowing she needs me to be her man before I can be her protector. After I give her what she needs to hear, then I can be both.

"Stop, Ari. I was right there with you last night. There was only one thing either of us could focus on. You're telling me now. That's all that matters."

"I wouldn't keep this from you. I wouldn't."

"Enough," I stress firmly. She jumps, sucking in a choppy breath. "Whatever you're thinking, just stop. I understand, baby. I know you didn't mean to. Now tell me what the fuck happened."

Her chin trembles, and her eyes fill with tears, but none spill over.

"I love you remember," I remind her, pulling her tight. "I'm right here, Ari. Let me shoulder this shit for you, and stop thinking about anything else."

"He stopped by Trend," she says so soft and meekly, I have to strain to hear her. "It was weird seeing him, but I think he really thought he was there for some sort of well check. He saw us. I'm not sure when, but he saw us together at some point. He knew what he was seeing, but for whatever reason, felt he needed to check. He said he needed to hear from me, after seeing my life on pause for so many years, that I was happy and moving on. It was awkward, more for him because he looked miserable with his own life, but not for me. Even knowing he had to have seen me often to know how long I was on pause. I didn't spare him the enormity of just how happy I am now and just who you are to me, but in the end, I made sure he knew just how happy you made me. He said some things that make me think he harbors a lot of sadness and regret, but he wasn't there long. He didn't even get close to me. Just sat across from my desk. Before he left, though, God … before he left, I told him to get control of London and make sure she stops her crap. He must have told her."

I stare at that text with her trembling in my arms and silently vow to do everything I possibly can to ensure she never feels this again. It looks like I had my investigator looking into the wrong fucking person.

"London do something to need you to have him stop her?"

She shakes her head, lines appearing between her brows. "No, I mean, I don't think so. There've been a few hang-ups at Trend, but nothing that would make me assume it was anything other than a wrong number. We've gotten them regularly enough over the years that I don't think it was her. She always came up on the caller ID. I said it to him because history indicated she wouldn't stop, no matter how long of a break she gave me between her bouts of crap. She would always come back and spew her venom."

"And the text?"

"I have no idea, Thorn. What does she mean by that? He must have made it sound like it was something it wasn't. Otherwise, it makes no sense."

"No clue. But I'm about to find out."

I lift her phone, jam my finger against the top of the text screen, and pull up the contact for her fucking sister. It's against my ear and ringing before Ari can stop me. Her wide eyes don't look away, her tits heaving under the shirt she pulled from my closet last night.

The line connects.

I know it's her sister. She had just enough time to get a syllable of Ari's full name out, and that was a second too long.

"You have some fucking nerve," I growl, my throat red hot with the rage I feel. She starts to speak, but I cut her off. "Shut the fuck up. You speak, it's when I've asked you a goddamn question, and I better not hear a peep otherwise. You sent that shit, but you better take fucking notes. You get near Ari, I'll destroy you. Do you hear me?"

"Yes," the sister replies. Instantly. Weakly. Fucking coward hiding behind her phone.

"You forget her number. Forget she even exists. Never again will you pick up that phone and so much as think about her with it in your hand. Do you understand *that?*"

"I-yes."

"You fucked up. Not her. You fucked up and then continued to fuck up. Either of you fucking contact Ari again, I'll have my team dig up everything they fucking can and bury both of you. I don't know you. You mean shit to me, but she means the world, and I promise you this, I get even an inkling that you're so much as thinking about Ari, I'll find you. No hole will be deep enough to hide in. No shadow dark enough to conceal you. No distance I won't travel to make sure you understand what *the fuck* I'm willing to do to protect my whole goddamn world. Do you get that?" My ears ring, my throat aches, and my heart pounds. I'm bloodthirsty to make this bitch pay for every second of the seven years Ari felt pain from the destruction her sister's actions set in motion.

"Y-yes."

This time, she sounds like she understands exactly what will happen if she so much as looks the wrong way while crossing the street. She seemed like she wanted to say more, but she wisely didn't. I know what I sound like when that kind of anger takes over. I hang up and toss Ari's phone down on the table, wishing I had shattered it against the wall instead. I hope that bitch takes heed of what I said. That's the only warning I'll ever give her.

I meant every fucking word. There's nothing I wouldn't do for Ari. If it came down to it, I'd step in front of any harm meant for her. Nothing, not one thing, I wouldn't do to ensure she's breathing that easy life I promised her months ago. Nothing.

"From now on, she doesn't exist for you either, baby. She and that motherfucker she's saddled with. I mean what I said; I'll put someone on both of them, and they won't ever recover when I'm done if they even think about continuing this shit with you. They don't get a part of our future. Not a single day. Not a minute. Not even thirty fucking seconds."

Ari wipes her eyes and nods.

"You need to talk about that shit?"

She shakes her head.

"You sure?"

"No. You're right. They don't get this. They took enough; they can't have this." She sucks in her breath, straightens her shoulders, and forces a smile. "Thank you."

"Told you, beats only for you, baby. I'll protect that until the day I die. Now, you want to try to eat something or get back in bed and start this day the right way?"

"A redo sounds good, honey. Then maybe breakfast."

"Anything, Ari. Anything for you."

THIRTY-ONE

Ari

You're something else

IT'S BEEN FIVE DAYS SINCE THE MORNING THORN UNLEASHED A wrath unlike I've ever seen on London. It was a brilliant display of power that I'll never forget. Seeing him like that, knowing it came from his love for me—wanting to protect me from what London's always done—made it easy for me to do just what he said before he took me back to bed. London and Thomas won't get a single piece of our future. Not when they've taken enough as it is. I've had my time to grieve the loss of London and, if I'm honest with myself, that happened before she stole the man I almost married. Heck, I should be sending her a fruit basket and thanking her for ensuring I was ready to receive the gift of Thorn when fate brought him to me.

It didn't hurt that I had a session with Dr. Hart two days after that call.

I've suffered enough. I've buried myself for too long under that pain. I'm done allowing them control over my happiness. They had that for seven long years, but I'm in control now.

I'll never stop missing my parents. I'll never stop grieving the loss of them. But I'll take each day I have left on this earth and live my life with Thorn's love knowing, if they were watching over me, they would be so beyond pleased with where my pain brought me in the end.

The only thing weighing on my mind now is Piper.

Well, the only thing on my mind *now* is Piper. I had a few days to process them, but that's it. Now it's all her.

The weekend I was supposed to spend alone with Thorn didn't go as planned. Friday and into Monday was spent with the stomach bug that's been breeding its nastiness for the past two months between Barcode and The Alibi. The same one that kept us apart for days in the first place. I went in to Trend Tuesday, but since then, I've only worked a few hours a day, not wanting to overdo it. I have competent and well trained employees, and I know they can handle it anytime I'm not there. There are still things that only Piper or me can do, which is the only reason I've felt a little guilty for not being able to be there longer.

I did find it terribly funny that, while I had spent a few days closing up the painful memories of my past, I had also been vomiting randomly the whole time. It seemed like a fitting time. Purging them from my life, literally.

Then there's Piper.

Through my days with the bug, I kept trying to contact my best friend.

Every single day since Saturday, I've called her, and it's so unlike her not to answer my calls. We've never spent more than a day without talking or, at the very least, texting. We didn't talk much after Thomas left either. I was in a rush to get to Thorn at the time, so it was even more out of place that she wouldn't at least pick up when I called.

I was worried.

I was beyond worried, and I needed to do something about it.

Which just brings me to the little monkey on my back. Or, rather, the fact that ever since my sister sent that text on Saturday, Thorn's been a constant shadow. He doesn't say it, but I think London's text, his call to her, and the visit I had from Thomas was just too much for him at once. It's better today than it's been. He finally went in to The Alibi to deal with things he couldn't ignore any longer, but that didn't mean I would head to Piper's without at least asking him if he wanted to come with me. A week from now, yes. But not when he's left me for the first time since that happened only hours before.

I pad through his house, almost tripping over Dwight when he darts out in front of me. I left my phone in the kitchen when I went to get dressed, intending to use Thorn's massive in-home gym after I cleaned some around the house. But that could wait until later.

"Thorn," he barks in the phone.

"Hey. You okay, honey?"

His phone picks up the rush of air that leaves his mouth. "Sorry, Ari. Just busy. What do you need, baby? Something wrong?"

"Nothing is wrong. Just wanted to let you know I wanted to head over to Piper's. I need to check on her. I know you've been working through some stuff, so I was calling to tell you what I planned in case you wanted to come with me."

"I didn't think it was that obvious." He laughs halfheartedly. "I'm fine, baby. With you getting sick on top of that other shit, it just fucked with my head. It was more because you got sick from that stomach bug than anything else. Didn't help when you told me you got so tired you were struggling to stay awake while driving home from Trend yesterday."

"I know. I understand it too, Thorn. I do."

"I can't get away. I would if I could, but I have to deal with this shit. If you want to go check on her, I think it's a good idea, but let me see if Wilder can drive you to ease my mind. With him there, I won't have to worry that you'll overdo it, causing that shit to come back."

"Okay, honey."

"I'll call you back if he can't; otherwise, I'll make sure he comes right over."

"Sounds good. Thank you for taking care of me."

"Nothing else I'd rather do. Love you, baby."

"Love you, too."

We disconnect, and I finish up the things I had been in the middle of before the need to drive to Piper became something I couldn't postpone a second longer this morning.

"How does that mess in the back seat not bother you?"

Wilder scoffs.

"It would bother me. And your windows aren't tinted. That's embarrassing, Wil."

"It's been a busy week," he grumbles.

"It was so busy that you couldn't pick up the sea of condoms in the back seat? Isn't there some warning about heat and direct sunlight making them ineffective?"

Wilder looks over at me in horror before focusing back on the road. "That's not funny."

I giggle. "Actually, it really was. You should have seen your face. Why *do* you have all those condoms back there anyway?"

The slight blush on his cheeks is ridiculously charming even when we're talking about condoms. This man watched Thorn give me a strip tease months ago, and he's constantly giving us a hard time about always being locked away with each other when we go for drinks at Barcode or even meet him for dinner. One thing he's never been is bashful. Well, unless the very girl we're headed to check on is around, that is.

"I didn't mean to have condoms back there, okay? Let's just call it a Costco trip gone wrong and leave it at that."

My lips twitch.

"Plus, you make it sound much worse than it is. There's probably only fifty or sixty of them."

"You need that many?" I ask in shock.

He looks over, blush gone and a wolfish grin in place. "Babe."

"God, you sound like Thorn."

"Taught him everything I know. Which means you shouldn't be surprised by Costco condom runs."

Now it's my turn to blush. He turns into Piper's neighborhood, and I stare out the window. I close my eyes, my cheeks getting hotter when he makes a sound of disbelief.

"You two are practically fused together, and you're getting shy on me over condoms?"

"It's not that." I giggle at the picture of Thorn and me fused together.

"Look, if you aren't ready for Costco runs, just dig into the sea back there," he jokes, laughing at himself.

"For your information, we don't need them."

I point at her house, and he pulls his car into the driveway.

"I'm afraid to ask why you don't need them. Mainly because this conversation is putting shit in my mind that has no right to be there, but also because I'm concerned your answer means I didn't teach that bastard a thing after all. Pride and ego, Ari. Pride. And. Ego."

"How about you just shut up about it and stop thinking about my sex life with Thorn?"

"Fucking hell. You two want to play with fire, go ahead. This conversation is stopping before I envision something I'll never forget."

"You're something else, Wilder."

He opens his door and turns to look at me with that wolfish grin again. "You don't need to butter me up, darlin'. I like you already."

I roll my eyes but ignore him, not wanting to egg him on further. "Come on. I've got a spare key, and I'm not afraid to use it."

"Thorn know you might go all breaking and entering if he misses some calls from you?"

"For your information," I call over my shoulder, "there haven't been just some calls missed. Over the past five days, I've called her over and over. Piper and I don't do that. So I'm here. And Thorn wouldn't ignore my calls." I don't point out that I can't break and enter into a house that I'll be sharing with him as soon as I can get my stuff moved in. I'll let Thorn have the honors.

"Whatever you say."

I unlock the door and step inside the dark house. The lights are all off and the blinds all pulled. The air still. Too still. A chill rolls down my spine, and I shake it off. Wilder is by my side instantly. He's alert with all signs of the jokester gone, hiding behind his stern focus. We move into the house, him in front of me. My eyes roaming the mess. A broken table by the front door, the one where she used to keep her keys and toss her mail on. A vase shattered near the living room, the flowers that had been in it all over the floor. I'm sure, at one point, there had also been a giant wet spot. We keep walking, more signs of something wrong scattered here and there.

We go through three more rooms before we find Piper. She's curled into a ball on her bed, tucked so tight I had missed her in the sea of pillows and bedding the first time I glanced into the bedroom.

"Piper!" I cry, rushing forward, but stop when Wilder's hand prevents me from moving anymore. "Hey!"

"Get pissed all you want. Wait a fucking second." He steps forward, leaning over her prone form, and pulls the comforter off her face. Tenderly, something so unlike him, he brushes the tangled hair out of her face. A sharp curse leaves him that has me moving. I don't care what he says. She looks away from him and blinks up at me with tears falling. One eye swollen and bruised, and a cut on her lip that's not fresh but still ugly. When she sees me, the tears start falling.

"Oh, Pipe."

"I …" She closes her eyes. "I think I'm ready to take you up on that offer now. That is, if you still need a cat watcher/plant waterer/ or whatever other excuse you tried to come up with to get me out of here. I'm so sorry I didn't listen to you. I'm so sorry."

"None of that, Pipe. I hate that I have to ask, but where is Matt? Do we have time, or should we rush?"

She shrugs one shoulder and winces. "He hasn't been back. Not for a few days. He shouldn't be … God, he's not been back. Not even to check that I was … he's …" She takes a shuddered breath.

"We have time."

God, my Piper.

"Shh," I coo. "None of that. Let Wilder get you sorted with some ice on that eye. You just rest on the couch, and I'll take care of everything else. You're safe now."

We both help her get up. She's moving slow, and even though I can't see any other visible injuries, I don't doubt there's more than the eye can see. Wilder leaves with her, the expression on his face sticking with me while I go about packing as much of Piper's life as I can fit in whatever suitcases, duffles, and totes I can find. We won't get it all, but I'll make sure there isn't anything here that she can't live without. Just in case.

I just finish zipping up the last duffle bag I found in her closet when Wilder walks back in the bedroom. I sway a little when I straighten, reaching out to grab the edge of the dresser to steady myself. Pressing my hand to my stomach, I pray the stomach bug isn't about to rear up and bite me again.

"You okay?"

I nod, swallowing the warm rush of saliva.

"It pass?" he asks when I drop my hand a minute later.

"Yeah. I think so, at least."

"Hmm," he hums.

"What?"

"Nothing."

"Wilder," I drawl.

"Hey, none of my business, remember? Just that everyone I know who got that nasty shit, it didn't ever just 'pass' for them. Not once while they had it. Guess you're lucky." He winks, but I can see past that and the anger that's boiling close to the surface over what we walked in on. "Or you have a different issue making you nauseous that Costco could've prevented."

"Oh, shut up. I'm on the pill!"

"Whoa," he grunts when I slap his hard stomach. "Just saying. Want some of that sea now? Just in case?"

"You're ridiculous. I'm putting this last bag in the car. You get Pipe. No more talking about condoms, sex, or *anything*!"

He laughs for a second before his face falls when Piper moans in pain from the other room, and then he gets serious, leaving the room. I heave the bag over my shoulder and walk to the car. All I let myself think about is Piper. She needs me. Once she's settled and I make sure she doesn't need medical help, then I can sit down and try to remember when I had my last period.

Shit.

When we get to my house, I help Piper get cleaned up. Aside from the eye and her lip, she didn't have any other injuries, but she desperately needed a shower. At least, she assured me that she didn't. Wilder didn't leave the hall outside the guest bathroom once. Not until I led her to my bed and tucked her in. He was at her side when

I stepped away, one finger gliding over the brow above her swollen eye, not touching her injury. She let him, her eyes closing, and I suddenly felt like I was watching something that wasn't meant for me to see.

He stepped back, moment forgotten, but didn't leave the room. Since Piper didn't exactly seem to want him gone, I chose to ignore him and sat on the side of the bed to ask her what happened. Three days she had laid in that bed alone after the argument with Matt that resulted in her being hurt, only leaving to use the restroom and try to eat. She was holding it together, but I also wasn't going to test that and push for more. Namely being where the heck Matt was. She was safe. That's what mattered.

When I left the room, Wilder followed. The second I closed the door quietly, he started moving like a man on a mission.

And he hasn't stopped since.

He pulled the stuff I packed up out of the car and moved it into one of the guest rooms. He even drove back to her house and loaded her car up with all the things from her closet I couldn't fit. I tried to hide the shock when he left for a second time. It only lasted briefly, though. The large pile in the middle of my guest room he'd created only grew as he continued coming back with more loads. When he heaved in a huge television that I know for a fact had been hanging on her living room wall, I decided not to even touch whatever was happening in his head. Clearly, something was driving him. Though, I'm pretty sure what they had successfully ignored over the months wouldn't be unnoticed any longer. I left the guest room and let him do what he needed. If he wanted to keep driving over there and take everything but the kitchen sink, I wasn't stopping him. I secretly hoped that Matt would cross his path while he was there, so Wilder could teach him a lesson.

"I think you got everything that matters … and then some," I tell him three hours later when he walked out of the guest room and didn't storm out of the house. Five trips. Apparently, that's all he needed.

"One less thing she has to think about."

"I'm not sure she's going to need the shelves from a bookcase without the actual bookcase, though."

"Couldn't fit the case, brought the shelves instead."

Goodness, what I wouldn't do to see the state he left that house in.

"Thank you, Wilder. You didn't have to do all of this, but it means a lot. I know it will for her too, even if she might need your help figuring out what to do with shelves and no case."

He shakes his head. "Is she okay?"

"She will be. Piper's not alone, and she's stronger than she thinks. She's safe, and that's what matters."

"Good. That's good."

His voice is strained and his face pinched tight, but I leave it be. I don't want to pry when I have a feeling he needs to figure out what he's feeling himself.

"How about I give Thorn a ring and then order us something to eat?"

He glances down the hallway to my bedroom before looking back at me. "Yeah, that sounds good. I'm sure he'll want me to stick around until he can get here anyway."

I don't confirm that he very well might. Especially since I'm pretty sure Wilder said that to justify staying to himself, regardless.

God, what a crazy day.

THIRTY-TWO

Ari

I'll never stop waiting

I NEED MORE HANGERS.

A lot more hangers.

I step back and blow a piece of hair out of my eye. The last dress that I needed to hang sways on the metal rod slightly. Next to that one, about twenty more from the same color family. I still have about half of my stuff left to transfer to Thorn's, but what's here fills so much of the empty space that had been here before, the transformation is shocking. No more sea of gray and black in here. Nope. Not with my colorful wardrobe.

The shoes, still sitting near his, make me smile every time I see them. There is tons of space to use the shelves near my clothes for them, but if he doesn't mind, I'm leaving some of my collection right there sidled up to his for a while. At least, until it no longer gives me butterflies when I see it.

Aside from some personal items, the rest of my closet's contents, and what few important furniture pieces I had from my parents, I had all but moved in. Thorn's spent every single chance he gets showing me just how much he likes that I'm here, too.

I stayed with Piper at my house for a week before she nicely asked me to stop coddling her. That was the same day Wilder showed up with a work crew and installed some super fancy alarm in the house. He said Thorn called him to let him know I was going home—to Thorn's—but he was lying. How he knew I was leaving, I still don't know. I just gave Piper a hug and reminded her I was only a call away. Her need for space was just a little greater than her desire to settle into the house that would become hers. When she was ready to deal with the paperwork of me giving it to her, that is.

Just like I told Wilder that day we brought her there, she's stronger than she realized. I hate what it took for her to realize what she couldn't accept before, but I know she'll pick herself up and find her way. Until she does, I'll be there every step of the way. Lord knows she's done the same for me over the years. So many times I lost count. Now I can return the favor.

I took her need for space and threw myself in it. Using the past two days that Thorn's been busy at work, I've avoided the huge elephant in my mind by moving my things into *our* home.

It was pointless to ignore what I knew couldn't be ignored. Not when I had five positive pregnancy tests hiding in my purse.

My stomach roils, and I close my eyes, a tear rolling down my cheek.

This is bad. Really, really bad.

It didn't matter, logically, that what worried me was that I fell in love with just the thought of what those positive tests meant instantly. Not when they could be the reason I lose everything else.

In the end, it didn't matter that Thorn and I loved each other completely.

It didn't matter that I knew that love was something some people never find. The kind that, without a doubt, we would still have for each other until the day we left this earth.

What mattered was how Thorn would feel when I told him that my birth control failed, and he was going to be a father.

A father he had told me he didn't ever want to be.

If I tell you I never want to ruin a kid by passing on the shit I'm made from, is that a deal breaker for you?

I swat at my cheeks when more tears fall, his words from the Mexican restaurant parking lot slamming into me. It wouldn't have been a deal breaker. I know that now in my gut. He would have always been enough. Fate, on the other hand, apparently had something else in store for us.

You've changed the way I look at things, a lot of things I never thought I would change my mind on, but I'm not sure kids would be one of those things even the beauty of you could fix.

The echo of his words keeps coming, and the tears speed up.

He has no idea. None. Knowing that he doesn't think he's worthy of bringing a child into this world is heartbreaking enough. It wasn't until he told me he wasn't sure the beauty our love gave him would be enough to change his mind that I realized how serious he was.

The only thing I know for sure is, no matter what happens when I tell him, this baby is made from love, and I'll do everything I can to prove to Thorn just how incredible he is … and how lucky our baby will be to have him as its father. If that doesn't work, I'll be crushed, but I won't be alone. I'll raise what our love created, my heart beating for his still—but also our child, and know I'll never find someone else to share that with.

"Ari!" Thorn calls, startling me from my thoughts.

Is it already six? Crap.

I grab my phone from the shelf I had placed it on and flinch. Quarter to seven. He's late, not surprising, since he's still short staffed at The Alibi.

His heat covers my back, and I pull in a deep breath, the scent of his cologne soothing some of my anxiety. His arms wrap around me, giving a little hug, then he drops them, and I know what's coming next.

"Babe."

I close my eyes, hoping they aren't too red, and turn. When I open them and blink up at him, the kiss he wanted is completely forgotten.

"What the fuck?"

"That obvious, huh?"

"That you've been crying? Yeah. Real obvious, Ari. What's wrong? Is it Piper?"

I shake my head. "Come on. Let's go sit down."

"I don't want to sit down. What I want is for you to tell me what's got you standing in the closet crying."

"Please, Thorn. Let's just go sit down."

"What. The fuck. Is wrong!" he bellows.

"I'm pregnant!" I yell back, the confession bursting forth sloppily when his agitation just kept growing and my already frazzled thoughts couldn't handle it. I should have taken care, though. I should have dragged him to the damn couch myself and been strong enough to hold back until I did.

"What did you just say?" He doesn't sound angry—but the lack of *any* emotion in his tone is scary nonetheless.

I exhale, long and loud. Thorn is standing so still, I wouldn't be shocked if I could just poke his chest and knock him down. Shock. Ha, funny, that word.

"You heard me."

"What did you say?"

"I know you heard me, honey. But, fine. You need to hear it again? I'm pregnant."

He walks around me and out of the closet. Silently. Scary silent. I bite back my tears and calm myself down, giving him a second before following. When I enter the bedroom, he isn't there. I check his home office, the library, and both sitting rooms before I finally find him. He's standing next to the pool, out by the grill, just looking off toward the mountains. The bottle of whiskey in his hand, no glass, is a pretty good indication of just how badly this is going.

"Thorn, honey, please talk to me," I plead.

"Ask me," he mutters.

"I'm sorry?"

"Fucking ask me, Ari!" he snaps, spinning and pinning me with his gaze.

"Ask you what, Thorn?"

"Ask me why my father is in fucking prison. Ask me what the fuck he did to get sent away for goddamn life!" He finishes bellowing his words, turns, and tosses the whole bottle against the house, shattering it on impact. "Fucking ask!"

I suck a choppy breath in but keep my resolve strong through my confusion and worry. "Why? Why is he in prison?" I quietly ask, the word so small, but I know packs something scary powerful with its answer.

Thorn steps close, his eyes wild. "Murder, Ari. He's going to rot in that cell because the man whose blood fills my veins—the blood I'll give that child—was capable of killing his own goddamn *son!*"

I jerk back, shock making me reach out blindly for something to steady myself. Thorn, even through his anger, has his hands on me, making sure I'm safe. Just as quickly as his hands landed on me, though, they were gone.

"I told you. I'm made from shit. Pure evil. A mother who loved her high more than her two boys. A father who was an angry drunk and an even angrier crackhead. She sat there and watched, my brother only five, crying because he was hungry and not once stopped that angry son of a bitch. I tried, but he hit me so hard I couldn't get back up. Just shook my brother. Shook him so hard he never woke up again. That's what made me! That's who I am. How can I give that to an innocent child? How can I be a father who's worth a shit when what made me was capable of taking his own son's life? All my brother did was have the misfortune of being born from that same blood. A child that I made would have that same blood, giving them what evil my parents gave me? What kind of life would they have?"

"You're wrong."

"I'm not."

I angrily wipe my eyes, not making a bit of difference with the number of tears I'm crying. "You're so very wrong." He pinches his lips together, and I'm not even sure he's listening anymore, but I keep going. "You're the most incredible man I've ever met, Thorn

Evans. You love me with gentle care. You worry about me unwaveringly. You protect me from any harm that could touch me. You have so much integrity inside that beautiful soul of yours, *our* child would be nothing short of blessed to get even a fraction of it. They might have made you, but they didn't make you the man you are today. You aren't who they were. You, the man who my heart came alive for, have no idea just how amazing you are. How lucky any child we have would be to call you dad."

"Ari," he grunts, but I shake my head, tears still rushing down my face.

"My heart breaks for your brother. My heart breaks for you. But my heart knows what kind of man you truly are. My heart knows that anything that our love made will be the most beautiful child ever created. Inside and out. We didn't plan this. It's just as big of a shock to me. But this child—your child—is a gift I'm so thankful fate has handed me. I love you. God, I do. I love you so much that I know it will break something inside me that will never mend if I have to walk away, but I will if you can't find a way to be okay with the child our love made."

He doesn't move. Now, he's got nothing left. All the steam just vanishing. He looks like he's carrying the weight of the world now. I close the distance between us, roll on my toes, and kiss his slack mouth.

"You brought me to life. You gave me beauty. I just didn't realize until I saw that positive test just how magnificent that beauty could get. I love you, honey, but I'm going to go stay with Piper … stay at my old place. I'll give you space to think about this. To … to think about what I've said. You take however long you need but know I'll never stop waiting." I press my hand against my flat stomach. "*We'll* never stop waiting."

I left Thorn's house last Wednesday, taking nothing but my phone and purse with me. I texted him two days later and asked him if I needed to come and get Dwight and Jim. All he said was no. Since then, nothing. I miss my boys, but the way I missed Thorn was something close to desperately. It grew each day I was without him.

When I got back to my old house, the one I hadn't even completely moved out of, I triggered the alarm. That was more than I could handle, and I just dropped to my knees crying while Piper silenced the alarm and answered her phone when the monitoring company called to make sure there was no trouble. Following that was a call from Wilder, but I was too lost in my sadness to pay any attention.

The whole night, she held me while I cried uncontrollably. The tears never stopped. I knew I needed to get it out so I could move on, so I didn't try hard to stop them either. I let myself have that moment of heartache, and the next morning, I didn't allow myself to wallow. I had to find the strength to be there for Thorn when he hopefully made his way back to us. And I had to find a way to be resilient to any pain that may follow, if he never did.

My life was worth it.

The child that I loved already was worth it.

And Thorn was worth it.

I would fight for all of us.

The only person who my pregnancy didn't immediately inflict

bad news on was Piper. That went a long way in helping me sort myself. It took me two days to be able to tell her what happened. Then we both sat there and cried for what Thorn had endured. It was at the end of the next day that I was able to stop the tears for the second time. It was also that night that I vowed that Thorn wouldn't be lost to us forever. He would come back to us, and I would spend every day loving him and this child so much there would never be a chance for him to ever think he wasn't worthy again. From that day on, there's been no possibility in my mind that this wouldn't work out. I meant what I said; we would wait forever if we had to.

It's that steadfast resolve that had me walking out of the doctor's a week after leaving his side, sonogram of our miracle in my hand, and feeling happiness for the first time since. I stood outside the well-known obstetrics practice under the warm sun with my hand on the belly that protected what our love made, feeling a sense of calm that everything would work out.

I had no idea that, at that moment of sheer happiness, I had just put my future in the hands of the devil. I stood there, the sun shining bright while I thought about what our child would look like, with darkness waiting in the wing. Blissfully happy and completely unaware that just hours from now, everything would change forever.

THIRTY-THREE

It was time

ANGER AND RAGE HAD BEEN NO MATCH FOR THE strength of Fury. Weak, they had been. So pathetically weak.

They had no clue that Fury had been waiting, hunting … plotting. Not until the opportunity made itself known, and it was too late.

When Fury stood in the distance and had enough with the plans the weak had thought clever, something purely sinister pumped through Fury's body, pushing the ominous soul to the forefront.

The sweltering heat that surrounded Fury while the car idled at a distance from the woman in the sun only amped that vehemence to insurmountable levels, fueling the ire, ensuring that no one could save the woman.

Anger's plan had been pitiful.

Rage couldn't do better.

Even that stupid perky Sorrow had tried to butt in. Attempting to save what Fury thirsted to slice so deep, feel the warm blood as it rained from that woman in the sun's body, ensuring that there would be no chance that the woman in the sun would survive.

Not now.

Not ever.

Fury was done waiting.

Fury had finished the hunt.

Fury was ready to feel the warm blood soak evil's flesh.

It was time.

It was time.

Regret felt the shift.

Grief felt the wicked air.

Sorrow was all that remained in the end. Not feeling, like those that had come before, but seeing for itself what kind of maliciousness was planned for the prey it hunted from the shadows.

Sorrow had tried to fix the out of control power that Fury had stirred up on the way out of hell. Sorrow had hurried, but still felt Fury's sting because of it. But even making itself vulnerable to the very one it was trying to save hadn't fixed anything.

There was too much pain.

Too many memories—the same ones that had kept Regret company for so long would be what brought everything down in the end.

Everything was out of control. Not just Regret. Oh, it was still there and stronger than ever.

Sorrow's fists clenched when a malicious grin appeared on Fury's face, and all it took was one glance at the woman in the sun to know just how bad this was.

Oh, it was indeed time.

Time to grasp on to that hidden sliver of hope, and for the first time in close to a decade, pray for help.

That's when Sorrow heard Regret's whispers. Heard each one, remembering the woman in the sun's hand on her flat stomach outside of the doctor's office and knew Regret was right.

It was Fear, however, that grabbed the phone off the seat and made the call everyone agreed needed to be made—the whole time following two car lengths behind Fury. Sorrow was proud that hindsight had ensured Sorrow knew who to call, stealing the information straight from the one who wanted to harm the woman in the sun.

"Thorn," the voice answered when the call connected.

Sorrow tried to answer the man, but it was Despair who rushed forward and did it in the end, giving the man the destination that registered instantly. When the man hung up the phone, everyone prayed that the man on the phone wouldn't be too late.

For, if he was, it would be too late for everyone.

And Hope would be lost forever.

Ari

Piper had gone back to work.

It has been almost three weeks since she had been there last—two weeks since her attack from Matt.

311

I told her not to worry about Trend. We would be fine for however long she needed, but she wanted to keep going and get back to her normal. I selfishly wanted her to wait and go back next week so that I wouldn't have to be alone after my doctor's visit. I wanted to share the news of the baby with someone who was just as ecstatic as I was. I had rushed home, completely forgetting that she wasn't there.

It was a shock to get back and be alone. I wanted to share the news with her, but I knew she wasn't the only one. Only I didn't just want to share the news with Thorn, I needed to desperately. Piper was doing what she could to be excited enough that I wouldn't feel his absence, but I did. How could I not?

He needed time. It hurt, but I understood. That understanding didn't take away from the fact that I needed him, and no matter what I said, it hurt not to have him. Not just his love, but his acceptance and happiness about our child. I didn't doubt anymore that he might not come back to me, but I still craved him. I just needed to be patient until he figured out his way back.

I spread out the printed pictures of the tiny little bean inside me on the kitchen island and smiled, recalling the sonogram I had. More specifically, when I heard the baby's heartbeat. I knew that Thorn would feel the same healing powers from that sound as I did when he heard it too. After all, both of our own hearts had been beating through life unconsciously until they collided and the love created when they merged had produced that indescribable little rapid thumping that echoed around me from the child in my belly.

I did what I had to do, what I knew needed to be done. I asked the tech to hand me my phone and waited long enough to make a recording of that beautiful noise, then sent it to Thorn with one simple message.

The beauty of us made a perfect love.

He didn't reply.

I didn't think he would.

When my doorbell rang thirty minutes later, hope sprang free, and I rushed to answer. Only, when I pulled the door open, thinking it would be Thorn, I allowed the devil right into my house.

"What the hell are you doing here?!"

I jumped and turned to run when I saw the dead eyes that looked at me, knowing that nothing good could come of that. I wasn't fast enough, though.

Thankfully, the same time that evil wrapped its claws around my neck and squeezed, the only man who could save me had already received a call that not only shocked him to the core, but guaranteed he would move mountains to get to me on time.

THIRTY-FOUR

Ari

You can't save her now

"**S**TOP! FOR THE LOVE OF GOD, STOP!"

I hear the voice. I hear the pleading. I can feel the desperation and agony in each one of the words.

"You're going to kill her!"

My vision danced with black spots. My lungs burned, desperate for the air that the hands on my neck were keeping from them. My nails clawed and scratched at the hands that were strangling the life from me. The only thing that kept me from submitting to the darkness was knowing my child's life depended on me to fight for both of us.

I bucked.

I kicked.

I fought with everything I had.

When the hands vanished, I threw myself to the side and rolled

314

away while gasping. It wasn't graceful, my crawl backward on my hands and knees, but I moved quickly, and when I turned, shock held me still when I saw the two people in my house.

One of them didn't surprise me; after all, I opened the door and let evil right in. It was the other, however, that I couldn't understand. Not after all this time.

"Why?" I croaked. "Why London!"

The other—Thomas—moves, but she blocks him, throwing herself in his path.

"No!" London screams. I wince. "You can't!"

I look back and forth between them, shocked at what I see. My sister, whom I hadn't seen in years, is only a shell of herself. She doesn't look even remotely close to the vibrant woman she had been when things were perfect in our worlds. She also doesn't look like a woman who was capable of what she had put me through, torturing me through years with calls and texts.

It was Thomas, though, the man who had looked broken under regret weeks ago, who made me gasp and feel the coldness of dread.

He wasn't broken anymore.

He looked absolutely sinister.

Nothing like that man who had come to see for himself that I wasn't still hiding from the world.

I don't understand what I'm seeing.

"You can't save her now." He pushes London away with a lazy swat, and she falls to the floor with a crash. "You can't ever save her."

My eyes widen and pure fear fills my veins when he pulls a gun from his pants and points it at me.

"You weren't supposed to leave," he strangely tells me. "I put up with your weak shit for years, wishing you would be what I craved—someone to break. You hid yourself from me, though, didn't you? Made me think you weren't strong enough for what I craved. I see it now. You practically pushed me to your sister. She wasn't timid. She had fire in her. Had. But she doesn't anymore, do you? I waited for fucking years, thinking it would come soon, but you gave it to that disgusting bastard instead? I got a virginal little bitch who only knew how to lay there like a dead bitch while I fucked her. I knew to bide my time, take the one who was ready for me to mold to what I wanted, and then when I finally had you again, I would show you what a real man does. I would ride the innocence from your body, break your soul, and turn you into what I wanted. That cunt," he screams, pointing the gun at London. "That cunt tried to save you. Played me for a fool. She was good with her act, I'll give her that. Gave me what I wanted just to keep me from you! You had no fucking clue what you walked in on that day, did you?"

I shake my head, tears falling and look from the gun to my sister and back at Thomas. "Thomas, you don't want to do this."

"All you had to do was wait. I was even willing to let you have a little fun until I was ready to slice her up and take what I wanted with you. I wasn't going to waste her fear, not until I used her up. London fucked that up when her guilt trips kept fucking up. Started trying to find ways to tell you to watch your back. ALL YOU HAD TO DO WAS WAIT!"

"Please. Stop!" London screams, lifting from the floor and charging him.

He lifts his leg and kicks her hard in the gut. She falls instantly.

His words and her text weeks ago making sense now. She had been trying to protect me. My God.

He steps over her, holding the gun in her face. "Should we play a game, wife? Should we show Paris what she had been too upset to see clearly that day she found us together?"

"Please don't," she begs, sobbing.

I go to stand, ready to run while he's distracted, but the second I get halfway up, Thomas is right there. He swings his hand back and cracks it against my face, knocking me back down with the force of his punch.

"Next time you move, I'll put a bullet right here," he warns, pressing the gun low in my belly. Right where my baby is. I cry harder, no longer able to see a way out of this. "Sit the fuck down and listen."

He goes back to London and grabs a fistful of her hair, dragging her to the middle of my living room. She doesn't even try to fight him. Her dead eyes full of grief, sorrow, and regret as they hold mine. She limply lets him drag her by her roots, falling with a crack of her head against the floor when he releases her.

"You would be surprised how good an actress sister dear is, Paris. Did you know all it takes is a knife against a bitch's cunt to make her turn willing in the arms of someone forcing her to take him? You walked in right after I warned her what would happen if she told you what I would do to *you* when you were my property. The tip of my knife ready to slide inside her if she didn't take me and make me believe she wanted it. I had no clue that your perfect timing would give me the wild cunt I hungered for. She was too afraid for herself and you that she gave one hell of a show. She fucked up, though. She saved you, but not herself when she showed me that.

I knew the second you found us, her going wild so I wouldn't hurt you, that I had what I needed. There isn't an inch of her I haven't ruined. But you," he bellows, pointing the gun back at me. "You were supposed to wait until I had finished breaking your sister's spirit. Until after I made her disappear. Then I wouldn't need her to keep calling. You would have been alone and weak when I brought you back to me and started all over!"

"Thomas, please! You don't want to do this. Put the gun down and let's talk."

I don't even recognize the look on his face now. It's too terrifying. He's a monster. My heart keeps pounding. Terrified of what he'll do, broken for what she endured, and frantic for a way out—for both London and me.

"No! You ruined it all! Talk? Fucking talk?" He brings the gun up, and I know, I *know* it's too late. I squeeze my eyes shut and pray that Thorn won't be broken by this. Pray that he'll find a way to move on and keep his beauty.

The gun blasts. A loud crash makes me open my eyes. I look down at myself, trying to find a bullet wound on my body but come up empty. My head whips around to see London on top of Thomas, my broken coffee table under him while she beats him with her tiny fists. He's fighting back, but his punches go unnoticed by her. I have no idea how she isn't feeling them, but she just keeps wailing her hands on his face.

"Get the fuck off me, you cunt!"

"I won't let you take her! I won't let you take the life she deserves! You ruined mine, you motherfucking asshole. You took everything from me, but it was worth it in the end to make sure she never felt the horror you had planned for her! I would do it every day for the rest of my life, all over again, to SAVE MY SISTER!"

My eyes go wide with her words, but when I see the red stain growing at her side, they take on a whole different meaning. She just … took a bullet for me! Now it's my turn to save her—save the sister I wrongly accused of so much over the years.

I move, crawling, and search for the gun that had to have fallen close if it's not in his hand anymore. I see it tucked just under the edge of my couch and grab it.

"London, move!" I scream. She turns and sees me with the gun, then throws herself to the side.

Thomas's insane eyes look at the gun in my hands, his blood-stained teeth appearing when his lips curl in an evil grin. "You don't have the guts, bitch. You don't have what it takes to kill someone."

"Wrong, Thomas! I have everything it takes. There is nothing that a mother wouldn't do to protect her child, but there's also nothing a woman wouldn't do to ensure the rest of her beautiful life is spent with a man worth fighting for. And there's nothing a sister wouldn't do to save her family. Something you should know!"

When I pull the trigger, my aim true and straight through his heart. The recoil of the gun makes me stagger back, tripping on the back of the couch and falling over it. Landing with the soft cushions at my back and my legs in the air. I rush to my feet, take one look at Thomas, and know it's over. Really over. I'm safe, London's safe, and Thomas isn't a threat anymore. That's all it takes for my whole body to shut down.

Right before the darkness pulls me under, I could have sworn I heard Thorn screaming for me.

If only it was real. My heart cries, reaching out for the man I wish was here to save me again.

THIRTY-FIVE

THORN

There is no end for us

NEVER, FOR THE REST OF MY DAYS, WILL I FORGET THE scene that greeted me when I rushed into Ari's house. The terror I felt for her from the second her sister had called, stopping my world right there in the middle of a fucking meeting an hour away, crippled me.

I saw the text from her ten minutes into my race to get to her.

She had to have sent it before what London assured me was happening soon, reached her. She had to have because there's no way London was lying. No one could fake that raw fear. All I could think, while I replayed and replayed the rapid swooshing heartbeat of the baby our love created, was how I would never forgive myself if I was too late. Hearing that sound and reading her simple accompanying text had affirmed what I had already started to realize since she left.

I didn't just want that baby. I loved it. Anything she helped make would never be unlucky. I would show her and our child a beautiful life.

If I lost her and our baby today, there was nothing left for me. Nothing.

I would never come back from that. Not ever.

I made the hour drive to get to her house in thirty-nine minutes. I jerked the wheel, the car slamming over the curb and crashing into the car parked in the driveway that I'd never seen before. I had the door open and was running at full speed into the unknown that waited for me, bellowing her name a second later.

"Fuck!" I yelled, seeing a man I didn't recognize with his very dead gaze fixed open to the ceiling. Blood in a heavy pool surrounding him. London said that motherfucker Thomas Vale was about to break into Ari's house. She said she would do what she could to save her sister from him. But seeing the man I assume is Thomas, very fucking dead, wasn't what I expected.

I should have had someone on them. Watching them. *Fuck.*

"She," I hear gasped through labored breaths. "She passed out, but she's not hurt. Ju-just a little banged up. S-shock, I think." I turn to the voice. London. Her breathing not coming easy, blood covering her chest and side. The striking resemblance to Ari gives me pause for a second. Even with the signs of a hard life, she's still beautiful; she just isn't Ari. Even if she was healthy, I would know the difference.

"Can you stand?"

She shakes her head. "I don't … I don't think so. Worry about my sister. I'll be fine and … Thorn, if I'm not, that's okay too. As long as she's okay, I will be."

Fuck me.

I glance over the side of the couch, seeing Ari's on her back, just shy of the couch and rush over to check her pulse.

Strong.

Fucking strong.

Thank God.

I could fucking cry. My hand moves, down to her stomach, and I rest my hand there. I have no way of knowing, but I have to believe it's not too late. That our baby is okay. That it's not too late for me to tell her how much I want this life we've made. I want to fall to my knees and thank God for not taking her—them—from me. But first, I need to make sure the sister who saved her life is around to tell Ari why she did what she did.

I move Ari, bringing her with me and resting her on the ground next to me while I keep a towel pressed tightly against the wound on her sister's chest. I keep my eyes on Ari, pressure on her sister, and pray the ambulance I called is here soon.

I was lucky I had all the connections in Vegas that I did because I wouldn't have to stick around and deal with bullshit questioning. The chief of police arrived at the same time the ambulance did.

"I'll take care of everything, Evans."

"'Preciate it."

That was all I needed. I jumped into the ambulance—the second one, the first had already rushed off with her sister—and took Ari's hand in mine. I didn't think of anything but Ari and our child. Even if I didn't have the chief in my back pocket cleaning that shit up, it was self-defense plain as day. It was just part of the life I led that ensured too many people owed me large debts. Ari wouldn't have to relive this day ever again. No questions asked. No investigation would be launched. By the time that motherfucker's body was gone, the only memory of this day would be the blood on her floor. That, too, would be cleaned before she ever left the hospital.

All traces of what transpired in her living room—gone forever.

The medic works around me, and I keep her hand in mine. I allow myself one fucking tear. One motherfucking tear. Then I silently promise whoever is listening that I will never stop being the man Ari needs from this moment forward. To be the man she deserves.

There is no end for us.

There's never an end for the two hearts that finally found each other.

Never.

THIRTY-SIX

Ari

The best stuff

I SLOWLY COME AWAKE.

The fogginess in my head jumbles everything together, making it impossible for me to decipher what is reality. Fighting exhaustion when it threatens to pull me back under because I'm so tired. So unbelievably tired.

"Ari?"

I jump, so out of it that I hadn't even realized I wasn't alone.

It takes work, but I manage to open my eyes a sliver and see Piper standing over me. She's crying but still smiling, so I guess that's a good thing.

"Don't move. I'm going to get him."

Him? Don't move? I can't even open my eyes completely, and she thinks I'm going to get up and *move*? I turn my head and look in the direction she just left. At least I was right when I thought I was in a hospital. The bustle of the nurses' station is visible through the open doorway.

I lose my view of the nurses when a giant body slams against the open door's frame in its haste to get in the room. I follow the body up, my eyes stopping when I see the bloodshot eyes and tired face of the man who carries my heart in his pocket. He takes three quick steps into the room before dropping to his knees at the side of my bed, his hands enveloping my hand closest to him, and with a heavy breath, he drops his forehead against our hands.

"Fuck, Ari," he breathes. "Scariest moment of my fucking life."

The memories rush me, and somehow, I manage to get a hold of myself.

"The baby?" I wheeze, my throat burning.

He looks up, and what was on his face when he rushed in and what I worried I would see the next time I saw him and brought up the baby, is gone. Instead, in its place is unadulterated joy.

"Perfect."

"Perfect?"

"Strong."

"Nothing's wrong? Not even from when I fell?"

He shakes his head, face soft and eyes full of love. "Not one thing is wrong. Our baby is made of some strong stuff, I've been told."

Tears fall from my eyes when he gives me my own words back. They continue to fall, getting lost in my hair. He called it our baby.

"The best stuff," I whisper, my voice trembling.

"Yeah, baby, the best."

"You're happy?"

The corners of his eyes crinkle, his smile is small but mighty, and he leans in to kiss my temple.

"You're okay. Nothing will ever hurt you again. The baby we made is perfect. There's not a fucking thing I could find not to be happy about right now. I'll make sure you don't doubt that, Ari. I promise you. I'll never let you and our baby down, not ever again. Only thing that would make me happier that you're both okay is getting you home."

"Our baby," I breathe.

"Going to love our baby, Ari. How can I not when it's part of you?"

"It's part of you, too."

"I'm told that's a good thing," he jokes. "But, yeah, baby. We made that baby, and no way what we have would be less than fucking perfect. I let you down when I couldn't see that. I let you down because I let my shit cloud what I never should have doubted. I should have been beating that door down and taking you home. I'll never forget that I was almost too late. Fuck, I'm so sorry, baby."

"None of that. We're okay—all three of us." I hiccup a sob. "I love you."

"Fuck," he breathes, dropping his lips to mine and lifting enough to speak. "And I you, Ari. And I you."

Thorn steers the wheelchair away from the bed; something the hospital insisted on even though they had already discharged me. They tried to tell him a nurse had to wheel me out, but he refused. I'm pretty sure he terrified everyone when he did that, which is why they relented. We made a left out of my room, and instead of heading down from the floor we were on, he took me up.

I'm not sure how he did it, but I know it was against hospital policy for him to take me into the room we entered. I might be family of the patient, but he isn't, and he definitely isn't a hospital employee. I didn't ask. I didn't care. I needed to be here.

My sister's eyes close, and a tear falls from her cheek when she sees me.

"You're okay?" I ask when he stops my chair next to her bed.

She nods. "Yeah. It hurts something fierce, but I'm going to be fine. They said it was a clean wound."

I reach out and take her hand. The warm tingle that goes up my arm from being near my twin after so long isn't missed. We're a part of each other. I hold her eyes and pray that our parents can see us finally making our way back together after so many years of pain.

"You saved me."

"I'd do it again and again, baby sister," she whispers, her voice low but firm.

"Why? Why did you do it, London? Why didn't you tell me?"

"I couldn't," she says brokenheartedly. "You don't understand."

"So tell me. I won't ever ask you again what made you do it, but I need to know … I have to know."

She cries silently but nods. "I never wanted to leave your side. He … he forced himself on me before that time you caught us. Not all the time, and the first time was well before the time that you witnessed it, but it had happened for a while. He kept saying things like I was the one ready to take first. I didn't understand it at first. He told me the first time that I had been asking for his firm hand by just wearing short shorts. I didn't realize what was happening until it was too late. H-he told me he would kill you if I told anyone, so I kept my mouth shut. He kept coming back, and I knew—could see it in his eyes—what he would do if I didn't give him myself. He wouldn't just take my life—he would take yours too. That day you found us, you couldn't see the knife he put against my body when you opened that door. I knew I had one choice—make you think I had betrayed you. I was already gone. It was too late for me. I had to save you."

"London." I sob. She lived through hell, and all this time, I hated her for something she didn't do.

"I made sure you believed it too. Year after year, it felt good knowing I kept you safe, even if I was hurting you more each time I had to do it."

"At what cost!" I yell.

"Worth every penny and every day."

"How can you ever forgive me for not seeing the truth?" I gasp, my whole body shaking with grief.

"I already have. You're alive and … now so am I." She glances over my head to where I know Thorn is standing, his steady and strong hand tensing on my shoulder. "You look at her like she's your whole world. Like she's more important than the air you need to breathe. Everything I always hoped she would find. Thank you. Thank you for making it worth it."

"Fuck," he hisses, and I hear the emotion in that one word, heavy and thick.

"I mean it, Ari. You, healthy and happy. The man who clearly loves you at your side, protecting you, that's all I ever wanted for you. I'm free. I'm finally free from my lies and my prison. You gave *me* that when you fought that monster. You set me free. You saved me. Only thing that would make it better is if we could find a way to fix us."

I stand, careful of her wound, and wrap my arms around her the best I can.

"I love you, London. I'll never be able to give you back what you saved me from, but I'll never stop trying. We'll find our way. I promise."

"I love you, too. I've got you again. That's all I've ever wanted, Ari."

Two weeks later, things were finally settling back to normal. Thorn still fretted, but I knew that was not something I could stop. He had taken the past two weeks off, not leaving my side once. I didn't mind the fussing when it meant I had him with me, loving me, loving *us*. He worried, yes, but he also used every second he had to make sure I knew just how happy he was about our baby.

The first day, Wilder had come over and closed that night. Then Harris came up from Florida. It's easy to see just how those two became such incredible men after meeting Harris. He walked in, smiled an easy grin that I bet still got the ladies, and told me he had always wanted a daughter. Just like that, he claimed me as his. Besides running The Alibi in Thorn's absence, he was settling in, and I secretly hoped he wouldn't rush back to Florida. Especially when I saw just how happy he made Thorn.

Thomas's death, just like Thorn promised, was swept away like it never happened. I don't ask for details because I don't want to know them, but also because I don't need Thomas touching any other part of my life. The police never came, and after Thorn took a call from the chief of police, he assured me they never would. It was done. Forever. London said that they came to her in the official capacity and said there had been an accident, but nothing else. Just like me, she never asked another question. Thomas was *finally* out of both of our lives.

The only thing that had changed since that day was the house. My old house, that is. Thorn took care of everything. He moved everything of mine that I wanted here—in our house—and placed the rest in storage for me to deal with later. Two days after that, my old house was on the market. After the listing agent left his house, I asked him about Piper. To my absolute shock, he told me that Wilder had packed her stuff up before the police had even left and basically kidnapped my best friend. When I called Piper about it, all she said was that she was staying with Wilder until she found her own place, and if he didn't let her leave then, she would beat him with the shelves that didn't have a case. Hearing her joke about those dang shelves was all the assurance I needed that she wasn't exactly there unwillingly.

I had asked for details about what was going on between them when they came for dinner a few days later.

I just didn't get them.

Not from Thorn, who just laughed.

Not from Wilder, who just glared.

And not from Piper, who just blushed.

I let it be. Matt was quiet, and my friend was safe and finding her happy. I could live with that.

I jump when a warm hand lands on my shoulder, looking away from the mountains I had been staring out at while I got lost in my thoughts, to see Thorn standing behind me.

"She's here, baby."

I give him a huge smile, turn to look at the stunning view one more time, and then head into the house with him holding my hand. Jim winds himself around my feet while I walk, making me look down at him and laugh, that is, until I hear Dwight hissing and throwing his evil attitude around. Not surprising, since sitting next to him on the couch is someone who looks just like his favorite human slave that he loves to torture. I keep my eyes on my ginger beast, getting an absurd amount of satisfaction when he volleys his cat glare back and forth between London and me, not sure what he's seeing.

"I think we broke your cat." London laughs softly.

"He was defective anyway," Thorn grumbles, walking us into the room. Thorn drops down into the lush chair near where London's sitting and pulls me onto his lap, his hand instantly moving to my stomach. Even with no signs of our baby, he is always touching my stomach when he's near me.

"How are you feeling?" I ask London, placing my hand over his.

She shrugs. "Physically, better. It's still sore, but I'm not taking the pain meds anymore, so that's something."

"And mentally?"

"Dr. Hart is helping with that. Thank you for getting me in with him."

"Lon," I whisper, leaning forward. This talk has been two weeks in the making, but when she called last night and asked if she could stop by, she mentioned that she and Dr. Hart had talked about her fears that I blamed her. I knew it was time to bring it up. "You know I don't blame you, not now. You were a victim. I'm not holding that against you, and you shouldn't hold it against yourself."

"I was weak. I was in over my head before I even realized I was drowning. I kept thinking that I would find a way out, but I never did."

"Not anymore, London. Not ever again. You saved me. Over and over. Now it's our turn to save you."

She wipes away her tears. Shaking her head and not understanding.

"I know you said you don't want to stay here. Thorn's got property in the mountains. We want you to move in there, get out of that house you lived in with *him,* and feel safe while you heal. You won't be alone. There's a guest house where he'll have one of his security guys stay to be near. Just in case, you need the reminder that you're safe now. For seven years, you saved me. It's my turn now. For as long as it takes."

"Ari," she whispers, looking behind me at Thorn. "I can't accept that."

"You will," Thorn, my bossy man, interjects.

A flash of spitfire shines through when she glares at him. "You know, you're really bossy."

I bounce in his lap when he laughs.

"Really bossy."

He laughs harder, and I can't help but smile too.

"You don't owe me anything, Ari. You know that, right?"

I pat Thorn's hand, letting him know I want up. He grumbles under his breath but releases me. I take the two short steps to the couch and drop down next to my sister. I take her hands, hold them in my own, and look her in the eye.

"I thought I lost you forever. I thought you hated me. Even before everything happened, I thought I would never have my sister back. I had no clue you were distancing yourself because he had been harming you for a year. You were stuck with a monster, and the whole time, I thought the worst of you. You might not think I owe you anything, but London, I owe you everything. You sacrificed so much for me, and because of that, I found him." I point at Thorn. "I have him, and he gave me this." I move both our hands to my stomach. "I owe you *everything*."

We embrace, both of us crying.

"If you keep making my girl cry, though, we might have to rethink a few things."

"Oh, hush." I laugh, grabbing a pillow and tossing it at his head.

"Family takes care of family, London. There's nowhere else that we would want you to be. I know you don't know me. I need to tell you, though, before everything that happened, I said some shit things to you, and I'm sorry for that. Need you to know how sorry I am."

She waves him off. "You might have said things, but you were protecting my sister. You showed me in one phone call that she was with someone worthy of her. That's not something to be sorry for."

I watch his throat move as he swallows. I know he's struggled with that, knowing just how deep London had been trapped and just playing the role her puppet master tortured her to do had only made him feel worse about that call he made to her.

"Nevertheless, I'm sorry for what I said. I wish I would have done more."

"Apology accepted. I don't want to hear anything else about it. There wasn't more you could have done, but Thorn, it worked out. We never bring it back up. Deal?"

"You going to be a sassy headache just like your sister?"

She looks at me, my heart swelling with happiness at having her—the sister I grew up thick as thieves with—back in my life.

"Probably worse." She laughs.

When Thorn's deep laughter mixes with London's, mine picking up and joining, my whole world rights itself and the last missing piece settles into place.

My heart wide-awake, full and bursting.

My sister back, healing and growing stronger every day.

The man who I live for, smiling at me with his heart in his eyes, giving me every dream I had thought was lost forever.

Our baby, safe and strong, growing inside my belly.

My heart wasn't unconscious anymore.

No.

Now it was beating for *everything*.

EPILOGUE

Ari

Simple as that

"I LOOK LIKE A WHALE."

Piper laughs, then proceeds to stuff another chip in her mouth. In the middle of Trend. Completely breaking the no food on the floor rule.

It's not like I can enforce it anyway. I laugh to myself, then pick up the burrito I had been craving all morning off the glass case at the register and stuff it in my mouth, moaning as I chew.

"It's really disturbing when you get all orgasm face over food. How much longer until He-Man's baby comes?"

I wipe my mouth, swallowing my bite. "One more month."

She looks down at my belly, her head tilting to the side. "If your belly gets any bigger, you're going to pop."

"Oh, shut up!"

"You should have seen her this morning when she was in the

back running inventory on some new arrivals. The pen she was using fell off the table, and she spent a good ten minutes trying to pick it up. The best part was, when she had enough of trying, she went to grab a new pen, only to drop that one too."

I jerk my head to my sister and narrow my eyes. "You aren't supposed to share that! It was a low moment for me."

"Literally." London giggles.

I pretend to be annoyed, but seeing her laughing like this, almost carefree, is a great feeling. It's been a long road for her, but she's coming along, and she's not alone. I think when she started working at Trend, things really turned around. At least, that's when I noticed a change in her sadness. She might not ever be back to the girl she used to be, but she won't ever be without the support she didn't have for too long.

She was still at Thorn's house in the mountains. Not far away, only a short drive, but far enough that it's allowed her to find herself again. Well, start to, at least. Thorn's guy was still there, living in the guest house. I can't help the nagging feeling that something's going on with him and my sister, but for now, I'm not going to ask questions. She's happy, and that's all I need.

When Piper and London start chatting, I ignore them so I can finish my burrito. My mind running away from me.

All the people I loved the most were working hard to change.

I was still seeing Dr. Hart, but we were only meeting once a month, and it felt more like me reading my journal out loud than therapy now. He helped me come to a point of acceptance and not feel guilty over what London had experienced. I'll probably always feel some of it, but I'll channel that in to helping London heal.

Thorn started going for his own sessions shortly after Thomas's attack at my old house. Not only did he feel a lot of guilt over not protecting me, but he also felt it from not following through with his gut feeling to keep an eye on the people who had caused harm to those he cares about. I can't imagine those sessions are fun. Between Thorn's bad habit of not liking to let others in to his personal thoughts and feelings and Dr. Hart's stubborn will to help others heal? I almost wish I could place bets on which will win before every session and watch from the sidelines.

Whatever happens each time he walks into that office is helping, though.

The biggest thing he was working on was letting go of a lot of the pain he had collected and carried around for years, which was all I could ever ask for. He did tell me that they had spent the past six sessions talking about the brother he had lost—Phoenix. It was an easy decision when we found out we were having a boy, who he would be named after. I wanted his brother's memory to be celebrated when Thorn brought his son into the world, no longer keeping him hidden and buried in painful memories.

Even though there had been ten years between them, Thorn had loved Phoenix and just wanted to be near him. With little else to do, the brothers grew close, and I knew the loss of him would never fade. The pain wouldn't cripple him anymore, though. Our son would give him some healing, I just knew it.

Piper started seeing Dr. Hart a few months after the attack. She's still struggling, but mainly because she's fighting off the attraction to one man while still trying to get over what Matt did to her. To be honest, I'm not even sure what's happening with Matt anymore, not since Wilder appointed himself Piper's bodyguard. He came around, but Wilder made sure he didn't come back. The last time I know about him coming around was four months ago. She asked me to stop asking about it, and I have. She's happy, and until I think otherwise, I'll respect her wishes. If there's something going on I need to worry about, Wilder would have told Thorn, and Thorn would have told me.

"Are you going to eat the wrapper, too?" Piper laughs.

"You know what? I'm not going to stand around here and be food shamed. I'm just giving my baby what my baby wants."

"What your baby wants is to end up like his He-Man daddy, that's what!"

"Oh, come on, Ari!" London giggles. "We're just joking. Plus, you can't help it that you've turned into a human garbage disposal."

I squint my eyes and glare. "I should have eaten you in the womb."

"You've certainly proved that you have the appetite to handle just about anything. Even the fetus of your sister in utero."

I toss my lunch trash at Piper, nailing her right in the head, and stomp waddle to my office. It really takes the steam out of a good attitude stomp when you're waddling, though. My feet scream at me while I move, the stupid flats I've been forced to wear since my belly gained its own zip code are the most uncomfortable things I've ever felt. I was born to wear heels. Just this morning, Thorn had to threaten me with no sex if I wore another pair of heels. I enjoy my heels, but I love sex with him a whole lot more.

I snatch my purse off my desk, leave everything where it was when I left to go have lunch with the girls at the register, and sneak out the back door before the food police catch me.

When I pull into the garage and see Thorn's bike in its spot, my grumpy attitude from Trend lifts instantly.

He's home.

I knew he had his session with Dr. Hart today, but when I asked him before leaving for work, he wasn't sure if he was going to be coming home before heading to The Alibi later.

But, this, I could work with.

I was waddle running the second my car door shut. Dwight, sensing his favorite toy is near, is sitting at the doorway when I open it. Right in the middle, making it impossible for me to step up into the house from the garage stairs. Not with this belly at least.

"Move, beast."

Of course, he hisses. I get a tail swish, but that's it.

"You see this?" I taunt, waving my cell phone. "Watch this, demon cat. I'm calling the vet. Kiss those balls bye-bye."

He really works on the next hiss. Puts his whole body into it.

However, he does move.

Dwight loves torturing me, but he loves his balls more.

I drop my purse on the kitchen island and head in search of my other two boys. Jim's developed a naughty little habit of hiding and jumping out at us. We laugh that it's his prank mode. It's sometimes scary just how much alike they are to the characters they're named after. Luckily, that isn't the case today. I'm pretty sure I would fall if he jumped out at me today; I'm that tired.

I find them both in Thorn's office. He's got his glasses on; something I didn't know he wore until I saw him working on his laptop for the first time. Now, if there was ever a version of Thorn that could beat the others without fail—it was when, at my request, he wore those glasses while I used my mouth to take him there. It was so hot. God, just remembering how he had gone from zero to sixty in seconds, losing control and taking me so hard I tingled between my legs for days, makes my panties get wet.

"You keep looking at me like that, and I won't give a shit that you haven't kissed me yet because I'll be fucking you."

I lick my lips.

Thorn growls, and Jim looks up from the nap he had been taking on Thorn's shoulder—his favorite spot since the very first day he clawed his way up there.

I also don't move from where I'm standing in the doorway because I've decided getting what he's offering sounds like a great plan. Well, that, and my feet really hurt.

"Ari," he warns.

"You know, your desk works for me. I wouldn't have to stand on my toes, pushing off our bed, while you took me from behind. You could just stay right there, let me stand between your legs, and just guide me in and let me bounce."

"Fucking hell, Ari!" he bursts out, tossing his glasses off and pushing away from his desk. Jim goes running the second Thorn moves the chair, not interested in finding out why his master is going insane. "Tell me you aren't wearing panties."

I lift a shoulder. "Find out, honey."

He rumbles his excitement, grinning down at me. "Around the desk, palms to the wood."

I give a little jump, beyond turned on.

He steps up behind me, his hands roaming over my huge belly. He doesn't stop until he finds what he's waiting for. The baby kicks his palm, and I look over my shoulder to see him standing there with his eyes closed, smiling huge. He doesn't move again until our son stops kicking his greeting against his palm. When the kicks stop, his eyes open again, and I see his love for me all over his face.

My dress is flipped over my bottom next, and I tremble when I hear the sound that leaves Thorn's lips when he sees that I'm not, in fact, wearing panties. Look, they're hard to deal with, and I'm as big as a house.

"You wet for me, baby? Or do you need me to eat this sweet pussy?"

"I'm soaked, honey. I ache for you. Please, fill me up."

His hand moves, the tips of his fingers grazing over my folds. He hisses in a breath. "Fucking drenched."

I hear his chair move, the weight of his body sitting, and I fight the urge to try to reach my clit around my huge belly. Thorn's hands rub up and down my legs, and I feel him move, jumping when his mouth kisses me right at the top of my thigh. When his nose presses against my wetness, and I hear him suck in a breath, I sway.

"Fucking sweet. Shuffle back and let me guide, baby."

I do what he says, moving my feet back the tiniest inch, waiting until he starts to lower me with the guiding hold of his hands on my hips. I feel his dick against my entrance, so I stop waiting and drop down on him. Every inch sheathed inside me.

It's been a few days since we had sex last, and I'm absolutely ravenous for him. I take over, rolling my hips, thrusting my body off and on him. The stretch and burn of my body taking his weight consumes me. I'm aware of nothing else in the room.

My cries get louder; the wet sounds of him moving inside me hit my ears.

"You know what I want, don't you?" he grunts, his words heavy with the desire I'm giving him. "Fucking, baby, this greedy pussy. You know what I want from you."

"I can't," I whine.

"You can. You will. I know I'm hitting that spot inside you, baby. My cock stretching you wide, tapping against where you want me the most each time you slam yourself on me. I just need to know if you need my hand between your legs or if you're going to soak my cock with your come with just me inside you alone?"

He tweaks my nipples, the jolt of electricity that zaps through my body driving me higher. He grabs both hands full of my boobs, tweaking, massaging, driving me up and up.

"Give me what I want, Ari." His hips power up from his seat. We're wild now. I can't even tell where I end, and he begins.

"Thorn!" I yell, giving him exactly what he wanted, and I feel the gush of my orgasm leaving with the burst of fluid that does, in fact, sound like it soaks him. He cusses, lifts off the chair until I have to stand on my toes and brace my hands on the desk. His hands go to my hips, traveling down each arm until he's lacing our fingers together. Then he takes me hard.

When I feel the last rough thrust, we both cry out. His forehead between my shoulder blades, his hands now supporting my body with a gentle hold on my hips. I lift my hand and push my hair out of my face, the bun from earlier destroyed by his hands.

Only, I stop short when I'm painfully slapped in the face with something blunt. Something that definitely wasn't there moments before. I pull my hand away from my face and see the huge diamond ring on my left ring finger.

"What the heck?" I gape.

Thorn laughs, his length falling from me, and I'm so hypnotized by the rock on my hand, I don't even move when our combined wetness starts dripping out of my body.

"Thorn, what did you do?" I question, so confused. I didn't

even feel him put this on my hand. It must have been when he was holding both of my hands. Understandable since that was the same time he starting giving it to me wild and raw, just how I love it.

"Pretty obvious, don't you think?"

He cleans between my legs with a tissue, then smooths down my dress and pulls me into his lap. One arm behind me, the other holding my left hand and moving the ring around with his thumb.

"I think you forgot something," I whisper, looking at his face.

He glances up and frowns.

"Did you forget to *ask* me to marry you?"

He tosses his head back, laughing loud and deep. The pain he used to hold himself back with nonexistent between us. He keeps laughing, and I just narrow my eyes and wait for him to stop.

"This isn't funny. You're supposed to get on your knee and ask!"

"Babe."

I know that babe. That's the babe that says he didn't ask for a reason. A cocky reason.

"You didn't ask because you knew I'd say yes?" I guess, knowing I'm right, but he confirms it when his smile just grows.

"You love me?"

"You woke me up and gave me my dreams. Of course, I love you."

"You know I love you?"

"Your heart beats for me."

"Simple as that then, don't you think?"

I smile.

Then I push my face into his neck and burst out into tears.

"Fucking hell, I should have known you'd start crying."

"Shut up. You can't make me feel this much love for you that I leak when that hole inside me that your love filled gets too full and then laugh at me."

"Babe, that makes no sense."

"It makes all the sense! You fill me up! You did it when I was broken. You just found that empty hole and made sure it was patched up, then filled it up every day with your love. And you've continued to fill it up even though there's no more room."

"Fuck," he breathes heavily.

"You're going to be my husband." I gasp, lifting from his neck and smiling at him through my tears.

"You're going to be my wife," he returns, the biggest grin I have ever seen on him rendering me momentarily speechless.

"Thank you for waking me up, honey. Thank you for loving me the way only you can. I can't wait to be your wife. Even though you didn't ask, yes, I will marry you."

He mumbles under his breath, and I watch his eyes get wet. "You're my everything, babe."

"I beat for you, Thorn."

"And I beat right back, baby. I'll never stop."

He pulls me close, and just like every single time I'm in his arms with my ear pressed against his chest, I feel his heart pounding louder and louder, calling out for the heart that was made just for it. The answering thumps grabbing on and answering each one of those beats with one of its own.

Beating for each other.

The two unconscious hearts that woke up to their everything.

The End.

The Hearts of Vegas series will continue with

BLIND
HEARTS

Piper and Wilder's story.

AFTER THE HAPPILY EVER AFTER

BONUS

ONE

Ari

Ask me why he's in time-out

"**I** THOUGHT YOU WERE HEADING OUT EARLY TODAY?"

I look over at my office doorway and smile at my best friend, Piper. She doesn't return the gesture, though. In fact, she doesn't even seem to act like she really wanted an answer anyway. She's headed over to the corner of my office with one thing on her mind.

Or, I should say, one person.

"There you are, handsome little mini He-Man."

I roll my eyes at her, but my smile stays in place when I hear my son cooing and babbling at her in response.

"You know, you could at least pretend that you care about me?"

She looks away from Nix long enough to roll her eyes at me, then returns to him and gives him a loud raspberry on his neck. My son, never one to shy away from affection, lets a squeal out before the most infectious giggles comes from his chubby little body. Just like his father, when my son laughs, he does it with every single fiber of his being.

God, I love that sound.

"So? What gives?" Piper asks a moment later, tucking Nix against her body, not caring that he immediately wraps his little fist around her necklace, pulling the expensive jewelry into his mouth.

"What gives about what?"

"You. You and Little He-Man being here when I know you planned on going home early today."

I lean back in my chair and let out a low chuckle. "Ah, that. Well, Nix and I decided that Daddy can wait a little while for us."

Piper sniggers.

"What now?"

"I bet he makes you call him Daddy, doesn't he?"

"You really have no shame, do you?"

Piper opens her mouth to, I'm sure, tell me something sarcastic and throw in a joke about my sex life, but when Nix gives a mighty yank, showing more strength than any six-month-old should have, she stops.

"You're no longer allowed to tell me I can't call him little He-Man, Ari. I swear, he almost just beheaded me with that yank."

I cock my head to the side and just look at her. What does she expect? She calls him Little He-Man because he's a huge baby, just like his father who she's been calling He-Man for over a year.

At six-foot-four with muscles on his muscles, Thorn is nothing to sneeze at. Even if I wasn't over a foot shorter and of small stature, he would still be a giant to me. No one was shocked when Nix, following his giant father's footsteps, came out well over ten pounds.

"Anyway," she says, after getting Nix to give up his prize and settle with one of his favorite teething toys. "Tell me why you and my favorite little guy are still here."

"Because I own Trend, and I should be here?"

"Ha! Yeah, right. You know the girls and I could run this place without you ever coming in. You told me yesterday that you were cutting out for an early start to your weekend."

"Fine." I sigh with a grin. "If you must know, I'm here because I know Thorn expects me home. He doesn't know it yet, but he's in trouble *and* he's in time-out."

"We're talking about the same Thorn Evans here, right? Your fiancé? The same massive beast of a man who can make you fall to your knees with just one deep, rumbled 'babe'? That guy?"

"Those 'babes' make even you pause, Pipe." I laugh.

"The point, Ari."

"The point is, my handsome husband thinks he can play God."

Nix fusses, and I reach out for him. Piper, though she loves my boy, won't ever argue about handing him over when he's fussy.

"Close the door, will you?"

She gets up, and I wait for the door to close completely before pulling my silk blouse up and lowering the cup of my bra to settle Nix on my breast. He doesn't hesitate, relaxing in my arms and blinking his emerald eyes up at me while he nurses. My heart swells, and I run my fingers soothingly down his cheek. It's hard to remember when I wasn't so full of love and happiness, even if it was such a short time ago, but when I've got my son in my arms, it's impossible to think of anything but just that. Even without the blessing of him, Thorn would have done that all on his own, but my heavens, am I glad he blew into my life and changed it with a thirty second bet.

"He wants another baby," I tell Piper.

"Another baby! You just had a baby!"

I laugh softly, looking away from my son when his eyes start to close, still nursing. I know from experience he won't let go of his meal until he's completely passed out.

"Which is why he's in time-out."

"I take it he didn't agree when you told him you didn't want another baby yet?"

"I didn't say I didn't want another baby."

Piper's face is nothing short of comical while she gawks at me. Her wide eyes going from me to my chubby baby, then back to me. "Look, I get how it might be easy to forget Little He-Man literally was just born months ago with him being the giant's spawn and all, but aren't you supposed to, I don't know, wait a year or so before growing another human?"

"Look at him, Pipe. How can I *not* want more babies with the man I love? Two years ago, I never thought I would have *this*— have Thorn and our son, and be so loved I wake up every morning thinking I'm dreaming."

"Uh, then what's the problem?" She frowns.

"The problem, my friend, is Thorn."

"Could you be any more confusing?"

"We aren't even married yet, for one. I would actually like to share a last name with my man and our boy."

"So get married. This is Vegas, Ari. You can be married in an hour if you want. That's a bullshit excuse, and you know it. What's the real issue?"

"Nix."

"What about Nix?"

"He's just a baby, Pipe. He's still nursing." I take a deep breath, the movement rocking Nix enough that he lets go and settles against my naked breast in his sleep. I maneuver him to pull my bra back up, standing from my desk to place him in his portable crib. After tucking my shirt back into my pencil skirt, I turn to Piper and shrug. "It hasn't been that long. I remember what it's like to feel like I was alone. I guess it's just new for me, feeling this full. What if I don't have enough love for another baby, and they both suffer because of it?"

Piper stands from her seat and walks over to me, placing her hands on my biceps and smiling. I feel like the weight of the world—my world—is resting on her telling me what I need to hear to ease my fears. She's right; everything I have been telling myself for the past three months since Thorn brought up another baby has been just masking the real issue—if I have enough love to give two children equally. Fears that have nothing to do with my sneaky husband, the fact that we aren't married yet, or our chats about another baby, and everything to do with the insecurities my heart still holds from the pain I lived before it started beating again from Thorn's love.

"You have so much love in you, Ari. You could have a hundred He-Man babies, and you would still have so much to give. If that's what this is really all about, stop thinking that and let Thorn give you more of that beautiful life. That man loves you and Nix so much, I'm not shocked he wants more, but I know he would be okay with just the one you have if you didn't want more. Don't forget that."

I sniff and wipe a tear away. It takes me about ten seconds of feeling the warmth of her words before I remember why this conversation started. I start laughing so hard she has to drop her hands. I hold my hand up, shaking my head and moving away from Nix over to the couch and drop down.

"Uh, you okay?"

"Ask me why he's in time-out, Pipe." I laugh, wiping a whole different kind of tears away this time.

"Right. Urm. Why is your forty-two-year-old man in time-out?"

"That, Pipe, would be because he started tossing my birth control three months ago. Two months before he even brought up the fact he wanted another baby, I might add."

"Stop it!" She gasps.

I let a few more chuckles out, shaking my head with a smile. "At first, I thought I was losing my mind. I was so forgetful right after I had Nix, it wouldn't have been a stretch. It was during my sugar pill week, so I just refilled the script the next day and moved on. When I went to start those, they were gone too. Luckily, I had another pack that I was able to take when I realized what was going on. It's been two months' worth of me placing a decoy pack down and just not mentioning it when I would find it gone later."

"Wow."

"Yeah, that's a good summary."

"So you're hiding out here, why?"

"I'm not hiding out. I'm just making him sweat a little. I called him at lunch and told him when he got home we needed to talk. I've been ignoring his texts and calls since then. I may have purposely waited until I knew he would be tied up at The Alibi, too," I add, smiling when I think about him being stuck at work—at the strip club he owns.

"I'm surprised that even stopped him."

"Oh, it didn't. At first. Then I sent him a text that basically said if I saw him before I got home, he wouldn't be happy."

"Empty threat," she deadpans, smiling and rolling her eyes.

"Completely. He doesn't know that, though. So he's at home, and I'll deal with him when I get there."

"That should be interesting." She laughs.

I just smile. Interesting? That's putting it lightly. By the end of tonight, it's not just going to be his world that's rocked.

"Enough about me. I've got about an hour to kill before I head home. How about you tell me what's going on between you and a certain man you've been spending more time with?"

Her smile drops when she snaps her mouth shut, and she narrows her eyes. It's the blush that hits her cheeks—a blush I haven't seen on her face since middle school—at the mention of who I know she's been spending more time with, that tells me everything she isn't.

"You know what else is interesting?"

Her eyes go to slits, but I know she's not embarrassed.

"Watching you two? Now *that's* getting interesting."

When she gets up and leaves my office without responding, her blush even deeper, I can't help but laugh so hard my belly hurts. Piper isn't ever at a loss for words, but one man sure does it for her.

Interesting indeed.

TWO

THORN

Just like every night

MY PHONE RINGS FROM ACROSS THE KITCHEN. I GLANCE UP at the clock and frown when I see the time. Ari was supposed to be home at four—two hours ago.

Fuck.

I've been sitting here with my goddamn thumb up my ass for the past three hours waiting. I haven't waited for Ari since the very beginning of our relationship when she slipped away from my bed the first time I had her. However, I knew she needed that space then, just like I know she needed it today. And just like back then, I have no fucking clue why she needed that space I was giving her.

"What?" I snap, the phone against my ear.

"What's got you pissed? You just spent the whole day watching girls get naked."

I feel the vibration in my throat before the growl leaves my lips.

"Or was it dick in your face and not pussy?"

"Shut the fuck up, Wilder."

"It was dicks, wasn't it?"

"No," I grunt.

"And you're pissed after a day of watching women get naked because?"

"Not one of them was Ari, Wil. I think you get what I mean."

His laughter comes over the line. "I thought Ari didn't get pissed about you seeing naked chicks all day?"

"She doesn't get pissed."

"So you've said, yet every time you open the doors to audition for new dancers, you're in a shit mood for a week."

I walk over to the medicine cabinet and pull some Advil down.

"She thinks it's fucking hilarious. Ari doesn't have a jealous bone in her body. She doesn't get pissed … I do."

This time, Wilder laughs so loudly, I have to pull the phone away from my ear. I drop it on the counter long enough to toss two pills in my mouth and swallow them with a long drink of water. By the time I pick the phone back up, he's still laughing.

"Not fucking funny, Wilder."

"You own a strip club, and you get pissed about chicks dancing for you?"

"Keep that shit up."

"Or what, Thorn?" he taunts.

"How's your lady problems?"

Wilder stops laughing.

"You done?"

"Well played, Thorn. Well played."

"She wants to talk. I was stuck at The Alibi all day with

appointments for new talent. I know she fucking planned the 'I want to talk' text because she knew I couldn't get out of that shit. I swear to fucking God, Wil, if she pushes the wedding back again, I don't care what she fucking says, Elvis is marrying us."

"Who says it's a bad talk, man?"

"The follow-up text that came after I kept trying to call her. I had some young chick shaking her ass on the stage trying real fucking hard to get my attention, but all I saw was her telling me I wouldn't be fucking happy if I didn't wait for her to get home."

"I take it the chick didn't get one of the open spots?"

"What the fuck do you think?"

"Did you even fill any of the spots?"

"The Alibi is the best goddamn strip club in Vegas. You think I didn't fill those spots even with my girl twisting my fucking head up? My pockets are fucking loaded because I can spot talent without seeing the naked body. If she's got to be desperate for my attention, she isn't The Alibi material anyway."

"Cocky bastard."

"Didn't hurt that I had Ari's list of favorites, so I didn't even need to watch a quarter of them anyway."

His laughter booms through again. "Ari's picking the dancers now?"

"Got a good eye, Wil. I wouldn't hire them without seeing it for myself, but she called each fucking one that I would have picked up anyway just from their submission videos."

"It's fucking weird that you guys bond over strippers."

"Female, Wil. Female strippers. Ari might not be jealous, but I sure as fuck am."

"Whatever, Thorn. Go enjoy your night and stop acting like

you have a vagina. Maybe she just wants to tell you she's moving the date up and not back."

"Unless it's tomorrow, it won't be soon enough."

I move over to the range at the same time I hear her car pulling into the garage under the kitchen.

About fucking time.

I finish stirring the sauce, then place the spoon down on the stupid little mini-plate Ari bought for spoons next to the range.

"Ari's home."

I disconnect the call without another word and lean against the counter, watching the door that leads up from the garage. I normally wouldn't let her open her door without being down there to help her with Nix, but fuck, she made it clear she wanted me to wait for her. Which I'll do, but the second she steps in this house, I'm done waiting.

A few minutes later, the door opens, and I hear my boy babbling my name softly. His sweet voice saying da da humbles me to the core every single time I've heard it since the first time he gave me that gift. My eyes hit Ari's when she steps into the room, but I glance away when Nix lets out a scream.

"Da! Dadadada. DA!"

"Babe," I say, looking away from Nix when Ari doesn't move to step closer—giving me what I need.

"Da!" Nix continues, getting louder than before.

I raise a brow. Rolling her eyes, she steps forward, dropping her keys and purse on the island before stepping around it and moving closer. Nix keeps going, getting more impatient by the second that he's not in my arms yet.

I feel you, Nix. I feel the same way when your mama doesn't greet me right, too.

"One of these days, I'm going to give you one of those babes and wait for you to come to me, Thorn Evans."

"No, you fucking won't. You're too hungry for me."

"God, you're cocky."

"So I've heard." She doesn't move, standing just out of my reach with Nix going nuts to be in my arms. "Babe. Last time you made me wait for it, I threw your teasing shit right back in your face when I didn't let you come for an hour."

She gasps and looks down at Nix. "Thorn, really? He can hear you."

"He doesn't know what I'm fucking saying."

"Whatever," she mumbles, stepping closer.

Nix starts grabbing fistfuls of my shirt, pulling himself up my chest, just like one of our cats has a tendency to do. I reach down, pull him gently from her arm, and help him get to where he wants to be, bending at the same time so Ari doesn't have to strain to give me what I want. The same time his open mouth lands on my jaw, her mouth presses against my mouth. I wrap my free arm around her body, pulling her closer, and we both open our mouths. I get one sweet as fuck lick of her tongue against mine before we pull away. Not even five seconds—that kiss—but fuck is that what I needed.

"Hi." She sighs, blinking up at me.

"Miss you, baby."

"Da!"

I look away from her beautiful face and smile at Nix. "Missed you too, my boy."

I watch my girl, that sweet as fuck smirk teasing her lips, while she dishes up our plates. I walk from the island she's standing at and grab one of Nix's teething biscuits before moving over to his chair. He starts talking a bunch of nonsense when he catches sight of Dwight, our oldest cat, but stops the second his diapered butt lands in his highchair and he's got that little cracker thing in his hand.

"He's hungry, Daddy," Ari mumbles, stepping up to the table and placing our plates down. I look down at her and cock my brow. "You're kidding?" she adds in disbelief. Not sure why, since she knows better.

"Feel like I'm kidding?" I pull her into my arms and grin down at her when she sighs the second my hard cock presses into her softness.

"It's strange that you get hard every time I call you Daddy. In front of our son, I might add. There's nothing sexual about that."

"Baby," I groan, leaning down and nipping at her exposed neck. "You calling me Daddy, in any context, is going to go right to my cock."

"Sit down, honey," she says breathlessly, pushing away and moving to go grab the cups I missed her filling.

I pull her back. "You sit. I'll grab our drinks. He good without some milk?"

"I nursed him before I left Trend."

I nod and walk over to fix our drinks. Jim—our other cat—jumps on the chair next to Nix at the same time I sit down. Nix ignores us instantly and starts rambling to the cat. Jim, always good with my boy, just blinks his cat eyes at Nix, giving a few meows.

"Swear to God, you would think they understand each other." I laugh.

"I wouldn't be surprised," she answers, her own giggles mixing with my chuckles. "How was your day?"

I shake my head but tell her how the auditions went. We spend the rest of the dinner talking about how things went at The Alibi and how her day was at Trend—her luxury consignment store. Today was one of the rare days she had Nix there longer than a few hours, but I wasn't shocked that he had a great day. He would; there's never a shortage of arms to hold him.

I wait, our conversation never stalling or straining even though her request to chat later is thick in the air. After dinner, I take Nix to give him a bath while Ari cleans up the kitchen—at her request. Not that I wouldn't be giving him his bath—I do it every night—but I normally clean up after dinner when Ari's worked a full day. Bath time, though, that's mine. Ever since he was born, even if I had to work late at The Alibi, I would come home to give him his bath. It's our time, and fuck, I love it. The only thing that has ever come close to the gift I got when Ari became mine is Nix. I never thought I could love someone the way I do Ari, but the way I love our boy? Indescribable.

Nix looks up over my shoulder and smiles a second before Ari's hand lands on my shoulder. She leans over, and I smell her perfume. God, she smells so fucking good.

"Is my handsome boy ready for bed?"

He beats his fists into the water, splashing us both as he laughs. We finish his bath together, and she heads to the living room to wait for us. Nix doesn't fight his pajamas like he normally does, his fist in his mouth telling me he's not fighting because he wants what his mama is waiting to give him.

"You aren't the only one, son."

I lift Nix from his changing table, his head landing against my chest the second he's in my arms. Feeling his weight against my beating heart only reminds me just how far I've come since Ari came into my life. He only lifts his head for a moment when we enter the living room. He hears Ari's voice scolding Dwight, but for what, I have no idea. One of these days, that cat isn't going to be able to escape the threat of losing his balls, though.

"Come here, baby," she coos at Nix, lifting up for him.

I groan, not even bothering to hide it when I see the small wet circle on her gray cotton sleep thing. She hasn't slept in her lace nighties since she was too far in her pregnancy with Nix for them to fit, but even that solid gray thing is fucking hot. The thin straps somehow hold up her full tits. There's not much shape to it, but when she stands, I know it hits her just under her round ass. It's how her tits strain against the top that makes me hard. Seeing the milk wetting the front shouldn't make me even harder, but it does. You fuck your woman once with that milk lubing the valley between her tits, and you'll never look at them the same again.

Nix starts to complain, pulling at her top and rubbing against her. I settle behind her and pull them both against my chest, watching over her shoulder as she pulls the top down. I reach around, my hand sliding under to cup her as she moves the rest of the material away. A drop of milk falls from her nipple to my fingers. I bite my tongue. She shifts her body, her tiny frame between my legs rubbing against my hardness. I push it back, just like I do anytime she's in my arms, and watch as our boy moves his head and latches on to her nipple.

She lies back on my shoulder, her hand resting against his head, and sighs. Just like every night. I hold them both, her nurturing our son and thank whoever will listen that I've got these gifts in my arms. I don't look away. I never look away. I watch him feed, eyes exactly like mine never looking away from me. Not when he pulls away, her nipple falling free, and I pull that cotton back over her skin. Ari shifts his weigh and moves him to the other side. This time, it's me who frees her. I swipe at the milk waiting to fill his belly while she moves him around, then I offer him her other nipple, and still, he never looks away.

Not until his eyes start to flutter.

"Want to tell me why you keep taking my pills, honey?"

Nix's eyes blink open, just for a second, but I swear it looks like he was laughing at me.

That night, it was me that looked away from him first. I drop my head, tighten my hold on them, and stare up at the ceiling.

Fuck.

THREE

Ari

Tell me what I want to hear

THORN DOESN'T MOVE WHEN I STAND AND ADJUST NIX. I walk away from him and head toward the nursery. Not once does Nix stir, though he never does. My beautiful boy sleeps just as hard as his daddy does.

I lean over his crib and place a kiss on his temple, breathing in his scent. A quick check to make sure his pacifier is in arm's reach before I pad out of his room, turning off the light and closing the door softly.

The house is silent while I walk from the baby's room toward ours. The lights dim, casting a warm glow around the large space. The glass door that opens to our private balcony is open, carrying me toward the dark night beyond.

The Strip shines in the distance behind me, giving us just enough light to see the mountains in front of us shadowed against the darkness.

It's my favorite view, especially when the man I love is in the frame of those shadows. His arms wide as he leans his weight against their hold on the railing.

I stop just outside the doorway and breathe in the desert air.

"This what we're going to talk about?"

My feet carry me forward, not answering him. When my hand lands on his back between his shoulder blades, his head falls forward, and he looks down.

"You have two minutes, Thorn. Two minutes to come up with a reason that will make me forget that you took my birth control without talking about *why* you did it. Or," I say, dropping my voice and pressing my front to his back, kissing the space my hand had just been. "Is thirty seconds all I should give you?" I whisper, reminding him of the time that we hadn't been where we are now … letting him know exactly what I want.

I pull away at the same time I hear him cuss under his breath and walk away, smiling the whole time I start counting in my mind, knowing I won't get far before he pounces.

One.

My steps move me toward the open doorway.

Two.

I hear him breathing heavily.

Three.

My foot hits the hardwoods.

Four.

Steel like bands of solid muscle surround me, wrapping from behind and lifting me off my feet.

Five.

Those arms finish turning me, and I wrap my legs and arms around Thorn's body.

"Twenty-five more, honey," I smart, leaning forward to nibble his jaw just hard enough to drive him wild. The vibrations from his chest make me rock my hips against him, loving the feeling of him enjoying what I do to him as it tingles my skin.

My back's against the bed before I can even think about counting again; his mouth against mine hungrily. My hands move to his thick hair when he lifts his mouth from mine. The dark locks messy from my hold. I let my hands glide from the top of his head to his stubbled cheek, pulling him back down to where his lips hover over mine.

"You should have told me," I scold, no heat in my words.

"I did."

My head moves against the mattress when it tips to the side to look at him in disbelief. "Hiding my pills was telling me you wanted another baby?"

"Tell you every night I hold you and our boy in my arms and feed him your tit, Ari. Tell you every night I make sure I'm here to bathe him." His mouth gives me a quick kiss before he's lifting back up to look down at me. "Tell you every night I fuck you so hard, you milk every goddamn drop from my cock ... and then again in the morning."

My breath shudders when he starts rocking his sweatpants-covered thickness against my center. My thin panties might as well be nonexistent; I can feel every inch of him against the wet material. His mouth drops to my neck as he starts kissing, licking, and biting the sensitive skin. My moans falling from my lips and my hands moving to the smooth skin on his back.

"Tell you with every single I love you, baby. But," he starts, waiting for me to open my eyes and look down to where he's moved. The second he has my gaze, he opens his mouth and bites the swell of my breast, just above my sleep dress before lifting and giving me one heck of a devilish grin. "It was *you* who told me when you started playing my own game against me."

I gasp. "You knew!"

"There's nothing you do that I don't see, baby. Didn't take your pills to be a sneaky bastard. Took them to see what you would do about it."

"I should've known better," I grumble.

His hand lifts off the mattress where he had been bracing his weight off my body, and his fingers trail down the strap of my dress, making my whole body come alive. He curls those fingers into the material that covers my breasts and pulls it down slowly, my sensitive nipple hard and begging for him. The strap of my dress digs into my shoulder, but I don't feel a bit of pain.

His eyes hold mine, his mouth opens—still grinning. Then his lips are wrapping around my nipple, the pressure of him sucking against my skin making me cry out. He groans, his eyes bright, and releases his hold on my dress to grab my breast. The pressure from his hold and the suction from his mouth releases my milk. His tongue swipes against the stiff peak, and he closes his eyes with a snarl against my flesh.

I can feel the material covering my other breast getting more wet as he continues to drive me insane. Every few seconds, he lifts off just enough that his lips give a tiny gap around my nipple and the milk falls slowly from his lips and over my skin to coat his fingers. I know what he's doing; the same thing he's done every night that he does this.

"Fuck," he grunts. His hand leaves my breast, and he shifts so that he's resting on his shins between my spread legs. He pulls the bottom of my dress up, exposing my panties, and presses the hand that hadn't been teasing my breast against my core. "Drenched," he mumbles to himself.

My hips move, the tips of his fingers running up and down my panties. His eyes move from my pussy to my tits with hunger in his gaze.

His hand lifts from between my legs, and he moves it to pull the waistband of his sweats down. His cock springs free—hard, thick, and long. He reaches up, leaving his cock free against his abs, the sweats pressed against his balls. Both hands pull my dress down, bunching it under my breasts. Then his hands are on each heavy, needy globe. He drives me insane with each flex of his fingers, each pinch of his fingers. I feel more of my milk leaving, coating his hands.

My breathing coming in rapid pants makes me lightheaded. His, mixed with the groans of approval as he gets what he wants, is just as fast.

I pull my lip between my teeth when he releases me and brings both hands to his erection, wiping the wetness from my milk on his length. He does this every night. It shouldn't be as hot as it is, but his enjoyment from my breast milk is something I will never grow tired of.

He keeps jerking himself, his cock wet and glistening. He makes sure to show me this, him pleasuring himself, because he knows I get off on it. I really could come just from this alone.

"You wanted to talk," he says, his voice strained and even more gravelly than normal. "You wanted me to admit that I took them, but I want you to admit you *wanted* me to."

"Honey," I whine, one of my hands moving down my body and slipping under my panties. He growls, his eyes watching as I start circling my clit.

"The only thing better than your greedy pussy sucking my balls dry is knowing that we could be making another beauty out of our love, Ari. Admit it, you want me to put another baby inside your belly."

He reaches one hand down and pulls my hand from between my legs.

"Thorn," I whimper.

He drops his other hand from his cock; it bobs, and I lick my lips. His hands are at my hips before dragging his palms down my legs, lifting them up and pressing them together to rest on his shoulder while he removes my panties. He follows the same movements in reverse until the cool air is kissing my wet pussy.

"You want my cock. You always want my fucking cock, baby. Your greedy pussy is begging to be filled, isn't it? You want it? Then you tell me what I want to hear."

"Stop being cocky about it, Thorn." I try to be firm, but my voice is as breathless as I feel.

"Ari," he hisses.

"I'm still mad that you didn't just talk to me about it."

"You aren't mad."

"Thorn!"

"Ari!" he mocks.

"I need you, honey," I whine.

"Tell me what I want to hear."

I move, pushing off the mattress and scamper to my knees before shoving his shoulders and pushing him on his back. His long legs almost making me fall over the other side. I caught him off guard, so I was able to get the upper hand before he even realized my intent. My legs straddle his hips, taking him into my body with one hand guiding his shaft.

"You aren't calling the shots this time, honey." I gasp, moaning low and long when he fills me completely.

He groans deep, the sound filling the room with the same kind of intensity licking across my skin when I start to move. His hands are on my hips, not to pull me off but to help me ride him faster. There's no more teasing. I take what I need, crying out when his thumb rolls across my clit.

His hips start to surge off the bed, pushing himself even deeper. Frantic movements and unsteady rocks against his body keep pushing my body higher. The tingles ripple up my spine, my pussy clenching around him with each thrust in.

"More," I beg.

My hands fall back to his thighs, and I move faster. His eyes down, looking at me taking him inside me. I use his body, pushing off him while he keeps me steady, and pumps up from the bottom, going impossibly deep when I drop my body down.

"Fuck," he hisses. "Give it to me, baby."

"I need—"

"I know what you fucking need," he growls, pulling me up so I'm no longer leaning against his thighs. My hands fly to his wrists as he starts to lift me off and pull me down. The coil of heat inside my belly springs loose and sets off an avalanche of ecstasy.

The only thing—aside from me calling out his name—that I

hear over the roaring of my thundering heartbeat in my ears is him answering my call.

"Ari," he grinds out, the heat of his release filling me.

When I collapse against his chest a moment later, his heartbeat against my cheek, I smile the second my own does what it always seems to do when we're skin to skin like this—answers each beat with one of my own.

FOUR

We're in front of fucking Elvis

"**Y**OU WANT TO GO CLEAN UP OR FALL ASLEEP WITH me inside you?"

She hums but doesn't answer.

"Ari?"

"I like having a part of you inside me."

Fuck. I feel that burn, one I'm well used to by now, start to warm my chest.

"You going to keep lying on top of me while we talk, baby?"

Again, she hums.

"I want to see your face, baby."

"You're comfortable. And I think you broke me."

She rocks on me when I laugh silently. The movement makes my cock fall from her body. I groan at the sensation of losing her heat, and she echoes the sound with a grumbled complaint that's cute as fuck. I'm not the only one who likes my cock inside that greedy pussy.

"Babe," I say in that tone that she knows well.

"Oh, fine," she grouses. She slides off my chest and puts an elbow into the mattress, resting her free hand on my chest. "I shouldn't have sent you that text knowing I was doing it on purpose to make you simmer on your thoughts."

"No, you shouldn't have."

"I'm not sorry about it, though, because that time-out I put you in ended pretty spectacularly."

I shake my head and grin at her. "I know you saw me take your pills, baby. I also know you had another pack in your purse. All I wanted was for you to talk to me about giving Nix a sibling, Ari. I tried to talk to you about it four months ago, and you shut down."

She sighs. "Four months ago, I had a two-month-old who was only slightly more demanding than his father, honey. I was also still dealing with my postpartum issues. I couldn't even think about having another one—not then. Until recently, I'll be honest, I worried another baby would mean Nix wouldn't get enough of me."

"And now?"

"Now, I know I was just being foolish with my worry. You, Thorn ... you give me everything I've ever dreamed of. I couldn't ever lack the love to give when you fill me full of it every single day."

I shift us, my hand going into her hair and resting against her head. I pull her tighter against my body and hold her gaze, searching her eyes and finding the love she gives me right where it always is.

"Just wanted to bring it to the table, baby. I wasn't asking you to get pregnant that day."

A tiny smirk makes her relaxed face go even softer. Her hands, resting against my chest, glide up and down slowly. "You would have been happy to, though, wouldn't you?"

"I love you, Ari. You bringing Nix into this world was the most beautiful thing I have ever seen in my life. Every time I look in his face, I see pieces of us both. Humbles me to my knees every day that I get you, and we made that. Nothing would make me happier than to fill this house with more children."

"Not even doing that as my husband and not my fiancé?"

"Only thing in this fucking world that would be sweeter, Ari."

"I have to ask, if you want another baby so bad, why not just bring it up again?"

"I knew you weren't ready then, and I think we both know why I might have been apprehensive."

She nods, a little sadness moving into her eyes at me bringing up the past.

"But taking my pills, Thorn?"

"Told you, knew you saw me. Not my finest move, but it was all I could think of to make *you* come to me and talk about it."

"How long were you planning on taking my packs?"

"Wait for you forever, baby. You know that."

This time, bringing up the past doesn't make her sad. She laughs softly, the sound going straight to my gut. Her whole face gets bright as she smiles.

"Lucky for you, you'll just have to wait another seven or so months."

My head jerks back, and I study her face. That smile still there, tears that I know aren't because she's sad filling her eyes.

"Babe," I breathe.

She licks her lips and her brow furrows, adorable as fuck. "I don't know that, babe."

"Not the time to be cute, Ari."

"You could have stopped taking my pills after the first month, honey, because *I* stopped taking them after the first time you did."

"Ari," I exhale, my heart pounding—my chest feeling too fucking small.

She leans forward, presses her lips against my mouth, and kisses me quick. Not once do we close our eyes. She leans back and presses her forehead against mine.

"I had my first appointment a week ago. I had almost convinced myself you got me pregnant the very day I tossed those pills away, but it was most likely about two weeks."

"You're pregnant?"

"I am."

"God, Ari."

"I love you, Daddy," she says, giving me a wink.

My cock swells, and I roll her to her back, sliding in slowly.

"I fucking love you, baby."

The whole time I take her, slow and steady, we never look away. I keep the pace, never deviating. When I feel her start to ripple against my cock, I know I won't be able to hold off—even when I just came as hard as I did before this. Not knowing the woman I love with everything I have is giving me another child.

She gasps, her pussy pulling me deep as it continues to constrict, and she comes with a soft cry of my name on her lips. Her watery eyes shining bright with love. I push in, my cock twitching, and groan low before taking her lips in a deep kiss.

I pull back, the whole fucking world under my roof right now, and give her the grin that I know always gets me what I want.

"Tomorrow, we're in front of fucking Elvis. My son in my arms, my baby in your belly, and you're going to be my wife. Not waiting another fucking day to make you mine—forever."

"Cocky." She laughs on a sigh.

"You love it."

"I do, honey. I do."

The **REAL** end ;)

98021059R00211

Made in the USA
Columbia, SC
21 June 2018